the other mothers

ALSO BY KATHERINE FAULKNER

Greenwich Park

the other mothers

mothers

a novel

katherine
faulkner

GALLERY BOOKS
New York London Toronto Sydney New Delhi

G

Gallery Books
An Imprint of Simon & Schuster, Inc.
1230 Avenue of the Americas
New York, NY 10020

First Gallery Books hardcover edition December 2023

GALLERY BOOKS and colophon are registered trademarks of Simon & Schuster, Inc.

For information about special discounts for bulk purchases,
please contact Simon & Schuster Special Sales at 1-866-506-1949
or business@simonandschuster.com.

The Simon & Schuster Speakers Bureau can bring authors to your live event.
For more information or to book an event, contact the Simon & Schuster Speakers Bureau at 1-866-248-3049 or visit our website at www.simonspeakers.com.

Manufactured in the United States of America

10 9 8 7 6 5 4 3 2 1

Library of Congress Control Number: 2022950935

ISBN 978-1-6680-2478-2
ISBN 978-1-6680-2480-5 (ebook)

For Emma and Maddie

Tash

WE MEET IN A room with no windows in a town of pebble-dash houses. The high street is lined with boarded-up storefronts and betting shops. They have taken me inland, to the nearest station, I assume. Here there is no crash of waves, no call of birds. No cheery stripe of blue peeping out from behind rooftops.

In the car on the drive down here, Tom and I had made a game of it for Finn. First one to spot the sea. I had seen it first, though I kept quiet to let Finn be the winner. Seeing that sapphire ribbon stretched across the horizon, my heart had lifted, despite everything. At the promise of a vacation. Days on the beach building forts and castles. Finn's feet making perfect prints in the wet sand of the bay.

I wondered if they might handcuff me, but they didn't. They seemed almost apologetic, the officers in the car. They kept asking if I was cold, if I would like a window open, a drink of water. I shook my head, tried to focus on the landscape outside the windows. I wanted to find a landmark, a place I knew. But I couldn't. And the farther we got from the coast, the more unfamiliar it became.

They opened the door for me when we arrived, offered me a hand, but I stepped out on my own. Overhead, the cold sky, speckled with a swirling milk froth of stars, was so beautiful I'd actually caught my breath. We never see stars in London. I had a sudden sense that I was only now seeing things the way they really were. And that I, too, was finally being seen.

Now we are inside the room. It's just me and Detective Pascoe, a gray PVC rectangle of table between us. His colleague, Williams, said she would go and get some tea. She said it like tea was the answer to my problems. When I look down, I see there is a dark smear of blood on the cuff of my sweater.

I find my voice is weak, like something far away.

"You are looking, aren't you? You need to look. On the cliffs. He fell, but maybe he's still . . ."

My mind forms the next few words, but I find my mouth cannot.

A loud buzz. The interview room door opens. Williams is back, holding a mug for me and another for Pascoe.

"Careful," she says as she sets them down. "Very hot."

There is nothing sensuous about Williams. She is slim as a Boy Scout, neat in her gray suit. She has a heart-shaped face, so pale you can almost see through it. Her hair is cut short, like a little child's. Like Finn's. I feel a twist in my gut. Finn.

Pascoe acknowledges the tea with a nod, then clears his throat into his balled fist, replaces his hands on the table in front of him.

"We're doing everything we can to locate him, Mrs. Carpenter. Should I call you that, or do you prefer Natasha?"

"Please, call me Tash." I am like you, I want to tell him. A professional person. I am a wife, a mother. I don't belong on this side of the table.

"Can we go over what happened tonight, Tash? On the cliffs?"

I try to focus on the details in the room. Count the ceiling tiles, one by one. They don't know anything. They weren't there. They can't know.

"I went for a walk."

We both know this is an opening offer. One Pascoe isn't likely to accept.

"Bit late for a stroll, isn't it? Especially on a night like this."

When we'd gotten down to the water earlier, the storm had already started. The wind was plucking napkins from the tables on the seafront, sending them dancing up the cobbled lanes. The sea was beaten to a seething green foam. The man at the boat-trip kiosk had shaken his head, offered Tom the money back. I'd scooped Finn into my arms, promised him we would go tomorrow. I suppose we won't now.

Of course, I scold myself. Of course we won't. The vacation is over. Everything is over now.

"I take it you're not local?"

I shake my head. "No. We're here on vacation."

"Where are you staying? Rental? Second home?"

I listen for an edge of hostility in Pascoe's voice. I used to vacation here with my family. Spoiled, middle-class teenager that I was, I couldn't understand why people would live in the gray towns we sped through on our way to the postcard-perfect coast. Why live in Cornwall, but here, rather than by the sea? As if it were simply a matter of choice, a kind of eccentricity on the part of the locals. Now I know the truth. What people like us were responsible for. A slow asphyxiation. Trimming away the prettiest parts for our Easters and summers, leaving the rest to blank-faced decline. The ultimate selfishness.

If the hostility is there, though, I can't hear it. Pascoe's face is stone-like, impassive; the face of a man who sees the world as it is, and does not see much point lamenting it. Behind it is a logical mind, concerned with material things. Which sees patterns, and notices when they are disrupted. Like when a middle-class mother strays from a vacation home at night, and ends up bloodied on a cliff edge, someone screaming for the police.

"It's called Crugmeer House," I explain. "It belongs to a couple we know. We've been staying with them, a few other friends." Friends. My tongue feels wrong as I say the word, my mouth emptied out of moisture.

"I see. Have you known them long, these friends?"

Less than a year. It doesn't sound like much, does it? But friendships are different when you are a mother. Your eyes meet those of another mother over the swings, the sandbox, the GP waiting room, and you just know. The lack of sleep, the exhaustion, the funny moments and the painful, the constant emotional wringer.

That was how it had been. Our lives had been so familiar to each other. I had known what they laughed about, what they worried about, what kept them up at night. At least, I thought I had.

"How do you know each other?"

I open my eyes now and force myself to meet Pascoe's gaze.

"We met . . ." It comes out as a croak. I clear my throat, start again. "We met at the playgroup."

The littleness, the innocence of the word almost makes me laugh out loud.

London Evening Post, November 21, 2017

WILD SWIMMING WARNING AFTER NANNY DEATH
BY Natasha James

A warning about the dangers of open-water swimming has been issued following the death of a young woman at a local nature reserve.

Sophie Blake, twenty-one, went missing on the evening of July 7, 2017. Miss Blake, who worked as a nanny, had been reported missing by her employers. Her body was found several days later in the East Reservoir. She had suffered a large cut to her head.

A pathologist who carried out the postmortem told the inquest it was possible Miss Blake could have sustained the head injury when she dived into the water.

The injury—combined with the water temperature, which had been cooler than usual for the time of year—could have left Miss Blake unconscious or dazed and unable to swim to the side, he said.

Miss Blake was known to enjoy open-water swimming. The alcohol levels in her blood suggested "a degree of intoxication," the inquest was told.

Coroner Victoria Carmichael said it was not possible to say for certain what had happened, but it was "likely" Miss Blake had decided to go swimming after drinking alcohol and had gotten into trouble in the water.

She said her death should act as a warning to others amid the growing popularity of so-called "wild swimming," which is not permitted in Woodberry Wetlands, a nature reserve comprising twenty-seven acres of reed-fringed ponds and dikes.

The reserve forms part of the Woodberry Down regeneration

site, one of Europe's largest building projects that will see forty-six hundred new homes built.

Dave Holt, the manager responsible for the reservoirs on the site, admitted that wild swimming had become popular in the nature reserve, which comprises the old East Reservoir.

"We have signs up to say that it is not safe," he added. "People just ignore them."

Miss Blake's mother said her daughter was "irreplaceable," and that her death was something from which her family would "never recover."

The coroner recorded an open verdict.

Tash

London
September 2018

THE NEW FLATS ARE still being built, right against the reservoir. The two completed towers loom above like giant Legos, glimmering rectangles of turquoise, their pale spines straight, their glass balconies mirroring the sun. As I stand on the wooden walkway, I can hear the faraway shouts of building workers, the clang of metal on metal. Red cranes sail back and forth, hauling metal pipes that glint in the light. A flock of geese, disturbed by the noise, takes flight over the surface of the water.

It was hard to avoid the feeling there was something uneasy about this place, even before the girl turned up dead. Most of the old public housing blocks are still here, sitting unrenovated just behind the new towers. They've been airbrushed out of all the promotional material, but if you walk around the back, onto the Seven Sisters Road, you see them. Big concrete balconies, damp stains creeping up the walls like hunched specters. They'll knock them all down in the end. They started on one last week. It's still there now, standing half demolished against the sky, like a piece of paper torn in half.

I walk past the towers and into the nature reserve along the East Reservoir. Autumn has filled the branches of the trees, making them heavy with seedpods and crab apples, a rust starting to creep through their greenery. Underneath the slats of the walkway, wading birds huddle for safety. The little rounds of their nests are long abandoned, the shells of their eggs washed away.

I stand for a long time, looking over the reservoir. The sun disappears behind the clouds. It is eerily quiet. A water strider disturbs the mirror flatness of the water. The reflection of the towers melts into ripples.

It's guilt, I suppose. The real reason I keep coming back here. I did a hopeless job that day, running out of the coroner's inquest halfway through the evidence every time my phone rang. I'd known deep down, when I dropped Finn off, that he wasn't right, and by the time I got to the coroner's inquest I had three missed calls from the babysitter. During the first witness, she'd called again, and I'd had to squeeze out, the others tutting as the door slammed behind me. Finn's temperature wouldn't come down, she said. I'd have to pick him up. I heard Finn wailing in the background, and her shushing him. I could see the court clerk had started motioning from inside the room about me using my phone. A familiar heaviness had settled on my chest. Looking back, that day was probably the beginning of the end.

Afterward, I kept thinking there must have been something I missed. Perhaps it would make more sense if I could just figure out where they found Sophie, where she was alleged to have fallen. Where was she supposed to have hit her head?

A flicker of movement on the far bank causes me to look up. There is a woman there, on the other side of the water, the nature reserve side. She looks middle-aged, maybe older. Oddly dressed for a walk around the wetlands—a long quilted coat, even though it's mild, an ill-fitting pleated skirt, and leather loafers. Her hair is wild and unkempt, her mouth clamped in a straight line. There is something unsettling about her eyes. I feel as if her gaze is fixed on me.

Automatically, I raise a hand in greeting, but the woman makes no response. Just keeps staring at me, like she doesn't want me out of her sight.

My phone rings in my pocket, and I jump. That will be Tom, wanting to know if I'll be home for Finn's bath.

I silence his call, shove the phone back into my pocket. As I look up, the woman disappears into the bushes. I can't work out where she went. It is as if she evaporated.

I leave the walkway and start to head around the reservoir, the path pebbles crunching underfoot. It seems to take forever to get to the other side. Then, as I move closer, I see a trail through the trees I haven't spotted before. That must have been where she went. Is it a bike track, perhaps? It seems to run along the side of a narrow waterway, off from the reservoir.

I follow the path. It quickly becomes muddy. Plants and weeds proliferate, a tangled canopy of branches blocking out the light. The stream on my right is clear and shallow, the bed a silty brown. Tadpoles dart over a collection of artifacts beneath the surface: a broken bike, a yogurt container, a length of pipe, a coil of police tape. On the other side a chicken wire fence is collapsing under the weight of ferns. Through its gaps, I catch glimpses of the reservoir plant and prefabs. A hum of machinery drowns out the trickle of the water.

The canopy becomes thicker and darker, brambles and cow parsley growing across the path. I have to push them back to keep going. A sign tacked to the chicken wire reads: Danger: No Entry. Maybe this was a bad idea. I think about turning back when I hear the sound of rushing water ahead.

Around a bend is a metal bridge, a grid underneath. A sluice gate leading out of the reservoir, a muddy water bottle in its teeth. A willow tree is hunched overhead, its fronds trailing into the sluice, pale leaves sucked into the foaming pool beyond. The sound of water is now a roar.

There is no sign of the woman. I think again about turning back. But then I see it, tied to the opposite post of the bridge. A lone bunch of flowers. The petals are large and shriveled, like wrinkled pillowcases. The flowers have been tied with a long pink ribbon, its fraying edge trailing into the water. But it is the photograph that holds my attention, enclosed in cellophane to keep off the rain.

When I turn the photograph over in its cellophane folder, I am startled to find the article with my byline on the other side. It has been cut out of the paper, the print blurred on one side where water has leaked through.

Wild swimming. That's what the coroner had said, so I'd had to report it. But it had been so vague. The copy had been hard to write; I'd had to put caveats everywhere.

I feel the ribbon between my thumb and finger. So is this where her body was found? Not in the reeds of the reservoir, as I'd imagined, but up against a sluice gate, in a pool full of rubbish, the roar of water in her ears.

It didn't make sense. If Sophie had been swimming, how did her body get here?

Tash

WHEN SHE KNOCKS ON my door a few days later, I don't remember her straightaway. I just see a woman, around my mum's age. Maybe a bit older. It is drizzling softly, and the woman's quilted coat has no hood. The rain is drawing a halo of gray-rooted frizz up around her temples.

"Hi."

I wait for the woman to explain herself, but for a few moments she just stares back at me, as if it is me who should be doing the explaining.

"Are you Natasha James?"

"Yes."

Actually, it is Natasha Carpenter now, officially, but the new name has never really stuck. It had suddenly felt important, when Finn was born, that the three of us would share the same surname, but then I'd found I couldn't shake my old one, or maybe I didn't want to after all. So I'm still James, mostly. Mrs. Carpenter festers in the closet, like a new dress I can't get comfortable in.

"Great. I was hoping we could talk. Can I come in?" I consider the woman. She looks like she's had a rough time of it somehow. Briefly, I wonder if she might even be homeless. On second glance, I decide she is merely unkempt. Eccentric, perhaps, rather than destitute.

"I'm sorry," I say, trying to keep my voice gentle. "Have we met?"

The woman ignores my question. "I only need a minute," she says. "I've come from Walthamstow." Her jaw stiffens. I detect a hint of menace. My hand tightens automatically on the lock.

"The thing is, it's actually not a great time," I say. "My husband is trying to get some rest—he's a doctor, he's been working nights—so I'm on my own with—"

"Mummy!"

Somehow I can hear in Finn's voice that he is standing in the high chair. Something about the manic pitch of it, or maybe I can hear he is higher up than he should be.

"I'm sorry, I really have to go and check on my son." I throw her an apologetic smile and start to close the door.

"Wait. This is about Sophie Blake."

I still my hand on the lock.

"I'm sorry?"

"I saw you," she says through the crack. "At the wetlands. I know you wrote that story. I'm Jane. Sophie's mum. I want to talk to you."

I ARRIVE in the kitchen just in time to lift Finn out of the high chair, where he's poised like a diver ready to jump. Jane Blake stands awkwardly by the fridge and watches me lift him down, wipe his face, tell him off. He whines a little as I carry him into the next room and place him on the sofa. When I reach for the remote control, the whining stops.

"You can watch one *Bing*." I wag the remote control at him like a finger. "Only one, OK?"

Finn's face breaks into a smile, his pale hair falling over his eyes, soft and fine as cotton candy. I reach out to push the silken strands behind his ears.

In the kitchen, Jane is still standing by the fridge.

"Have a seat."

I motion to a chair, but she ignores me, fixes me with a cold stare.

"You don't remember me."

The moment she says it, though, I do. "You were at the reservoir," I murmur. "The other day."

"That's right." She lifts her chin. "I seen you there before. Looking for the place where my daughter died. I want to talk to you. About all this—this rubbish you wrote."

She tosses the article onto my kitchen table. For a moment, neither of us moves.

"Why don't you have a seat?" I ask gently.

Jane eventually sits gingerly on one of the kitchen chairs, ending up with her knees pushed up against a table leg. Our kitchen is so narrow we could only assemble one half-moon of the circular dining table we bought from Ikea when we moved in. The other half is folded down permanently next to the wall. I rummage in the cupboard for my notebook, a working pen, then sit down opposite Jane. She is unfolding the crumpled printout on the table, flattening it with her hands.

"Jane, legally, I had to report what the coroner found. Which was that Sophie's death was most likely an accident. That she had—"

"I know what the coroner said," Jane spits. "It didn't happen."

"So what do you think happened?"

"My daughter was murdered, Natasha. Someone killed her. They killed her, and they put her into that water."

As I open my mouth to reply, Finn reappears.

"Mummy, *Bing* not working." He starts fussing at my knees. There is a ghostly outline of milk around his mouth. I pluck a wet wipe from the packet on the table and bat at him with it.

"I'm really sorry," I tell Jane as Finn twists away in protest.

Once the TV is reanimated, I return to the kitchen. Jane shifts in her chair. Her eyes drift down to my leggings, where a glob of Finn's porridge has been deposited on my right thigh.

"I called your office." Jane is still looking at the blob of porridge. "They said you didn't work there no more."

"Yes," I say. "I left. Quite soon after . . . after the inquest." I start wiping the porridge off my leggings. I don't elaborate. I really don't feel like getting into the whole miserable story.

"So you don't actually have a job, then?"

"No, I mean . . . yes, I do, but I'm freelance now."

"Oh." The corners of Jane's mouth have turned down.

"It's a good thing," I add, a bit too quickly and with a touch too much brightness. "It means I can place stories anywhere."

Jane can see that there is a degree of spin at work here, but she stays silent. She plucks a photograph from her handbag, sets it on the table. A peace offering of sorts, perhaps.

I haven't seen this picture of Sophie before. She looks younger than twenty-one. An elfin face. A smattering of summer freckles across her nose and cheeks.

"She was a lovely girl," I say.

"She was."

She was. And now she is dead. There is a shameful part of me that wants to recoil from Jane, just because of the terrible truth that she is proof of. This could happen to me. My child could die. Maybe that explains my feeling when I saw her on my front step. The tightening of my hand on the lock. You can smell it on a person, that sort of damage.

I look up at Jane, place my pen down for a moment. Finn calls out in the other room. I ignore it.

"Do you have any idea who would have done such a thing, Jane?"

Jane glowers at me.

"I wouldn't be here if I knew that, would I?" She leans back in her chair. "Anyway. That's your bit, isn't it?"

"I'm sorry," I say. "I don't follow."

Jane's eyes narrow. "I thought you said you were still a journalist."

"I am, but . . ."

"Well, then," she says, tapping a finger on the table. "You need to investigate. You need to find out who killed my daughter."

Sophie

Fifteen months before

AFTER I GOT OUT of the water, I sat on the banks awhile. Usually the runner came around this time, but today there had been no sign of him. I kept missing him these days. I felt sure he'd be here today, but perhaps I had mistimed it. I'd been thinking about other things.

It was six years to the day since Dad. I knew I should call Mum, that I was going to have to call her at some point. But every time I pulled my phone out, I ended up not doing it. I couldn't think what I would say.

It was Dad who first got me into swimming like this. It wasn't called wild swimming then, didn't used to be something other people did. It was just our thing. He took me to so many places. You can swim anywhere, he told me. Don't let anyone tell you you can't.

Dad had shown me how under the water the cold can't hurt you. You can become the same as it. He taught me not to worry about reeds and plants, the wriggling creatures that live in mud. Sometimes you feel something against your foot, or you think you do, but it's no good looking for what. Eyes don't work down here. Their world, not ours. Only blindness and noise. You can't stay. Your air runs out, and you have to go back, into the light.

Then you come into the air and it's better and worse. Your lungs can fill; the sound of everything is clear and distinct in your ears. A plane overhead. The shuffle of the reeds at the banks. Far away, the sounds of traffic. Then you go under the water again, and it's a different noise, the noise of everything that's in it.

Afterward, as I walked out, the banks always felt steep, my limbs heavy. You have to dress quickly or the afterdrop comes: a deep cold, more frightening than the water, because it is a cold inside. You shake, faint sometimes. Dad had seen it happen.

Getting dressed was always the worst part with Dad, our hands awkward, eyes finding anything else but each other, until it was done. But then there would be blankets, and a flask of tea, just me and him and the good feeling. I missed it, the happy silence between us.

It wasn't the same anymore. The ends of my hair were wet against my neck, my hands cold and clammy to the touch. The reeds moved around the water, like silk sheets.

I took my phone out again. The gold case was shiny in the light.

"Sophie."

"Hi, Mum. Just thought I'd call."

"Uh-huh." We were quiet for a minute. I scratched the ground with my sneaker. Somewhere there was a bird. I looked, but couldn't see it.

"Doesn't feel like six years, does it?" Mum said.

I knew what she meant. And yet sometimes I found it hard to remember the details of Dad. I was left with pieces. The soft, warm heft of his back. A soapy smell. The rough skin of his hands.

The bird again. A soft, squeaking call. Dad would know the bird, beckon me to see. *C'mere, Soph. C'mere.*

The bird went silent. I listened to Mum's breathing on the line, the slight wheeze of it, like music.

"He'd be proud to see you now."

This had all been said before. There was nothing else that either of us could say.

"How's things? You still taking your pictures?"

"Sometimes."

My camera was next to me on the blanket. Last time there was a kingfisher here, a heron on the far bank. But today there was nothing that made me want to lift the lens to my face.

"I saw the picture of the forest wall thing you made at the playgroup. Looked lovely."

"Thanks." It took me weeks to finish that. I came in early every day to cut out different leaf shapes, twisting the paper in my hands to make the wobbly edges of oak leaves. I showed the children how to fold paper butterflies in half, to cover both wings in paint. I cut all the shapes out before playgroup started, so they would look exactly right. I made other things, too. Shiny cardboard stars and sequined planets to hang from the tiles in the ceiling. A tissue paper sea of silvery tinfoil fish, with ribbons of green seaweed.

"I'm glad it's working out there for you." The truth is Mum had wanted more for me, whatever that means. Couldn't see why it was what I needed, the simplicity of my singsong days with the children, their duckling-soft hair, their sweet, fat little hands. Their love offered up so easily, without complications.

"Sophie," Mum said. "Will you come home and see me soon, love?"

Silence on the line. Overhead, the *tick tick tick* of a helicopter in an empty sky.

Then, beyond the trees, I saw him. His T-shirt first, the orange one he always wore. He was in his shorts, his earphones in. I'd never gotten close enough to hear what sort of music he listened to. I smiled to myself. So I had timed it right after all.

"I'll call you back, Mum." Even as I said it, I pressed my thumb to end the call. I always liked this part, the moments before he saw me.

When he reached the gravel path snaking around the East Reservoir, our eyes met. His face was pink, the ends of his hair damp, his chest rising and falling as his lungs caught up with his heart. He raised a palm and smiled, his face open, like a child's. I smiled back.

Then he brought his hand up to one ear, as if he was about to take an earphone out. For a moment, I thought this was going to be it, that he would speak to me. But something made him change his mind, a frown tugging at the side of his mouth. He looked away, picked up his pace, shook his head a little. And then all I could see was the back of him, the muscles under the skin of his calves.

Tash

———⟨ɷ⟩———

I BAG A TABLE at the park café. Before we had Finn, Tom and I used to go for lavish brunches at a place called Ruby's, with big mango-wood tables, pendant lights with filament bulbs. These days we're broke, and Finn is impossible in indoor cafés, so we trudge to Clissold Park most Saturdays, shiver at the same hard metal outside tables while Finn tears about on the grass.

Despite being barely two, Finn is terrifyingly fast on his balance bike. Tom runs behind him with the ludicrous, crouching gait of the anxious parent of one. I see my husband's mind scroll with a checklist of danger—dogs, climbing frames, low walls, electric scooters. No one tells you how much of loving a child is to fear his death. The dread of it flickers constantly at the edges of our existence, like a light we cannot look at directly.

Tom catches up with Finn, lifts him off the bike and slots him into the high chair.

"Did he have much breakfast?"

There is never any need to ask which "he" Tom is asking about. Finn is our shared deity, the creature around whom our two lives orbit. Sometimes parenting feels like being part of a two-man cult only Tom and I know the rituals of.

"Two Weetabix and a banana."

"Nana?" Finn looks at me inquiringly. I sigh and lean to retrieve the emergency banana from the stroller.

"Long week." Tom yawns. "I wish this one would learn to sleep in his own bed."

"Tell me about it." We both smile ruefully at our son, so beautiful and oblivious in his high chair, who has woken us at four in the morning every day this week.

"You look tired, Tash."

"Oh, thanks," I croak. I peel the banana and pass it to Finn. "Say, 'Thank you, Mummy,'" I tell him pointlessly as he mashes it into his face.

"Sorry." Tom laughs. "I just meant, you look like you need some sleep."

I nod, let it drop, rubbing my eyelids with my fingers. I think about the crow's-feet I noticed in the mirror yesterday, just starting to pinch at the corners of my eyes. The bags underneath that seem to have become a permanent feature.

"Did you get any further with your gentrification thing yesterday?"

"The what?"

"Your article about the wetlands."

"Oh, yeah." I'd told Tom that the reason I kept going to the wetlands was that I'd been working on an article about the gentrification of the area. It wasn't exactly a lie—I did think it would be a good subject for a piece, and I'd pitched it a couple of times. I hadn't mentioned the Sophie Blake case to him yet. I guessed it would probably come to nothing.

"Fine. I mean, not great. It's just difficult, you know. Finn's still so un-happy going to playgroup in the mornings. I just . . . feel guilty about it. Can't focus."

Tom reaches out to Finn, squeezes his chunky leg.

"You still don't like playgroup, mate?"

"Finn no like it playgroup," Finn says, lowering his eyebrows. He starts twisting in the high chair, and I can see he is going to try and stand up again. He is too big for high chairs anyway. I pull him out for a cuddle. His foot gets stuck and he cries in protest until Tom dislodges him.

"Oh, Finney." Tom ruffles his hair, then turns to me. "I thought you said most kids settle down within a few days?" Tom always talks as if I'm some sort of expert on these things.

"Well, not Finn, apparently," I murmur, tucking Finn's head under my chin. "He still screams the place down every morning."

"But it's been weeks!"

"I know that, Tom!"

The playgroup drama is so frustrating. I can't work out where I'm going wrong. I thought Finn would love St. Mark's. It reminded me of the local church playgroup of my own childhood: the cozy, primary school smell of Play-Doh and glue, battered picture books, custard and floor cleaner. The walls of the inside rooms were covered in a sugar-paper forest of paint-blob butterflies, cut-out ladybugs, parrots with yellow tissue paper wings. Outside there were raised vegetable beds, a weather station with twirling windmills, a rainwater gauge.

Everyone said we were lucky to get a place, that it was always full. But Finn starts to cry as soon as the stroller turns the corner and he sees the church building. Yesterday I had to force his hot fists open with my thumbnail to retrieve the strands of my hair he'd grabbed in a bid to hold on as I handed him over.

"Oh, Tash, it sounds like it's been so tough," Tom says.

"It has." Two breakfast plates and a smoothie are placed between us. Tom ignores them, reaches for my hand under the table and squeezes it. I squeeze back, attempt a smile, then pull my hand away to push Finn's hair out of his eyes, wipe a smear of banana from his cheek.

Tom picks up the smoothie and stirs it thoughtfully with the straw. "Wasn't the woman in charge there . . . what's her name?"

"Elaine?"

"Wasn't she saying it might be a good idea to fix up some playdates, so he can get to know the other kids a bit?"

I reach over for a crust of toast, trying not to react to Tom's implication that "playdates" are my domain. The pressure to befriend the other playgroup mums makes me feel on edge. They already seem to have dispersed into chatty little circles at the gates, even though term only started a few weeks ago, and every time I've struck up a conversation with anyone, I've had to abandon it instantly to deal with Finn's campaign of resistance. We usually end up on the floor by the coat pegs, Finn wailing and me grinning and rolling my eyes to reassure everyone it is all under control, while other mothers file past, politely looking away.

I met one other mum in the first week who'd seemed nice. Her name was Christina. Her little strawberry-blond girl, Eliza, was a bit clingy and reluctant, too, and we'd bonded over the shared settling struggle. When I'd asked Christina about a playdate, though, she'd made a pained sort of face.

"Sorry—I'm a lawyer, and I work pretty full hours. You could ask Sal. She's my babysitter. She picks Eliza up most days, and some of the other kids." Christina had pointed me in the direction of a harassed-looking woman in lumpy leggings, pushing a huge double stroller. I'd felt downgraded.

Since then, I'd noticed a clique of three mothers who always seemed to leave together and disappear off somewhere. If there was a social hierarchy at the playgroup gates, I suspected these three were at the top: the willowy one with messy blond hair and the stylishly vacant stare of an off-duty model; the one with a shiny black ponytail who carried a water bottle and always looked midway through a run; and the third, an English-rose type with chestnut hair and a closet of stunning coats. I'd often watched them leave, wondered where they were going. Last time, I'd even walked the same way a bit, hoping I might catch up with them enough to say hello. But I'd been too far behind, and they had disappeared behind the shimmering leaves of the horse chestnut trees in Clissold Park, the sound of their laughter scattering after them.

"You're right," I tell Tom. "Finn would be happier if he knew some of the other children. I'll make an effort with that this week. I'll get to know the other mothers, try and find him some little mates."

Tom smiles. "I think that's a good plan. I'm sure it'll all settle down."

"I hope so," I say. "It sort of has to, doesn't it? If I'm going to ramp up the freelancing work."

I'd persuaded myself—and Tom—that having childcare would be a revelation. But so far, by the time I've recovered from the trauma of dropping Finn off, gotten home, eaten, showered, and tackled our mess of a flat, our mountain of laundry, it always seems to be time to pick him up again.

The egg in the bottom of my shakshuka has started to congeal. Finn rubs his eyelids with the backs of his hands. I glance down at Tom's feet.

Despite the cool weather, he is wearing shorts and sneakers. And he's only had a smoothie for breakfast.

"Are you going running, Tom?"

Tom has the grace to look a bit sheepish.

"I thought I might. Just while Finn's having his nap. Is that OK?"

I pick at the skin of my cuticles. I know Tom needs downtime, too, but childcare is my domain all week. By the weekend, I'm desperate for a break from wiping the high chair down, washing scrambled-egg plates.

"Sure, OK."

"I won't be long."

Soon after, Tom jogs off, and I head home with Finn. By the time we are there, it has started to drizzle, and Finn's long eyelashes have already fluttered closed under the rain cover.

I transfer him to his cot, then message my friend Grace to see if she is free to come over. But she doesn't respond, and then I remember she will still be on her honeymoon. I've seen the pictures she has posted on Instagram. Her and Ben climbing zigzagged streets of multicolored houses, eating ice creams, gazing from a wrought iron balcony over an azure sea crisscrossed with white speedboat trails.

I decide to use the free time to shower and wash my hair instead. I brush my teeth, tiptoeing around the bathroom rug that is always unpleasantly moist, averting my eyes from the grubby sink tiles that need regrouting. I go to get dressed. The bedroom of our flat, as usual, is freezing cold. When I reach into my sock drawer, I find there are no clean pairs. As I fumble around for a pair of Tom's, I spot a piece of paper tucked down one side of his balled-up socks, next to his passport and driving license.

It's the photograph of Sophie. Jane must have left it on the table. Why is it in Tom's drawer?

I feel cold again, all over. I snatch up some socks and turn the photograph facedown, and place it back where I found it. I keep my thumb to the edges, not wanting to mark her pretty face, then close the drawer, quietly, so as not to wake my sleeping son.

Tash

———— ❦ ————

HALFWAY UP THE PATH to the playgroup entrance, it starts. Finn stops walking, his hand suddenly limp in mine.

"Finn no want to, Mummy."

I had wanted to be on time so I could chat to some of the other mums, like I promised Tom. But as soon as I arrive I can see that we are really late. The chatty circles have dispersed, and the churchyard is silent.

Tom had seemed almost cross with me when I'd finally mentioned the Sophie Blake case, and told him I was planning to spend the day looking into it.

"Sounds like a wasted morning to me," he'd muttered, wiping porridge smears from the half-table. "If a coroner has already ruled it was an accident, what more is there to say?"

Tom has a point. It's not likely that the coroner has got it wrong, but it's not impossible. It has to be worth a day's work at least—chasing the police and the coroner's office for any more information, going over the inquest witnesses, checking Sophie's social media for clues.

"I think the mother could be onto something, though, Tom," I told him. "It's not obvious how Sophie could have hit her head around the reservoir. And there was no conclusive evidence she'd drowned. Look at all those true crime podcasts, where they go back over a cold case and find out what really happened. This could end up being like that."

Tom snorted. "This isn't some TV drama."

"It could still be a case where something was missed," I said stubbornly. "Police are under pressure, coroners have had their funding cut . . ."

Tom raised his eyebrows.

"What?"

"I just think you should be careful with this grief-stricken mother, that's all," he said, holding up his hands. "She'll be vulnerable. She might not be thinking clearly."

"I know that. I'm just checking it out, that's all. I'm not exactly over-whelmed with other ideas at the moment." I took a sip of my tea. "By the way, I found the photo of Sophie Blake in your sock drawer."

"What?" Tom picked my plate up too quickly, sending the knife clattering across the table.

"A photo of Sophie Blake," I repeated. "Jane Blake left it on the table the other day, when she came round. I found it in your sock drawer."

Tom had turned away from me, stacking the plates on the side-board.

"Did you?"

"Yep. Any idea how it got there?"

I saw Tom's shoulder blades rise and fall. "Weird," he said. "No idea. Maybe Finn redistributed it."

It was true that Finn had developed a habit of messing around with my work papers—tearing them or scribbling on them if I left them lying around in his reach. But the idea that he'd actually taken one and hidden it in a drawer seemed unlikely to me. I had thought about pressing him more, but then I'd looked at the clock and seen that we were already late. It had buzzed at me all the way to playgroup drop-off, though, like a fly inside my brain.

Finn's lips are pursed in a way that means he is trying not to cry.

"Finn no want go in dere."

"Oh, darling. Come on, let's see if they've got the police car out." I scoop him up in my arms, trying to mimic the brisk confidence I have watched other mothers display at these moments. "It'll be fine," I tell him, pressing the intercom. "Shall we have hot chocolate later, when I pick you up?"

Finn's eyes widen in horror. "Mummy, no go away!"

Elaine, the playgroup leader, is at the door. I do the usual awkward smile through the glass window while she works the heavy lock on the other side.

"Hello, Finn," she says, and smiles. He writhes into my chest.

"Sorry," I say. "He's a bit . . ."

Elaine is used to this routine by now. She brings her face close to Finn's. "Shall we find the police car?"

"Already tried that one." I try to laugh, but it comes out as a choked sort of cough. Finn twists closer into me. His cheek, Play-Doh soft, is pressed against my neck. I feel the hot needles of anxiety along my arms as Elaine holds out her hands.

I force myself to say a cheery goodbye, and start to hand him over. The siren sound of his crying starts. He digs his fingers into the skin at the tops of my arms so tightly I gasp.

"No, Mummy! No go away, Mummy!"

The other children look up from the play tables and stare at Finn. The playgroup suddenly looks dreary and colorless, bare and institutional, compared to the soft coziness of our messy flat. Why am I forcing him into this?

"No go away, Mummy!" His face is red now, streaked with tears and snot. Elaine is still holding her arms out. I hesitate. Finn has always been such a happy child. He is never like this. Surely you aren't expected to leave your child like this. He is only two.

"I know it's hard, but you should go. Really. He'll stop crying the moment you do."

I turn to see who is speaking. The petite, chestnut-haired mother—the third of the glamorous-mum trio—is at my side. A smile of perfect teeth, pink lipstick, a pair of brown boots at the end of her extremely skinny jeans.

"Really?" I ask weakly.

"Definitely." Her voice is smooth, syrupy, like a late-night radio presenter. "He'll be fine." She reaches out to Finn's face and brushes his fringe out of his wet eyes. "Hello, little one. I'm Laura. What's your name?"

I look from Laura to Finn. He squirms into me and away from her, the heel of his hand pressed clammily against a tear-filled eye.

"Oh dear. Poor little bean. That's my boy Oscar, down there, by the way." Laura gestures to a stocky little boy in a striped top, clutching a plastic dinosaur in each hand. "Oscar," she says loudly. "This is your new friend . . ." She looks at me, one eyebrow raised.

"Finn," I say.

"Finn," she repeats. Finn stops crying. The two children look blankly at each other.

"You have to just tell them they're friends," Laura explains in a stage whisper, winking at me. "They're simple creatures at this age, boys." She returns her voice to its former pitch. "Come on, Oscar. Give your friend Finn one of those dinosaurs. You like dinosaurs, don't you, Finn?"

Oscar hesitates, then selects his least favorite dinosaur and reluctantly holds it out to Finn. Finn sticks out his bottom lip and shakes his head, but his eyes have drifted to the toy.

"I just think," I say. "Maybe if I stay for a—"

"Stay nearby," Laura says. "There's a café across the street. I'll come with you—I could do with a coffee. Bye, Elaine!"

I open my mouth to protest, then close it again. Laura looks from Elaine to me and smiles, as if she has solved everything, then gives Elaine a nod. And before I know it, Elaine has taken a whimpering Finn from my arms, Laura's hand is at my back, and I have been ushered out, the heavy fire door shutting behind me, muting my son's howls as he is carried away.

Tash

AT THE CAFÉ, TWO cappuccinos arrive in tall glasses, a little cookie in a cellophane wrapper beside each.

"Feeling OK now?" Laura lays her coat over the back of the chair opposite me, followed by a sea-green pashmina that she pulls from her neck, tossing her hair free.

I swallow a lump in my throat. Laura looks at my face and laughs.

"He'll be fine, Tash! Stop worrying. What you need is caffeine."

The heating in the café is on full blast, and the windows are thick with condensation. Steam rises from the umbrellas and stroller covers slung over the radiator by the door. Through the window, I look over at St. Mark's. Hunched under a metallic sky of thunderclouds, its walls darkened by the rain, it looks drab and cheerless, even eerie. Beyond the churchyard, the asphalt paths in the park are slick with rain. In the distance, two high-rise blocks of the new Woodberry Estate loom like watchtowers. I itch to call Elaine to ask if Finn is all right.

Laura leans back into her chair and raises her coffee in the air like a champagne flute.

"To freedom."

"Freedom." I force a smile back, let my shoulders drop a little. "Thanks for making me do it, Laura. I have been on the edge of giving up."

"I get it," she says. "I know it sounds awful, but you just have to dump and run."

She is right, of course. Everyone says so. I'm being overprotective, need to relax.

"How old is Finn?" Laura asks.

"He was two in May. So two and four months. How about Oscar?"

"Oscar isn't two until January. He's just big for his age! He is one of the younger ones—he, Beau, and Lissy were all born the same month. We all did prenatal classes together."

I nod, although I have no idea which children she is talking about. I start to take Laura in properly. She is wearing perfume and mascara, and a silk top with fluted sleeves. The top is pale and pearlescent, like the inside of a shell. She is looking at the large, gold face of her watch.

"I can't stay long, annoyingly," she says. "My shift starts soon. In fact, that's what I meant to say—I think I know your husband, from the hospital where I work. Tom, right? Tom Carpenter? He's on rotation in Accident and Emergency, at the Whittington?"

"That's him. Are you a doctor, too?"

"I am. Tom and I have been in A&E together since he started." She pauses, tilts her head to one side. "Did Tom never mention me?"

"He might have—sorry, I can't remember."

I think I detect a flicker, a little pilot light of annoyance behind Laura's eyes, but as soon as I notice it, it is gone. She picks up her coffee cup. Her nails are short and round, painted the color of calamine lotion. Her wrist twinkles with a thin gold bracelet. I think I had imagined all the female doctors Tom worked with were like our friend Abi—brisk, practical, with hair permanently tied back and a face scrubbed free of makeup. I had never imagined Tom working alongside this sort of person.

"I've been there a few years now," Laura says. "It's a fab hospital."

"Are you not rotating, then?"

Laura's forehead creases. I sense I have said the wrong thing.

"I'm just a basic staff doctor." She shakes a smile back onto her face. "I did apply for the residency position, but . . . this way has worked out better, actually. I can work slightly more regular shifts, so it fits in better with Oscar. Is Tom working today?"

"He's on nights this week."

"Oh, bad luck. It's such a nightmare, isn't it? It's so lucky for us that Ed has a really flexible job. He usually does the pickups. Have you met him yet?"

I nod, realizing I know which one Ed must be—he is one of the few dads who does regular pickups. He's always seemed very friendly, usually turning up slightly late, in his running gear, a bike or scooter over his shoulder, smiling apologies for having forgotten Oscar's hat or coat or water bottle. I hadn't known he was Laura's husband, and wouldn't have matched them. She seems so put together, whereas Ed is quite scruffy and unshaven—although I suppose he's quite good-looking, in a used-to-be-in-a-band sort of way.

"He seems like a great dad," I say truthfully. "I wish Tom would do a few playgroup runs."

Laura smiles, then changes her expression to something else, somewhere between a smile and a frown.

"Same hospital, same area, boys the same sort of age," she says. "How funny we've never bumped into each other before, Tash."

I clear my throat. "Well, Tom and I don't live around here, exactly."

Our street is barely a mile north of here, but feels a world away from these neat, tree-lined avenues and pretty coffee shops. All the houses on our road have front gardens full of weeds and builders' rubble, bricks studded with satellite dishes and broken burglar alarms. The high street is all phone shops, money transfer places, kebab houses. Not pretty coffee shops like this.

Laura sets her cup down. "What do you do?"

"I'm a journalist."

"Really? Wow, interesting job." She sits back in her chair. "Working on anything at the moment?"

I hesitate. "Not really. I've got a few ideas. Hopefully I'll be back in the swing of it when Finn is, you know, a bit more settled."

Laura smiles sympathetically. "He will settle, Tash, I promise. In a few weeks' time he'll be skipping there in the mornings, and you'll have your life back." She checks her watch again. "Yikes. I should go. But, hey—let's get them together soon, shall we? Finn and Oscar? I bet Elaine's bent your ear about playdates—but she's right. They do help."

I look up, pleased.

"Thank you, Laura, she has, actually. And I think it would really help Finn. I tried to arrange something with Christina, but, um . . ."

"Ah, Christina. Let me guess." Laura grins, raising a groomed eyebrow. "She was too busy with her top job to fit you in?"

I laugh. "Well, she did say her babysitter might be free . . ."

"What? Sal, you mean? She subcontracted you to her babysitter?" Laura shakes her head. "Oh, Christina! I'm sorry, Tash. Never mind. Let's get Finn and Oscar together for sure. When suits you? We could come over to your place, if you like?"

I open my mouth to reply, then close it again. I imagine Laura squeezed up against the chipped counters in our galley kitchen, eyeing up the cheap, wonkily fitted cupboards, the broken extractor fan in the corner.

"If you'd rather come to ours," Laura says gently, glancing at me, "we usually have a few kids over on Friday afternoons?"

"Thanks, Laura," I say gratefully. "That sounds perfect."

Tash

DAVE HOLT'S PREFAB SMELLS of German shepherd and damp carpet. Outside, it has started to rain. Wind rattles the cabin, as if trying to work out who is inside. Dave makes us two mugs of tea and sets them on a melamine tray next to his old desktop computer.

Dave is the man who found Sophie's body. He was a witness at her inquest, but they hardly asked him any questions. I'm still not totally convinced that this is going to amount to a story, but it's worth having Dave on tape, just in case. It is the sort of interview that provides good color—the gritty reservoir bloke, describing how he stumbled across a corpse.

"Thanks for meeting me, Dave," I say, checking the recorder.

"No worries." Dave presses the tea bag to the side of the mug. "Makes a change from the people from the new flats forever coming round, moaning about the machinery noise."

I am relieved I didn't mention the noise myself. It's awful, like a low whirr, a constant hum of dread.

"Are they nice, the new flats?"

Dave wrinkles his nose. "Not my kind of thing. Don't like them floor-to-ceiling windows. Give me vertigo."

"What do the old residents think about them?"

Dave shrugs. "No one around left to ask."

I had read that nearly all the old residents have been moved out now. "Decanted," the developer's website calls it. Just a few still remain. The ones who aren't having it. The ones who are refusing to go.

I feel my phone vibrate in my pocket. I know, even without looking, it will be Jane again, asking for an update. I flick it onto silent.

Jane is so sure that Sophie was murdered that I find her conviction rubbing off on me whenever I speak to her. The trouble is, she has no proof, nor any idea who might have wanted to hurt Sophie, or why. I'm starting to sense that her knowledge of her daughter's life in the years before she'd died is hazy, that Sophie was keeping her at arm's length. She thinks it is possible Sophie had a boyfriend, or was seeing someone casually, but doesn't really seem to know whom. She doesn't know who Sophie's friends were.

Dave leans over to pass me a chipped mug, sucking in his belly.

"So," Dave says. "You want to know about that girl I found last summer." Dave gestures outside. "I found her over there, by the sluice, facedown. I called it in straightaway. They sent a police constable, just a kid really. Didn't even bring any waders." Dave sighs. "We got in, turned her over, and . . . well, it wasn't very nice."

"Why . . . what, in particular?"

Dave hesitates. One of his two German shepherds is fussing at his knees. He holds out a flat, pale hand, and the dog licks it.

"You ever seen a body that's been in water?"

I shake my head.

"You don't want to, believe me." He starts rubbing the dog behind its ears. "It's a shame. We do have the signs up about swimming. Not that people take any bloody notice. Ever since they started calling it a 'nature reserve.'" Dave makes the quotation marks in the air with two pairs of fat fingers, rolls his eyes at me.

I smile faintly. An accident, then. I glance down at the recorder, disappointed.

"I told them it'd be trouble," Dave continues. "Especially now it's the trendy thing, all this open water swimming. They forget how cold it can be, even in summer. The surface water might seem still, OK for swimming. As you're getting in, where it's shallow, it doesn't feel so cold. But under that, the temperature drops fast. You get into the middle, suddenly you're in water only a couple of degrees. You get in trouble in no time at all."

Dave carries on in this vein for a while, saying nonpodcastworthy things about the dangers of managed waterways. I glance down at the tea in my own mug, moon-pale, the bag still floating. I think of Sophie's bloated skin. I imagine her terror, unable to breathe, water filling her lungs.

"Were you not surprised, then, by the conclusion of the inquest?"

Dave pauses before replying. "What d'you mean?"

"I mean, you didn't see anything—I don't know. Odd about it?"

Dave considers this. "Well, the police looked at it, didn't they? They said it was an accident."

There has been a shift in Dave. He is looking at me differently, and his words have slowed, like he is choosing them with more care.

"I just wondered what you thought, really."

"Well . . . we do get it from time to time in the reservoirs," Dave says. He gazes out into the darkness. "I mean, it was a bit of a strange one."

"Strange how?"

Dave screws his face up. His two dogs are at his knees, clamoring for him, their wet, panting mouths open. Dave hauls himself up, rattles biscuits into two bowls. The dogs rush to them, pushing past one another in a double helix, mirror images of each other.

"Usually," Dave says, his back to me, "we find the clothes before the body."

"Clothes?"

"Every other time I've known about, we've found the clothes. A little pile by the water. Nine times out of ten, that's how we know. Body usually turns up later."

"And you didn't? With Sophie?"

Dave shakes his head as he sits back down in his chair.

"She had all her clothes on. Somehow that didn't seem right to me. Who goes for a swim with all their clothes on?"

I frown, trying to remember if there was any mention of this at the inquest. I'm sure there wasn't. I'm sure I would have remembered.

"What about the head injury?"

Dave shifts slightly in his seat, glances to the side.

"They said she could have gotten it jumping or diving in," I prompt. "I can't seem to work out how it might have happened."

Dave is staring down at the dogs.

"I looked at that, too," he says quietly. "I walked all round. If there was something, I wanted to have it made safe. But you're right. There's nothing she could have hit her head on."

For a moment, there is silence. The dogs have settled at Dave's feet, their wet noses pressed against his steel-capped boots. Dave reaches down to stroke the ear of one, as if for comfort.

I hold my breath, glance down at the recorder between us, check it is on. I suddenly feel like maybe the podcast idea wasn't so far-fetched after all.

"Did the police interview you, Dave?" I ask. "Did they seem to be investigating it?"

"They did. They seemed to be, for a bit. But then they said it was an accident. I figured they'd gotten some other evidence. By the time I found that phone they told me they didn't need it for anything. They said now that it was with the coroner, it was no longer a police matter."

I look up. "Sorry, Dave—did you say a phone?"

"Yeah. Hang on."

Dave hauls himself up again, pulls open a drawer, and takes something out. "We dredge that area occasionally," he says. "This was among the shopping carts and whatnot. Could be nothing to do with it. But I just thought the timing seemed to fit. And it looks like a girl's phone, you know?"

He passes it to me. I cradle it in both my hands, like a jewel.

"Might not have been hers, of course. I thought they'd want to check. But they told me no, the case had been passed to the coroner, so they didn't need it."

I turn the phone over in my hands. The glass of the screen is cracked, the edges covered in a layer of silt. When I gently scratch the back of it with my fingernail, the dirt comes away. Underneath is a glinting case, shiny as a golden ticket.

Tash

"THIS? YOU WANT ME to fix this phone?"

The Turkish man at the counter picks the phone up between his thumb and forefinger and dangles it in front of his face.

"Careful with it, please," I mutter, gritting my teeth.

He raises his eyebrows, puffs out his cheeks. He rummages under the counter for a charger that fits. He plugs the phone in. At first, nothing happens. Then, after a few moments, the cracked screen illuminates, a perfect square of blue light. I place my fingers lightly on it, feeling the thrum of life inside. I feel as if I have witnessed a miracle.

"Yeah, I think so," Jane had said when I asked her about the phone. "She did have a gold case for a while, I think. She liked gold. Why?"

"Just checking a few details," I'd told her, my pulse quickening. The phone had to be Sophie's, then. It had to.

Now I have agreed to pay this man a hundred quid to remove the passcode security. He hasn't told me how he has done it, and when he emerges from his shop, I don't ask.

"Here you are."

I almost snatch the phone, thumbing it greedily. I check the messages, WhatsApp, photo reel. But there is nothing. I flick miserably through the apps, but find just the basic stuff that came with the phone. It's all empty. No photos or videos, nothing in the calendar. There are no contacts in the address book, there's no call history. It looks like all the apps have been removed.

"I don't understand. There's nothing on it."

The man folds his arms. "I said I'd remove the security," he says. "I didn't do nothing else."

"I'm not paying you a hundred quid—you've wiped the phone!" I grip the counter until the skin around my nails goes white. The phone man narrows his eyes. I can tell this job is proving more trouble than it's worth to him.

"I told you, that wasn't me."

"Are you saying this happened because of the water?"

He looks down at the phone. "No, water won't do that, but—"

"So why is there nothing on here?"

"Swear on my life, babes, nothing I done will have wiped that phone. It must've been wiped before."

"Before what?"

"Before you lost it in that river."

"Reservoir."

"Whatever."

I force myself to think.

"Can you recover stuff?" I ask. "Stuff that's been deleted, I mean."

The man makes a whistling noise, rubs the underside of his manicured beard with a flattened palm.

"Possible," he says. "Sometimes. I know a guy." He gives me a hard look. "But it's not cheap."

"TASH! YOU made it!" Laura trills. "Welcome to the madhouse. Can you fit the buggy in?"

Mine is the third or fourth that has been squeezed into the hallway—I have to yank it over to one side, adjust the push bar to make it smaller. Laura's hallway is light and elegant, a huge cloud of flowers on the side table, a smell of pomegranates. I feel intensely aware of all the scuffs on the frame of my stroller, the stains on the seat fabric, the squashed rice cakes in the footwell.

I pick Finn up and follow Laura into her kitchen. I hear female voices in the living room next door. My underarms feel hot in my new top that keeps riding up, my black jeans still a little too tight, even all this time after he was born.

I put Finn down and look for something to distract him with. To my relief, he ambles off happily toward Oscar and starts to play alongside him with the cars.

"So," Laura is saying. "Tea? Coffee?"

"A cup of tea would be great."

"Oh God. Isn't it time for wine yet?" I don't recognize the muffled voice that calls from the other room.

"Sure," Laura shouts back, giggling. I join in with the laughter, try not to feel that it is directed at me.

Laura pulls at a long handle on the wall, revealing a fridge that opens via some hidden French doors. Laura plucks the wine out by the neck.

"Glass of white?"

"Oh, sure."

"You can have tea if you like, it's fine."

"No, no. White sounds great."

Laura goes to locate three wineglasses. While her back is turned, I run my hand lightly over her gray-painted cabinets. On the shelves are a rainbow of cookbook spines, a neat line of glass jars filled with different pasta shapes. The smell of Bolognese sauce bubbling on her stove makes my stomach contract with hunger.

"Oh," I say, remembering my offering. "I got you something, Laura." I head back to the hallway to retrieve the small but outlandishly expensive box of chocolates from the shop on Highbury Barn. I reach under the stroller, my arm skimming the cool Victorian tiles of her hallway.

"Oh wow, thank you," says Laura. When I place it on the counter, I notice the box has gotten slightly squashed. Laura sets down the wineglasses and picks up the box, then puts it down again, as if she is not sure what to do with it.

"No worries," I say awkwardly. I instantly wish I'd just left the chocolates in the stroller.

Laura hands me a glass, holds up her own for me to clink. When I bring it to my lips, I realize I am longing for it, anticipating its taste and temperature, the softening of the muscles in my neck and jaw as I take my first mouthful.

In the living room are the two other mothers. The tall blond one is on the sofa. The sporty dark-haired one is standing by the fireplace, a small baby in a carrier on her front. The children play at their feet on a wooden floor scattered with brightly colored Lego bricks. As well as Laura's boy, Oscar, there are two others: a dark-haired girl and a pale child with shoulder-length strawberry-blond hair, whose gender I've never been able to determine.

"Right, Tash," says Laura, handing me another wineglass. "Do you know everyone? This is Nicole, mum of Lissy, who Finn might know . . ."

"Hey." From her voice I identify Nicole as the requester of wine. She is bouncing in a slight squat, her thumbs hooked around the straps of the carrier like belt loops. Her baby has a strikingly full head of dark hair, like her. The dark-haired girl sitting with Oscar must be Lissy.

"Thanks," Nicole says as I pass her the glass. She has an American accent. She stops bouncing, takes the glass, and tips it straight into her mouth.

"And this is Claire, who is mum of Beau. Claire, Nicole, this is Tash and Finn. Finn's new at playgroup. Tash's husband, Tom, works with me, at the hospital."

"Lovely to meet you, Tash." Claire throws me a full-beam smile, blinking away a thick, platinum-blond fringe. She is tall and slim and sort of frail-looking, like a giraffe. She is wearing the stealthily expensive uniform of the thirtysomething mother—white sneakers, jeans cut off before the ankle. Her white linen T-shirt fits exactly right.

The strawberry-blond child, who must be Beau, starts to fuss mildly at Claire's feet. "Mummy, I want milk." Claire plucks the child from the ground and lays it across her lap, brushing its fringe back from its eyes. Then she yanks up her T-shirt and pulls a small, cream-colored breast out of her black lace bra. Tucking the nipple between two fingers, she takes the child by the back of the head and pulls it onto her, inserting the nipple into its mouth. The child sucks contentedly, its left hand pressed against her other breast, its green eyes wide open. I become very aware of the muscles in my face.

"Are you all right, darling?"

I realize Laura's words are aimed not at one of the children, but at Claire. Laura's hand is resting lightly on Claire's temple as she feeds, tucking a hair behind Claire's ear. There is something so intimate about the gesture that I look away, embarrassed.

"Just a glass of water, please," Claire says quietly. "Thanks, hon."

I decide to sit down near Nicole. The baby on her chest is asleep now, snoring slightly, its tiny nose pointed upward.

"Congratulations." I nod at the baby. "Girl or boy?"

"Girl," she murmurs. "Charlotte. Thank God. I never wanted boys." She glances at Finn. "No offense," she adds halfheartedly.

I laugh, unsure whether she is joking.

Nicole tells me she works for an investment bank, but is on maternity leave. She and her husband, John, live in Highbury, "right by the fields." The husband merits little comment, but on the subject of her friendship with Laura and Claire, Nicole proves to be an expansive talker. The three of them met at prenatal classes, she confirms. "We all clicked right off the bat," Nicole adds pointedly. "We've been super close ever since." I force a smile as she produces story after story signaling their shared history, her prior claim on Claire's and Laura's friendship.

My focus drifts from what Nicole is saying. I find my eyes drawn to Claire, who is listening, with a bland smile, to some story that Laura is telling. She occasionally closes her eyes and purses her lips, as if trying to identify a sound she can hear from a long way away. She keeps Beau—a boy, it turns out—at her breast as Laura talks, stroking his hair without looking down at his face. Claire is one of those people who is so beautiful she is almost strange looking. It is the sort of brittle, catwalk beauty that women admire more than men: her torso hard and boyish, her breasts so small her muscular toddler son is able to cup one fully in his hand as he suckles from the other.

The wine is dry and cool. I drink one glass, then another. When Laura begins spooning spaghetti and sauce into small plastic bowls and arranging toddler tables and chairs, my stomach starts to growl. Too embarrassed to ask for a bowl for myself—they don't seem like the sort of women who eat much—I sneak a couple of mouthfuls of Finn's when no one is looking.

When I carry his bowl to the sink, I find my head is swimming. I wash up the bowls, even though Laura calls at me not to bother. I rinse out Finn's cup and fill it with water, which I gulp down in one go.

I ask Laura where I can find the bathroom and she directs me upstairs. I think I've followed her instructions, but when I open the door, it is clear I've got the wrong room. Ed, wearing the workout gear I recognize from pickups, is sitting at a desk in a darkened study, a large screen glowing blue in front of him.

"Oh, hi, Ed."

"Tash! I didn't know you were here." Ed is smiling, but he looks flustered, guilty. His eyes flick from my face to his screen, his hand jerking forward to his mouse to click a browser window closed.

"Sorry to disturb."

I feel my face flushing red. Was he watching a film?

"No, no, you're fine. Sorry. I was just in the middle of something." He clears his throat. "Is Finn downstairs?"

"Yep, yep, they're having a lovely time."

"Oh, great, that's great."

I wonder why this feels so awkward, why I feel as if I've wandered into something intimate—his bedroom, rather than his study. It certainly smells more like a teenage boy's bedroom. Ed's battered sneakers have been kicked off under the desk. It is as if he's come straight from the gym or a run, and sat down at his desk without showering.

Ed clears his throat. "If you're after the bathroom, it's the next door on the left."

"Right," I say. I stumble backward. Ed watches me, the grin still fixed to his face, as I close the door.

Tash

WHEN I GET BACK to the living room, I feel disoriented. I notice the darkness at the windows, the orange glow of streetlamps. I whip out my phone and am startled to see it is late. I have three missed calls from Tom.

Laura has put some music on in the living room. It feels slightly too loud to me. The wine is starting to give me a headache, pressure building behind my eyes.

"I should go," I tell Laura. She smiles vaguely and I wonder whether I had been outstaying my welcome anyway. Laura appears to be sinking slowly into the sofa, her eyelids drooping. I have the distinct sense that a transition has occurred from day to evening without me realizing, that I shouldn't be here anymore.

"Would you like a lift?" Claire asks me mildly. "Jez is picking me up in a minute." I assume she is talking about her husband, although I do fleetingly consider the possibility she has some sort of driver.

"Thanks," I say, raising my voice slightly over the music. "But, uh, I don't have the car seat. For Finn. We'll be absolutely fine on the bus. Thanks, though."

Finn looks up at me and rubs his eyes and I suddenly long to be cuddled up on the sofa at home with him.

"Come on," I tell him. "Let's get home."

There is a knock on the door. Laura hauls herself up and heads toward the hallway. I notice a slight wobble as she navigates the corner. I hear the muffled sound of her greeting, a man's voice in reply, followed by a different laugh from the one I have heard her use before.

"It's Jez," Laura calls through to the living room.

"Daddy!" Beau clambers to his feet and dashes into the hallway.

Claire smiles after him. A few moments later, Jez walks into the room, carrying Beau upside down by his ankles. Jez is wearing a suit, no tie, his top button open. An air of work, energy, and money has followed him into the room, like a breeze from an open window.

Beau is giggling uncontrollably. His T-shirt has slipped toward his face, leaving his pale tummy exposed. His strawberry-blond hair, caught in static, has fanned out at his father's knees, like a dandelion clock.

Once he has set Beau down on the floor, Jez pulls himself up to his full height, looks at the bottle of wine, and grins, raising his eyebrows at Nicole, Laura, and me in turn.

"Oh dear," he says. Everybody laughs. The joke feels funnier than it really should. "Is Ed here?" Jez asks.

"He's working upstairs," Laura says quickly. "He's been flat out all day. Hey, Jez, this is Tash. She's a journalist."

I flinch slightly at Laura's introduction. She sounds like she might have had too much wine. Jez's eyes move from Laura's face to mine.

"Hello, Tash the journalist." Jez locks his gaze on mine and throws me an amused smile, flicking a quick glance at Laura in a way that implies he shares my suspicion about her and the wine. I am ashamed to find I am thrilled by the way Jez invites me immediately into this private confidence. I surprise myself with how willingly I participate in it, how readily I return his smile, at the expense of the friend who invited me here, to her home.

"Nice to meet you," I say before I find I am forced to look away.

Finn presses a forehead against my leg. He is starting to flag now, his nerves with the other children fraying, the frequency of toy-snatching incidents increasing. We have stayed far too long. I ruffle his hair, start mentally locating my bag, Finn's shoes, his coat. Just as I'm about to stand up, Laura fetches Jez a beer and he sits down beside me, opposite his wife, rolling the neck of the bottle between his hands. I am tilted toward his body as his weight sinks into the cushions.

"I was just asking Tash," Claire says vaguely, "if she wanted a lift."

"It's fine," I say again. "I don't have the car seat." I have the strange sense no one can actually hear me.

Jez turns to me, the sofa sinking further. "Where do you live?"

"Down at the bottom of the park. One of the roads before Manor House. Near . . . do you know the new development? Woodberry Down?"

I think I see a muscle flicker in Jez's cheek, just for a second, before his genial expression returns.

"Know it well. Sure you don't want a lift? I can always come back for this lot."

"It's fine," I tell him firmly. I force myself to meet his gaze. His eyes are ice-cube pale.

I stand up, say my goodbyes. I haul the stroller outside and gulp in the cool evening air like a drink of water. I wait until we are out in the street to strap Finn in. I hand him my phone to play with, hoping it will keep him quiet on the way home, gambling that he won't drop it and smash the screen like he did last time.

Nicole passes us with her girls, headed for a shiny black car across the street. She has pulled on a black baseball cap, puffer jacket, and backpack. She smiles and winks at me.

"Good to meet you, Tash," she calls over her shoulder as she lifts her children into the darkness of her car. "Nice to have you in the club."

I smile back with an effort. My head is pounding. My vision swims. I reach out for the top of the front garden wall for support.

"You good?"

Jez is at my side. His tone is casual, but his voice is lowered, and as he says the words, I feel him slip his hand onto the small of my back, where my skin is exposed between my top and jeans.

"Fine," I say breathlessly. "I'm fine, thanks."

His fingertips move over my skin, lightly, toward the bottom of my spine. The next moment, he is gone. Afterward, I can't tell for sure whether the touch really happened, or whether I imagined it somehow.

SOPHIE'S IPHONE 5s

Deep Retrieval (earlier data not present)

7/7/2017

MISSED CALL: 4:06 p.m.

FROM: +44XXXXXXX422

MESSAGE RECEIVED: 4:16 p.m.

FROM: +44 XXXXXXX422

TEXT: Hi Sophie, where are you? Was expecting you here 20 mins ago.

MESSAGE RECEIVED: 6:34 p.m.

FROM: +44XXXXXXX761

TEXT: Hey Soph, just wanted to check you were ok earlier? You didn't seem yourself. We've missed you and T. Call me soon. L xxx

MESSAGE RECEIVED: 8:45 p.m.

FROM: +44XXXXXXX669

TEXT: Hey can u call?

MISSED CALL: 8:51 p.m.

FROM: +44XXXXXXX669

MISSED CALL: 8:52 p.m.

FROM: +44XXXXXXX669

MISSED CALL: 8:54 p.m.

FROM: +44XXXXXXX669

MESSAGE RECEIVED: 9:06 p.m.

FROM: +44XXXXXXX669

TEXT: I don't think u shud use it Soph. U don't no what they'll do.

MISSED CALL: 9:22 p.m.

FROM: +44XXXXXXX669

MISSED CALL: 9:31 p.m.
FROM: +44XXXXXXX669

MESSAGE RECEIVED: 9:36 p.m.
FROM: +44XXXXXXX669
TEXT: SOPHIE CALL ME PLEASE. No ur angry, but this isn't the way.
I shud of never given u that. Call me.

MESSAGE RECEIVED: 9:37 p.m.
FROM: +44XXXXXXX669
TEXT: SOPHIE CALL ME PLEASE

MESSAGE RECEIVED: 9:39 p.m.
FROM: +44XXXXXXX669
TEXT: I'm just worried about what they might do

11:59 p.m.: FACTORY SETTINGS RESTORED (ALL DATA DELETED)

REPORT ENDS

Tash

"ARE YOU STILL THERE?"

I snatch the phone back up, Finn's coat and shoes in one hand.

"Yes, yes, I'm still here," I tell the police press officer. "As I said, if I could just speak to—"

"Remind me," the press officer says. "The investigation into the death of this person was discontinued."

"Yes—"

"In September of last year."

"Yes, but—"

"And the inquest concluded in November."

"Yes . . ."

"And now you've found a phone."

"Yes, and—"

"In a reservoir."

"Yes, that's correct." I try to stay calm, ignore the sarcasm in her voice.

The retrieval guy had only managed to get hold of a few messages—the last ones, all from the day that Sophie disappeared. But even these few seem intriguing to me. There is something really unsettling about them—not to mention the fact that they were deleted in the first place, along with all the other contents of her phone.

Surely there was at least a chance the police might look again at her case. And if they agreed to do that, then not only would Jane be satisfied, but I'd have an exclusive story to sell to the nationals. I just had to get this hopeless press officer to listen to me.

"The mother of the dead girl has identified the phone as hers," I say.

"Perhaps it would be a good idea to give the phone back to her?"

"Yes, but you're not listening, there's stuff on the phone that I think—"

"Listen, Miss . . . Can you remind me of your name?"

"It's Natasha Carpenter."

"And the news organization you work for?"

I clear my throat. "I'm freelance."

"I see." The temperature seems to drop about five degrees. I glance at the clock; we should have left for playgroup six minutes ago.

"Look," I say. "Can you please just arrange for me to have a two-minute conversation, at a time of his or her convenience, with the officer who . . ."

Finn has sensed that I am distracted. He has spotted the sugary fruit puree I mix into his porridge on the counter and has grabbed it in both hands. I lunge to intercept it, but fail. He starts sucking the puree straight from the packet, grinning behind the plastic spout.

"The officer is not available to discuss this," the press officer says. "I can only suggest you—"

"Are you seriously telling me that the Metropolitan Police has no interest in a new piece of key physical evidence relating to the unexplained death of a young girl?"

There is a pause.

"Can you hold again please?"

"Oh no, please don't—"

The hold music starts up again before I can even finish my sentence.

CHRISTINA ARRIVES at the playgroup on her bike seconds after me, with a squeak of brakes, Eliza strapped into the child seat. I consider waiting for her, but she is still fumbling with her bike lock, so I bypass her and usher a reluctant Finn inside.

Christina catches up with me on my way out.

"Hey—how's it going, Tash?"

"Good, thanks."

"Oh, I'm glad to hear it." Christina is making no move to leave, but is fiddling with the clip of her helmet, her long dark hair tangled in the back of it. It is obvious there is something she wants to say.

"So Finn is settling in OK now?"

"A bit better."

"That's great to hear." Christina takes a breath. "Look, I just wanted to say I'm really sorry about before, Tash—when I told you to talk to Sal about a playdate. I didn't mean to imply I was too busy to hang out with you . . . I didn't think about how it sounded."

I smile, appreciative of the apology. "Honestly, it's fine. Hanging out with me and my socially awkward two-year-old is not the most tempting prospect for anyone."

She nods. "Eliza struggles with shyness, too. I know it can be difficult."

There is something stiff in the way she says this that makes me wonder whether Eliza's shyness might be genetic.

"I wondered," she continues tentatively. "Are you free for a coffee by any chance? I'm on a rare day off and I haven't much planned. I thought I might go to Ruby's."

"Sounds lovely," I reply. "I'm actually on my way there now. I'm meeting some of the others—Laura, Claire, and Nicole. Why don't you join us?"

In a development that I find quietly thrilling, I seem to have been given a standing invitation to join Laura, Claire, and Nicole for post-drop-off coffees at Ruby's. The three of them appear to think nothing of going there most days, despite the fact that even the croissants cost about a fiver.

As soon as I mention the others, though, the smile falls from Christina's face. Her shoulders tense.

"No, thanks," she says shortly. "Another time, maybe." I open my mouth to ask why not, but Christina is already walking away, pulling the bike helmet a little too firmly back on her head.

UNDER THE table at Ruby's, I tap out a message to Jane Blake, asking if we can push our meeting back by half an hour.

"Anything interesting?"

Nicole is staring at me over her black coffee. Claire and Laura look up, too.

"Oh, sorry," I mutter. "Just a boring message about work."

"I'm sure it's not boring!" Claire says enthusiastically. "Your job must be so fascinating."

I smile awkwardly, but somehow I can't imagine bodies of dead girls, phones fished out of reservoirs, and dodgy Turkish phone shops on Blackstock Road are the sort of thing these women usually chat about over their morning coffees.

"It's just an invoice I need to chase," I insist. "Seriously. Very dull."

"Were you chatting with Christina before?"

I look up at Nicole. Was she there when Christina and I were speaking?

"She wasn't trying to palm you off on the babysitter again, was she?" Laura laughs, tells the others the story before I can protest.

"No!" Claire and Nicole look horrified. Laura rolls her eyes.

"It wasn't a big deal," I say. "She seems nice."

"If you say so." Nicole raises her eyebrows.

"You . . . don't get on with Christina?"

Nicole gives a little shrug. "I barely see her. I just think it's a bit strange to go to all the trouble of ordering donor sperm on the internet to have a baby . . ."

"Nicole, shush!" Laura admonishes, suppressing a chuckle.

". . . to then barely ever pick her up from playgroup." Nicole shrugs, brushing croissant crumbs from her fingers.

I clear my throat. "Well, her job sounds pretty intense—isn't she a lawyer?"

"A public defender kind of lawyer," Nicole says, flapping a hand dismissively. "A lone working parent. It's her whole thing."

"A lawyer and a single parent? That's impressive, no?"

I can instantly see I've said the wrong thing. Laura looks uncomfortable and glances at Claire. Claire touches her hand lightly to her forehead. Laura nudges a glass of water in her direction and Claire smiles at her weakly.

"I'd steer clear of the babysitter, Sal, anyway, Tash," Nicole says.

"Unfortunately, I agree," Laura says, an exaggeratedly pained expression on her face. "Sal's not good news, Tash."

I want to ask what about Sal is so objectionable, but the bill arrives on the table, and I am forced to suppress a wince. I still haven't even worked out how I'm going to tell Tom about the cost of that report I had done on Sophie's phone—let alone this new brunch habit I seem to have developed.

"Any plans for this week, anyone?" Claire asks brightly, changing the subject.

"I'm spending as little time at my house as possible," Laura groans. "We're having our kitchen redone." This is baffling news. There is nothing wrong with Laura's kitchen. "That reminds me—Claire, can you host a playdate on Friday? Our place will be too much of a state."

"Sure." Claire nods, but she doesn't return Laura's eye contact.

The waiter asks us how we want to split the bill.

"Oh God," Laura says, cupping her cheeks with her hands. "I've forgotten my purse."

"Again?" Claire exhales sharply. Laura looks wounded.

"I'll get your share," Nicole purrs. "It's no problem."

"Thanks," Laura murmurs, smiling gratefully at Nicole. "I'll pay you back on Friday."

"Can you make it, Tash?" Claire asks, her eyes fixed on me. "Friday, at my place?"

"Love to," I reply. I pick up my bag and tap my card for the waiter, silently praying that it won't be declined.

JANE IS already there when I reach the park café on Highbury Fields, by the enclosure full of grubby plastic toddler equipment and broken tricycles. Jane said it had to be somewhere outdoors, so she could smoke, but I am already regretting the choice of venue. It is windy, and the lids keep blowing off our takeout cups.

Jane reads the phone data report, stirring her tea with one of the little wooden sticks. She has a plastic laundry bag with her today—one of those red-and-blue-checked ones you sometimes see homeless people dragging around. I help her compare the numbers one by one against her phone address book, me reading them out, Jane stabbing at her phone keys with a single yellowed finger.

"Nope," Jane says eventually. "Don't recognize any of these."

"Are you sure?" I ask, disappointed. "Do you want to check again?"

She shakes her head, pushes the report back over to my side of the table.

I take it from her, deflated.

"Well, anyway, I'm hopeful the police might look at the case again in light of this," I say. "This last person sounds almost fearful for Sophie—don't you think?"

Jane's chin starts to wobble, and immediately I see that I misread the reason for her silence. Fat tears start to roll down her cheeks. She reaches a trembling hand into her battered handbag, takes a tissue from a small polyethylene packet and presses it against one eye, then the other. This whole routine is something she barely even notices she is doing anymore, I realize. Managing her grief is now part of her muscle memory, like a smoker lighting up, a mother wiping her baby's face.

"Leave it to me," I tell Jane, putting the report away in my backpack. "I'll look into it, even if the police don't."

Then Jane starts to talk, properly, for the first time. About what Sophie was like, as a child. How she loved drawing and painting and dressing up and animals and photographs and children.

"Did Sophie go straight into nannying?" I ask.

"No, she did a childcare course, then started as a nursery worker. She did her training at St. Mark's."

I put down my coffee. "Sorry—St. Mark's?"

"The playgroup," Jane says. "It's very highly thought of."

I swallow. "That's—that's my son's playgroup."

"Oh." Jane looks at me, and for a moment I am not sure what to say.

"When—when was Sophie there?"

"She left the summer before she died. In 2016."

I count the months back on my fingers. We looked around the play-group when we were searching for childcare options for Finn—yes, it must have been that summer. Finn would have been a few weeks old. Could we have seen Sophie there, while she was still alive?

I try to think. There was a girl who worked there, who spoke to us, wasn't there? A blond girl. She was talking to Tom. Tom had Finn on his front, in the carrier. I remember seeing the girl putting her finger in Finn's tiny palm. I only saw the back of her. Could it have been Sophie? I try to remember the playgroup worker's face, but my mind draws a blank.

"Are you all right?"

"Yes, sorry," I mutter, recovering myself. "So—she worked at St. Mark's. And then . . . ?"

"A couple poached her from there. Hired her as a nanny."

I feel suddenly exhilarated, then quickly remember it can't be any of the mothers I know. All our children started this term.

"Do you remember their names?" I ask Jane, opening my notebook. "The couple she worked for?"

Jane frowns, then shakes her head. "I don't," she says. "Sorry."

"What did Sophie say about them? Were they good employers?"

"I don't know. Sophie said they had a beautiful house."

"Anything else?"

Jane sighs. "She didn't say much about them, really. It was the two boys Sophie always talked about."

Two boys. I make a note.

"Did you ever visit Sophie at their house?"

"No." Her face spasms with pain. "It wasn't always easy, between me and Sophie. Especially after her dad died. Heart attack. Sophie was fif-teen. We were . . . a bit lost, for a while. I drank. Too much."

I didn't know Sophie lost her father, at the same age I did. Same as me. Out of a clear blue sky. Jane pulls out a cigarette and lights it.

"Do you think Sophie had a boyfriend?"

She blows a plume of smoke sideways from her lips.

"I think she was seeing someone at one point," she says. "But she never told me much."

"Anything she might have said about him?"

"Only that she met him on . . . one of those app things."

I lean forward. Nothing was said at the inquest about any boyfriend.

"Did she definitely never mention a name? How about where he lived? What he looked like? Where they met up?" I pause. "Anything at all would help, Jane."

Jane shakes her head. "Like I said, Sophie was private. She didn't speak to me about it. She only mentioned it once, and then . . . I got the feeling it maybe fizzled out anyway."

"I see." I put my pen down. Jane glances at me, seeing my disappointment.

"Look," she says gruffly, pushing the laundry bag toward me. "I brought you all this. I dunno if it might help. It's . . . Sophie's things. The stuff she left behind."

I stare at the bag. My fingers itch to unzip it, but I resist when I see that Jane's eyes are reddening again.

As I try to think of the right thing to say to her, my attention snags on something in the background. There is someone standing on the path, on the other side of the railings from where we are sitting. A creak as they push the gate.

It is Sal, with the twins' battered double stroller. It looks like she is on her way through to the toddler play area. But she has stopped, and is staring straight at Jane and me, her mouth a tight, pinched line, her heavy frame casting a pool of shadow.

I meet her gaze and attempt a wave and smile. But Sal does not smile back. She looks from me to Jane, down to the laundry bag, then back to me. When she meets my eye again, her expression is one of horror.

And then Sal closes the gate, hauls her squeaking stroller back onto the asphalt path, and walks straight back the way she came.

Tash

"WHAT IN THAT BIG bag, Mummy?" Finn's hands, covered with to-mato sauce, are reaching for the zipper of the laundry bag. I pull it to the other end of the table.

"Nothing, sweetheart. Eat your pasta, please."

I push Finn back onto his booster seat, the smell of some other woman's perfume in his hair again from playgroup. It makes my heart lurch.

Finn chews thoughtfully, his cheeks smeared with red, still staring at the bag.

"It's a present for me, Mummy?"

"No, darling."

"It's Paw Patrol?"

"It's not a present. It's not your birthday today, remember? No, Finn!"

I gasp as he lunges for it again. I lift it, with an effort, to the kitchen counter, out of his reach.

"It's not for playing with, Finn, OK?"

Eager to get started on Sophie's things, I rush through Finn's bath and bedtime, caving immediately when he refuses to have his hair washed, pulling him into his favorite pajamas wordlessly, limb by limb. Halfway through his story, Finn notices he is being shortchanged.

"Do voices, Mummy!" He turns to examine my face, as if he is un-sure whether I am really there.

"Sorry, sweetheart." I brush his hair with my fingers and make myself slow down.

Here comes a dad, with a spade in his hand.
Stick Man, oh Stick Man, beware of the sand . . .

Finn stops me, points a stubby finger at the picture of the beach, the family building sandcastles. "Finn go dere, Mummy? In seaside?"

He asks the same question every time we get to this page. I'm dying to take him on a proper beach trip. I think back to my last conversation with Tom about it. He'd said we should just go to Mum's in France for the holidays again, that it was a vacation as far as Finn was concerned, that he wouldn't know the difference.

"But I want to take Finn somewhere with a beach," I'd told Tom. "He never stops going on about it."

There was no beach where Mum and Claude were—unless you counted their weird local lake that smelled of trout and chemicals and that Claude insisted people swam in. In any case, a summer vacation with my mother and her partner in middle-of-nowhere France was an absolute last resort, and Tom knew it. It was true that Finn liked it at Mum and Claude's—feeding the chickens, riding his trike around their big, messy garden. But it wasn't the same. Especially last year. We'd planned to spend our summer vacation there, but then Tom hadn't even been able to get the dates off work because his rotations had gotten messed up, so Finn and I had ended up going without him. It had been miserable.

"Look, I'll leave it up to you," Tom had said in the end. "But we need to start saving money at some point, Tash, if we're going to move to a bigger place, try for another baby. Isn't that more important than all the other stuff?"

Whenever Tom and I argued about money, the conversations always ended with this, the weight of the obvious solution to the problem hanging between us. We both knew what he was talking about—how we could get money for a vacation, or a deposit on a house, if we really wanted it.

When my dad died, his photographic works were held for me in a trust. Nearly two hundred of his best and rarest pictures, signed originals, sitting in storage at his agent's offices in Mayfair. Over the years, I'd sold the odd one to pay tuition fees, or for my journalism training, or when we needed the deposit on our flat. But I know he would have wanted me to keep them, and so the bulk of the collection is still there—all the stuff from the Gulf War, the one that won a prize; and his last shots from Iraq, which were found after his death.

Tom understands how I feel about the photos, and he has never openly said he thinks I should sell them all. But I know that if it were him, he would. And these images of mostly dead people, in places I have never been, weigh on us, lingering darkly in the background of our arguments, like shadows.

Finn looks up at me, searches my expression.

"Of course we can go to the seaside, darling," I tell him.

"In sea?" His soft little face lights up.

"Yes, of course we can. We'll go in the summertime."

WHEN FINN is asleep, I head to the fridge and carve out a chunk of the lasagna I made for his dinners. The yellow square of the microwave light hums in the darkness. As I wait, I pull out the inquest documents Jane placed on the top of the bag to read as I eat.

The pathologist's report is like trying to read another language. I keep finding words I need to put into a search engine: "hematoma," "petechiae," "hypoxia."

The section marked "Cause of Death" states only: *1.a. Unascertained.* I skip to the end, to a handwritten section marked "Commentary."

Body has undergone some decomposition. Drowning cannot be ruled out as cause of death. No fluid present in lungs. Evidence of head injury, no skull fracture. No other positive sign of injury. Possible signs of minor petechial hemorrhage found under right eyelid. However, full examination of these features impeded by extensive lividity (body found in facedown position). One broken fingernail present. No foreign DNA present under fingernails. Examination for hematoma/subtle injury impeded by condition of the body at time of examination.

I pull out my laptop, open a browser window, and type in "petechial hemorrhage." Images pop up of bloodshot eyes, speckled blood marks under the eyelids. I click on the eyelid picture. The article is entitled "Effects of Asphyxia." *Asphyxia.* Could Sophie have gotten that from drowning? This article isn't about drowning. It is about cases of suffocation. Or strangling.

The chair is starting to hurt my back. I carry the bag over to the sofa in the front room and start going through the rest of the contents. There is a pile of battered childcare textbooks—these must have been from Sophie's college course. Most of the rest just looks like clothes, a battered washbag.

I pick up one of the textbooks. It is about child psychology. One dog-eared page falls open. It is a section about avoidant attachment, which doesn't mean much to me. In the margin, someone has written: *Jude?*

I make a note in my pad—*WHO IS JUDE?*

Before I can go through the rest of it properly, though, my phone vibrates loudly on the coffee table.

I snatch it up, not wanting it to wake Finn. I expect it is an update from Tom, who told me earlier he'd swapped his shift so he could go for a birthday drink with his friend Ravi. But the message is from an unknown number.

STOP DIGGING.

I startle, so much so I drop the phone, sending it clattering under the coffee table. I pick it up. Adrenaline pulses through me as I read the message again.

I stare at the images on my laptop, the pathology report by my side.

Then a flash of light at the edge of my vision distracts me.

The security light outside our basement flat has flicked on.

Sophie

Fourteen months before

WHEN HE FIRST STARTED at playgroup, Jude never seemed to want to play with me. He never wanted to play with anyone. When he arrived in the morning, he sought out the toys he wanted, and lined them up on the table in front of him. He never, ever asked for help. I'd never met a two-year-old quite like him.

I found myself drawn to him, this little person who was always in his own orbit. I started to sit down next to him and talk about what he was doing.

After a while, he stopped ignoring me, started giving me sideways glances, to check if I was still there. Then he started to play near me, on the floor, occasionally showing me things. Then he started to watch me with my other children. After I'd given them some attention, he would go over to each child and knock over their tower of blocks, scribble on their picture.

Elaine just thought Jude was naughty. "You need to spend time with your other key children, too," she'd said. I sensed there was something wrong, though. I spent my weekends reading up on it. I searched my textbooks, highlighted the passages that seemed to fit.

"Is that his mum, the woman who picks him up?" I asked Elaine one day. She was tall and pretty, dressed like a model, but always looked sort of lost, like she'd ended up at the playgroup by accident.

"Stepmum," Elaine said. She gave me this look like we both knew what that meant.

I started keeping more of an eye on her, this stepmum. I noticed she didn't ask me much about what Jude had been doing. She always seemed stressed about him putting his coat on properly, making sure he had all his things. Neither of them ever seemed very pleased to see each other.

"Thanks for that, Sophie," she said to me once after he'd refused to let her help put his shoes on. She looked tired, and I suddenly felt a bit sorry for her. "I'm sure you've noticed," she added quietly. "Jude is . . ."

She seemed to be struggling to get to the point.

"Unusual?"

She pursed her lips. "Oh. Is he? Unusual? I was just going to say he seems fond of you."

I clamped my mouth shut, regretted saying anything, pretended to fiddle with the little backpack on Jude's peg.

"I suppose I don't really know what's, you know . . . normal." She put her head to one side. "Is Jude not normal?"

I glanced at Jude. He didn't seem to be listening. I took my time, chose my words carefully.

"He is very independent, for his age," I said slowly. "Has he—has he always been like that? Resisting you helping with things?"

"I think so." She nodded, scratching at a thumbnail. "I just . . . I find it hard to know what he wants."

"That can be hard with toddlers anyway," I said. She threw me a grateful smile.

I bit my lip, wondering why I didn't feel I could tell her the truth.

Tash

———⟨⟩———

I SIT PERFECTLY STILL, frozen to the spot, wait for the sound of Tom's key in the lock. But it doesn't come.

The light flashes off, then on again.

The security light doesn't come on unless someone is really close to the house. I try to remember if this has happened before. Is the light broken?

Then I hear a sound outside. A shuffling noise, like footsteps, on the other side of the window.

I feel my stomach contract, a hot flood of dread. Someone is breaking in. Tom might not be home for hours. It is just me and Finn. The door of our basement flat is not even double-locked. Why do I never lock the door properly, like Tom always tells me to? I should have let him put that chain on it. We still haven't even gotten that bathroom window fixed.

The light flashes off, then on again.

I should just look outside the window, but I find I physically can't, that some deep and unfamiliar instinct has wrested the controls. My body has gone completely rigid, my legs locked to the floor, as if I can stop things happening if I stay as I am.

For a moment, there is nothing. Only the breeze, the low hum of traffic. Across the road, I can see the familiar constellation of red and green in the neighbors' shrub, Christmas lights they never seem to take down.

I ease myself from the sofa and creep into the hallway, pulling my hoodie tighter around me. I edge up to the front door and slide the bolt across, muffling the sound with my hands. On the other side of the glass, the safety light is still on. I can't see anyone. But the silence feels thick, as if someone is holding their breath.

I edge back from the door, feeling for my phone in my pocket. I can hear the throb of blood in my ears. I pass Finn's room in the hallway, and push the door open to check on him. He is there, sleeping and perfect, his hair falling over his face, his skinny wrists and ankles poking from the too-small animal pajamas he refuses to abandon.

I step out into the hallway and look toward the front door. I feel a twist of terror as I hear something again. Something like a shuffle, or a scrape.

I'm sure this time. Someone is there, close to me. It is the rustle of human movement, of shoe leather against stone. The light flicks off, then immediately on again.

My hands shaking, I feel again for the hard edges of my phone in my pocket, like a talisman. Trembling, I pull it out and call Tom. It goes straight to voice mail.

The noise comes again, unmistakable this time. Footsteps. Not the soft footfalls you'd hear from the pavement. Sharp, distinct, close. Someone is on our basement steps. Then there is a smash, loud as a shotgun.

I hear myself scream before I'm aware my mouth has opened. I leap back into Finn's room, slam the door shut behind me. I pull the nearest thing—his toy chest, overflowing with plastic cars—against it, but it's not heavy enough. I reach for more things, anything. Books, a lamp. A toddler table. Why does none of this stuff weigh anything?

Finn is awake now. He rubs his eyes and looks at me blearily.

"Mummy, Mummy? What, Mummy?"

I resist the urge to scoop him into my arms. I need to stay by the door. If I can keep the door shut, nothing can happen to him.

"It's all right, Finn," I whisper, as calmly as I can. "Go back to sleep." I can feel tears pricking at my eyes as I pull my phone from my pocket and try to dial 999. The screen is unresponsive, my fingers refusing to work.

"This is 999, which service do you require?"

"Police. Please."

It comes out as a whisper. I don't know if I'm trying not to scare Finn or trying not to scare myself. My heart feels like it might explode in my chest.

Finn is jolted awake at the word police. His eyes widen. "Police mans coming, Mummy?"

I press a finger to my lips. I recite my address, my name, for the person on the phone.

"And what is the reason for your call?"

"S-someone is . . . at my house," I stutter into the phone. "I think maybe—"

The line cuts out. I stare at my phone in disbelief. My battery is dead. My heart is pounding so fast my chest hurts.

"Mummy, what's happening?" Finn's mouth is turning down at the edges.

"Stay quiet, sweetheart," I say, shushing him. "It's going to be fine."

"But what's happening, Mummy?"

"Shh, Finn. Please."

I realize I haven't heard anything for a minute or so. The terror fades a little, my heart slows. I listen again. I can't hear anything. I put my ear to the bedroom door. It doesn't sound like anyone is inside.

"Mummy?"

I pull the duvet over Finn, kiss the soft skin behind his ear. "Everything's OK," I tell him. "Mummy was just checking on you. Sleepy time." It is the magic, sleep-training word. To my astonishment, his eyelids flutter shut, the pull of sleep thick on his little body. Within moments, he is snoring softly.

Carefully, I start pulling things away from the door. When I step into the hallway, the security light is off, the front door locked shut, the glass unbroken. There was no one there. But I heard glass smash. Could they be somewhere else?

I stand in the darkness and listen. But there is nothing. The safety light stays off.

When I am at the front door, I listen for a couple of moments. Then I slide back the bolt and open the door.

The air is cold on my face, the growl of the traffic on the main road thicker in my ears. I look around, and find nothing.

Then I take a step forward, and pain slices through my foot. The sensation is white hot, like lightning.

Gasping, I stagger back, lowering myself down just inside the front door, and take my foot in my hand. The red is everywhere. It doesn't look real. A vivid scarlet line from the bottom of my big toe to the arch of my foot. I am only vaguely aware of a clipped police siren, a blue flashing light.

"Ms. Carpenter? Are you all right?"

I look up to see two police officers on our basement steps. They are staring down at my feet, at the pool of blood, and our front step, which is covered in huge, jagged pieces of broken glass.

Introduction to Child Psychology for
Early Years Professionals, p. 162
This edition first published June 2006

Avoidant attachment: some key signs

   —No distress caused by mother's absence
   —Shows little interest when she returns
   —Avoids eye contact
   —Shuns physical touch
   —Excessive independence
   —Resists help to complete tasks

Avoidant attachment may be the result of abusive or neglectful caregivers.

Tash

THE TWO NICE POLICE officers have left by the time Tom comes home. He finds me in the front room, my leg propped up on cushions, blood still soaking through the bandage the officers helped me tie around my foot, bits of lasagna on a plate on the floor. As soon as I see him, I burst into tears.

"Tash! I came as soon as I saw your message. I saw the glass—are you OK?"

He pulls me into a hug. I swallow. "It's fine, I think. Can you have a look?"

Tom pulls away and gently unwraps the bandage. I cry out.

"Sorry— Oh, Tash! You should have gone to the hospital; this looks deep!"

"I couldn't go with Finn here, could I? Anyway, I've bandaged it up."

"Not very well, you haven't."

Tom is already going to find his kit. I can hear him rummaging in the top shelf of our closet, washing his hands, pulling on latex gloves.

"You'll need stitches." He produces a needle from the bag and starts filling it with a clear liquid. "Lidocaine," he says, seeing me looking. "It's local anesthetic. Sharp scratch, OK?"

I press my lips together. I feel the metal scratch of the needle, then the coldness of the liquid passing under my skin.

"Are you really allowed to have this sort of stuff at home, Tom?"

"Of course. All doctors do."

I gasp at the pain.

"Do you always make sure it's where Finn can't— Ouch! That really hurts."

"Sorry. Hold still." He is putting the stitches in now, black thread pinched between his teeth, his fingers red with my freshly shed blood.

"How did you manage this, then?"

I tell him the story. The light, the noises I heard outside. How sure I was someone was there. When I tell him I called 999, that the police had been over, he looks up from applying the dressing, his eyes wide with horror.

"Jesus, Tash! Were you that worried? Did Finn wake up? What did the police say?"

As I recount my conversation with the police, I watch Tom's expression shift from sympathy to skepticism.

"Oh. So—the police thought it could have been a fox?"

"The police were hopeless. It wasn't a bloody fox, Tom. I heard footsteps. It was a person. How would a fox have covered our front step in broken glass?"

"I guess—could someone have chucked a bottle down the stairs? Maybe that's why you heard footsteps? Or maybe it was a drunk bloke, looking for somewhere to piss?"

"It really didn't feel like that to me." I hesitate, then decide to tell him. "And look. Just before it happened, I got this."

I pull up the text, hand Tom the phone.

He reads it, then stares at me. "What the fuck? Who sent that?"

"No idea. The number's not in my contacts." When the police left, I also checked it against the numbers on the report on Sophie's phone. But nothing matched.

"Haven't you called the number?"

I shake my head.

Tom locks his jaw, then taps on the number to call it.

"Tom, wait . . ."

"What? Let's find out who this is."

Tom holds the phone to his ear. He looks furious. I hear the muffled sound of an automated message. It says the number's out of service.

Tom takes a deep breath, then sets the phone down. I feel myself shiver. Tom picks up a blanket from the sofa and pulls it around my shoulders.

"It could just be a wrong number, I guess," he says. "Or a prank."

"Bit of a weird prank."

Tom frowns. "The alternative being what?"

"That someone wants me to stop digging into the death of Sophie Blake."

Tom is uncomprehending. "What—the inquest case? The girl who died in the wetlands?"

I nod.

"Is that what you think?"

"I don't know what else that message could mean." I shift position, wincing with pain. My foot is throbbing. "I really do think that someone killed her, Tom."

Since the police left, I have been turning it over and over in my mind. I keep coming to the same conclusion. Sophie's head injury that couldn't be accounted for; the fact that she was wearing clothes; the phone that had been wiped before it ended up in the reservoir, the deleted messages that suggested someone was worried about her on the night she died. And now, an anonymous message to me, telling me to stop digging. A person outside our home, broken glass that felt very much like a threat.

I hadn't told the police officers any of this when they came around earlier. I didn't see the point. I could see they didn't even really believe me that there'd been a real person there. They'd kept going on about foxes. But I know there was someone there. Someone trying to frighten me. The same person sending the messages. And the more I think about it, the more I can think of only one possible explanation. Someone killed Sophie Blake, and they got away with it. And now, that same person—or someone linked to them—is trying to frighten me off.

"But I don't understand," Tom says slowly. "How would anyone even know you were looking into her death?"

"I don't know," I say more quietly. I try and remember who knows. Jane Blake. The reservoir guy from the wetlands. One police press officer. No one else. Unless there is someone else. Someone watching me.

Tom takes my hand, interlaces his fingers with mine. "Don't you think a discarded bottle is a bit more likely, Tash? If you'd just gotten that message, it's understandable you'd be on edge about a noise outside, but—"

"Tom, I honestly heard someone, right outside. There was a smash . . . it sounded controlled. Deliberate."

Tom looks at me for a moment. "OK," he says. "Well, in that case, maybe we get a stronger lock on the door. I've said before I think we need bars on the windows, too."

I look away. I have always protested about the bars. But now, I'm not so sure.

"And maybe one of those doorbells. You know, where you can see who's at the door? Ravi's got one at his new place. You can see who's outside your house through an app on your phone."

I laugh at this. "Ravi's moved to the suburbs with his huge brood and turned into a nosy neighbor."

"He loves a gadget." I can see that Tom has had a nice evening with his friend. His shoulders have dropped. He is smiling more.

"Thanks," I say after a pause.

"What for?"

"For not telling me to stop doing my job."

"Come here." He pulls me into a hug. "I'd never want you to do that," he murmurs into my hair. "I'm sorry I was out with Rav and you had a scary night. I feel bad I'm doing so many nights at the moment, too. It won't be forever."

"I know. It's OK. Let's just go to bed."

I LIE awake for a long time, the weight of Tom's arm around my waist, my foot throbbing, adrenaline still fizzing underneath my skin. The fear I felt earlier hardens into outrage. Who is this person who wants to frighten me, to make me feel my family is not safe? Who wants me to just shut up and disappear?

I've been a reporter long enough to know that when people start threatening you, it means there's something there. But the threats usually take the form of lawyers' letters. Not anonymous text messages. Not people trying to break into my flat late at night, while my son sleeps.

Stop digging? No chance, I think, shifting myself from under Tom's arm, curling onto my side. *I'm going to find out who you are, and what you did. I'm going to expose you.*

Tash

I FEEL DIFFERENT SINCE the broken glass, my nerve endings heightened, as if I am missing a layer of skin. Every time my phone sounds, I snatch it up, heart pounding, in case it is another anonymous message. I have started jumping at slammed doors, motorbikes revving on the street.

My foot is still throbbing as I make my way to Claire's for the Friday playdate. It's the first time I have been to her house. Everything about it is huge; the windows, the front steps, the stone lions on either side. As I limp up to the front door with Finn, I have the sensation of us both having shrunk. Finn stares at the gold Victorian knocker, shaped like a human face, with a crown of leaves in its hair and a heavy ring in its mouth. He looks worried.

"Mummy, what's that face?"

"It's a knocker, darling. Do you want to knock it?"

Finn shakes his head, so I do it instead.

Jez answers. "Tash! Good to see you. Hi, Finn." Jez is wearing a crisp white shirt and suit trousers, a red tie balled and stuffed in his trouser pocket, just the tip of its tongue protruding. On his neck, just underneath his ear, is a tiny razor cut.

We follow Jez through the front room and into the kitchen. I try not to limp. I'm sick of being asked what's wrong.

"What can I get you to drink?"

I forget to answer his question. Their house is unlike anything I have ever seen, except on the property finder app I'm borderline addicted to. The huge front room, with its marble fireplace and tall bay window, seamlessly turns into a kitchen, which gives way to an enormous dining space, contained in what looks like a floating glass box. The house appears to have no wall at all at the back; the glass box is part of a huge double-story addition, with a grid of slim Crittall windows and a black metal staircase. Beyond it is a wall of green, a jungle of mature trees and plants.

I put Finn down and immediately take his muddy shoes off, shoving them into a plastic bag in my backpack. I find his cup of water and zip the bag back up. I wonder about leaving my backpack on the floor, but it looks wrong and messy against their furniture, so I pick it up and put it back on. I imagine how I must look to Jez: a frumpy mother, bent over a backpack, clattering around with bits of toddler plastic.

Finn has already wandered into the front-room area and has his hands on a cream, vintage-style ride-on car.

"Finn, that's not yours."

"He's fine." Jez smiles over at Finn, who has frozen, legs already on either side of the seat. "Help yourself, mate."

Finn grins at me triumphantly and plonks himself down onto the car. I glance nervously at the wood floors, the marble fireplace, the powder-painted ceiling roses. *Please,* I think, *don't break anything.*

"Can I get you a drink, Tash?"

"Oh, no, thanks." Truthfully, I'm not a huge fan of how much daytime drinking these playdates seem to involve. I keep returning home with a throbbing headache.

"A coffee, then?" Jez is at the kitchen island, next to a cherry-red espresso machine.

"I'm fine for coffee, too, actually."

"Oh, that's a relief." He throws me a conspiratorial smile. "I don't think I actually know how this works." He touches one of the levers and it clatters onto the marble counter. He feigns a look of terror, followed by a grin that reaches every contour of his face. I burst out laughing.

"I wouldn't mind a tea. Do you know how to make tea?"

"Tea I can do."

He flicks the kettle on and starts to whistle something, a song I know, but can't place.

"Your house is beautiful." I feel I can't not say it. I can't take my eyes off the glass at the back of the house, the garden beyond. It must be a hundred feet long or more. Banana trees arch overhead; wisteria coils around a wooden pergola. Tucked at the far end, I spy another glass-fronted building, a garden room of some sort, painted a tasteful pale gray. A light is on inside.

"Thanks. We like it. So, how's the world of journalism?"

"Oh, it's fine." The words come out less convincingly than I'd hoped, with a sort of sigh.

"Oh God." Jez laughs. "That sounds bad."

"Sorry." I make a face. "It's just—freelancing. I'm constantly chasing payments, basically begging for work. I do sometimes wonder if it's worth the effort, really."

"Oh no. Don't give up, Tash. You must never give up."

I hesitate, unsure how to respond. Before I can reply, Jez comes to stand very close, close enough for me to smell him. I can't work out what he is doing. I can actually feel his breath on the surface of my cheek. The memory of his hand on the small of my back. His wife is, presumably, here somewhere, likely to appear at any moment.

"I just need to get the milk," he explains.

I jump back, as if I've been scalded. I am standing in front of the fridge. The cupboards all look the same, I can't tell. I step farther away, farther than I need to, a blush creeping up the side of my neck. When I look up, Jez hasn't opened the fridge. He is still looking straight at me.

"Here you both are. Hi, Finn!" Claire is in the kitchen, wearing a loose kimono jacket in patterned red silk over a white vest and jeans. I wheel around, smiling. I am sure she must see the color on my neck.

"Hey," I gabble. "You look lovely, Claire." She does look different—tanned, perhaps.

"Thanks, Tash."

"Have you been away?"

"We had a few days in our Cornish place." Claire rolls her eyes dreamily. "We had amazing weather. It was quite hot for this time of year! We were so lucky." She leans on the counter, her silk sleeves settling about her arms like butterfly wings, smiles the smile of someone who is used to being lucky with the weather. "Can you pop us another bottle of fizz, please, Jez sweetheart?" She winks at me behind his back.

"We'll go at Easter," she adds. "To Cornwall. With Nicole and Laura, too."

"Sounds wonderful," I say honestly. "Finn is desperate to go to the beach." I think again of Finn's little fingers pointed at the picture of the beach in his favorite storybook.

"You should totally come, Tash!" Claire's eyes are wide. "We'd love it!"

"Oh . . . no!" I protest. "I didn't mean—"

"You must! Bring Tom and Finn! The house is finished now, so there's loads of room. You can walk right onto a sandy beach. Imagine them all there playing together! Finn would love it!"

Jez pops a bottle of champagne from the fridge, starts to pour. I pause, try and work out whether Claire is serious. I have never known people who throw gifts around like these women do—playdates, brunches, spa days, champagne, vacations. I allow myself briefly to imagine us all in Cornwall together—those big open skies, sparkling blue coves, Finn running around with a bucket in the waves with his new friends, us drinking wine around a beach campfire, like models in the Boden catalog.

Claire has already moved on, though, so perhaps it wasn't a real invitation. She is holding the stem of her glass delicately, the tiny bubbles sparkling behind her fingernails.

"How's Finn finding playgroup now?" she asks as she takes a sip.

"So much better, thanks." This is true. The playdates with Oscar, Beau, and Lissy have really helped him. He's particularly keen on Oscar, who is very chatty for his age, and shares Finn's love of anything with wheels.

"That's such great news. I knew he'd be fine." Claire beams. "It's a really great place. Elaine always works wonders."

I glance at her, wondering what she means by this. But Claire has turned away, gathering the champagne bottle and the flutes between her slim fingers.

"Right," she says. "Shall we go downstairs?"

THE BASEMENT is full of stylish chairs and low tables, like the foyer of a Scandinavian hotel. Laura stands up to greet me; Nicole is bottle-feeding baby Charlotte in an armchair. She waggles her fingers with her free hand, but doesn't get up.

Claire pours more champagne, and the children play while we sit and chat. Later, I ask to go to the bathroom, desperate to have more of a look around their house. I feel as if I'm on the set of a film.

"Sure," says Claire. "We'll keep an eye on Finn."

I'm sure there is a bathroom on the basement floor, but I want to see the rest of the house, so before Claire can protest, I take the staircase up from the front hallway. The stairs are painted a deep indigo, with a pale runner in the center, a little brass rod holding it in place on each step. Off the first landing, I see what must be Beau's bedroom—except it seems very grown-up for a not-quite-two-year-old. It has no pictures on the walls, or soft furnishings. Just a few toys thrown haphazardly in a basket. If it wasn't for the dinosaur quilt cover, you wouldn't even necessarily think it was a child's bedroom.

I make my way along the upstairs hallway. The floorboards are stained white, the walls papered with the palest pink ticking stripe. The brushed-gold light switch is cold to the touch. I am sure I hear a door closing, soft footsteps on the landing, but when I look around, there is no one there.

At the end of the long corridor, I spot what must be Jez and Claire's bedroom. The room is light-filled and magazine bright, the bed plump with pillows and cushions and covered in patterned throws. Dark green walls, silk lampshades, a sheepskin on the floor. The air is cool, and there is a scent of fresh flowers.

I step into their en suite bathroom. My fingers feel for a switch, but instead, soft lights appear in the walls, sensing my presence. I place my hands under the tap and water appears, the temperature perfect. The hand soap in a glass pump bottle smells of tangerine peel. I look around for a towel, but seeing none, I try the drawer under the sink.

There are no towels in there, though. Just bottles. Dark brown pill bottles with white plastic lids. Rows and rows of them, packed tight into the drawer, neat as an army. I stare at them, stunned. This is no normal family medicine cupboard, with half-full bottles of Tylenol, cough syrup, Band-Aids adorned with cartoon characters. This looks like the inside of a pharmacy.

I pick the bottles up one by one and hold them up to the light. They don't have prescription labels. Surely if they were prescribed, they would say for whom? The drug names don't mean anything to me, either. *Diazepam, temazepam, zopiclone.*

Behind the bottles, there is something else. A paper pill packet shoved right at the back of the drawer. I lever it out with my fingernail. As I do, I can see that it is a packet of contraceptive pills. They are the ones I use myself. I recognize the purple stripe on the side of the box.

Unlike the bottles, though, this packet does have a pharmacy label, peeling at one edge. I turn the box over to read it.

When I see the name, I nearly drop the box. This can't be right.

It says these pills were prescribed to Sophie Blake.

Sophie

Thirteen months before

"I'LL WRITE MY CELL number on here, and a few details," she said, taking a piece of paper. "This is the sort of salary we were thinking."

I was finding it hard to concentrate on what she was saying. I was distracted by her house: the high ceilings, the shiny kitchen cupboards, the glass at the back, the black-and-white photographs on the walls in frames.

"You have a beautiful house, Mrs. Henderson."

She didn't seem to hear me right. "Yes, the house. You'd be in the annex."

I looked at her blankly.

"It would be a live-in position. We think that would work best, for us. And Jude."

She handed me the piece of paper. I looked at the number she had written down. I tried not to show how shocked I was. It was more than twice my nursery salary. Was this how much nannies were paid?

"Obviously we could negotiate," she said quickly. "If it's, you know, not what you were expecting."

I look up from the paper.

"When you say, live-in," I begin, "you mean . . ."

"You would live here."

"In this house?"

"There's an annex," she explained. "You'd have your own space."

I still didn't know what she was on about—annex sounded like something out of Anne Frank—but then I thought of my shared flat above a kebab shop on the Archway Road junction. The extractor fan that smelled of doner meat. The thump of the parties in the flat next door. The scream of sirens at night.

"I'm sorry my husband isn't here, Sophie. He very much wanted to meet you, but he had a meeting he couldn't get out of."

I nodded, wishing she had said her husband's name. I couldn't remember it, couldn't remember him ever coming for pickup. The playgroup mothers were all distinct in my head—I knew them by their coats, the shades of their catalog-perfect strollers—but the husbands were so dull, so colorless. They tended to shape-shift in my mind, like ghosts. I could never be sure which one was which, which child to hand over to whom.

"What do you do for work?" I asked.

"I teach yoga a bit. I have a studio, out in the garden." She gestured vaguely to the back of the house. "But I'm not really doing much at the moment, not with . . . well. You've probably noticed by now."

She was smiling self-consciously, one hand on her belly. Her stomach was curved, just slightly, a little cantaloupe-sized bump. You'd never know unless you were looking for it.

"Congratulations."

"So, you see, I'm afraid I'll definitely need some help." She was looking down now, fiddling with a fold of her dress. She seemed to find this part shaming, I thought. The fact that she needed help, not because she had a career, like the other playgroup mothers, but because she just needed it.

"So." She looked up, fixed me with her steely blue gaze. "What do you think, Sophie?"

I paused. I already knew that I would take the job. There was no way I wasn't going to take the job. The money was double what I was paid at playgroup, plus I wouldn't have to pay rent. But something was preventing me from saying yes, and I wondered what it was. Not the house—so beautiful, so full of light, little toys tidied away at the edges of the rooms in wicker baskets. Was it her? She didn't seem so bad, the stepmum. She seemed quite sweet, really. She just wasn't used to things being hard, things taking time. I guessed that it wasn't her fault. But there was something here, nonetheless, something in the particles of the air between us. Something that was making me hesitate. Why hadn't she asked me any more questions? Didn't she want to know about my experience, my qualifications? Didn't she want to know who I was?

I rehearsed it in my head, the idea of handing my notice in. Elaine would be angry, but she'd get over it. One more disappointment to add to her life's little pile. Casey and Tara would have something to say. I was sure of that. *Good luck with that kid*, I imagined Casey saying. *I hope they're paying you enough.* Tara would be too nice to say anything, but she would think it was a bad idea. She'd told me once that you should never live in. *People take advantage*, she'd said. *Once you live in, it's like you're never off duty. You'll be babysitting every night. You won't be able to get away from them.* But what would I want to get away from, in this house?

"OK," I said.

Her face broke into a hopeful smile. "Really?"

"Yeah. I mean, I'll have a think about it. I'll let you know."

She nodded vigorously. "Of course, of course," she said. "You must take your time, Sophie. You just let us know." She stood up.

"Thanks, Mrs. Henderson."

"Oh, honestly, Sophie." She waved her hands, did a jangly little laugh. "Please. Call me Claire."

Tash

I SLUMP ONTO THE edge of the bath, the pill packet in my hand. My hand is trembling, my legs unsteady. Sophie Blake had been here. In this house. Had she been Claire's nanny? Or was there some other reason they had her pills in their drawer?

I look at the drawer of pills, then back at my reflection in the glass, trying to work out what on earth is going on. But before I can make sense of what I am seeing, I hear Finn scream.

I know instantly in my gut that it is a real cry—something has happened to him. Even though I am two floors away, I can see his face exactly in my mind, crumpling like a crushed paper bag. I run down the stairs, through the kitchen, and back down into the basement, his crying getting louder and louder.

JEZ IS kneeling at the bottom of the metal staircase. My screaming son is writhing in his arms. Laura is leaning over them both in doctor mode, her hands on Finn's cheeks, trying to look in his mouth. The other women are standing around, staring at him, like participants in some gruesome tableau. There is blood on the carpet. Finn's face is white. As soon as I appear, everybody, including Finn, fixes their eyes on me.

Jez passes Finn wordlessly to me. I hug my son tightly, then pull away to look at his face. The blood is coming from his mouth. I shush him, put my fingers inside to feel for his teeth. They are all still there. His bottom lip is split.

"Muh. Mee." Finn is crying so much that he is gasping for breath.

"Put this on his mouth."

I am vaguely aware of Jez's voice, of one of his hands on my shoulder, the other pressing a cloth, wrapped around something cold, against Finn's face.

"Shh, shh. All right, darling. All right." I hug Finn into me, feeling his blood soaking through my top. I turn to Laura, Claire, and Nicole. "What happened?"

They all open their mouths, but Laura speaks first.

"He fell down the stairs. We didn't get there in time." She takes a deep breath. I can't help glancing over at the table, the almost-empty bottle of champagne.

"I'm so sorry, Tash. We were talking and . . . I'm so sorry."

I try to steady myself. Finn is still sobbing, but the screaming has stopped. He feels puffed out, like a collapsed balloon.

"I had a look, it's not bad," Laura says, coming close to me. She places her hand lightly on the back of Finn's head. "It looks worse than it is. Lip injuries bleed a lot but heal quickly. I don't think it needs a stitch. He'll be fine."

"OK. Thanks. I think I need to get him home." I know it's not her fault, but I can't force myself to meet her eyes.

I take Finn upstairs. He sobs softly as I zip him into his coat. "Muh. Mee. Carr-ee."

"You know I can't, Finney. It's too far for me to carry you and I need to push the buggy."

His face crumples again. "No buggy, Mummy."

"Come on, please, darling." The urgency in my voice makes him cry harder. I pull my phone out and try to hail a taxi. But the app produces nothing. The first ride cancels. The next says seventeen minutes. I hear footsteps on the stairs, a presence behind me.

"Tash? Let me drive you both home."

I open my mouth to say no to Jez, but then the hopelessness of my situation dawns on me. It is rush hour. We might have to wait for two, maybe three buses before there is space for the stroller. Finn is in pain, and tired. We have no car. I have a sudden pang of longing for our little car—the red Vauxhall Corsa that gave up the ghost a year or so ago. It broke down when Tom was driving it, and he said we didn't drive enough to justify a new one.

"OK," I say. "We'll take a lift. Please. Thanks."

I pack Finn into the car seat in the back, fumbling with the unfamiliar straps. He is strangely calm now, distracted by the novelty of riding in a car. His swollen lip looks awful, upturned and fat, like a raw sausage. I try to smile so I don't alarm him.

"Are you comfy, sweetheart?"

He doesn't reply. I tuck my bag in next to him, zip open, so he can reach the snacks. There's another car seat beside where Finn is, so I get into the front. The seats of Jez's car are a soft leather, the color of a milky coffee. Two iPads are strewn casually into the footwell. The passenger seat feels very high up, like a sort of throne.

As Jez pulls out of their drive I think again about what I found in the bathroom. Sophie Blake. Her pills were there, in that house. But why? Had she been there? Had she been in this car, in the passenger seat, where I am now?

"Thanks for this," I tell Jez.

"Honestly, Tash. It's the least we can do."

Jez is a careful driver. He doesn't lurch, like Tom does, at the speed bumps on their long road. He looks straight ahead, his hands firmly on the wheel. His forearms are tanned, the hairs sun-bleached. I turn to look at Finn. I can see he is about to fall asleep, the shadows of the plane trees flickering over his cheek.

I rack my brain for a way to ask Jez about Sophie, about the pills. But before I can think of one, he speaks.

"So how did you become a journalist?"

At first, I mumble single-word answers, too rattled to think properly about Jez's questions. But somehow, as we drive on, I find myself relaxing. He is easy company, and I find myself telling him the whole story. The story I hardly ever tell, about why I really became a journalist. The story about my dad, and what happened in Iraq, just before I started my GCSEs. And how we found out after he'd died that he'd fixed up this work-experience placement for me at his paper. And it was as if he'd known exactly what I was made for.

"Hang on," he says. "We're not talking about Dom James? The war photographer?"

I stare at Jez. "You've heard of my dad?"

Jez's eyes are wide. "I've got all his books. He was a legend. Wow—you must be so proud!"

To my alarm, I feel a tightening in my throat.

"Oh God." He looks at me, horrified. "Sorry, Tash. I didn't mean to upset you."

I shake my head, force myself to swallow. "It's fine." I exhale, recovering myself.

We sit in traffic for a while, the snake of cars edging forward painfully, the light starting to fade around us. Jez reaches across me to the glove compartment, opens it with one hand, extracts some gum.

"Would you like one?"

"Thanks." As he replaces it, I spy a packet of cigarettes and a lighter. "You smoke?"

Jez makes a face. "Rarely. I mean, I was a social smoker. But Claire hates it, so I try not to." He glances at me. "You?"

I smile. "Similar. Journalists are terrible for smoking. But yes, Tom doesn't like it, so I haven't for a long time."

We inch forward.

"Were you ever tempted to go to war zones and stuff?" Jez asks. "Like your dad?"

I make a face. "No," I say. "I mean, you have to be a top reporter to get that sort of gig. I never made it to a proper national."

I think about the time a few years back, when I got a few weeks of shifts at a national. There was a top table of reporters there—a table that had its own coffee rounds, its own in-jokes, its own rules about who sat where, who talked to whom. I'd sat on the periphery, at my temporary desk, and watched them. Blokes mostly, older than me. None of them worked as hard as I did. But that didn't matter. If a big story broke—a royal scandal, a terror attack, a Russian spy killing—I watched them open their little black books and call contacts they'd lunched and nurtured over decades of drinks and dinners, never worrying once about childcare.

"You might still get there," Jez says.

I laugh. "I won't."

"I'm sure you're being modest."

Jez's smile, his absolute self-confidence, irritates me all of a sudden. "You don't know anything about it, actually."

The words spill out before I even know I've said them. Jez fixes his eyes back on the road.

"I'm sorry," I say quickly. "That was rude and unnecessary."

"Not at all," he says gallantly. "You're quite right. Sorry I said anything."

We are nearly at the flat now. Jez brakes and signals. I mentally grapple for something to say, a way to smooth things over.

"What about you?" I ask awkwardly. "I haven't even asked about your job."

"Oh, don't bother, really. It's nowhere near as interesting." Jez slows down, gestures outside. "Here we are—it's just here on the left, isn't it?"

I look out of the window. "Oh, yes. Thanks." I turn to face him. "Jez, thank you. For the lift."

"It's nothing."

"I'm honestly—I'm very grateful. And I don't know why I reacted like that. Why I was so rude, I mean. When you asked about my work."

"Really, Tash," he says. "You've had a horrible shock." He glances in the rearview mirror at Finn. "It's fine."

It does not feel fine. I hesitate, not wanting to leave, wanting to explain, to redeem myself somehow.

"I think I just feel a bit lost at the moment," I blurt.

I clamp my lips together, my tongue feeling suddenly thick in my mouth, my throat constricting. I have, I realize, never actually said this out loud. When I dare to look up at Jez, he's nodding thoughtfully.

"I think," he says carefully, "that everyone feels like that from time to time."

I take a deep breath. I should get out of the car. I should go home.

But somehow my hand, which I have placed on the door handle, doesn't move. "Tash," Jez says, very softly. "It's all right."

Finn makes a noise in the back. Something in the atmosphere is broken. I start to feel around for my bags, Finn's coat. I pull at the door handle, but the child lock is on.

"Oh, sorry. Here."

Jez releases the child lock, but then realize I still have my seat belt on.

"Sorry, I'm still strapped in."

"Ah. Right."

I move my hand to release the seat belt. In my haste, my fingers miss the clasp, and brush against Jez's.

Even though the contact only lasts a moment, it seems to linger on my skin. Long after I have opened the passenger door, hauled my sleeping son out of the car seat, carried him home, and closed my front door safely behind me, it feels like it is still there. His touch, on my hand, like the brush of a stinging nettle.

Sophie

Twelve months before

THE RAIN THIS MORNING had painted the paths with a mirror shine. Clissold Park smelled washed and clean and of itself. As I walked through the gates, Mum called.

"Oh." She sounded surprised I'd answered. "Is that Sophie?"

"Er, you called me, Mum."

"I know, love, sorry. I'm just . . . pleased I caught you."

I felt a stab of guilt. How many times had I ignored her calls this week?

"So how is it, love?"

"Fine." I pinched the phone between my ear and my shoulder, changed hands on the push bar of the stroller. "I'm just walking Jude. He's sleeping."

"Oh. Does he still sleep in the day? I thought he was three."

I bite my lip. Not you as well, Mum, I think.

"Sometimes."

Mum pauses. "They treating you all right?"

"Of course."

"What's your room like?"

"Nice."

The annex, as they called it, had turned out to be better than nice. It was more like a separate house, stuck on one side of the main one. It had its own front door at the bottom of some basement steps, a small kitchen at the back looking out to the garden. It was my own little home.

"And you're not finding it a bit much?" Mum asked. "Being there, all the time?"

"It's fine." I had more of my own space now than I did in the house share before. It was plenty of space for just me. It wasn't as if I had anyone else to bring home. I thought briefly about the runner. The wet ends of his hair, his dark eyelashes.

"And she's a nice person?" Mum asked. "The . . . wife?"

"Yeah."

"And what's the husband like?

"Nice as well," I said evenly. "Friendly."

I wasn't used to being around a man like Jez, let alone living with one. When he got home, he scooped Jude up in his arms, cuddling and kissing him, calling him his "best boy," joining in with his games, even if he was still wearing his suit. In the evenings, he tied an apron on over his shirt and cooked their evening meal from scratch. He had shelves and shelves of books, and he told me I could borrow any of them I wanted. I had a pile of them stacked by my bed, ready to start. I imagined myself dropping them into conversations with him, just casually. And him giving me that look he did sometimes, surprised and impressed, like he was still trying to figure me out.

It became very important to me that Jez thought I was doing a good job. I had decided to start making him espressos in the morning, so he didn't have to buy one on the way to work. I had been practicing with the machine when they were out. I got the grind amount just right, a perfect biscuit-colored foam on top.

"Wow! No one never makes me coffee," he had said with a grin, and Claire had pinched him teasingly at the bottom of his stomach.

"Well, why would I bother to learn to use the machine now, when Sophie does it so beautifully?" She'd turned, still touching him. Winked at me.

"It's fine," I told Mum. "It's all going well. Really well."

"You know you can always come home. If you miss your home comforts."

"I know." Yeah, right, I thought. Beige food, nights on the sofa that smelled of cigarette smoke, watching her crap TV. No, thanks.

"What do you do all day, then?"

Mum didn't believe good things like this just happened. She didn't believe in people like Claire and Jez. I could tell she didn't trust them.

"I told you all this, Mum. I get Jude his breakfast, take him to the playgroup—"

"But what about *while* he is in playgroup? What do they expect you to do then?"

In truth, I did find that part a bit weird. Not having anything to do all day. That morning I'd asked if there was anything I could do while Jude was at playgroup. Anything that needed doing in the baby's room, maybe?

Claire had looked up, smiling at me. "I'll do all that, hon." She was lounging at the window seat, eating protein yogurt from the tub with a silver spoon, her bump cocooned in a stripey dress, like a mother from an advertisement. "You just chill. Help yourself to anything in the fridge, if you're hungry."

"But there must be so much—"

"Honestly." Claire had shaken her head. "You'll have more than enough to do when the baby's here."

I guessed that maybe the reason Claire didn't think it was strange me not doing very much was because she didn't do much, either. She was constantly in motion, flitting mothlike in her silk kimono and floaty skirts, dancing around to Blondie songs in the kitchen, not caring whether I was there looking. What she actually *did*, I couldn't quite put my finger on.

"There's not that much to do in the day," I admitted. "But they don't mind."

"Hmph." Mum exhaled noisily into the phone. I imagined the air battling through her tar-threaded lungs.

"What?"

"Well, I'd keep myself busy if I were you, Sophie. Can't you do their washing, or—"

"I didn't ask for advice, Mum."

"You never do. More's the pity."

I hung up, pressing harder than I needed to on the screen.

We walked through Clissold Park, past the café in the big grand house, along the shining asphalt paths by the water fountain, the straggly rose bushes. Down the hill, past the bottom of the park, you could see the strange old castle building that used to be a waterworks, and beyond it, the shimmering cranes on the Woodberry Estate.

By the time I left the park it was starting to rain again. The trees dripped, their branches meeting in an archway over the middle of the road, like interlinking fingers. I hurried up the stone steps and felt for the house keys in my pocket. It still seemed strange to me that I owned a key to a door like this, on a street like this. That I could just let myself inside it.

Claire was at the door. She helped me in, glancing at Jude's closed eyes. I whispered hello. Claire looked at her watch, then back at Jude, then at her watch again.

"I just find he's a bit happier in the afternoons, when he's had a nap," I whispered, an attempt at explanation.

Claire hesitated. "It's fine," she said after a few moments. "You do whatever you think, Sophie." She was smiling, but I was starting to suspect that what Claire said wasn't always what she meant.

I couldn't understand why she wouldn't want Jude to sleep. He got exhausted otherwise. But it was her call, I reminded myself. She was the stepmum. It wasn't my business.

I heard Claire closing the garden doors on her way out to the studio. I wondered if she was annoyed about the sleeping thing. It made me feel jangly all over. Maybe I should tidy the house, make it up to her.

I made my way from room to room, ending up in the new baby's nursery. It was twice as big as Jude's room, and finished already, months ahead of time. Claire had had wallpaper shipped from Italy and got a man in to hang it properly, so all the pieces fit perfectly together. It wasn't like normal paper—it felt soft to the touch, like cotton. The pattern had bamboo fronds and vines in the palest greens, monkeys and giraffes positioned at just the right height so they seemed to be peeping over the cot.

I ran my fingers along the bars, pausing at the part where Claire had fastened pale gray bumpers, with ribbon ties. I had read that you weren't supposed to put newborns in a crib with bumpers, but I pulled my hand away. Claire's baby, I reminded myself. Not mine.

I gave the surfaces a quick clean, plumped the cushions on the pink armchair. Claire had left some baby things on the seat, still in paper bags from the little shops on Upper Street. Among the velvety sleepers, tiny soft towels with bear ears on the hoods, I spotted a patterned dress, a pink stuffed rabbit. They didn't know what they were having, and Claire insisted she didn't mind. It was obvious, though, that she was hoping for a girl. I'm not sure you can expect to keep secrets from someone. Not if they come and live inside your house.

Tash

TOM DOESN'T BLAME ME for what happened to Finn's lip, or even really ask what happened. On the scale of disasters he has seen, a split lip barely even registers. He does think it needs skin glue, though, and seems annoyed with Laura for not doing anything with it.

"She should have erred on the side of caution." He pulls his bag down from the high shelf in the bedroom closet.

"I'm sure she meant well," I say. "Maybe she didn't have anything on her—not every doctor carries around a bag of all this hospital-grade gear."

Tom tells Finn to close his eyes, then holds a needle to his lips. "So how did this happen, Finney?" Tom asks.

We both look at Finn. His face starts to crumple again.

"All right, sweetheart," I say soothingly. "Maybe we shouldn't make him relive it, Tom."

"OK. Sorry. Little scratch, buddy." Finn screams.

"It's all right, love." I breathe into the perfect swirl of Finn's ear, kissing the edge of it. Tom starts with the glue. Finn's screams curdle into sobs.

"Nearly done," Tom murmurs. I try to watch, but find myself forced to look away. "Do you think he'll have a scar?"

"I don't think so. Try to hold still, Finn."

"Daddy, stop!" Finn howls. I feel a sob rise in my chest as I clutch him to me.

"I'm sorry, kiddo," Tom says gently. "Not long now."

"It was my fault," I murmur. "I should have been watching him."

"Nonsense. You can't watch him all the time." Tom looks away from the lip for a moment to lock eyes with me. When he sees my face, he reaches out, squeezes my hand. "Hey—it's not your fault! You're the best mum, Tash. The best."

I smile gratefully. Eventually, Tom finishes, packs his bag.

"All done," he tells Finn, ruffling his hair. "Brave boy." He gives my hand another squeeze. "Now, do you want to have some TV and ice cream with Daddy?"

TOM HAS a shift first thing, so he goes to bed early. I pour myself a glass of wine and sit in the kitchen. It feels as if I have been holding my breath.

I type out a message to Jane.

Could Sophie's employers have been called Claire and Jeremy Henderson?

She doesn't reply. I suppose it is too late to call. I toss my phone onto the table in frustration. But then I remember about the report on Sophie's phone.

I look up Claire's cell phone number and go through the ones on the report. The first one is a match. It's Claire's cell number.

Hi Sophie, where are you? Was expecting you here 20 mins ago.

Claire sent that message the day Sophie disappeared.

I pull out the heavy bag of Sophie's belongings to have another look through them all. I sifted the clothes properly, pulling out each item one by one.

The majority are cheap T-shirts, jeans, and leggings. But some other things are quite different. A beautiful, long cashmere cardigan, impossibly soft to the touch. A jacket in fawn-colored leather, smooth as butter. A sea-green clutch with a pearl-studded clasp. A belted trench jacket. A dark lace dress, cut low at the back.

My fingers slow. I check the necks, the insides. I find designer labels, the sort I've only ever heard about, never seen in real life, never touched with my own hands. I take my index finger and trace the silk folds of the clutch bag. Are these really Sophie's clothes?

When I move the bag closer to place the clothes back, I realize what is making it so heavy. The thing I thought was a wash bag is actually a camera case, something heavy and angular nestling inside.

I open the zip and reach inside. The camera is an old-fashioned one, the metal casing cold to the touch, the weight of it so heavy I barely trust myself with it in my single hand. I lift it out, run my fingertips along the markings on the aperture ring, the metal shutter speed dial. It reminds me of my dad's camera so much that for a moment I think it must be his. Even the battered leather strap looks the same.

A vintage Nikon. This is a proper camera. It would have cost thousands. Had Sophie really bought this?

I pull out the small metal lever to manually wind the film reel, then flick the door open. But there is no film inside.

A message arrives from Jane.

Yes I think that was there names.

I set the camera down, catch my breath. Sophie was Claire's nanny. She lived in their house.

Immediately, another message comes through.

She spoke more about the boys. There names were unusual. I think there baby was Bo or something like that. The older 1 was Jude.

But I thought Claire only had one boy, not two. So where was this other boy? Where was Jude?

Sophie

Eleven months before

CLAIRE HAD HAULED A load of shopping bags into the hallway.

"It's just my old clothes," she said when she saw me looking.

"Can I help?"

"No, that's all of them."

I peered inside one of the bags. A leather jacket. A lace dress, a silk clutch. The stuff looked brand-new, maybe even designer. Some had obviously never been worn. They still had the tags attached.

"Do you think you could stuff them under the buggy?" Claire was frowning at me. "I guess you could do a couple of runs."

"To where?"

"The charity shop." She stretched her arms over her head, her fingers interlinked. "Need to make space for my glamorous new maternity wardrobe." She rolled her eyes at me to show she was joking.

I hesitated. Claire gave me a funny look.

"What?"

"Nothing, I just . . . they look brand-new, some of them. Have you thought about maybe putting these on Depop? You could make a fair bit of money."

"Depop?" Claire pursed her lips. "What's that?"

I looked at her. "You must have heard of Depop."

Claire burst out laughing. "Wow," she said, putting her hand on her hips. "You make me feel very old sometimes, Sophie."

I laughed. "Sorry. It's an app. You buy and sell clothes. You just take pictures on your phone—it's super easy. I can show you."

"Thanks, but honestly, I'm far too lazy." Claire smiled. "Just take anything you want, Sophie. Really."

Later that night, in my bathroom, my hands searched greedily through the bags. I slipped the black lace dress on first. I had known it would suit me, but was startled by my reflection in the glass. I looked older, taller, more whole somehow. An adult.

I found my heels, rummaged in my makeup bag for a red lipstick, a dark eyeshadow. I held my phone up and snapped, pouting like I'd seen Casey and Tara do in their Instagram shots. I lay on my bed awhile, fiddling with the filters, and by the end I looked like someone else entirely.

Lately, it really did feel like I was becoming someone else. It still took me a few seconds to remember where I was when I woke in the mornings. To recognize the swirls in the ceiling plaster, the dancing pale golden light on the walls, as belonging to a room of my own. My key ring suddenly had loads of keys—front and back doors of the house and the fob for their Land Rover—just for getting stuff in and out. I didn't know how to drive, although Jez had said he'd be happy to teach me. I had started to make my way through the little stack of books Jez had loaned me, too. At breakfast, I had begun to eat the same things as Claire. It seemed to make her feel better about me cooking if I ate with her. At first I found the things she liked strange, but now I was used to them. Smoothies with kale and ginger, buckwheat porridge, sweet potato pancakes, thick clots of Greek yogurt with seeds and fat, round blueberries.

I wasn't actually paid to start work until eight, but Jude would usually wake before six in the mornings, and there would be no sign of Jez or Claire. I didn't really mind. I was used to early starts, and Claire needed her sleep.

One morning, I decided to take him to play in the garden, so as not to disturb her. I wasn't dressed yet, but I guessed they wouldn't be up for ages. It wasn't really cold, but I grabbed a cardigan from the bag of Claire's clothes in my room and pulled it on over my pajamas. It felt so soft in my fingers.

I held Jude's hands as he stepped into his red-and-navy wellies, then pulled the handle of the glass doors. The summer air was cool and wet with the smell of plants.

Jude ran outside ahead of me, and I was surprised to see Jez in the garden room, dressed and sitting at the desk. He smiled, raised a palm in hello. I pulled the cardigan tighter around myself, feeling suddenly self-conscious.

"Jude, maybe we should get you some breakfast," I called to him. "Shall I make you porridge, with honey?"

But Jude was running off, looking for his ball. He ran over to the solid door at the end of the garden office, the one I'd assumed was some sort of storeroom. I followed him, but Jez got there first.

"Not in there, buddy," he said, picking Jude up under his armpits. He turned to me. "He can't go in there. It's a darkroom," he explained.

"A darkroom, for photography?"

"That's right," he said. "You can't let the light in. I mean, you could, I guess, but I'd have to kill you."

He smiled at me to show he was joking, and I found myself averting my eyes, like you would from a light that was on too bright.

"That's so cool that you have a darkroom."

I instantly cringed at my words. I sounded like such a baby.

Jez tilted his head. "Are you interested in photography, Sophie?"

I cleared my throat. "I used to be. I mean, I used to take pictures a lot. For art projects, when I was at sch—college." I coughed. "I've never been in a real darkroom, though."

Jez's eyes were fixed on my face. I tried to picture what I must look like to him. My bare, unwashed skin, my hair pulled up in a ponytail. The grass was wet on my ankles, where the pajama bottoms were too short.

"Sorry that I'm still in my . . . Jude came into my room again and woke me up."

"Don't apologize."

I thought Jez would look away then, but he didn't.

Jude started singing to himself, picking up stones from the gravel path, looking at each one in turn and putting them back again.

"He never used to sing like that," Jez said, looking over at Jude. "He's happier, Sophie."

"I'm glad."

"I mean it. The way he is with you, he is hardly like that with anyone. Just my mum, I guess. He loves his gan-gan. And you. That's it."

I looked down, embarrassed. I noticed he hadn't said anything about Claire.

"So, you're a photographer," he said. "A multitalented nanny. Do you have a good camera?"

I nearly said yes, but then I realized it probably wasn't that good a camera after all, even though it had been the best my dad could get. "My dad bought me one when I was thirteen. I—don't know if it's really a very good one." I felt a twist of guilt in my gut as I said it. *Sorry, Dad.*

"What's the model?"

I told him.

"Oh. Not bad." I thought about Dad, saving up to get it on special offer from a place on Tottenham Court Road. How he had edged it across the table to me on my birthday, the red-and-gold diagonal stripes of the cheap paper he'd wrapped it in. How he couldn't look at me properly while I opened it, and I knew that it was because he wanted me to like it so much.

"If you want to try something different," Jez said, "you're welcome to borrow one of mine, Sophie."

"Really?"

"Absolutely. Hang on."

Jez jogged back to the house, ruffling Jude's hair on the way. I stood there for a while, watching Jude pile stones from the path around the raised beds into a plant pot. Jez returned, something metal in his hands and a leather strap coiled around his wrist. He held it out with one hand, as if it were a throwaway camera he'd picked up at the chemist.

"Here you go."

I looked down. It was a vintage Nikon. It must have been worth thousands.

"Are you serious? I can use this?"

"Sure."

"Don't you need it?"

"No, it's fine. I haven't had much time for it lately."

"What do you take pictures of?"

"Buildings." He grinned. "I love buildings. Boring or what?"

Jez had told me about the glass towers they were building by the wetlands where I swam sometimes. He said they were part of some huge plan for a new community or something, but I'd found it difficult to focus on the details. He had kept saying words like urban regeneration, cultural ecosystem, social capital, splaying his fingers wide, drawing the estate for me in the air with his hands. It made me imagine him as an orchestra conductor, drawing the tall blue-green towers out of the earth, the muscles in his back flexing underneath his shirt.

"Are they your photos in the hallway?" I asked him. "The black-and-white ones?"

"Afraid so."

I wanted to say something about them, but I was worried I would sound really stupid or basic. I wouldn't use the right words. So I ended up saying nothing, except that was sort of worse, because I could see he was disappointed I hadn't even said I thought they were good, or anything like that.

"Keep the camera as long as you like," Jez said eventually. "Maybe you could take some pictures of Jude. I'll help you develop them in the darkroom if you want. Here, take it."

He held up the camera again. This time, I took it into my hands. The cold weight of it caught me off guard, and Jez's hands closed around mine to stop me from dropping it.

"Sorry," I mumbled.

"No worries. It's heavy! Oh, your hands are cold. Here."

Jez hooked the leather strap over my shoulder so I didn't need to hold it anymore. Then he took my hands in his, cupped his own around them, and brought them to his face. Jez blew gently, his breath warm against the skin of my hands.

I looked at him, surprised. He smiled. "It's a hand house," he said quietly. I suddenly felt very aware of the space between our bodies.

"Fee! Come!"

It was Jude. "Coming!" I called. I pulled my hands away, realizing I had been holding my breath.

When I turned around to face the house, I saw Claire inside. She was standing at the kitchen window, her hair loose around her shoulders, her dressing gown undone. She was cradling her bump in one hand, a toy of Jude's in the other. She was looking straight at us.

Tash

TOM WATCHES ME FROM the barbecue. I'm at the table he wants to lay with food, cradling Sophie's camera in my hands, tracing the shape of it with my fingers. The inquest papers are spread out in front of me, my laptop humming between us.

Tom turns from lighting the kindling. "You want a drink?"

I put the camera down and guiltily push the laptop shut.

"I'm fine, thanks. Sorry—let me move these." I push the papers aside to make room for the food Tom has made. I promised him I'd do the salads, but I see he's given up and done them himself without complaint, basil already scattered over the panzanella I said I'd make. He has prepared elaborate marinades with garlic and lemon and sumac for the wet, pink slivers of chicken he has neatly slid onto skewers.

Grace is coming over today, with Ben. I had intended to tidy the flat and help Tom with the food, but I've been distracted by the breakthrough I had this morning. I have just found Sophie's profile on a dating app. It hasn't been deleted. Creepy that they don't get rid of these things when someone dies. But then, I suppose, who would have known to ask them to? Her profile picture is a selfie, taken in a bathroom with a long mirror. Sophie is wearing postbox-red lipstick and what I'm sure is the black lace dress from the bag Jane gave me. She doesn't look much like a playgroup worker in this shot.

I need to find out whom she met on this app. If she was killed, then statistically her killer is likely to have been someone close to her. Most likely of all—given the contraceptive pills—a boyfriend. Surely Claire would have known if she'd been dating someone. Maybe they even discussed the dating app. They were living in the same house, after all.

The thought of asking Claire directly about Sophie makes me feel uneasy, though. My friendship with her still feels too new and fragile—definitely too unsteady to weather the confession that I am looking into the death of her former employee. And anyway, it's not as if I seriously think she or Jez could have had anything to do with Sophie's death. The idea seems utterly ridiculous. The soft-spoken, chamomile-tea-drinking mother who practices extended breastfeeding, and her thoughtful, charismatic husband? I couldn't see it. But if Claire found out I was looking into Sophie's death, she'd wonder why I hadn't told her that—or, worse still, she might assume it had been the reason I had become friends with her in the first place. I had endured enough comments over the years to know what most people thought journalists were like.

I decide that the best thing would be to try to talk to Laura first. I feel on safer ground with her, somehow. If Claire, Laura, and Nicole had all been so close—as Nicole had been at pains to tell me the first time we met—then surely Laura would have come across Claire's nanny. I could imagine Laura making an effort with someone like Sophie, a younger woman who might lack confidence or feel unwelcome. It wasn't impossible that Laura would remember Sophie mentioning dating, or a boyfriend. I was dying to ask Laura about Jude, too. Where was this secret son that Claire and Jez were hiding away?

"Ben says they'll be here in ten," Tom says, looking at his phone. "I'm just going to shower." I see him glance at my laptop one final time, but he doesn't say anything.

I clear the table, wedge the back door open. I find the hammock at the bottom of the shed, dust it off, and tie it up between the tree and the fence post. Our tiny back garden is still full of Finn's toys, but Tom has cut the grass, and with the sun shining it is not an entirely depressing scene. There won't be many more days like this, I think, flopping into the hammock. Already, the leaves on the tree next door are turning gold, scattering themselves over our grass.

Tom returns from his shower with two bottles of beer. He passes one to me, and brings the other to his lips.

"Cheers," he says.

"Cheers," I say. "It's a shame Ravi and Abi couldn't make it."

Tom shrugs. "I guess it's a bit of a schlep for them now, with three kids."

I'm secretly pleased they declined the invite. Ravi and his wife, Abi—a child psychologist or psychiatrist, I can never remember the difference—have three children under five. It's quite hard work having them all over.

"How's the foot today?" Tom runs his hand along my elevated leg. His touch feels affectionate rather than professional. He'd started kissing me in bed last night, sliding his hands under my clothes, but I just hadn't felt like it. I'd told him my foot was still really hurting and he'd made sympathetic noises, but I could tell he thought it was an excuse.

"Still really sore."

"Ah well." He gives my ankle a squeeze. "I'm sure you'll be back in action and getting smashed with the Desperate Housewives again soon."

I haven't told Tom yet about what I found. The fact that Sophie was Claire's nanny. The mystery over the other son, Jude. I knew he'd say that I shouldn't be hanging around with them if I was investigating them at the same time. And to be honest, he would probably be right.

"They are not housewives," I say with a laugh, swinging in the hammock. "Housewife isn't even a thing these days, Tom. Don't be sexist."

"Why are they all free to sit around and drink sauvignon blanc all afternoon, then?"

"Well . . . Nicole is on maternity leave and Laura works in shifts, as you know."

"What about the other one? Claire?"

I'm still not actually sure whether Claire has a job. I can't see anything obvious online. It feels like an indelicate thing to ask. Along with a growing list of indelicate things I'd like to ask her. I change tack, look at Tom over the top of my shades.

"How come you never mentioned Laura before? She seems really nice."

Laura has been brilliant this week. She has been meeting Finn and me on the way to St. Mark's in the mornings, so that the two boys can walk in together. She somehow knew this was exactly what Finn needed.

It is really helping. I don't actually have many other friends with children, and it's taken me by surprise how much of a difference getting to know Laura has made.

"What?" Tom has his back to me now, the barbecue smoke floating away over his shoulder. I take my sunglasses off and shade my eyes with my hand, to get a better look at him.

"Laura always makes out you know each other quite well from the hospital. That you're friends."

"We're colleagues, that's all." Tom turns to the garden table and starts pulling open a packet of burger buns. He seems to be struggling with the cellophane.

Before I can ask what he means, the buzzer rings. Tom goes to answer it, and I stay in the hammock. I listen to him greeting Grace and Ben. Soon they appear in the garden, Grace wearing a lemon-yellow dress and sandals, her sunglasses pushed up into her curly hair, the tips of her cheeks just a little sunburned. Ben is wearing a linen shirt and a straw hat, as if he's just strolled off the set of *The Talented Mr. Ripley*.

I get up to kiss them both. "You two look very tanned and happy."

Grace gives a little half-twirl. "Thanks. Hey, I love your new hair!"

"Oh, thanks."

I feel a bit guilty about how much I'd ended up paying for my hair. I'd let myself be talked into honey-colored highlights, as well as a cut and some sort of expensive Brazilian conditioning treatment Claire had told me about, which had made my hair so soft I couldn't stop touching it. I couldn't really afford it, obviously, but hanging around with the playgroup mothers had left me feeling drab and in need of a pick-me-up. I'd decided to make an effort to get my figure back, too. After all, I couldn't play the baby card forever. The other mothers all had perfect arms and washboard stomachs, and it wasn't as if I'd just given birth—Finn was two and a half now. I couldn't keep wearing black leggings and a greasy ponytail for the rest of my life. I needed to get a grip.

"Good honeymoon?"

Grace smiles dreamily. "Perfect. You have to go to Positano."

I only met Tom because of Grace. She introduced us when I came to visit her in our first term at university. Homesick in my halls at Cardiff, I'd taken a bus to see her, secretly hoping she'd also be having a terrible time at Oxford, and that we could spend the weekend commiserating over wine and pizza, like we used to. But instead she'd been happy and glowing, and had led me excitedly into a wood-paneled bar and introduced me to a new boyfriend, Ben, plus a string of posh new mates. They'd all nodded vaguely in my direction, then turned back to conversations Grace didn't realize needed translating, and I was left cradling my cheap red wine and feeling like an impostor.

After a while, though, I noticed Tom, glancing at me across the table with a sort of shy interest, tilting the wine bottle in my direction inquiringly when it was his turn to take a glass. He had a northern accent and he had made me laugh. And he was quite good-looking, if you ignored his clothes. He told me he was studying medicine, and I'd rolled my eyes and laughed into my drink.

"What?"

"Sorry, I was just thinking about my mum. How ecstatic she would be if she knew I was being chatted up by a good-looking Oxford student who was planning to be a doctor."

"I'm not chatting you up!" Tom had gone bright red, and I'd laughed even more.

"Oh. Aren't you?"

I had been drunk enough by that point to make a flirty mock-disappointed face, lowering my lashes, sticking out a glossy bottom lip. Tom had smiled and looked away.

Later, after a lot more alcohol, Tom had pulled me to him and kissed me as we danced, sweaty and drunk, on the sticky floors of some awful club. In the morning, I didn't remember much about it, but Grace had been delighted. "He's such a nice guy," she'd whispered into my ear as we hugged goodbye at the bus station the next day.

Tom and Ben start loading meat onto the barbecue. Grace comes to sit next to me. "Where's that cute godson of mine?" she asks. "I bought him this. I knew you'd hate it." She hands me a stuffed neon-green crocodile with sunglasses on and a T-shirt that says I Heart Capri.

"Thanks a lot." I laugh. "I'll wake him up in a bit."

"Yes, please. You know I don't come here for *you* anymore."

"Of course."

Tom serves the kebabs he has made, the homemade lamb burgers with tomato and halloumi. There is a spell of quiet while everyone eats, cupping hands to chins as the juices spill over.

"Well, when you said you were cooking, I was a bit worried," Ben announces. "But these burgers are almost as good as the Van of Death."

Tom laughs. "Cheers. Means a lot."

I keep a polite silence. Even though I didn't go to Oxford, I know Ben and Tom are talking about the open-all-hours fast food truck where they, Grace, and the rest of their gang used to go for cheesy fries and burgers at the end of a night out. Sometimes I wonder whether they've actually forgotten I didn't go to university with them, or whether they just don't think that's enough of a reason not to talk about Oxford all the time.

"Obviously, Tash would have done a much better job than me," Tom says with a supportive nod in my direction. "But she's been otherwise engaged today."

"Oh yeah?" Grace pivots toward me, puts her burger down.

"Just work," I say vaguely.

"How is it all going, then? Freelancing, I mean."

Even though she's my best friend, I have found that lately I feel a tiny bit self-conscious talking about my work to Grace. She and the rest of the Oxford gang are all such high achievers. It didn't matter so much when I was doing well on my own terms. But since I left my job to go freelance, it has felt like more of a sore point.

To be honest, I have been privately stunned by how rapidly I have been downgraded since leaving my staff job at the *Post*. Within a few months, I seem to have gone from star reporter to a freelancer whose calls news desks can't be bothered to return. I have lost count of the precious playgroup hours I have spent on the phone this week, begging news desks to pay me for stories they'd used ages ago. The invoices are so modest it sometimes feels almost embarrassing to ask for the money.

This week's episode had particularly stung. I'd been really proud of the story, about women being refused pain relief in childbirth. When I'd first pitched it to the *Sunday Times*, the news editor had loved it. But last Sunday morning, when I rushed to look online, I couldn't find it. Thinking perhaps they'd held it for print, I had walked to the newsagent's and grabbed a paper, but it wasn't the splash story as I'd hoped, or even any of the other smaller stories on the front page. It had taken me ages to find my article. It had only made four hundred words on page nineteen.

Still, I sent Louise, the news editor, a cheerful email first thing on Monday. I thanked her for using it, checking how much I should invoice for. Two days later, her secretary had gotten back to me. She suggested three hundred pounds, plus VAT. Would that be all right?

I called Louise, assuming there was some mistake. She had had the grace to sound embarrassed, at least. "I'm sorry, Tash," she'd said. "We just can't pay more than that for a back-of-the-book page lead."

"But I thought you said it had a shot at the front."

"It did, it did. It's just, we had a minister resign on Saturday, and then . . ." On the line, I could hear the call for a news conference, Louise saying she had to go. I'd kept the phone to my ear as the call had gone dead. I focused on the blinking cursor on my screen, trying to work out how many hours I had spent on my story. It probably wasn't even minimum wage.

The sun dips behind the clouds. Next door the neighbors have started playing rap music inconsiderately loud. Ben and Grace are pretending not to have noticed. I bet this doesn't happen in Laura's and Claire's back gardens. I notice a line of ants, trailing from the patio underneath the hammock to the garden shed. As soon as I see it, I am sure I can feel them on my skin.

"Another drink, anyone?" Tom asks.

"I'll get them." I stand up and immediately wince. I keep forgetting about the foot.

"Tash, let me," Tom says.

"No," I snap. "I'm fine."

I limp back into the house, pull the fridge open with more force than

I need to, and stare at the contents. Beers have been angled in between bags of vegetables, leftover bowls of pasta for Finn. I miss the fridge we used to have before him, filled with expensive cheeses and pesto from the deli, seafood from the fishmonger, a bottle of gin chilling on the door for spontaneous G and Ts. Now the gin is shoved in the cupboard to make way for milk and juice, and the shelves are full of the cling-filmed failures of meals Finn has refused to eat.

I should wake Finn up. It is definitely time. I know if I delay, he'll sleep badly tonight. But in this moment, I can't muster the energy. I consider more painkillers, then reach for the warm wine sitting on the counter instead.

"Are you OK, Tash?"

Grace has followed me into the kitchen. She is leaning against the kitchen cupboards, her head tilted to one side.

"Fine," I say.

"Really? You seem quiet."

"Really," I repeat, firmly. "Want some of this wine?"

Grace looks away. "I'm OK, thanks. I'm going to grab a Coke."

I watch as she takes a can from a bag she and Ben brought over. I can't remember Grace ever drinking a Coke before. She faces me as she pulls the tab.

"Hey—did you think any more about that copywriting work?"

Grace first suggested this a while ago. The bank where she works, Schooners, is looking for a copywriter to help with internal comms, or marketing, or some other dull-sounding thing. The first time she mentioned it, I thanked her but politely declined. If I was going to do copywriting, I was sure there would be more exciting firms to work for than Grace's bank.

But today, before I start on my thanks-but-no-thanks speech, I pause. I checked my overdraft this morning and actually winced. Even bearing in mind the payments I was overdue for stories, it didn't look good. At first I couldn't work out what I'd been spending so much money on. Then I'd realized. It was the other mothers. It was relentless. Their version of coffee is more like extended brunch, with endless pastries ordered that mysteriously never got eaten, often moving seamlessly into the glasses of fizz or colorful cocktails that they seemed to feel were more socially acceptable than daytime wine. I had tried just not drinking, but it made hardly any difference—the bill was always split. Claire has also invited me to a spa day at the Corinthia for Nicole's birthday, and Laura keeps talking about the four of us having dinner. I am so touched to be asked that I keep agreeing to it all. But it is costing a fortune keeping up with them. Then again, I love the idea of Finn being included, of him having his own little gang of friends.

"Oh please, think about taking the work," Grace says. "The guy who's been doing our copywriting is *hopeless*. We'd pay you a good day rate, and you could work from home. You're such a brilliant writer—you could do it with your *eyes* closed."

I have had the strong suspicion that Grace is not, in fact, desperate, but has worked out my freelance career is going nowhere, feels sorry for me, and is trying to do me a favor. Maybe this is what all my friends secretly think—that my postbaby professional life is a disaster zone.

"I'll think about it," I say, forcing a smile.

Later, when I am washing up, I spot the ants again. They are inside now, making their way in a wobbly pencil line across the counter toward the fridge. I feel faintly sick. What do you do about an ants' nest? My mind flicks through various possibilities, like a macabre brochure. Chemicals. Bleach. A boiling-hot kettle. *Move*, my mother's annoying voice says inside my head.

I sweep my papers and Sophie's camera up away from the ants. As I returned the items to the bag, I feel something hard among the fabric. Something small, like a battery, or a lighter. It is inside the pocket of Sophie's buttery leather jacket.

I pull it out, unzip the pocket, and reach inside. It is a roll of camera film. One that is yet to be developed.

Sophie

Ten months before

THE SAFETY LIGHT WAS red on my hands, the smell of chemicals thick in my throat. I made an effort to concentrate, tipping my photograph paper in the tray like Jez had shown me.

"Like this?"

"That's it. You want to agitate it. Just a bit. But don't let it spill."

I held my breath, tried to focus, but I still tipped the tray a little too steeply. Jez's hand was immediately on my wrist, steadying it.

"Here, not quite so much. That should be enough. Get it in your stop bath now. Next one along."

I hesitated. I needed to step to the left, but I didn't want to rub up against his arm.

"Ah. Sorry." He looked up, moved away. I quickly pulled the paper out and laid it facedown into the next bath.

"I still can't believe you have a real darkroom," I said.

"Yeah, it's fun. And it seemed like a good use of this—well, it's just a cupboard really." I noticed Jez and Claire did this a lot. Tried to make out the things they had weren't that amazing. It was like they were always trying to pretend they weren't rich.

"Do you always do portraits?" Jez asked me.

"I guess. Mainly."

"Of your family, or . . . ?"

I paused, thinking about Jez's parents, Michael and Wendy, who had come to take Jude out for a day that week. They were like grandparents from a TV commercial. They had emerged from a taxi they'd taken from what they excitedly called the "West End," Michael in chinos and a button-down shirt, Wendy blow-dried in a linen dress and flowery scarf. When they'd seen Jude, Michael had made a silly face, and Wendy had dropped to a crouch and spread her arms and fingers wide for him, her face aglow with love, the shopping bags she was laden with all clattering to the floor.

"My dad's dead," I told Jez. "And my mum's . . . a bit of a screwup. She drinks."

Jez raised his eyebrows, blew a big breath out from his cheeks. "Wow," he said. "I'm sorry."

"It's all right." I rubbed at an imaginary mark on my cardigan sleeve, trying to dismiss the guilty feeling. As soon as I had said the thing about Mum, I regretted it. I think I only said it because I wanted to be impressive, miraculous in some way, to him, to both of them.

"What about your boyfriend?"

I froze, feeling a blush creeping up my cheek. Had he really just asked me that?

"I'm not really seeing anyone at the moment."

I decided to change the subject. "Have you taken any good pictures recently?"

Jez shook his head, sending a lock of hair falling into his eyes. "Nothing I'm proud of."

"I really like the ones in the hallway."

"Oh yeah?" Jez looked up, as if he was genuinely pleased to have my approval. I'd been studying the prints closely. Most were of glass towers, bridges, cityscapes I didn't recognize, from other parts of the world. One was a shot of Claire on a balcony somewhere, in side profile, a glass of wine in her hand. I had looked at that one a lot. It seemed like a strange sort of picture to have of your wife. She just looked like any beautiful woman. You couldn't really see her face.

The best one was a picture of Jude. He was being held upside down, his corkscrew hair fanned out, his dimpled grin. He looked about eighteen months old in the picture, chunkier than now, his features still soft and babyish. I couldn't help but wonder whether it was his mother holding him in the picture, or whether it was taken after she died. Emily, her name had been. I had heard Jez say it on the phone to his mum, when he thought no one was listening. If there were any pictures of Emily in the house, though, I hadn't found them.

On Fridays, Jude didn't go to playgroup. I had started taking him to a stay-and-play called Cuckoo Club, where lots of other nannies and babysitters went. I was the only one of them who lived in. One of the babysitters was Sal. I recognized her from playgroup pickups. Her own boy, Billy, went to the playgroup with Jude, and she had just started looking after a baby girl called Eliza, too.

"How are you getting on, living with Mr. and Mrs. La-di-da?" she asked me. Sal seemed fascinated by the idea that I lived with the family. She was deeply suspicious of all the wealthy mothers like Claire. When we went to Cuckoo Club, Sal spent most of the sessions eyeballing the ones she particularly disliked, laughing as their overpriced clothes got vomited on and the organic snacks they had packed got thrown straight on the floor.

"It's all right," I told her. "Claire's pretty nice."

"I'm surprised. I always thought she was a bit stuck up."

I hesitated. "I mean, she is a *bit* la-di-da."

Sal and I exchanged looks, then laughed. I looked down at my jeans. They were actually a pair of Claire's, from the bag she'd given me. I felt a little squeeze of disloyalty in the pit of my stomach.

"What about him?" Sal asked. "Her feller, whatever his name is?"

I looked away, pretended to watch Jude. I could feel Sal's eyes on me, like cold air on the surface of my skin.

It had occurred to me, obviously, to wonder whether it was OK that Jez and I were spending so much time together. We were in the dark-room a few evenings a week, developing pictures of Jude.

I wondered why he kept coming. I didn't particularly need his help anymore. He'd shown me how to do it. We didn't have very much to say to each other, really. There was just the buzz of the light, the chemical slosh of the water in the bath trays. We always went out of our way not to touch each other. I wasn't sure what it all amounted to, whether it amounted to anything at all.

"Jez?" I shrugged, trying to sound casual. "He's not so bad."

"Good-looking, isn't he?"

I averted my eyes. "Is he?"

Sal gave me a hard stare.

"What?" I could feel my cheeks burning.

"Be careful there, Soph," she said. Then she hauled herself up, went over to pull a snatched toy out of Billy's hand.

I think I was too young and stupid to really understand what she meant, to see the danger I was in. In my quiet moments, alone in the annex, I sometimes thought about Jez now, in the way I used to think of the runner. Dared to imagine there was more to him avoiding touching me than just being polite, or careful. Sometimes, touching myself at night, I would let my thoughts unravel to their logical conclusion. Imagine him touching me, at last. I knew these thoughts were shameful. But the mind can't be controlled like the body, can it? It goes to the places it shouldn't, even if you tell it not to.

Tash

———————

THE PHOTO PLACE OPENS at nine. I am their first customer. I pay extra for the one-hour service, and go to sit across the road in the chain coffee place, checking the time every few minutes. When they finally hand me the envelope, I walk back across the street to the coffee place and tear the packet open.

I spread Sophie's photographs out on the table. The pictures are all of the same curly haired boy. Here he is with a tower of blocks, in a ball pit, on a climbing frame in Clissold Park. This boy must be Jude. And then, around five pictures in, I find Claire. Seated at her kitchen table, making glittery Christmas cards with the little boy by her side.

I examine the picture carefully, taking in all the details. They are wearing matching aprons, Claire's tied neatly over the bump that must be Beau. Jude has paint and glitter all over his hands, while Claire's are clean. The portrait is nicely shot, the colors Instagram-bright. But there is something strained about Claire's smile, the bags under her eyes deeper than I ever remember seeing. Jude is not smiling at all. He is looking intently into the lens, his mouth slightly open.

I couldn't understand why Claire had never mentioned Jude. Where was he? Why did she never bring him on playdates? I think about the page in Sophie's textbook. The passage on avoidant attachment, the suggestion that it could be caused by neglect. Surely Sophie had gotten it wrong. But then I think of that tiny, sparse box room I saw off their hallway, and I feel the hairs on the back of my neck stand up.

I move on to the next picture, of Jez and Jude, sitting in a café I recognize as Sunbeam on Blackstock Road. Finn loves Sunbeam, but I am surprised to see the Hendersons in such a plastic-menus, chips-with-everything sort of place.

In the picture, Jude looks happier. He is grinning, his face pressed against Jez's chest, a striped straw in his hands. Over their heads, the back of the café's awning is visible, with the word Sunbeam, and a beam of light is pouring in next to them. It is a clever picture, playful with the light and the setting, and capturing a real moment between father and son. Sophie had talent, I realize.

The last photo in the pile just seems to be another picture of the same scene, in the café. This time, though, the image has been taken at an odd angle.

In this photo, a pregnant Claire is seated next to Jez and Jude at the table in the window. It looks to have been taken just a few moments after the last image; Jude still has the straw in his hand. Now, though, they don't look happy. Jez is staring blankly at Claire; she is looking down at her phone; Jude is rubbing his eye, as if he might be crying.

All the other pictures are so carefully composed, but this one feels blurry, amateurish. The three of them don't even seem to be the focus of the picture this time. A whole load of random people in the café are in the shot, too. The composition is odd, with no obvious focus. It is almost as if the picture has been taken by accident.

I look at the image for a while. There is something unsettling about it, after all the others. I can't imagine such a careful photographer as Sophie taking this image by mistake.

Sophie

Nine months before

ON THE MORNING OF Jude's fourth birthday, Claire asked if I knew anywhere we could take him for a special breakfast. I blinked at her. Had she and Jez really not made plans for his birthday?

"Well," I said. "He likes a place called Sunbeam on Blackstock Road."

Claire had made a face. "Blackstock Road? Where's that?"

I could tell straightaway that it had been a mistake to mention Sunbeam. Claire would hate it. "It will probably be too busy anyway," I said. "How about I make us something?"

"No! Let's risk it," Jez said cheerfully, half overhearing. He was steering a delighted Jude around the kitchen on a new scooter. "If that's Jude's favorite, then Sunbeam it is."

A week earlier, when I'd asked Claire what they were planning to get him for his birthday, she had thrown her head back in exhaustion, her icy-blond ponytail flopping over the back of the sofa. She was looking more pregnant now, her bump round above her jeans, her breasts newly full of blue, marbly veins.

"Oh God, Sophie," she'd said, rubbing her eyes. "I haven't given it very much thought, to be honest. What do you think we should get him?"

It was pretty obvious, I thought. Jude needed a scooter. He must have been the only preschool kid in north London who didn't have one. Whenever he saw a child on one, his little eyes followed it down the street, his lips pressed together. If it were up to me, I'd have gotten him one ages ago, a blue one, which was his favorite color, one of the ones with light-up wheels, and a horn-cum-flashlight that played different noises—police sirens, fire engine, rubbish truck backing up.

Claire had frowned. "A scooter? Do you think? I bought him that bike, and he never rides it."

It was true that Jude hated his balance bike, which Claire bought for him at great expense from Selfridges because, she told me, she had loved the look of the vintage cherry-red color, the little woven basket on the front. But Jude didn't have the coordination to steady himself with his feet, nor the confidence he needed to push against the ground and trust himself not to fall. Also, he didn't like red. I could have told her that much.

I decided to order the scooter with the debit card Jez had given me for household shopping, complete with light and matching helmet. I was sure Claire would be grateful—she seemed stressed out about the whole birthday thing. Also, it was less than a hundred pounds which, I was learning, wasn't a lot to the Hendersons.

When it arrived, Claire was confused. "Did you order this?"

I looked up at her. "Is that OK? I thought . . . I thought you wanted me to help you find him something."

"Oh, right," she said, picking up the box.

"Sorry, did I misunderstand? I thought you meant you wanted me to get him something."

Claire put the box down, then smiled. "It's fine. Thanks, Sophie."

"Shall I wrap it for you? I bought some paper."

Claire's smile faded just for a second before reappearing. "Nope, that's fine. I'll do it. Thanks, though."

AS I feared, Sunbeam was much busier on a Saturday. Jez had to raise his voice as he spoke into the waiter's ear to ask if they had space. To my relief, the family at the table by the front window was just leaving. The man at the door asked us to wait until they could clear it, but Claire sank down heavily into the booth seat, muttering that her feet were killing her. The waiter had to reach around her bump to clean up. She watched blankly as he squirted surface cleaner over the abandoned plate of chips in front of her, the smears of tomato ketchup. I could see she already hated it. The pressure of having made the recommendation felt like a hand on my throat.

I had enough items in my backpack to keep Jude occupied until the food arrived, if we ordered straightaway—a packet of crayons, some action figures, games on my phone if things were really desperate. But Claire stared at the menu as if it was written in another language.

"Sorry," she told the server eventually. "Can you just give us a few more minutes?" Under the table, I dug my fingernails into the seat cushion.

I decided to distract Jude by letting him sit on my lap and play with Jez's camera, even though it put me on edge. Children always knew what was precious, I found. It was always those things they wanted to touch. It was as if they wanted to feel their power. Jude fiddled with the lenses so the focus went all wobbly. Click, click, clicked away, even though there was no film loaded.

"Easy, Jude," Jez said. "That's a nice camera."

Claire got up to go to the toilet. "I'll have the salad bowl, please, darling," she muttered to Jez as she left. I pulled Jude into my chest, moving my knees to one side to let her pass.

"So." Jez brushed at some crumbs on the table. "Why was it that you ditched the photography course, Soph?"

I shrugged. "I guess I realized it was, you know, not an easy thing to get into. Someone basically told me you have to work for free for like, years? And anyway, I didn't know anyone who would give me the . . . work experience or whatever."

Jez looked at me, then away, rubbing his palm up and down his arm. "I see."

I pulled the camera off Jude. "Here you go, sit with Daddy." I picked him up under his armpits and lifted him onto Jez's lap. I loaded a film inside and threaded the strap around the back of my neck. I positioned myself about two yards away, to the side of the café, and stood on tiptoe to get more height.

"You're standing on tiptoe," Jez said, laughing.

"I want to shoot you from above and I'm five foot nothing."

"That tall?"

"Be quiet."

"You're the same height as Kylie Minogue."

"Who?"

"Oh, don't tell me . . . All right, I get it. I'm completely past it." Jez did an exaggeratedly pained expression. "Are you going to take this picture or what?"

It thrilled me a little bit, the feeling of having him in my power. "Ah, the light's all wrong," I said. "Hang on."

I crossed the café, stood near the wall so I had a good shot of them both, with the light and the letters on the awning behind. Jude was getting bored now. He started to squirm. He took the red-and-white-striped straw from the juice on the table, bent it and stuck it up Jez's nose. Jez laughed. I pressed the shutter.

When Claire reappeared, Jez seemed to forget about the photograph. He stood up to let her into the comfortable seating of the booth, helped her to ease herself down.

I lifted the camera again, hid my face behind it. When Jez sat down again, I trained the lens on his face, making sure I had the focus right. As I watched his face through the lens, though, I noticed his expression change. His features flattened, his easy gaze stiffened. I dropped the camera from my face, and followed his eyes across the café.

On the other side, near the pass-through, was a woman. She was tall and dark, her long hair loose over one shoulder. She was staring straight back at Jez. Her cheeks were pink, as if with exertion. Without thinking, I brought my camera to my face and pressed the shutter again.

Later, after I had put Jude to bed, I came down to find Claire asleep under a blanket on the sofa. The dishwasher was humming, and Jez was doing the last bits of washing up, his sleeves rolled up above the elbow. I went to help him. There was something soothing about the slosh of the water, the rhythm of our drying and stacking.

"Did you know that woman, in the café?"

I tried to make my question sound casual. I rubbed along the surface of the plate, being careful not to look directly at Jez. He didn't reply, but his arms had stilled in the washing-up water.

"What woman?"

"I thought there was a woman staring at you, in the café. Tall, with dark hair?"

Jez was looking away from me, so I couldn't see his face. He pulled the plug, and seemed to wait until the water had stopped gurgling before he spoke.

"Don't think so."

He dried his hands on his jeans, headed to the fridge, pulled out a beer, and strolled off to the garden room. I watched the reflection of the glass as he switched on the lamp, painting a little yellow square of light into the darkness of the garden. I wondered why he was lying. And also, why I felt so crushed by it, almost as if all the air had been stamped out of my lungs.

Tash

THERE IS A CRASH of thunder as I leave the library. Outside the sky is darkening, the torrents soon dense and unstoppable, buses and cars throwing dirty water over the roads. I walk as close as I can to the walls, ducking under shop awnings, but by the time I reach the playgroup, my expensive new leggings are splattered with mud.

Elaine's face tells me I am late again. She is standing with her coat already on, her face as thunderous as the sky. Rain is coursing down the church roof, bubbling down the drainpipe. I mumble my apologies, but Elaine is already looking away, turning the key in the lock from the inside.

Finn is in a hyper mood, laughing giddily, refusing to put his coat on or swap his sneakers for wellies. He starts to splash in the little rivers of water running down from the church steps into the gutters on the road, his sneakers getting soaked.

"Look, Mummy! Muddy puddles! Jump! Jump!"

"No, wait, Finn, you need to put your—Finn!"

Laughing, Finn barrels straight past me onto the grass where the gravestones are. I dash over and yank him up by the elbow, but it is too late. He has slipped into a puddle and emerged with his trousers and the bottom of his sweater covered in mud. He is soaked, his hands streaked with it, his sneakers caked.

Through the pelting rain, I glance back at the church doors, but Elaine must have gone out the back way. All Finn's spare clothes are on his peg inside.

"I cold, Mummy." Finn starts to shiver. I hear another crack of thunder, the clatter of rain picking up on the iron bike-shelter roof.

"Oh dear."

I look up and see Sal. She is wearing gray tracksuit bottoms and a cheap-looking waterproof parka. Her hair is pulled back, her makeup-free face puffy and threaded with burst blood vessels.

"Yes, ahem. Bit of a disaster." I have to shout over the rain. I feel flustered, caught out in my inept parenting. "I think I'll just . . . call a taxi."

"A what?"

"A taxi. I'll get an Uber."

Sal looks us up and down. "An Uber won't let him in like that."

"Flag a black cab, then."

"Oh yeah? Where do you reckon we are, Piccadilly Circus?"

The wind picks up. All of Sal's charges are appropriately dressed. Eliza, Christina's daughter, is dressed in a neat yellow raincoat and boots, holding one side of the double stroller. A blond boy of about six on the other side is wearing a waterproof Spider-Man onesie and wellies.

"Bring him over to my place," Sal says, looking at Finn. "Don't want him getting cold. I'm only over the road."

"Oh, it's fine, I, er . . ."

Sal's hard gaze moves from Finn's face to mine. "It's Tash, innit?" she says. "I'm Sal. Come on. I need a word with you anyway."

I follow Sal to the housing estate at the side of the park. Hers is the last ground-floor flat, an empty washing line swinging in the front. There is a gurgle of rainwater, a splash of overflowing drainpipes. An orange cat is asleep on a plastic chair under the shelter by the front door.

Sal opens the door and shoves her stroller inside, and I follow with mine. There are toys all over the floor, clothes strewn over sofa arms and the backs of chairs A plastic table is set out with poster paints in garish colors and pots of the sort of glitter I hate getting out at home in case Finn makes a mess.

"Sorry about all the crap everywhere." Sal pulls her stretchy top down over her midriff, then reaches into her stroller and hands me a pack of baby wipes for Finn's hands. I take them gratefully. She gestures at the kids and introduces them, briefly.

"The twins are Ada and Aiden, and this is my son, Billy. Say hello, Billy." The boy in the Spider-Man getup grins. Sal pulls out a packet of chocolate buttons, takes a handful for Eliza and Billy, then hands Finn the rest without asking me. Finn's eyes go wide. He tips them all into his mouth before I can object.

Sal unclips the twins from their stroller and sets them on the floor with a crate full of noisy plastic toys. Aiden starts to mash the buttons of one with his palms, while Ada takes a small tambourine and starts staggering around with it. Sal plucks a TV remote control from a faux-leather armchair and jabs it at a huge television on the far wall. Eliza clambers onto a sofa, tucking her skinny legs underneath her, her face pointed at the TV. Billy sits in front of her on the floor, his legs crossed. They look tiny and slight beside the huge sofa, like little elves.

"I'll go and get some clothes for Finn," Sal mutters in my direction. The twins' two sets of blue eyes follow Sal down the hallway, their necks craning to see where she has gone.

I lift Finn into the middle of the room and start to peel off his wet clothes. I feel dampness on my clothes, too, my shoes, socks, the ends of my hair. Finn feels so little with only his underwear on. Sal returns with a colorful tracksuit with cartoon characters on it. The fabric is thick and soft.

"Are you all warm now, sweetheart?"

I try to scoop him up for a cuddle, but he is craning his neck around me to see the TV screen. I sit him next to Eliza, pulling a bobbled zebra-print blanket over his legs, trying to ignore the cat hairs, the smell of animal. I could really do with a hot drink.

"Shall I make us some tea?" I say.

"You can if you want."

I head to Sal's kitchen and flick on the kettle. When I pull the fridge door open the handle is sticky to the touch. The orange cat appears on the counter, rubbing its cheek against the edge of the fridge. I try not to look at the corners of its eyes, full of yellow gunk.

In the fridge are Peppa Pig yogurts, those plasticky cheese sticks. A tray of Rice Krispie treats Sal has obviously made with the kids. A bag of carrot sticks. A leftover Chinese takeout, its orange noodles coiled like snakes. A pint of milk, a half-drunk bottle of white wine.

Sal comes into the kitchen, rummages in the freezer, and pulls out a box of fish sticks, which she lines up one by one with surprising delicacy on a tray, then shoves into the grill. She then takes the bottle of wine out of the fridge and pours herself a glass.

"Don't worry, I'm not having it now," she mutters. "I just like to have it out on the side. For motivation. Finn like fish sticks and chips?"

"That's so kind, but we'll be fine, thanks, Sal."

"Did you say you wanted tea?"

"Only if that's OK with you."

Sal raises her eyebrows, then reaches for mugs and a box of teabags.

"Nice leggings." Sal is staring at my legs.

"Oh. Yes. Thanks."

"They're like those ones Nicole's always wearing."

I feel a blush spread over my face. "Oh, are they?" We both know they are.

The noise of the kettle rises, then lowers to a bubble. I glance at the Coca-Cola clock on her wall. It is barely four.

Sal perches on top of one of the kitchen stools.

"Saw you in that French place the other day. You, Nicole, Claire, Laura."

"Yes, that's right."

"You can get coffee for free at Cuckoo Club, you know. Three quid and there's tea, coffee, toast, the lot."

"Oh, right."

"I'm just saying. It's a lot cheaper."

I can imagine Sal at Cuckoo Club. It is run by volunteers in the community hall, and the vibe is quite similar to that of Sal's front room—a free-for-all of garish stuff I don't want in our flat. Walkers that play tinny nursery rhymes, huge plastic garages for toy cars, those bouncer things with flashing lights and jangling jungle animals, a neon-pink slide. Three pounds pays for unlimited slices of toasted white bread smeared with margarine, and tea that tastes like it has been made from a barely hot tap, served by grannies through a weird 1970s window.

Sal plucks a cloudy glass off the counter and fills it from the tap.

"I saw you talking to Jane Blake," she says.

I look up. My mind replays it again, how she'd frozen at the gate of the play area. The strange look she'd given us.

"You know, I'd watch it, if I were you, Tash."

I stare at her. "Sorry?"

"Talking to Jane. Hanging around with those other mums."

"I'm sorry, hanging around with . . . ?"

"Laura, Claire, Nicole. I would just watch yourself, around them."

I wonder if this is some sort of joke. But Sal is not smiling.

"Look, I ain't going to spell it out." Her voice is low now, barely audible. "I am just telling you, I know what you're doing. And you really need to watch your back. OK?"

Sal takes a step toward me. She is tall and broad, meaty as a buffalo. She would be the wrong woman to pick a fight with in a club. I think about the anonymous message. *Stop digging.*

"Haven't you asked yourself," Sal murmurs, lowering her voice further, "why they suddenly seem so keen to have you in their little gang?"

It feels clammy in the kitchen. The windows over the sink are steaming up against the rain. I make a face, tried to feign nonchalance, but I feel my neck coloring.

"You've got no idea what you are getting into, Tash," she says. "Absolutely none."

"Sal, I'm sorry," I say. "Is this—are you talking about Sophie Blake?"

At the mention of her name, Sal glowers.

"Sophie was a nanny, like you," I say, working it out. "She was a friend of yours, wasn't she?"

Before Sal can reply, there is a knock on the door. It is as if the sound breaks a spell that has been cast over the room. Sal gives me a final glare, then disappears to the front door.

I hear a muffled conversation, footsteps in the hallway. The rain outside, a drum roll, like a warning. The tea mugs sit forgotten beside the kettle.

When I look up, Christina is in the kitchen. She has obviously come from work. In her smart black trousers, jacket, top, and full makeup, she looks intimidating, which is perhaps the point of it all. I see her glance fleetingly down at my mud-splattered leggings, my baggy sweater.

"Hello again, Tash."

"Oh, hi, Christina. How are you?"

"Fine, thank you. My court case was adjourned early today, so."

She is being a bit stiff. I wonder again why she reacted the way she did when I suggested coffee with Laura and the others.

"Mummy!"

Sal has pushed the sliding door back, Eliza balanced on one hip. Christina's face softens and illuminates as she reaches for her daughter. "Hello, sweetheart. Have you had a lovely day?"

"I'll just go and get her things," Sal tells Christina. She disappears down the hallway.

Finn bounds into the room. "Mummy," he asks breathlessly. "Can I have more sweets from dat lady?"

"No," I tell him. "We're going home now, Finn."

"No, Mummy!"

Finn likes it here, I realize—the annoying, noisy toys, the TV-and-snacks routine.

"Finn, we need to get your wellies on now, please."

I clip Finn into his stroller, taking longer than I need to fit the rain cover. I want Christina to leave so I can continue my conversation with Sal. I want to ask her why she was so weird about Jane, and what she knows about Claire, Laura, and Nicole. But Sal and Christina remain in the kitchen, so eventually I leave, backing out of the hallway with the stroller, closing the door softly behind me.

When I glance back through the window, I can see Christina in the kitchen holding Eliza, chatting to her about her day, pushing stray strands of Eliza's pale hair out of her face. I wonder if I've seen Christina, in a different context. There is something familiar about her dark eyebrows, her strong jaw, her hair falling over one shoulder, dark as an oil slick.

Later that night, it comes to me.

I get up out of bed and find the photographs again, the ones that Sophie took. I find the last one, the blurry one. The one I thought had no obvious focus.

I can see it now, the thing that Sophie was aiming for. At the back of the café, there is another woman, wearing an expression entirely distinct from those around her. She is staring straight at Claire and Jez. And she looks furious.

I looked at the picture closely. The eyebrows, the cheekbones, the hard set of her mouth. The small, quick, glinting eyes.

The woman in the picture is Christina.

Sophie

Eight months before

SAL AND I SAT on the playground bench together, watching Billy and Jude race each other up the climbing frame, baby Eliza tucked up asleep in a smart, pebble-colored stroller. The air was frosty, but there was something pleasant about being out in the cold and the rowdy noise, away from Claire.

Eliza was making little soft snoring noises. "She's so cute," I told Sal.

"I know," said Sal. "And she's so easy. I got a good gig there."

"How did you get it?" I asked. "The job, I mean. How did you meet her mum?"

Sal didn't reply. After a while, I saw she was looking over at Billy.

"I never told you about Billy's dad, did I?" she said eventually.

"I should have asked," I replied. "Billy ever see him?"

"He'd struggle," she said, lowering her voice. "He's in prison."

I winced, shook my head. "Sorry," I whispered. I wasn't sure what else to say.

"Don't be," she muttered, brushing an imaginary crumb off her T-shirt. "We're all better off, trust me."

It had started out all right, she told me. Gifts, compliments, lifts to work. He was a builder, seemed honest. Put shelves up in the flat, redid the floors. Then once she was pregnant, things changed.

He made her stop seeing her friends, said they were bitches, jealous of her, that they talked about her behind her back. "And when they started telling me he was no good, he just said, 'There you go, there's the proof.'"

He accused her of talking to other men. One time, when he saw her speaking to a neighbor in a shop, he waited till they got home, then held a teaspoon in a boiling kettle and pressed it against her neck until she screamed.

"Still got the mark. Just here." Sal pulled up her earlobe. There was a coffee-colored mark, the surface of her skin shriveled like an overripe fruit.

"But . . . you were pregnant?"

"That was nothing. That was just the start."

A clump of hair. A skull cracked against a fridge. Then the thing that happened at the end, a few months after Billy was born. The attack that made her hit him back. Then pack her baby into his stroller, her hands shaking as she fastened the clasp, and run.

"He tried to do me for assault," she said. "They threw it out, though. Thanks to Christina. Eliza's mum."

"That's how you met her?"

"She was assigned to my case," Sal said. "She was pregnant then, massive. Barely fit in the family courtroom." Sal laughed, then looked sad. "You don't get legal aid for the custody part. I didn't have anything to pay her, but she did it anyway."

Eliza stirred, and Sal handed me her phone so she could rock the stroller.

"But how did you end up looking after Eliza?"

"She suggested it." Sal looked away. "I think she realized, you know. That I needed money. She came round once and—well, they'd messed up my benefits. I had nothing in. Not even milk for a cuppa for her."

Sal scratched at a mark on her arm. I tried to imagine what that would be like. The anxiety, the shame. Then I thought about the boxes of expensive salads that Claire rarely finished, her smoothies that cost five pounds each.

"Christina said maybe she could help. She knew I'd worked in a nursery, like you, back in the day. I was qualified to be a babysitter. She asked me if I fancied it. She helped me do my paperwork and that. She told me I was doing her a favor, that she'd rather have someone she already knew.

She was going back to work straightaway after the baby—barristers don't get no maternity leave, apparently. And she's a single mum."

"Really? No other half on the scene?"

"Not my business." Sal said this in a way that told me she knew exactly what the story was, but that she wasn't going to tell it to me. "So yeah. I started looking after this one." She lifted a whining Eliza from the stroller, sat her on her hip.

"Just like that."

"Just like that." Sal bounced Eliza on her hip and we made a song of it. Just like that, just like that. Eliza stopped crying, reached out and curled a finger around the gold hoop in Sal's ear.

"Sad for her that her dad didn't stick around," I said.

Sal glanced at me. She knew I was being nosy. She looked away, untangling Eliza's finger and kissing her on the nose. "Yeah, well. Christina's the cleverest person I know, but turns out she's about as thick as I am where blokes are concerned."

Tash

THAT NIGHT, WHILE TOM is watching TV, I stay in the kitchen, combing Sal's social media. I have to scroll nearly to the end of her posts before I find what I am looking for.

Like most of Sal's pictures, it has been taken by her on selfie mode, blurry and poorly composed, but just distinct enough to see that she is with Sophie. The two of them seem to be walking in Clissold Park, long shadows stretching in front of them. Sophie has a baby on her front. I can't make out her expression—the photo is too blurred. I was right, though, I can see that much. Sal and Sophie knew each other. They were friends.

Later, Tom finds me in the hallway, double-locking the door. I feel his eyes on me as I pull the bolt across.

"I'll sort those bars out this week," he says, sounding a bit guilty.

"OK." I still don't love the idea of the bars on the windows of our flat, but since the broken glass, I haven't voiced any objections.

"I'm going to bed." Tom is looking over at me, yawning. "Will you turn the lights off?"

"In a bit."

I return to the kitchen and sit back down at my laptop. Tom follows me, watches me as he pours a glass of water. "Is it that Sophie Blake thing still?"

I nod without looking up.

"You seem to be working so hard on all this, Tash."

"So what?"

"So . . . are you sure there's going to be a story in it, at the end of it all?"

I shrug. "It's too early to say."

Tom folds his arms. "I know you love a good mystery, Tash. But just bear in mind her mum might not be telling the full story."

"I know what I'm doing, Tom. I have done this before, you know. This is what I do."

"I'm just saying, you don't have all the facts."

I roll my eyes. "You never have all the facts, Tom. That's not how being a reporter is. You have to piece the story together, as best you can."

Tom looks hard at me. "Is that really what you're doing here, then? A story?"

"What do you mean?"

He runs a hand through his hair. "I mean, is this journalism, or are you trying to solve a murder—a murder you don't even know was committed?"

I look up at Tom. I see now that he has built up to this speech, that he is choosing his words carefully.

"I can tell you think I'm being negative," he says. "But I just can't see how a newspaper could print an article speculating about this, Tash. It feels to me like you're putting a lot of energy into something that's very unlikely to work out. Do you think—I don't know. Maybe your judgment's a bit off, or something?"

I stare at Tom. "Why? Because I've had a baby, and now I don't know what a story is anymore?"

Tom frowns. "I wasn't saying that at all. Give me some credit."

"Well, whatever you were saying, you're wrong. There is a story here. I know there is."

Tom raises his eyebrows. "OK. You know better than me. I would have thought from a legal point of view you don't have enough."

"Well, I guess I'd better keep digging then, hadn't I?"

It comes out harder than I mean it to.

"Let's get some sleep," I say in a stab at an apology. We don't argue much. Neither of us likes it.

"Let's."

"I love you."

"Love you, too." Tom leans over and kisses me, but his mouth misses mine, lands between my upper lip and nose. He turns away and heads to the bedroom alone.

Back at the kitchen table, I pull up the photo on Sal's Facebook again and look at it for a long time. It's the first picture I have seen of Sophie with Beau. He is strapped on her front in a carrier, his face toward her chest. There is something about the way she is wearing him, so close to her body, one hand protectively over the back of his head. No one seeing her wearing a baby like that would think she was the nanny. She looks like the baby's mother. I think of Finn, how his hair sometimes smells of another woman's perfume when I pick him up from playgroup. Had Claire minded Sophie carrying her baby like that?

I look at when the picture was taken: March 2017. Beau would have been tiny, just a couple of months old. Five months after this picture was taken, Sophie would be dead.

I look for Christina next. She doesn't seem to be on social media. She strikes me as that type. All I can find is her professional website, with details of her legal career. A black-and-white headshot, a tight, cold smile for the camera. I save the links, decide to call it a day.

As I'm putting my laptop away, my phone vibrates, the lit-up screen announcing a message.

It is from an unknown number, a different one this time.

I WON'T WARN YOU AGAIN.

Tash

THE NEXT MORNING, IT is blowing a gale, the stone path stained black with wet. The mothers at drop-off are hunched, harassed, avoiding eye contact.

"Ugh, isn't it horrible," Laura complains when she sees me.

"Yep." I am looking over Laura's shoulder. It's not her I am here to see. It is Sal, who has just arrived.

"No time for coffee today?"

"Afraid not."

Sal is by the entrance, unzipping Eliza's coat. Little tendrils of dark hair are plastered to her neck with rain, or sweat.

"Shame," Laura says. "You and Tom are still coming for dinner this Saturday, though?"

"Oh. Yes, lovely." Laura had suggested this last week, but I hadn't been sure if it was a definite invitation. "Sure. Thanks. Looking forward to it."

When Laura is gone, I watch Sal return to her stroller under the bike shelter. She glances up at the darkening sky, then reaches into her coat pocket for her phone. As she does, I press call on the number that sent the latest anonymous message.

I feel a hot flood of adrenaline. What if I am right, and her phone rings? What is my plan then? But her phone stays silent, and she replaces it in her coat.

She could have used a different number, I tell myself. Doesn't mean it wasn't her.

Sal looks up and sees me staring. I walk over, pulling my hood over my fringe.

"All right, Tash? Off for coffee with the yummy mummies?"

"No," I say. "I'm not. I'm here to talk to you. Do we have some kind of problem, Sal?"

Sal looks at me, surprised and curious, rather than affronted.

"It wouldn't have been you sending me strange text messages in the middle of the night, would it?"

Sal screws up her face. "What? I don't even have your number."

"Well, we're both on the WhatsApp group."

Sal rolls her eyes. "If I've got something to say, I'll say it."

It is not obvious to me that she is lying. But I'm sure she is keeping something from me.

"What did you mean before, Sal? When you told me I needed to watch my back?"

"I meant what I said." She works her chin defiantly. "If you don't wanna take no notice, that's up to you."

I consider Sal, her sweaty hair, her plasticky coat. Maybe she is one of those people who enjoys any sort of drama, who pretends they know more than they do.

"Is all this to do with Sophie?" I ask. "Sophie Blake?"

Sal opens her mouth, then closes it again.

"I know you were friends," I continue. "Why wouldn't you want me to find out what happened to her? Why wouldn't you want me talking to Jane?"

Sal shakes her head slowly.

"Jane don't know anything," she mutters eventually.

"You do, though, don't you?"

I take a step closer to Sal. Her eyes widen.

"You two talked. You'd have known who she was seeing. Who her boyfriend was."

It's an educated guess, but it hits the mark, I can tell. Sal looks up, horrified. The rain is pelting down now in thick, icy rods, rattling the corrugated-iron roof of the bike shelter.

"Has he said something?" I ask her. "Is he the reason you think I need to be careful? Is he the person who's been threatening me?"

Sal stares at the ground, saying nothing.

"And what about Christina?" I ask. "Why was Sophie so interested in her?"

At the mention of Christina, Sal's head snaps up. "Look, Tash. I don't know who's been sending you messages. I'm not threatening you. I'm trying to do you a favor. If you've got any sense, you'll listen, OK?"

She flicks the brake of her stroller up with her foot.

"Keep your nose out of it, Tash. Stay away from it."

"From what?" I raise my voice over the rain, exasperated. But Sal is already heading away.

Sophie

Eight months before

I NEVER REALLY LIKED the women from Claire's prenatal classes. Whenever they came around, I was expected to act as a sort of waitress.

"Just in case people need anything," Claire had said the first time. "Drinks, or whatever." She was in the hallway, plucking flowers from a long, slim cardboard box and arranging them in a vase. The flower boxes arrived every week—it was like a subscription. Claire had told me to leave them, that she liked to arrange them herself, but sometimes she forgot, and they wilted on the side for days before she noticed them.

"I'm really happy to help with anything, you know I am." I shifted my weight from one foot to the other. "It's just, I promised Jude we'd go to that music class he likes, with Billy and Sal, today." It was the last class of the term, the Christmas special. Sal said they usually got the caretaker to dress up as Santa and hand out presents. I was excited to see Jude's face.

"Do you really think he'll remember?" Claire adjusted her hair in the mirror. She was wearing another new maternity dress, a soft white waterfall cardigan over the top. Her body lotion smelled like watermelons.

I didn't say anything. I knew Jude would remember.

When Claire turned around, she looked almost surprised that I was still there, that the conversation hadn't finished.

"Oh, Sophie. Look, I should have told you," she was saying now. "But don't worry, it won't be a lot of work. Plus, Laura and Nicole have said they'll come early, to help."

Laura—one of the new prenatal group friends—arrived early, beaming, her bump enormous under her dungarees. She seemed delighted to have been asked to help.

"Hey, Sophie," Laura said brightly. "Lovely to see you again!" She made a show of closing the door quickly so the cold air didn't get in, then rolling her sleeves up and asking where things were in the kitchen.

I couldn't honestly see what there was for her to help with. Jez had been tasked with putting up endless fairy lights and setting out sickly scented candles that said things like Winter and Cinnamon on the side. Claire had bought all the food—cold dishes from the deli on Highbury Barn, where they measure the salads out to the gram, like uncut diamonds. Some overpriced mince pies and cupcakes had been delivered in large white boxes. The only thing Claire had made herself were some date-and-coconut flapjacks she claimed were healthy. I watched her bake them yesterday, staring at the screenshotted instructions from a food blog on her phone, mouthing them to herself and frowning. It took her the best part of a day to finish them. She had left all of the bowls for me to wash up.

Nicole, the other so-called helper, arrived only a few minutes before everyone else. By that time, everything had already been laid out.

"Hi, I'm Nicole," she said when she saw me. She shivered dramatically as she closed the door, then held out a heavy fur coat for me to take. I decided it was best not to mention that she'd met me a couple of times already.

Nicole glanced disapprovingly at the cupcakes—I wondered if, like Claire, she was one of these women who never ate sugar but constantly tried to push it on others—then turned to me.

"Can you fix me a drink, please?" she asked, stroking her bump. "Just any kind of mocktail."

"A what, sorry?"

Nicole blinked.

"A non. Alcoholic. Cocktail. If you don't mind."

I made her a drink, silently. After I handed it over, I went over to the sink, and poured myself a glass of water. I finished it, then stood for a moment holding the cold glass against my cheeks.

Others started to arrive. Soon, a line of big-bellied women was gathered at the kitchen island, plucking the best bits out of the expensive salads and piling them greedily onto plates. Claire had set the flapjacks out on a plate at the front, but nobody was really eating them. Claire kept glancing over hopefully. I willed someone to take one. Eventually I saw one of the women pick one up and bite into it, but she immediately spat it out into a napkin.

I felt a bit protective of Claire, but also irritated. I didn't see why she was trying so hard to impress these gossipy women who gaped at her addition when her back was turned and whispered about how much it might have cost.

When I went upstairs to check on Jude he had fallen asleep on his bed, a Christmas film still playing on his iPad, his full lips parted, curly hair spread out on the pillow. I pulled his duvet over his chest and wished I could just stay with him.

Halfway back down the stairs, I heard Laura, Claire, and Nicole in the front room. It took me a moment to realize that they were talking about me.

"I honestly don't know how you stand it," Nicole was saying in a stage whisper. "I would absolutely loathe having someone in my house."

Claire cleared her throat. "I mean, look, it . . . can be awkward sometimes."

I held my breath.

"Is she around, like, all the time?" Laura was asking now. "What about over Christmas?"

"Well, we haven't really worked out . . ."

"Surely you have a rule that she stays in the annex after, like, 7 p.m. or something?"

"Well, not exactly, but—"

"See?" Nicole interrupted, shaking her head. "This is what I keep saying. You're *way* too nice, Claire, that's your problem. You need to set some boundaries. Firm boundaries. This is your home! She needs to do things your way."

"Well, I don't know." Claire was twisting a strand of hair in her fingers.

She sounded uncomfortable. "She does work hard. Jude likes having her around—he really loves her. So, you know. I guess we just have to put up with it."

I don't know if it continued after that. I couldn't listen to any more. I turned around and went back the way I'd come. I found myself walking right up to the top of the house, where the nursery was.

I felt hot. I could feel my throat closing over, the sting of tears. A fizzing feeling under the surface of my skin. Something close to rage.

I looked for somewhere to sit, but the bloody baby clothes were still on the chair in shopping bags. They still had their tags on, the tiny hangers still in the shoulders. They had been there for weeks now. They needed sorting out. New babies' clothes needed washing and drying before they were used, to avoid skin reactions. All my textbooks said so. Someone needed to do the right thing in this house.

I took them out of the bags and started pulling the tags off, one by one. Then I gathered them all up, took them to the utility room on the first floor, and stuck them on a hot wash. I threw the labels away in the trash, scrunched the pretty shopping bags into balls. Then I went back to the nursery and pulled at the ribbons of the bumpers and tore them from the crib, leaving the bars of the baby's crib bare.

Tash

LAURA HAS MADE A chicken dish with tomatoes and olives and feta cheese. She sets it down in the middle of the table beside a steaming bowl of new potatoes.

"Cheers." Laura holds up a glass of red wine and smiles. Her lipstick is the same color as the wine. It makes her smile look as if it has been drawn onto her face.

"Cheers." Tom and I raise our glasses, to clink with her, Ed, Claire, and Jez. "Thanks so much for all this, Laura," Tom says.

I smile gratefully at Tom. He really hadn't wanted to come. He'd said that if we were going to the trouble of getting a babysitter, we should go out somewhere nice, just the two of us.

"It's been ages since we went into town," he had said. "We could go to actual London! Soho or somewhere. Have cocktails. Get drunk!"

"That sounds amazing," I'd agreed, wrapping my arms around his waist. "But can we do that another time? Laura really wants to hang out with us."

"But I see Laura all the time at work as it is!"

"People are different outside work. And besides, we should make an effort with the playgroup gang. They've been nice to me, especially Laura, and they've helped Finn out, inviting him to playdates. He's enjoyed getting to know the other kids. It's made a big difference to him settling."

Tom had pulled away from me, an eyebrow raised. "I think you just like hanging out in their fancy houses and pretending we're rich like them."

"That's not true!" But of course, Tom wasn't entirely wrong. I couldn't deny I found their company fascinating, even slightly thrilling. I had always thought motherhood was a great leveler, but the more I saw of Claire's, Laura's, and Nicole's lives, the more I could see how transformative money was for parenting. It had the power to magic the mothering experience into the very Instagram perfection I always thought was just a fantasy. Before I met the other mothers, I had known nothing of weekly flower subscriptions, macrobiotic recipe boxes, private family clubs, maternity nurses who would do all the night feeds for you. Housekeepers who morphed into nannies when needed, then faded into the background when you returned—changing sheets, tidying toys, keeping every surface gleaming. It made me realize what hard work my own life actually was. No wonder they all looked glowing, while I looked exhausted and haggard. I had been doing it all wrong.

"All right, all right," Tom had said eventually. "We'll go. I'll even make small talk with that husband who judges me for never being at playgroup pickup."

I looked at him, amused. "Ed, you mean?"

"Yeah, Ed." Tom chuckled, making a face. "You always go on about how much of a hands-on dad he is."

"That's not true. I mentioned once that he does a lot of Oscar's drop-offs! Once!"

"Hmm. Well, anyway, you did find him watching porn that time, remember, so maybe he's not a hundred percent perfect."

I frown. "Tom! I didn't say it was porn!"

Tom looked at my face and burst out laughing.

"Oh, Tash," he said. "From the way you described it, that was *one hundred percent* porn he was watching."

Thinking about what Tom said about the porn is making me look at Ed with a new fascination. What sort of father watches porn with his child awake and playing downstairs?

Ed catches me staring at him over the table, and throws me a questioning glance. I look away quickly. My eyes alight instead on Jez, who is in a shirt and no tie, a new splash of designer stubble on his cheeks. "Yes, this looks great, Laura," he says. Laura smiles, waves her hand over the food.

"It was easy. I just went to Sainsbury's. It's all out of a package."

"I saw you buying it in the deli on Highbury Barn," Claire mutters. "Where everything costs a fortune."

Heads snap up, eyes fix on Claire. She looks unusually severe in her black dress, her hair tied up.

"Sorry," Claire mutters. "It—it all looks lovely. Cheers, everyone. Nice to meet you, Tom." When she leans forward to lift her glass, her dress slips from her bony shoulder.

"Yes, cheers, Tom," Jez says. Both of their eyes seem fixed on Tom for just a beat too long. I wonder why they seem so interested in him.

Ed has already started eating. He spears a potato with his fork and transfers it straight into his mouth without touching his plate. "Cheers," he says, looking up. "Nice to have you all over."

Laura starts to serve with a large silver spoon, but drops it onto a plate as she leans over. The clanging noise makes me jump and grab on to Tom, my pulse racing, fingers digging into the flesh of his leg.

Jez catches my eye over the table, lowers his voice. "You OK, Tash?"

"Fine. Yes, fine. Sorry."

Tom reaches for my hand under the table, and I take it.

I haven't actually told Tom about the latest threatening message yet, the one Sal denies that she sent. I wanted to let things settle a bit after we argued the other night. In the meantime, I need to get a grip, stop jumping at everything.

"More wine, anyone?" Laura is asking now. "Tash and Tom brought this lovely . . . Oh, I'm not sure what that is."

"It's a cabernet sauvignon," I say defensively. It is a nice bottle. It cost us thirty pounds. I have also had my hair blow-dried, and my petrol-blue dress is new, although I told Tom I'd had it for ages.

"Of course. So, Tash, how's work?"

"Fine," I say. "Quite hard work, actually. I was complaining to Jez the other day."

I say it without thinking, then immediately regret it, feeling the dreaded rise of color underneath the skin on my neck. Tom doesn't look up, but I am sure I feel one or two curious glances in my direction. When I risk a glance up, Jez is smiling at me across the table.

"I was telling her she mustn't give it up," he says.

Now Tom looks up at me. I've never mentioned anything to him about giving up journalism. I shake my head slightly, tell him with my eyes that we'll discuss it later.

"What sort of journalism is it you do anyway, Tash? Magaziney stuff?" Ed asks his question through a napkin. He seems to be in a hurry to eat.

"No. I was a news reporter."

He places the napkin down. "Crikey. You're not doing an article on us, are you?" Ed laughs at his own joke.

"Tash works for the national press, mate," Jez interjects. "I'm really not sure your life is interesting enough for her." He leans over to fill my glass, catching my gaze and rolling his eyes in Ed's direction. I find myself smiling back gratefully, tilting my glass in his direction.

"What about you, Ed?" I ask. "I think Laura told me you worked in the city?"

According to Ed's last LinkedIn update—I have, of course, googled everyone here extensively—he works at the same investment bank as Grace, as a trader. I'm intrigued as to how he manages to work from home in such a high-powered job. Grace is always complaining about the bank's hours.

"Nah, I left there a while back. I work with Jez now, doing his financial stuff."

I glance at Jez, hoping he'll elaborate, but he is staring into his wine, swirling it in the glass.

"Tom, can I get you some potatoes?" Laura is speaking more loudly than she needs to, like she wants us to change the subject, or stop looking at Ed, who looks like he might be a bit drunk. He is pushing a potato around his plate with his fork in his right hand, scowling as it keeps eluding him.

Laura gestures to Tom to hold up his plate, like a child.

"So, Tom." Ed turns to him, speaking slightly too loudly. "You're the one who took Laura's residency position, is that right?"

I try and work out whether Ed has just made an honestly misjudged joke, or whether there is a vein of passive aggression beneath the remark. Tom looks intensely uncomfortable. Laura glares at Ed, the corners of her red-painted mouth downturned.

"Ed! It wasn't my residency position. Obviously."

Tom is smiling tightly. "I was very fortunate to get it," he says. "Most doctors don't get one the first time."

"I bet you did, though, didn't you?" Ed says. "Oxbridge boy, I'm guessing?"

Tom blinks. When he speaks, his voice is glacial. "I did go to Oxford, yes."

After an awkward moment, Laura breaks the impasse. "Oh, Ed!" she says. "Stop being so silly! Tom's a complete superstar. We're bloody lucky to have him. He'll almost certainly get promoted to consultant next year, and he'll deserve it." She gives a modest little smile. "I was disappointed not to get the post, but it worked out for the best—you know it did, Ed. We both needed more flexible hours, you see, with Oscar. I wouldn't have been able to commit to it as fully, not while he's little. There's always more time to, you know—'lean in,' or whatever the phrase is!"

Laura forces a laugh, shoots a supportive smile at Tom, but I notice that Tom drops his gaze from hers at the earliest possible moment. I wonder why Tom never mentioned that he and Laura were in competition for his position.

"Tash, more wine?"

"No, thanks." Laura doesn't seem to hear me. She tilts the bottle so much that it glugs, filling my glass nearly all the way to the top.

After dinner we take our drinks into the front room. Laura has lit a fire. I find myself looking at the wedding picture on their mantelpiece. Laura looks beautiful, and I'm struck by how handsome the younger Ed looks in the photograph, too. In his dapper suit, he reminds me of a band member from the Britpop era.

"We met at a gig in our first term of uni," Laura says, seeing me looking at the picture. "I was a fresher, and he was playing the bass guitar. I was smitten. Tragic, isn't it? Think how much shagging around we both missed out on."

I laugh. "Tom and I met when we were students, too. Although not at the same uni. I wasn't at Oxford." I don't know why I'm making such a point of it. I clamp my lips shut and ease myself down onto Laura's red sofa.

"Whoops!" Laura wobbles down beside me. "I feel a bit tipsy! It's that wine you brought. Too delicious!"

"I'm glad," I say, even though she is clearly overcompensating on the wine front.

"I love your dress by the way. Is it new?"

"It might be," I whisper. "Don't tell Tom."

"It's very hot." She nods approvingly. "Don't worry. Your secret's safe with me."

Claire is in Laura's kitchen, making coffee. Tom, Jez, and Ed are standing around the vinyl player, chatting about some band I've never heard of. I glance nervously at Tom, but the awkwardness with Ed seems to have passed. They look like they are getting on well enough now. Jez sees me looking at them. He catches my eye with a smile. I quickly look away, not wanting him to think I was looking at him.

"You look very serious, Tash," Laura says, cradling her wineglass in her fingers. "Is everything all right?"

"Of course," I say. I pause, biting my lip. "Laura, can I ask you about something?"

"Course."

I take a breath. "The thing is, I've been looking into something. A story. Well, I don't know if it's a story. Tom doesn't think it is. It might be nothing." I shake my head. "I'm not explaining it very well."

"Go on. I'm intrigued!"

"OK, well . . . There was a girl who worked at the playgroup, a while ago. Sophie Blake. She was friends with Sal, I think, and then—I think she went to work for Claire, for a while? She died—she drowned. Did you . . . did you ever meet her, or anything like that?"

As soon as I say Sophie's name, Laura's face changes. The smile falls away, a line appears between her eyebrows. She glances at the kitchen, to where Claire is. She lowers her voice to a whisper.

"OK," she mutters. She glances again at the men. "Look, Tash—I can talk to you about it, but not here. And whatever you do, don't ever mention this to Claire, or any of the others."

I blink. "OK, but—why not?"

Laura clamps her hands around her wineglass.

"They . . . don't talk about her. They don't like me talking about her."

"Why?"

Laura shifts in her seat, pulls herself up. "To be honest, I don't really know. All I know is, we're not supposed to speak about it. About her."

She smooths her skirt uncomfortably.

"Look, Tash, come over Monday, after drop-off. It'll be just us." She stares down at the floor. She looks close to tears. "I'd like to know what you've found out, Tash. I . . . I want to know."

"You want to know what?"

Laura glances toward her kitchen, then back to me. She speaks in a whisper.

"I want to know what really happened to Sophie."

Sophie

Seven months before

AS HER PREGNANCY CREPT on, Claire seemed more and more on edge. I felt as if I was always in her way—cooking for Jude when she wanted to make a smoothie at the kitchen island, in the family bathroom with him when she wanted to get in for a soak in their big clawfoot tub. She was enormous now, her bump reducing the space between us more each day, so that our kitchen interactions felt more and more claustrophobic. She seemed to just want me out of the house as much as possible, Jude, too.

I turned the conversation I had overheard between Claire, Laura, and Nicole over and over in my mind, like a scab I couldn't stop picking at. In a way, I could understand how Claire felt. I felt it sometimes, too, how tricky it was to see the edges between her life and mine. Was it OK that Jude came through the connecting door to my annex and crawled into my bed in the morning sometimes? Was it OK that I washed and dried Jez's underwear for him, and folded it away in his drawer? Was it OK that I had seen the soppy messages inside Claire's and Jez's birthday and Valentine's cards to each other, which had been left standing on bookshelves and mantelpieces for months?

It didn't occur to me that I needed to protect the edges of my own life, too. That if I didn't, I might be treading a path to disaster.

Sometimes, after being off with me for a few days, Claire would see me doing something for her, and I'd see her face soften. "Thanks, Sophie," she'd say. "I don't know what we'd do without you."

I didn't know what she would have done without me, either, to be honest. I seemed to be doing more and more for her and Jez, as well as looking after Jude. Washing the paint-spattered clothes and urine-soaked pants that Elaine shoved under Jude's stroller for me to deal with. The marital bedsheets, smeared with human fluids. Jez's sweat-soaked gym bag, decanted from his work bag. Claire's thongs and her comfortable pregnancy pants. In the family bathroom each morning, I wiped the thick tideline of skin cells around the bath, the black pattern of Jez's shavings in the sink, Jude's slivers of toothpaste and spit.

One night there was a knock on the door. It was Laura, bundled up against the cold in a thick woolen maternity coat.

"Oh, Sophie, hi."

I could see straightaway that something was off-kilter with her. She was wearing more makeup than usual. Too much, I thought. It was making its way into cracks in her face that I hadn't noticed before. She had overdone the blusher, and her cheeks didn't quite match. Despite the concealer under her eyes, I could see they were purplish and tired. Her smile was too wide, the lipstick too dark for her face. I spotted a bottle of what looked like Prosecco poking out of her bag, the edge of a squashed box of chocolates.

"Is Claire in?" Laura asked, glancing behind me. "Or, um, Jeremy? I was hoping we could, er . . . have an early Christmas drink. Nonalcoholic," she added quickly, cupping a hand to her bump. "Although, I mean, the babies are so well cooked by now a small glass can't hurt, in my medical opinion." She coughed, looked down, then up at me again. "Are they around?"

"I'm sorry. Claire is already in bed."

"Oh, poor thing. I don't blame her." Laura's face didn't match her words, though. She looked annoyed.

"And Jez is still at work, I'm afraid."

This wasn't quite true, but he did say he needed to work, and I doubted he'd want to be disturbed by a friend of Claire's—whom he presumably barely knew—dropping over for a chat.

Laura didn't seem to be listening. She was looking past me, up the stairs, as if she thought I might be lying.

"When . . . do you know when Jez will be back?"

I tried to think if Jez had ever been around when Laura was here. What did she want Jez for?

I shook my head. "Sorry."

It seemed to me there was nothing more to say, and the air was cold, a breeze shifting in the bare branches of the plane trees overhead. I wanted to close the door, but Laura showed no signs of moving. She was gripping the strap of her bag tightly with one hand. Her arm seemed to be trembling slightly, her teeth-gritted smile slipping. Were the edges of her eyelids pink? Had she been crying?

"I really need to see them," she said. Her voice startled me. It came out as a sort of squeak.

"I'm sorry, Laura. I'll tell them you came. Could you come over to-morrow?"

"I'm on double shifts all week at the hospital." Laura rubbed one eye. Her shoulders sagged. "I need to see them tonight, Sophie."

I paused, shifted on my feet.

"Maybe you . . . could try calling them?"

Laura paused a moment. Then I watched her pull herself up, straighten her spine, as an act of will.

"OK," she said brightly, forcing a smile. "No problem! Bye, Sophie."

I watched as she retreated down the road, the clack of her brown ankle boots sounding farther and farther away. After I had closed the door behind me, I kept wondering what she had wanted. What the question was that Laura thought they were the answer to.

Tash

WHEN GRACE WALKS INTO the pub, I spot it immediately, a tiny curve under her gray work dress. I gasp. She is grinning.

"I didn't know you and Ben were even trying!" I splutter.

Grace laughs. "I thought you'd work it out straightaway when I wasn't drinking at your barbecue. Then again, my boss still hasn't noticed. I'm nearly fourteen weeks!"

I hug her to me, smelling her familiar perfume, her curly hair tickling my face. She sits down on the bar stool next to me.

"Do you want to sit somewhere comfier?"

"I'm fine."

I ask all the usual questions about dates and ultrasounds and how they found out. She hands me her phone to show me the impenetrable black-and-blue pattern of her ultrasound photograph.

"You'll have to tell me what the hell I do. And ooh, I haven't told you—we finally bought a house."

"You bought a *house*?"

"Yeah! I didn't want to say anything until it was all definitely happening. But it is! We've just signed the contract! And it's really near you, in Highbury!"

Grace starts flicking through a gallery of pictures from a real estate agent's site. It is a small Victorian terrace, three bedrooms—"The third is just a box room really—but we could do the loft one day, I think." There is a lovely bright window at the front, an apple tree in the overgrown garden. I push away a familiar stab of envy.

"It's perfect," I tell her.

"We're so excited." She grins, puts her phone away. "Anyway, how are you? Is the copywriting going well?"

"It is, actually."

I agreed to try it, in the end. To my surprise, I am actually quite enjoying it. It is nice to feel appreciated, to get paid on time, to feel I can do something so easily and well, even if it is a bit dull. And it's easy to fit it in alongside my Sophie Blake research.

"Oh, I'm so glad. I know it's not the dream, but you're really good, Tash. Everyone at work has been very impressed."

"That's great." I pause. "Speaking of Schooners . . . Have you ever heard of a guy called Ed Crawley?"

Guilty as it makes me feel, Ed is the real reason I've finally gotten around to arranging this long-overdue catch-up with Grace. It had nagged at me how weird Ed had been the other night, when I'd asked about his job at Laura's dinner. I checked again after I went home. As I thought, his LinkedIn profile claimed he still worked at Grace's investment bank, in the same division. But then, the day after the dinner party, the whole profile disappeared. Something about him didn't add up.

"Ed Crawley?" Grace looks a bit pale. "Is that what you wanted to talk about?" She rolls her eyes. "I could tell from your voice there was something, Tash. It's like being friends with a bloody detective."

I grimace. "Sorry, Grace."

"Why do you ask about him?"

"He's my friend's husband. She . . . mentioned he'd worked at your bank once."

"Oh Christ." She is glancing nervously over my shoulder, as if he might be around here somewhere. "You know his wife?"

"Yeah."

"How well do you know her?"

I consider this. The truth is, I see more of Laura than I do of Grace these days. Or my mum, or any of my bridesmaids. I know where she keeps her mugs, her cookies, her Band-Aids and Tylenol. I've started to share things with her that I have never been able to talk to Grace about—stuff to do with becoming a mother, and working. The guilt I feel all the time. The worry about how little time it leaves over for Tom and me. And she is always so welcoming, so happy to have us at her lovely home. It's so familiar to me, now. I know which is the key for her back door, which of the new kitchen cupboards still sticks a bit.

"She's a pretty good friend." I pause again. "You know Ed?"

"Not personally," Grace says. I can't read her expression. "I mean, everyone at work sort of knows the name."

"Why?"

Our drinks arrive. Grace takes her lemonade, brings the straw to her lips. "There were . . . stories about him," she says.

I frown. "What kind of stories?"

"About him and . . . women."

I stare at her. "What? Really?"

Grace looks down at the floor. "Sorry," she says. "I feel bad for your friend. I think the reason he left Schooners was . . . something to do with all that."

I think of the attentive Ed I see at the playgroup, high-fiving Oscar over the splotched artwork he waddles out with at pickup, slinging Oscar's tiny rucksack over his shoulder. But then another image comes into my head. Of Ed clicking the browser window closed in his office that time. Tom's words. *From the way you described it, that was* one hundred percent *porn he was watching.*

"What happened?" I ask. "Why did Ed leave the bank?"

"I don't know exactly. It was a couple of years ago. Nothing was ever said." Grace sucks the glass empty. "Lot of rumors, though."

"Saying what?"

Grace pauses, rubs her temples. "I honestly don't know, Tash."

"But you said there were rumors . . ."

"Which might not be true."

Grace sits back, a hand floating to her little bump. She shifts on her sit bones, a gesture I remember from being pregnant with Finn. I remember that empty, jittery feeling of early pregnancy, wondering if things were OK all the time.

"All I know," Grace says, "is that it must have been something serious, because one day, he was just gone. His desk was cleared. No announcement, just an out-of-office reply to his email saying he'd left the firm." She looks at me and rolls her eyes. "Yes, all right, before you ask. I will try and find out."

"Thank you."

She raises an eyebrow. "This isn't to do with that dead girl case you were looking into, is it?"

I avoid her gaze. "It's just something I'm looking at."

"You're looking at your friend's husband in connection with a girl's death?"

"Well, not—"

"You think Ed could have been involved?"

"No. I mean, not necessarily. It just . . . might be relevant."

Grace puffs her cheeks out. "All right. I'll see what I can do. This is all very dramatic for a Tuesday night, Tash."

"Sorry."

Grace shakes her head at me, smiling fondly. "Don't worry." Her eyes drift to the menu. "Anyway. Can we order now, please? I think the baby wants chips."

When I get home that night, I pull out my laptop, log into the dating app where I found Sophie's old profile, and run a search.

I had a feeling about it, but I still catch my breath when I see the picture come up. He is using a fake name, but it's definitely him. Ed Crawley, on Sophie's dating app. The app even tells me where he is. He is 1.4 miles away. When I look at his profile, it says he is looking for a girl, aged eighteen to thirty. Blond, petite.

A girl, in other words, like Sophie.

Sophie

Seven months before

THE INTERNET DATING HAD been Sal's idea.

"You need to get out of that house," she told me. "It's not normal, you spending so much time cooped up with Mrs. Misery Guts."

Sal was right. I needed to get out, even if it was freezing, Jude having to be bundled up in his puffer coat and woolly hat for the playground. Claire was close to her due date now, her frustration mounting, her moods erratic. Her belly seemed improbably huge and round at the end of her long, thin arms and legs. It made her look spiderish, unbalanced.

"Here," Sal said. We were sitting on the playground bench, thick scarves knotted at our necks. Sal had the dating app open on her phone.

"You use this?"

Sal smirked. "I have used it."

"Meet anyone who wasn't a dickhead?"

"No, to be fair," Sal said with a sniff. "But that's me. I attract them. Anyway—stop changing the subject. There's a million blokes on that app. Must be one you like the look of."

I had never told Sal about the runner. I hadn't told anyone about him. Not that there was anything to tell. But I felt like it would ruin it somehow, to have it as something me and Sal laughed about.

He'd spoken to me, for the first time, the other day. It had been cold and sunny, and I'd been hanging around in the café, killing time before Jude's pickup. He'd run right up to the café and tapped his hand against one of the pillars outside, then hung his head, catching his breath. His cheeks pink, his exhales forming little clouds of steam. It made me laugh a bit, how he'd tapped the pillar like that, like he was playing a game against himself, like Jude would. First one to the café wins.

He'd bought a bottle of water and a coffee, then slumped into a chair at the table next to me. Then he'd turned and seen me, and smiled.

"Oh," he'd said. "Hello. You're the swimmer, right?"

Afterward, I kept going over all the stupid things I'd said, all the funnier, cleverer things I should have thought of to reply. How I'd then let the silence get awkward, because I couldn't think of anything else. And then he'd said bye, lifted up his hand to wave, and I'd seen a ring on his finger. And felt sad in a way that didn't make any sense, not really.

Sal was still at it with the phone, hands clad in fingerless gloves, swiping through picture after picture of men on ski slopes, or with their T-shirts pulled up to show off their rippling abs, or holding a beer, as if that proved something.

"Do I have to do this? I'm not bothered about finding a boyfriend. And even if I was, look at the state of these. I read somewhere that, like, half the guys on dating apps are married."

"You don't have to marry any of 'em," Sal said distractedly. She snatched my phone, started flicking through, looking for a picture of me.

"Hey!" I objected. But she'd already found the selfie I'd taken when I'd put on Claire's black lace dress.

"Too late!"

"What? You haven't!"

"Your phone is going to be on fire."

"Sal!"

She was squinting up at Billy on the climbing frame. "Oh, don't get the hump with me. You're only young once, for god's sake. You need some fun."

I suspected there was more to Sal's internet dating campaign than concern over how much, or little, fun she believed me to be having. I think she sensed the danger I was in with Jez, and this was her way of trying to steer me away from the rocks. I didn't think she had any cause for concern. I wasn't stupid. I knew what the boundaries were. I wasn't a child. I knew that thinking and doing were two very different things.

That night I lay on my bed in the annex, flicking through the faces of unknown men on the app. Flick, flick, flick. No one.

Then, suddenly, I found him. I would have known him anywhere. The eyes, the dark lashes. He looked so different from the others. Hardly anything on his profile. None of the usual nonsense. It was the runner.

I looked at his location. Barely a mile away. It had to be him. But I'd seen him wearing a ring. Why was he on here? Was he separated, perhaps? Divorced?

I took a breath and swiped right, left my phone on in case he replied. As I went to sleep, I imagined the whole thing. We'd go to the pub on Highbury Barn for our first date, or a walk on the heath. I would casually mention his name in front of Jez, and then I would watch him be forced to think about me with another man. Touching him, kissing him, possibly fucking him, with the black lace dress hiked up to my waist. I wanted to see it on Jez's face. I wanted to light the match of it underneath him, and watch how brightly it burned.

Tash

LAURA FINALLY AGREES TO meet me the following week. I am relieved when she suggests her house. The terrible weather has continued, and going anywhere feels pointless. Plus, in a grim verdict on our finances, Tom says we have to stick to twelve pounds each per day for the rest of the month. My bank balance can't take many more unnecessary cappuccinos.

"Claire doesn't know you're talking to me, then," I say gently.

Laura bites her lip. "No," she admits. "She doesn't."

"I see." I need to tread carefully here, start with the easy parts. "Did Claire hire Sophie when Beau was born?"

Laura shakes her head. "They already had Sophie before Beau came along. Sophie was hired to look after Jude."

"Jude?"

Laura stares at me. "Yes, Jude, Claire's stepson. Jez's son from his first marriage. Sophie was hired to look after Jude, then help Claire with Beau when he was a new baby."

Laura is talking as if I must know who Jude is. But he's never been around when I've visited. Not that I'm aware of, anyway.

"Did you know Jude's mother died?"

I frown.

"Jez's first wife," Laura says. "Her name was Emily. She was a lawyer, brilliant apparently. They found the cancer when Emily was pregnant with Jude—one of the blood tests picked it up. She insisted on holding off chemo to have him. She left it too late."

I set my pen down. "Oh God. That's terrible." I pause. "Laura, Claire doesn't seem to mention Jude much." Ever, in fact, I think. "How old is he? Does he still live with them? I wondered if he was at boarding school or—"

"Oh no," Laura says, shaking her head as if this was a ridiculous idea. "Jude wouldn't go to a— He's six this month. He's at home."

I take this in. "OK. But I never see him. Claire doesn't bring him to playdates, or the park, and I've never met him, or heard her talk about him. Have you ever . . . found that a bit odd?"

Laura looks away. "I don't know. I guess he's at home less in the day, now that he goes to school. He goes to a private place, over in Barnsbury. I think he does after-school clubs, that sort of thing."

I nod, but it doesn't feel like a whole explanation to me. I think again about Sophie's childcare textbook, her concerns about him. Laura's cleaner appears in the hallway and starts vacuuming the stairs, yanking the hoover up behind her.

"So after Emily died . . . ?"

"Jez met Claire. Claire moved into the house."

"The house that was Jez and Emily's?"

Laura makes a face. "Yeah, I know. They married within months. Claire adopted Jude. Jez had been getting his parents to look after Jude while he worked—they adore him, the grandparents—but Claire told Jez she didn't want their help. She wanted to do everything herself. She was madly in love, determined to make it all work, she told me."

"And then?"

Laura looks down. "And then it was hard, she said. Jude was difficult—probably grieving his mother on some level, although he was so little. Claire didn't know how to manage it, how to manage him. You remember what it's like before you've had your own. You don't know what to do with them."

"That's why she got Sophie?"

"That's right. When Jude turned two, Claire and Jez started him at the playgroup. Sophie was his key person. She seemed to be able to relate to Jude like no one else could. Jez said that if Claire didn't want the grandparents around to help, then maybe she should ask this Sophie person Jude was always talking about whether she'd come and work for them, full time, as a live-in nanny."

"What was Sophie like?"

"She was really nice." Laura sounds a little choked. "She was lovely."

The kettle boils and flicks off. Laura stares at it, as if she has forgotten what it is doing. She eventually stands and makes two instant coffees, slopping the milk in without much attention.

"Do you know what happened the night she died?" I ask. "At her inquest, it said she was at a party in the Angel, and then she wasn't seen after that."

Laura sets the coffees down on the table, then slowly sits back down opposite me. "It was Jez's fortieth," she says quietly. "They'd hired out an art gallery near the Angel. It was an amazing party."

I stare at her. "Hang on—it was Jez's party? You were there? You—and Ed?"

Laura blinks. "Yes, we were. All Claire's friends were there. Sorry. I thought you'd have known that. We all had to talk to the police afterward." There is a waver in Laura's voice. It has gotten under her skin, her family's brush with horror. I think again about what Grace said about Ed. I wonder how much Laura knows about it. Or whether there had been anything on Ed's record. Whether the police ever suspected him.

"Did you see Sophie that night?"

Laura shakes her head. "Hardly. She only stayed a bit. Then she took the boys back to the house. Claire didn't stay late at the party either—I think she had one of her migraines."

So Claire left early. Went back to the house. Sophie was there. They were there, alone, that night. Did the police think this was suspicious, that they'd been alone together in the house before Sophie disappeared?

"Claire told us that when she got in, Sophie seemed totally normal," Laura says. "Claire said good night to her and went to bed. Then Jez came home later and went to sleep in the spare room, and didn't see either of them."

I try not to betray my shock. Surely this means neither Claire nor Jez had a proper alibi for a good part of the night Sophie died. Only each other. Didn't the police think this was worth investigating?

"The next morning," Laura continues, "Sophie was gone. And someone—someone found her in the wetlands a couple of days later. I mean, poor Claire and Jez. They were beside themselves." Laura is shaking her head a little, as if she still can't quite believe it. "Such a terrible thing. And it was extra horrible for Claire and Jez because . . . well, because of how things were left, at her inquest."

"What do you mean?"

Laura hesitates. "I mean, don't say that I said this," she says. "The coroner said she probably went swimming and drowned. Claire and Jez said it was a hobby of hers—the wild swimming thing. So I'm sure that's right, I'm not suggesting . . ." Laura scratches at a patch of dry skin on her wrist. "I just . . . I think some people felt that the evidence made it seem like it wasn't clear whether . . . whether it was really an accident or not."

"What do you think?"

Laura starts fiddling with her cuff again. "I don't know," she admits.

"Did Sophie ever mention a boyfriend, or anything like that?"

Laura looks away, considers this. "I think Claire thought she'd been seeing someone. The police asked us all a lot about that. But I never heard about him. And Claire had no idea who it was."

There is no way around it, then. It sounds like the only person who really knew Sophie was Sal.

"Laura, when you told me a while ago to steer clear of Sal—what did you mean?"

Laura shifts in her chair. "I shouldn't really say. But just between us, I think Sal has got some . . . mental health issues. It's very sad." Laura hesitates. "Why do you ask about Sal, Tash?"

"I just wondered if she was worth talking to." I pause. "Look, Laura, I'm sorry. I had no idea when I started looking into this that you'd known her, that she was Claire's nanny."

"It's OK," Laura says uncomfortably. "Like I said, I'm happy to talk about it—I just don't want Claire to know, it would be so awkward." She makes a face. "I know it sounds strange—but after the inquest, Claire told me and Nicole she didn't want to speak about Sophie anymore. Not ever."

"Why not?"

"She said she found it too upsetting. Someone mentioned Sophie's name once after that, and honestly, Tash, Claire had—I'd class it as a full panic attack."

"Oh. That seems kind of extreme." I wonder if there's a possibility Laura could be exaggerating.

Laura purses her lips. "Look. Claire is quite sensitive. It's not my place to say, but . . . well, I'm sure you can see she is a . . . fragile sort of person. After Beau was born she was . . . well, I imagine she will share that with you, when she is ready." She pushes her hair behind one ear. "I think the reason she is sensitive is that one of the police officers once insinuated something to Claire, that was the impression I got. Something that made her . . . feel she was being accused of something."

"Of having something to do with Sophie's death, you mean?"

Laura nods. "It's ridiculous, obviously. But I guess they were always going to have some questions for her." She holds the mug to her mouth, pauses before she takes a sip. "I mean, she was the last one to see Sophie alive."

Sophie

IT WAS A WEEK or so before the baby finally arrived that I heard them talking about me.

It was a sodden day, the sky like a bruise. I was clearing up the remnants of one of Claire's failed activities for Jude, an overpriced Christmas craft kit. Claire seemed strangely fixated on this Christmas, as if it was some sort of test she needed to pass. She had ordered matching aprons for her and Jude, tubes of glitter that I knew would get absolutely everywhere, and set them out excitedly on the table.

"Come on, Jude. Let's make the reindeer!" Claire had sat down awkwardly, her belly pressed up against the edge of the table, fanning herself with her hand. Despite the cold weather, she kept complaining about how warm it was, removing layers of clothing and leaving them strewn around the house. Her pale cheeks were flushed with broken capillaries, like a piece of china blown too hot in the kiln.

"Let's start by cutting out the shapes." She held up the little squares of colored card, smiling like a *Blue Peter* presenter. She was trying, I could see she was. I took some sweet pictures of them, tried to encourage Jude gently to go along with it. But Jude just didn't like stuff like that. Within a few minutes, he'd poured all the green glitter onto his paper and started smearing it around in the paint and glue with his hands, and Claire was shouting.

"Oh, Jude, no, not the whole tube. Oh, it's everywhere. We just do a little bit—Jude, I said no!"

Jude looked up at me, trying to work out what he'd done wrong.

"Oh dear, Jude." I wiped around him, trying to calm things down. "Shall I just put a big mat on the floor and stick him in some messy clothes, Claire, and then he can use his hands if he wants to?"

Claire frowned. I could see this was not what she wanted. She wanted something to show from the activity: an Instagram picture of her and Jude getting just the right amount of messy, glittery decorations like the ones on the side of the craft kit package, which she could cut out and then photograph hanging out to dry on the little string with wooden pegs she'd purchased.

She sighed. "We're fine, thanks, hon."

Before long, glue was dripping onto the floor, and Jude's sleeves and trouser legs were covered in splotches of red and green paint. Claire kept trying to tidy up bits of his picture. I could feel the whole thing ebbing toward an inevitable meltdown, like the *tick, tick* of a stopwatch.

When Jude had calmed down, and the screaming had stopped, I gave him a cuddle and sat him on the sofa in front of the TV, his paint-stained thumb stuffed into his mouth. I could feel already that a bruise was forming on my cheekbone, another on the top of my forearm, from where he'd lashed out and I'd had to lift him, kicking and screaming, from a horrified Claire, who had recoiled from him, clutching her bump.

I rubbed at the table with a damp cloth to try and get the paint marks out. Then I went over to the sink and rinsed the paint pots and started to tackle the dishes that were still there from breakfast. They could easily have been the same dishes I washed up yesterday, and the day before; the scrambled egg pan, the small plate with smears of butter and toast crumbs.

After a few moments, I heard the sound of talking over Jude's cartoons. Jez and Claire were in the hallway.

"I'm sure she just thought she was being helpful," Jez was saying. "Please don't get so wound up about it."

"But why does she always swoop in like that—always at the precise moment that I'm having a difficult time? Is this what she's going to be like with the baby?"

"Maybe she is trying to make things easier."

"Make me feel useless, more like. She makes this face—I can't bear it. It's so obvious she thinks I'm doing the wrong thing all the time."

I held my breath, my face stinging. Claire lowered her voice. I turned the tap off, so I could hear her better.

"She took them off while I was out and hid them somewhere! I'd just tied them all on, made the crib all ready and cozy for the baby. Why would she do that?"

"Well..."

"And the baby clothes, Jez! Who takes new clothes someone has bought for their baby, rips the tags out, and sticks them on a boil wash? It's just a weird thing to do."

"Maybe she was trying to save you a job, Claire. I think you are supposed to wash new baby clothes—I remember Emily doing that when—"

"Don't. Don't go on about Emily, not now. Please, Jez."

"Claire, I need to go to work. Let's talk about this later, OK?"

As I dried my hands on a kitchen towel, I noticed they were shaking. I decided I couldn't be bothered to pretend I hadn't heard. I walked into the hallway to meet them. They froze, stared at me.

"The bumpers are in the bottom drawer in the baby's room, Claire," I said quietly. "I meant to talk to you about it. You are supposed to wait until babies are rolling. They can be a suffocation risk. I learned about it at college. But I'll put them back if you like."

I paused. Jez looked at me, then at Claire.

"I'm really sorry if you didn't want me to wash the clothes," I went on. "I just know you are advised to, and I thought it would be such a stress for you. You'd left them out for a while—I thought maybe you wanted me to do it. They are all like new, except for the tags. I'll ask next time. I didn't mean to upset you."

Jez was still looking at Claire. Claire glared at him, then looked at me, then at the floor.

"I'm the one that should be apologizing," she mumbled eventually. "I can see you were trying to help."

"Look, it's a lot, having someone live in your house when there's so much going on," I said. I felt a lump in my throat now. But I forced the words out anyway. "If you need some time just the three of you. If would prefer me to move out, I would understand."

Until I said it out loud, I don't think I had realized how precarious my life was now. What if they said yes? I'd be homeless, as well as jobless. Elaine wouldn't have me back—she pretty much ignored me now when I went to pick up Jude. I'd have to go back to renting, find a house share somewhere. Or back to Mum's. I couldn't go back there. I just couldn't.

So it was a relief to see it, I have to admit. The look of sheer panic on both of their faces.

"Absolutely not," Jez said. "We want you here, Soph. You are part of this family now. Isn't she, Claire?"

"Of course," Claire says. "Of course." But her eyes told a different story. And so did her hands, clamped firmly around her belly.

Tash

ON THE LAST DAY of term, the playgroup holds a nativity play. Claire has invited the parents for mulled wine and mince pies afterward. She has extended the invite to the entire WhatsApp group in a message accompanied by a string of festive emojis, from tiny snowmen to trees to presents to candy canes. After its arrival, my phone had pinged all afternoon with enthusiastic replies. Even Christina is coming.

Laura has saved spaces in the church for Tom and me. I sit down awkwardly next to Ed, who grins at us. Claire is sitting just behind, wrapped in twinkling jewelry and Christmas-ad cashmere, beaming at the stage. Jez is beside her, his arm slung round the back of her bit of bench. Nicole and what must be her husband, John, whom I have never seen, are on the other side, sitting apart from the others. Nicole is focused on the stage. John has not even removed his coat and scarf. He is jiggling one leg, stealing surreptitious glances at the phone in his lap.

Finn and Beau take to the stage, hand in hand, stuffed sheep under their arms and tea towels on their heads, looking deeply confused. I look back and Claire catches my eye, and I try to ignore the hot sting of guilt about meeting Laura behind her back. Laura is beaming at Oscar, who is center stage as Joseph, his arm around a terrified-looking Eliza, who is supposed to be Mary, and whose blue *Frozen* dress is slipping off her shoulder.

Christina looks smaller and softer out of her work clothes, in her sweater and jeans, her dark hair in a loose ponytail. I overheard her in the lobby telling someone she had scheduled the day off to watch the play. She is right at the front, glowing with pride as she watches Eliza.

I notice she keeps glancing over at us. I wonder if she feels excluded from our group. I think again about Sophie's photograph of Christina.

How is she connected to all this? I watch her burst out laughing and realize Eliza has dropped the plastic Jesus. Seven minutes later, the whole thing is over.

Claire and Jez's tree shines out into the street like a glowing Christmas card to the world, all tasteful pale lights and Scandinavian-style wooden decorations. A huge wreath twisted with dried oranges, cinnamon sticks, and holly is ribbon-tied to the gold knocker. The hum of music and chatter reverberates from inside.

"Looks like a nice party," Tom says. "Good of them to invite us." I smile to myself. Tom hates parties, especially when he doesn't know many people. He is doing this for me, I know. I give his arm a squeeze.

We wait for Claire to answer the door. Finn is looking up with horror at the knocker. He turns away from the door, his hand tightening in mine.

"I don't want go in dat house, Mummy."

It is an unusually articulate sentence for Finn, and he has said it with real feeling.

"Beau's house? Why not, darling?"

"Don't want to."

It's odd that he should feel shy at Beau's house. We've been spending a lot of time with Beau and Claire lately. Tom scoops Finn up on his hip.

"It's all right, Finney." Tom takes the tea towel off Finn's head, and his cardboard shepherd's crook. They look so little in his adult hands.

"It's Beau's house, Finn," I tell him. "You love playing with Beau."

But Finn presses his forehead into Tom's neck.

"I wonder if he remembers about the . . ." I trail off, gesturing at my lip to Tom.

"He's probably just tired," Tom says. "We'll just stay for one quick drink."

Despite all the complicating factors, I am quietly excited about being invited to Claire's fancy Christmas party—even though it has necessitated another new dress I can't afford. I am almost sure that the food—and the company—will be better than at our actual Christmas, at Mum

and Claude's in France. I am already bracing myself for their seasonal on-
slaught of heavy red wine and slimy pâté de canard, of the strange hand-
made presents Mum and Claude have picked up for Finn at some craft
market that will inevitably disappoint.

I am also hopeful that, with Claire's house full of people, I might be
able to slip away and poke around a bit. There must be stuff in the house,
more clues about Sophie. If I can figure out where to look.

Claire answers the door. She has shed her cashmere and is now
wearing a silk shirt, her cheeks flushed.

"Tash! Come in, come in! Finn, you superstar—you did so well!"
She crouches down to give him a high five.

Claire and Jez are so kind, so hospitable. The more time I spend with
them, the more inconceivable it is to me that either of them could have
had anything to do with Sophie's death. But that doesn't mean there
won't be clues here—especially if Claire was, as Laura said, the last person to see Sophie alive.

A little boy emerges from the front room, an iPad in one hand. He
looks around six, a thick mop of curly hair. I can see instantly that this is
the boy in Sophie's pictures, except he is taller and slimmer, as if the
chunky toddler in the pictures has been stretched. He eyes us suspi-
ciously.

Claire touches his hair, lightly. He flinches.

"Have you met my stepson, Jude, Tash?"

I shake my head, hoping I don't look too guilty. "Hello, Jude."

Jude doesn't respond.

"Jude, don't be rude. Say hello."

Jude looks at Claire, then runs off, up the stairs. Claire's smile wilts,
and she lets out a half sigh. I want to smile at her to show it doesn't matter, but am forced to turn my attention to Finn, whose bottom lip is
wobbling. When I try to take his coat off, he won't let me touch the zip.

"What is it, Finn?"

"I don't want to, Mummy."

"Come on, Finney," Tom says. "Let's see if there's a cookie for you."

Tom carries Finn inside. Claire heads to the kitchen island and dips a copper ladle into a pot of mulled wine. There are silver trays of miniature mince pies with a snowy dusting of powdered sugar. Ed is standing on his own, transferring chips from a bowl wordlessly into his mouth, flicking through his phone in a way that can't help but make me think of the dating app.

I take a glass of mulled wine and join Laura by the open fire. The grate is stuffed with boughs of fir trees; the room smells like a burning forest.

"This is so nice," I say.

"Isn't it?" Laura brings a hand to her mouth. "Claire loves Christmas," she says through a mouthful of mince pie. "She's obsessive about it. Oh, Tash—your dress tag's hanging out. Let me get it for you."

Before I can say anything, she yanks off the tag I'd deliberately left on the expensive dress so I could return it after the party. My stomach turns.

"Thanks," I say weakly.

"No problem." Laura looks pleasantly around the room. "I can't believe Claire invited the whole WhatsApp group."

"Kind of her to include everyone."

"Yep." Laura glances at Christina. "Even the weird ones."

Laura gestures to where Jez is standing by the Christmas tree with three or four playgroup mothers buzzing around him. They have swapped their usual leggings and sneakers for blow-dries and makeup— two are even wearing heels. Christina is standing slightly apart from the group, staring into a glass of water, twisting her ponytail around her finger.

I catch Jez looking in my direction. His gaze tilts down over my body, and then he locks eyes with me. I look away, hating myself for realizing I am slightly thrilled by the flicker of approval I saw on his face.

"What are you guys doing for Christmas?" Laura asks.

"We're going to France, to stay with my mum and stepdad. You?"

"Working, sadly." Laura gives me a rueful smile. I feel awkward. It does sound like she gets the short straw when it comes to shifts at the hospital, compared to Tom.

"Tash." Laura lowers her voice. "Did you ever get anywhere with the . . . thing you were looking into?"

Automatically, I glance over at Claire, who is chatting with Tom at the island.

"Not really."

I am somewhat regretting letting Laura in on the fact I am looking into Sophie's death. She appears to be as keen as I am to ensure the others—Nicole and Claire—don't find out. But I don't want her noticing me sneaking upstairs at the party to scout for evidence.

"I've been really busy with other stuff," I lie. "And—I don't know. I guess I feel a bit uncomfortable about it all, given that she was Claire's nanny." Not half as uncomfortable as you should feel, a voice in my head says.

Laura looks disappointed. "I thought you said you wanted to try and find out the truth."

I open my mouth to reply, but Nicole and Claire have come to join us by the open fire. Nicole is still talking about Lissy being passed over in favor of Eliza for the part of Mary.

"It's because Lissy's got an American accent, that's what it is." She is glaring into the cup of mulled wine she has been handed by Claire. I watch her reach in with a red-varnished fingernail to pluck out a clove.

"I'm sure that's not true, Nicole," Claire says. Beau is tugging at her top. She leans over to pick him up, and instantly he goes limp in her arms, his head on her shoulder, his eyelids at half-mast, like a much younger baby.

"How else can you explain it? Eliza couldn't even hold Jesus up straight!"

"Well, Eliza is a little bit older than our guys," Laura says gently.

"Hmph. I bet they only chose her because she's blond."

"It's more of a strawberry-blond coloring, isn't it?" I say neutrally. "Like Beau's." Claire is ruffling Beau's reddish hair. She seems to be brushing it over a bruise on his head.

Jez appears between Claire and Nicole, collecting their glasses, even though they are still half full. "Let's have some more mulled wine, shall we?" he is saying. "And music. I'll put some music on."

"Beau's nearly asleep, Jez," Claire says in a stage whisper. She wanders off to the kitchen island. Jez doesn't seem to hear her. "Alexa, play Christmas songs," he commands the air. The room is filled with the sound of "Jingle Bell Rock."

I swallow the last of my mince pie and look around for Finn. Tom is at the kitchen island, saying something to Claire. When I walk over, Claire smiles and motions that she is taking Beau upstairs.

"Claire is so nice, isn't she?" Tom says, as she walks away. "I was interested to hear about this free vacation in Cornwall we're going on, which you've failed to mention to me."

I look up at him, but Tom looks amused rather than cross.

"It sounds great! Why didn't you say anything?"

I clear my throat. "I wasn't sure if Claire was serious about that."

"Oh. Well, she says she is. Don't you want to go?"

"I . . ." I can't think of anything to say. "Of course. I mean, I think Finn would love it."

"Great! Let's do it then, as long as I can get the time off. It sounds like they have some huge place—she's invited quite a few people—but I guess we can always sneak off just the three of us sometimes if it gets too much?"

I am not listening to him anymore. I haven't seen Finn for ages.

"Tom, have you seen Finn?"

"I thought he was with you."

I go to search for Finn, and eventually find him in the hallway, sitting on the floor by the front door, his knees tucked under his chin.

"Finn! What are you doing here? Oscar and Lissy are in the front room. Don't you want to play with them?"

Finn looks at me but doesn't respond.

"Can you go in that room with Daddy for a bit?"

Finn's head is down, bottom lip out. I can see he is upset about something.

"What is it, Finn?"

"I don't like it in dis house."

"Why not, sweetheart?"

Finn suppresses a sob, the sides of his mouth twitching. "Don't want play in dis house. Don't want play with dat boy."

"Which boy?"

"Dat boy."

I follow Finn's pointed finger through the doors to the front room. In the far corner, away from all the other children, is Jude. He is playing on his iPad, headphones clamped around his ears. It is Jude that Finn is pointing at.

"Finn, darling," I say into his ear. "Why don't you want to play with that boy?"

His lower lip is wobbling. "No like dat boy," he says. "Dat boy hurted my face."

"What do you mean, darling? When did he hurt your face?"

Finn is speaking quietly now. I can hardly hear him.

"Dat boy push me," he whispers. "On the stairs."

Sophie

Six months before

THE NIGHT CLAIRE WENT into labor was the coldest of the year. They left in the middle of the night. The house was still and quiet with just me and Jude. I watched my phone, waited for news all Saturday, but there was nothing. I canceled the first date I'd planned with the runner so I could eat pasta with Jude, snuggle up and watch a film with him under a blanket.

On the second night, I put Jude to bed, then settled on the sofa to watch TV. Neither of them messaged to ask after Jude, or to say how it was going. The house was so quiet. It had started to feel as if they were never coming back.

I tried to get into a film, but found I was distracted, scrolling through my phone, waiting for news. I could reschedule that meal with the runner, I thought. Yet something was making me hesitate. We'd still only spoken over the app, but I was finding it harder to push aside the feeling he wasn't telling me the whole truth. He said his marriage was over, but had admitted he was still living with his wife, the mother of his child. "It's complicated. We have a son. I need to find the right time."

The next morning, I woke up to a message from Jez. They were coming home. I opened the shutters. The morning sky was mercilessly blue, the cold crushing. When I put the trash cans out, the steps were icy, and I nearly slipped. I imagined Claire falling, her arms clamped around the baby. I scattered salt on the stone, my breath coming out in little puffs of steam.

Jez came in first, beaming, gripping the handle of the car seat, the sleeping baby strapped inside. The baby was so limp and tiny, all slumped in on himself. Jude pressed his face into me. Jez bent down, cocked his head at Jude.

"Look at your baby brother," he said. "Just look at him. Isn't he great?"

Jude peered into the car seat, his curls flopping forward over his face. He looked huge, all of a sudden, compared to the baby.

"You're a big brother, mate. Isn't that great? How does it feel?"

Jude looked at his dad, then back at the baby.

"He is very little now," I told Jude. "And he'll sleep a lot at first. But when he's bigger, you can play together."

Jude looked at me. "Can you and me play now, Fee?"

"Of course."

Jez watched Jude walk away. His brow creased a little. Then he went back to get Claire. It was obvious it had not been quite the moment he'd been hoping for.

When Claire walked in, I was shocked. She was walking like an old woman, pressing the tips of her fingers against the hallway wall. I hadn't known she would still look pregnant, only slightly deflated, like she had a slow puncture. Her skin looked blotchy and gray. I later found out she'd had an emergency Caesarean, that she had lost four pints of blood.

"Claire, congratulations! He's so beautiful."

She smiled thinly. "Thanks."

I puffed the cushions on the sofa in preparation for her to sit.

"Can I get you anything?"

She shook her head and limped toward the sofa, wincing in pain. "Where's the thing, Jez?" she muttered. Jez produced a doughnut-shaped cushion from under his arm, and Claire sat down on it. Jez placed the baby on the floor next to her in his car seat. Claire closed her eyes. I thought perhaps she'd want to see Jude, but when she didn't open her eyes, I ushered him into the kitchen.

I fed Jude his tea, got him bathed and ready for bed. It was starting to snow. Claire was with the baby, and Jez was at the store, so I read him both his bedtime stories. I chose one of our favorites, *Stick Man*:

Stick Man is lonely, Stick Man is lost.
Stick Man is frozen and covered in frost . . .

Jude seemed to cling to me harder than usual. I told him we'd build a snowman together, if there was still snow in the morning. He was asleep before I even turned out the light.

Downstairs, Claire was sitting on the sofa, looking out at the snow. The baby was on a sleeping nest in front of her on the floor, curled and upturned like a little beetle. His fingernails were long. He was clawing at his own face.

The baby started to whimper, then to cry. His eyes were pinched shut, his mouth a little "O" of need, searching for her breast. Claire was still staring out of the window into the darkness. When she finally looked down, she seemed surprised by the sight of her own child.

The baby's soft face was getting red now, from all the crying. Finally, Claire picked him up. I realized I had been twisting a tea towel in my hands. I was gripping it so tightly I could see the bones of my knuckles through the skin.

Claire held the baby to her and turned her face to the wall while she rocked him. But the crying didn't stop. I felt as if the noise was sucking the oxygen out of the room. I was finding it impossible to take a whole breath.

Claire put the baby to her breast to feed. Seconds later, she cried out, her face contorted. I rushed over.

"Are you OK?"

Claire looked up. There were tears in her eyes. "Surely he can't have teeth?"

I looked at her, confused.

"He doesn't have teeth," I said.

She looked down at the baby doubtfully. Stuck a finger in his mouth to break the seal around her breast, and ran it along the inside of his mouth. The baby's eyes were open. They looked jet black.

"It feels like he has a mouth full of teeth," Claire said.

The baby was starting to cry again. I handed her a glass of water. "Let me get you some ibuprofen," I said. "And how about a chamomile tea?" I brought it to her, sweetened with honey, a couple of cookies on a side plate. Later I found them sitting there, uneaten.

The next morning, when I carried Jude down in his pajamas, Claire was already on the sofa, the baby at her chest. She looked exhausted, haunted. The baby squirmed on and off the breast, doing great gulping cries. Claire didn't seem to notice Jude come in.

"Jude," I called. "Come and have your porridge."

There was a sound of a key in the front door. Jez came in, a red scarf wrapped around his neck, sleet on the shoulders of his winter coat. He was clutching a grocery bag of fancy pastries. I could hear two voices, and I realized he was with Wendy, his mum.

Jez came into the living room, bouncing around in his sneakers. "Mum's here to see the baby, Claire," he said.

Jude's ears pricked up, and he ran to the hallway to see his granny. I heard the muffled sound of her picking him up and squeezing him, asking him about playgroup.

Jez walked over to Claire. "Almond or plain? I wasn't sure. They had ham and cheese, but . . . Anyway. I got you a coffee."

He put croissants down in front of Claire. As he did so, he lingered, bent at the waist, to coo at the tiny face staring up from her lap. When Jez saw the baby, it was like a light coming on in his eyes.

"You take him," Claire muttered to Jez.

Jez looked at her. "I thought he was hungry."

"I can't see your mum. I can't do all that right now. I need to sleep!" Claire almost shouted. Jez paused, silenced.

"Just running to the loo," Jez's mum called from the hallway. Jude came in, racing up to me to show me a children's magazine she'd bought him.

"Oh wow! Breakfast first, though," I told him gently, lifting him onto a stool, ruffling his hair.

Jez scooped the baby up. "Come here, son." Held against Jez's shoulder, he looked so tiny, like a baby rabbit. I suddenly longed to hold the baby. I felt it like a physical ache in the center of my body.

"Does he have a name yet?" I looked at Claire. Jez looked at her, too.

"I'm not sure," Jez said. "Are we going to go with Beau, Claire?" Jez was bobbing at the knees. The baby seemed soothed. His eyes were starting to close. "Claire, darling? I thought Beau was your favorite for a boy."

Claire exhaled heavily. "I don't know," she said finally.

"But I thought—"

"I don't *know*, Jez!" Claire was shouting now. Jude looked up, alarmed, from his porridge. "I don't know what we should call it. I can't even decide about the croissant. I didn't think it would be a boy."

IN THE days after, people came to the house. Midwives and health visitors. Never the same one. When the first one came, I played with Jude on the carpet while she talked to Claire and weighed Beau. Claire undressed him and handed him over to the midwife without kissing him or anything. His hair was pale and fluffy, like a duckling. He was so vulnerable. He could not do anything. He could not even hold his head. When Claire picked him up, I couldn't help but think that she was not supporting his neck.

"He's lost," the midwife said.

I looked up, not understanding what she meant. I saw Claire do the same.

"Eleven ounces," the midwife said, pointing at the screen on her scales. "We'll need to keep an eye on it. Are you feeding him every two to three hours? Setting alarms at night?"

Claire stared at her. "I feed him constantly," she croaked. "It feels like he never stops. When I lay him down afterward, he screams. Why would I set alarms? Not one of us is ever asleep."

The midwife packed away her scales. "I'll be back in a few days to weigh him again." She made it sound like a threat.

When she came back, Beau still hadn't gained enough weight. She asked Claire how she was finding breastfeeding.

"Agony," Claire snapped. "It's agony. It can't be normal. It just can't."

The woman asked if Claire was sure she was doing it right. She told

Claire all the things Claire knew already, all the stuff about nose to nipple, tummy to tummy. I could see that Claire was gritting her teeth.

"I take it you never breastfed your older son?" The midwife gestured at Jude, playing with Legos on the floor with me.

"He's not my son," Claire muttered.

Jude looked up, straight at her.

"Hey, Jude, let's build something together," I said. I tried to distract him, show him how to put a long piece on top of two stacks of blocks to make a house. Anything to move on from the ugly words about him that hung in the air. But Jude didn't look upset. He didn't look anything. He just went back to stacking the blocks, one on top of the other.

Tash

CHRISTMAS AT MY MOTHER'S converted barn—"semiconverted," as Tom muttered when he saw the state of our room—is a qualified success. Finn is intrigued by all its ramshackle nooks and crannies, and loves ambling about the cold, sunny courtyard, down the lane to where the neighbor keeps his pigs. Claude, who was hopeless with Finn as a baby, is marginally more interested now that he can talk. He speaks to him as if he is an adult, gruffly ordering him to fetch chicken feed and help him brush the yard.

It is freezing, though. I dress Finn in layers, even to sleep. And we have to watch him on the stairs, which Claude made himself and are a potential death trap.

I keep thinking about what he said at Claire's party, that Jude had pushed him on the stairs. Finn is a straightforward sort of boy, with little imagination. He doesn't lie much, and when he does, it is obvious. If Finn isn't lying to me, that means the others—Claire, Laura, Jez, and Nicole—are.

Laura told me he had fallen, and none of the others had corrected her. There had been no mention of Jude, or a push.

The uncomfortable thought occurs to me that perhaps I have been focusing too much on the things I have been keeping from Laura, Claire, Nicole, and Jez. Maybe I should think more about the things they might be keeping from me.

"HOW'S THE free-writing going, Natasha?" Mum asks after dinner the first night.

"Freelancing, Mum."

"I haven't seen your name anywhere lately. I wondered if you were still doing it."

I grit my teeth. "I email you the links to all my articles, Mum. You never reply."

"Oh, darling, don't be sensitive. I do click on them, but they are always behind those paywall thingies."

"*Sunday Times,*" Claude bellows. "Murdoch paper." He encloses a log in his meaty fingers and throws it into the fireplace. Tom puts his hand on my knee. It's not clear to me whether he is applying support or restraint.

When Mum and I do the washing up, she asks where Tom has gone.

"For a run," I tell her.

"Now? In the dark?" Mum raises her eyebrows.

"What?"

"Well, is everything OK between you two?"

I look at her. "Fine. Why do you ask?"

"Oh, I don't know," she says. "I suppose he seems a bit quiet."

"Does he?"

Mum laughs. "He's your husband. Haven't you noticed?"

Annoyingly, I realize she is right. Tom has been quiet lately. I struggle to think of a single conversation we've had since we left for France, outside of functional ones about Finn.

"He is always tired this time of year," I tell her. "Winter's tough in his job, you know that."

"Of course. Poor Tom," Mum simpers. "Such a hero."

I hate that it winds me up so much, all this NHS hero stuff. I know Tom works hard, but after all, it is his career. He's not the one stuck at home, cleaning splatters of food off the floor multiple times a day. A job for which I do not get paid.

Mum drifts away from the sink, dropping all pretense of helping me with the washing up. She is off looking in the mirror now, checking how her hair is falling over her face.

"I take it you still won't sell your father's pictures? Try and buy yourselves somewhere a bit bigger?"

Ever since she married Claude, Mum has referred to Dad in this way, as if he is nothing to do with her anymore. *Your father.*

"Your father wouldn't have wanted you to struggle, Natasha," she goes on. "He could never have dreamed that things would be so difficult for you young people." She comes closer, placing a hand on my sweater sleeve. "If your father had known all that, I'm absolutely sure that he'd have wanted you to—"

"Enough," I say quietly. "Please. Let's not, Mum. I don't want to fall out."

"No," she mutters. "All right." I fix my eyes on the dishwater as I hear her pouring another glass of wine and wandering off to watch TV.

THE DAY after Boxing Day, Mum suggests Tom and I leave Finn with her and go for a walk to the local town. She says she needs bread, and that their dog, Cassis—the Gordon setter that Tom adores—needs a walk.

It is quite nice walking Cassis over the plowed fields, the frozen clumps of earth underfoot, the big, flat skies of central France clear and blue. When we reach the sleepy town square, the café is closed, the outside tables empty. But the boulangerie is open, a smell of dough and sugar rising from the vents in the pavement. In the window is a kitschy, twinkling snow scene display. Tom unclips Cassis so she can drink from the bowl of dog water by the door. "I'll see if they'll do us a coffee to take away," he says.

I sit down at one of the outside tables, zipping my coat up to my neck. The potted plants are festooned with colored Christmas lights. Tom emerges with the bread Mum wanted, plus a paper bag of warm croissants and two hot chocolates in lidded cups. They are outrageously thick and sweet.

"This reminds me of our skiing trips." I smile at Tom.

He laughs. "I'm surprised you even remember those." Skiing trips with our friends belong to a life before Finn: drunken nights out in the resort, tales of bed-hopping at breakfast, pounding hangovers on the cheapest possible Ryanair flight home.

Tom passes his hot chocolate cup between his hands. His breath turns to steam in the air.

"How are you, husband?"

"I'm fine."

"You seem a bit quiet."

"Do I? Sorry." He dusts croissant crumbs from the metal surface of the table. "Work's been stressful lately."

"More than usual?"

He looks away. "Yeah. More than usual." He rubs his beard. "I was thinking I might not apply for the consultancy post at the hospital."

"What? Why?"

Tom scratches at a bit of melting snow with his sneaker. "Just the hospital. Some of the other doctors, the staff."

I stare at him. "You've never mentioned any of this."

"It's not that big a deal." He sniffs. "I'm going to apply for other places, that's all. Keep my options open."

"Hang on," I say. "When you say the other doctors, you're not . . . you don't mean Laura, do you?"

Tom pauses. "Not just her. But yes, I do find Laura a bit difficult."

"Did you and she fall out because you got the job she wanted?"

Tom is silent.

"Tom? Come on. I won't say anything."

"It wasn't that—at least, I didn't think we'd fallen out over that. It was something else. I caught her doing something she shouldn't."

"What sort of thing?"

"A breach of prescription protocols."

"A minor thing?"

"Not really, Tash." Tom runs a hand through his hair. "These things are serious. I spoke to her first. She asked me not to report it."

"And did you?"

"I had to, Tash. To protect myself."

"Oh."

I privately wonder if Tom really did have to report Laura. Tom does everything so by the book. He finds it hard to understand when other people have a more relaxed approach to rules; it doesn't always mean they are bad. I can imagine that if someone didn't know Tom, he could come across as a bit abrupt about stuff like that.

"Laura didn't seem to see that I had no choice," Tom says. "She was very cross with me, and she's just been really difficult and short with me ever since. And because she's been there longer, and she's so chummy with the nurses—they all seem to think I'm the bad guy as well."

He sets his cup down on the table, places his palms on either side of it.

"The weird thing is," he says, "whenever you're around, she goes out of her way to be nice. I don't know, Tash. I don't trust her, that's all."

I shift on the metal chair. I trust Tom, of course I do. But I can't square any of this with the Laura I've gotten to know. I wonder if there is a possibility he is being oversensitive, or has misunderstood. Laura has been nothing but kind to us, as far as I can see. If it weren't for her, Finn would probably never have settled at the playgroup.

"I'm sorry," I say. "About the work thing. It sounds stressful." I pause, unsure what else to say, so I try a joke. "I thought it was just my mum driving you mad."

We both laugh. "No, she's all right," Tom says. "She winds you up more than me. I think she's pretty funny most of the time."

Tom takes my fingers and presses them between his palms to warm them. The light is starting to seep away, and with it the small warmth of the watery winter sun. I pull my coat tighter around myself. For the first time, I feel sad that we are going home. Tom and I need to get away more.

"We should head back." Tom zips up his coat, pulling the neck right up to his chin against the cold. He whistles to Cassis.

"OK," I say. "Can you remind me to take my birth control pill when we get home? I need to be better at remembering."

"Sure." I wonder if Tom might say anything about trying for another baby, but he doesn't. I try to work out whether I'm relieved or a tiny bit disappointed.

"Any other New Year's resolutions?"

Keep digging, I think.

Tash

IN THE DAYS AFTER we get back from France, London feels silent, emptied out of people. All the cafés are closed, the roads clear. Finn and I cut lonely figures on the swings and climbing frame. The trees are bare and leafless overhead, the sky pale and featureless as an unpainted wall.

I was hoping to enjoy some time with Finn before playgroup starts again, but typically, after months of nothing, I have had a bite on one of my freelance pitches this week. To my surprise, one of the newspapers wants the gentrification story I pitched ages ago, about the wetlands. With no playgroup until next week, I have no idea when I'm going to write it, but it's the first bit of freelance work I've had in a while, so I will just have to make it work.

"Yeah, it's dead, we've got a lot of space to fill over the New Year," says the assistant news editor, who has obviously drawn the short straw over Christmas. I bite my tongue, try not to feel offended. "Obviously, it would be great if you could dig into the money a bit," he adds. "And can you file by Thursday?"

"Sure," I say brightly. "No problem."

At the weekend, while Tom looks after Finn, I make my way down to the wetlands to try and get some first-person accounts. It is bitingly cold, a white mist over the reservoir. I can't see the middle of the water. Geese emerge from the pale cloud like specters, their black heads and necks just visible, their feathered bodies fading into white.

I manage a few quotes, but my heart's not really in it. An old lady in a poky ground-floor flat is desperate for company and invites me in, but after a few minutes, she starts repeating herself, getting confused, so I politely make an excuse and move on. A few people glare at me, tell me to fuck off as soon as I say I'm a journalist.

Next, I head toward the new towers. The mist has lifted, but the light is starting to fade. Needle pricks of rain are starting over the reservoir. Across the water, the lights of the city glint like illuminations from a far-off planet.

As I pass the playground at the foot of the towers, I see Christina and Eliza. They are the only two figures there—hardly surprising, given the weather. Christina is pushing Eliza on a swing.

Christina arranges her features into a half smile, gives me a curt nod. "Hello, Tash."

"Hi, Christina. How was your Christmas?"

"Fine, thanks. Yours?"

"Oh, you know. Exhausting."

Christina is barely making eye contact. Her eyebrows are knitted together, her coat belted tightly. It feels like she is pushing the swing harder than she needs to.

"Do you live here?"

Christina looks at me warily, as if I have asked her something extremely personal.

"I only ask," I say, "because I'm writing this piece, and I was—"

"Look, Tash. I don't mean to sound rude, but I know what you're writing about. Everyone does."

It takes me a moment to realize what she means. She thinks I'm here about Sophie.

"Sal told me what you were doing. I can't help you, OK? So please don't ask."

There doesn't seem much point correcting her. "OK," I say. "But, Christina—can I ask why you wouldn't want to talk about it? About Sophie?"

Christina ignores my question. She grabs the swing. "Come on, Eliza," she says. "It's getting dark."

"But, Mummy, you said—"

"I said no." It comes out as a bark. Christina yanks Eliza out of the swing and grabs her hand.

"Christina, I—"

"Don't bother. Sorry, I'm just not talking to you about this, Tash. Not now, not ever."

THAT NIGHT, I work late to finish the piece on time. The flat is dark except for the yellow puddle of light from the desk lamp I've dragged into the kitchen.

I use my credit card to pay for access to Companies House, the financial records I'd always been able to view for free as a staff reporter. I pull the records of Woodhill, the company leading the development. It's a privately owned company, but looking to go public in the near future. I try to work out how much money Woodhill has made on the wetlands development, but the structure behind the project is complicated. A lot of work has been subcontracted to other firms. I start sketching out the relationships between the companies on my pad, but I quickly run out of space.

One firm appears more frequently than others: Graphite Security Solutions. I start tracing all the transactions between the two. Graphite has been paid millions by Woodhill. And yet there are transactions the other way, too—Graphite has bought up millions of pounds' worth of property in the development.

I do an internet search on Graphite Security Solutions. It seems it is a subsidiary of another company. I click on that company's website, and I realize I have been here before. I click the tab that says "Who We Are," and am met with a list of directors, with their profile photographs and potted biographies. Five are listed.

The first is Jeremy Mark Henderson.

Tash

THE WOMAN AT THE Corinthia spa reception has the glassy expression of a doll. I lean over her marble slab of desk, her lit scented candle, trying to read her screen. I make an effort to keep the white heat of panic from my voice.

"I d-don't . . . I don't think it's quite that much," I stutter. "I paid a deposit. And it is just a massage, a manicure, and a pedicure . . ."

"That's right," the woman says. "Three treatments, a day pass for use of the facilities, and lunch also. Plus your friend advised us that the three of you would be splitting the cost of Ms. DeSouza's food and treatments—as a birthday gift?" She pauses. "Would you like to see the breakdown?"

I grip my card. The embossed numbers are sharp against the pads of my fingers.

"Can I just cancel my treatments?" I ask quietly.

"I'm afraid the cancellation cost is the cost of the treatment now. You'd need to give us twenty-four hours."

I feel a plummeting sense of panic.

"You can pay when you leave, if you prefer."

"No, now is fine—I just, um . . ."

"Did you want to pay by card?"

I can feel there is someone else behind me waiting. There is nothing I can do. I start to hold out the credit card, a slight tremble in my fingers. Then an arm appears over my shoulder, a flash of black plastic between outstretched fingers.

"I'll get this, Tash. It's on me."

Jez looks like he has just come out of a shower. His hair is wet and he smells of shower gel. A sports bag is slung across his body. I feel myself adjust to his presence, like you might to a change in altitude. I hold up my palm.

"Honestly, no. Jez, that's very kind, but it's far too much."

Jez waves me away. "My treat," he says. "For Nicole. I forgot about her birthday. I'd like to get it."

I feel my face coloring. "I can't let you pay for this, Jez," I say firmly. "It's not appropriate."

"Please don't worry. Claire and I are members. We get better rates." He pauses. "You can pay us back, if you really want." He tilts his head to one side. "You might as well take the discount, no?"

Jez shoots an authoritative nod at the woman behind the desk, who has been holding his credit card in the air. She smiles shyly at Jez and places his card in the machine. As I hear the payment go through, the tick of the receipt printing out, my panic is replaced by unease. The woman hands me the receipt, and I shove it into the pocket of my dress.

"I'm sure Claire really appreciates you coming."

"But I . . ."

Jez drops the bravado, places a hand lightly on my arm, and lowers his voice for a moment. "Tash, please don't worry."

His eyes meet mine, and we look at each other for a moment. I open my mouth to say something, but before I can think of anything, Claire and Laura appear.

"Great, you're here!" Claire smiles. "Nicole's inside already. Let's go."

AS I make my way through the underground maze of the spa, there is something about the low lights, the hushed voices, the mirrors, that gives me a bad feeling, that tells me I should turn back. All the women look identical, disguised in white gowns, hair towel-wrapped, padding noiselessly in slippered feet.

After I change, I can't see Laura and Claire, so I head into the spa. Nicole is in the center of a pool, floating on her back. Her eyes are closed, her black hair spread ink-like around her. The arch of the roof meets its reflection in the water below, like jaws. Nicole's body is motionless. Then her eyes snap open, and she looks straight at me.

"Hello, darl," she says. "You look like you've seen a ghost."

She flips over, a curl of water following her body under the surface. I watch her shimmering darkly at the bottom of the swimming pool, gliding toward the side. Then she emerges, slick with water, strong and muscular as a lynx.

As I watch Nicole dry off, I shift in my dressing gown. My expensive new costume feels tight on my shoulders, the skin between my legs still sore from the wax I'd had to spend thirty-seven pounds—and a precious childcare hour—on.

I avert my eyes from Nicole's taut body and fix them on her face. "Have you had a nice birthday so far?"

"Yes, thanks. I love it here. Everything OK? You want a frozen grape?" Nicole passes the tiny bowl to me.

"Thanks." I pop the grape into my mouth. It bursts open, the frozen flesh on my teeth causing a cold, metallic pain behind my eyes.

"Are the others not here?"

"They went to the pods," Nicole says, gesturing down a corridor at one side of the pool.

"Pods?"

"Sleep pods. You never tried them?" I shake my head. She explains what they are. I get the sense she is enjoying the fact I don't know. "I don't like them, though," she says, making a face. "They remind me of coffins."

She swings her dark, wet hair over one shoulder to brush it. Then she interlaces her fingers and stretches them above her head, the muscles in her arms revealing themselves from underneath her coffee-colored skin.

"So Laura tells me you've been asking questions," she says. "About Sophie Blake."

I cough, nearly choking on my frozen grape.

"I'll tell you one thing. Well, three things, actually."

I freeze, unsure what to say.

"One," she begins. "If you're thinking Sophie Blake was some kind of angel—you'd be wrong. Two, I really wouldn't ask Claire about it if I were you. She's been through enough already."

I chew the grape, my teeth stinging again. "OK."

"And three," she continues. "You and I never had this conversation, OK? Oh, look." Nicole plucks her phone from her dressing gown pocket. "Nearly time for our massages. I need to shower first. See you on the other side." She makes what I imagine is intended as a little excited smile. It sits uneasily on her face, like a badly hung painting.

I find it difficult to relax during my massage. The pressure feels uncomfortable, the Tibetan bowl music irritating, the padded circle around my face making my cheeks hot and clammy to the touch. It is difficult not to think about how much the experience is costing per second. My thoughts are also still spinning with what Nicole has just said. What was the purpose of the conversation? Was she warning me off? And what did she mean about Sophie?

Next we are led to a line of white leather recliners, like seats in a private plane. A woman in a mask hands me a key ring thing with a string of fake fingernails in different colors attached to it. I'm relieved when I'm sat next to Claire, and not Nicole. I select the same dark red as Laura. Nicole chooses a molten eggplant purple, Claire a milky coffee color. We lie back as the women slough off bits of our skin and rub orange-peel scrub into our foot arches.

"Is everything OK, Tash?" Claire asks.

"Fine," I murmur. I find myself unable to look at her, unable to look at anything except the dots of colored polish, swimming in front of me like inkblots.

"I'm really looking forward to Cornwall." Claire flicks through the kaleidoscope of dismembered fingernails. "It'll be so much fun having them all at the cottage."

I keep telling myself that we can always pull out of this trip if we need to—it's ages away still, and it's not like we are paying anything.

"Finn will love that," I reply uneasily. It's true—he would. "I guess vacations just the three of us must be a bit boring for him really."

I pause.

"It must be nice for Beau," I say. "Having a sibling to play with."

Claire shrugs. "I guess," she says. Then she smiles, leans in. "Between us, Jez is desperate for another."

"Oh." For some reason, I feel heat rising to my cheeks. "And you're not . . . you're not keen?"

Claire's smile fades. "Just a bit anxious, I suppose." She looks down. For a moment, we sit in silence, watching as the masked women paint our nails in neat brushstrokes, left, middle, and right, as gentle as butterfly wings.

"Did you . . . did you have a hard time with Beau?"

"I had postnatal depression. It was quite severe."

I glance at her. "Oh, Claire. I'm so sorry."

"I didn't admit it for a long time. I think the midwives knew early on." She pauses. "One of them asked me outright, pretty much. She could see I was a terrible mother."

"I'm sure you weren't . . ."

"I was. I didn't love him."

I am silenced. There is a hardness in Claire's voice I haven't heard before. She glances at the nail technicians, straightens her back, then speaks more quietly.

"I mean, look. If he was on a sofa, or a bed, I'd make sure he didn't fall off. But that was it. He could have been anyone's baby. He didn't feel like mine."

"And you never said anything?"

"I thought they'd take him away, and then Jez would be heartbroken."

I exhale, put my hand on hers. "I'm so sorry, Claire. I can't believe no one helped you."

"I think on some level I was waiting for someone to ask the right question, whatever that might be. But whatever it was, no one asked it." She has looked away, like she isn't talking to me anymore. "It was awful. I felt like nothing was normal. I felt full of absolute dread. Terrible thoughts got trapped in my mind, which I couldn't seem to shake."

She is leaning forward, now. I look down and can see the hairs rising on my arms.

"I used to think—when he was a tiny newborn, his head still all wobbly—I used to think about what would happen if I just picked him up and his neck just snapped, backward, like that, like a tree branch."

I look up, shocked.

"I could imagine the whole thing in my mind," she says, looking straight into my eyes. "I could see it so vividly that I sometimes thought that this was actually going to happen. Or had happened already. Or that it was something I was going to do." Claire bends her fingers toward her, blows on the drying polish. "I mean, can you imagine what it was like, being inside my head? With thoughts like that?"

Sophie

Five months before

THE CRYING WENT ON all night. The noise made me grip the sheets on top of me, the surge of adrenaline that rose to greet each new scream shutting off my sleep. I listened to Claire and Jez upstairs, shuffling back and forth, shushing and hissing at each other, like noisy ghosts.

The house seemed to be in a constant state of crisis. Claire spent more and more time in her bedroom. Jez spent hours walking up and down the house with Beau on his chest, shushing him and rocking him while he cried. It was impossible to talk to either of them.

I was sure that Jez must see that something was wrong, that Claire was not behaving normally, that she wasn't doing any of the things she was supposed to be doing. I also wondered if he'd noticed Jude's indifference to the new baby, and whether that struck him as odd. I longed to talk to Jez about things like I used to. But there never seemed to be a quiet moment.

The last midwife that came was called Fatima. She had a black head-scarf and long fingernails painted dark red. They talked, the baby asleep between them in a Moses basket. I had made sure his temperature was right, his blanket tucked in at the sides. Fatima had her notes fanned out on her lap.

As she placed the band on Claire's arm to take her blood pressure, I saw Claire hold her breath.

"Try to relax," Fatima said.

Claire exhaled. The machine beeped.

"It is a little high," Fatima said.

"It's just because you're all here," Claire muttered, looking at me.

"So," Fatima said to Claire. "How are you feeling emotionally?"

Claire didn't say anything. I watched her carefully. I wondered if I should say anything. And what that would be.

"Claire?" Fatima prompted her gently. "I was asking how you were feeling emotionally."

The weight of the silence was heavy and thick, like a dam about to burst. I willed Claire to say something. Anything, rather than nothing.

"It's normal to feel tearful, or overwhelmed," Fatima told her kindly. "It's a lot. Especially your first time."

Claire looked down, as if her throat was stuck.

"Do you feel like you've been able to bond with the baby?"

I looked at Beau. He was so tiny still, so curled up and squashed. His head was scaly with cradle cap, red spots on his cheeks. He did not look like a baby in a book or an ad. Claire was looking at him, too. I could see in her eyes what the answer to the question was.

"We don't have to discharge you today," Fatima said. "We can put you on a longer-term visiting plan, with extra support, regular mental health check-ins. If you think you'd benefit from that."

Claire looked up from Beau, as if awoken from a dream. "No," she said firmly. "I don't need anything like that."

And so nothing happened. No one came, and it got worse and worse. The days felt so long, with so little light. Jez was back at work. Laura and Nicole—both still pregnant—had called around, their hands full of presents and flowers, eager to meet the first of the new babies. But Claire made me send them away, make an excuse. She and I were on our own in the house. From four in the afternoon to seven in the morning the sky was dark, and Beau just cried and cried and cried.

Tash

AFTER MONTHS OF PREVARICATION, the police press office has finally come back to me. The officer in charge of the original investigation into Sophie's death is willing to have a look at the phone. It feels like a breakthrough.

I arrive at my appointment at Tolpuddle Street. The officer on duty holds Sophie's phone daintily between her gloved thumb and forefinger before sealing it in a clear evidence bag.

"Thanks." She smiles blandly, indicates that I can leave.

"But . . . what happens now?"

"I was told to tell you to put any questions to the press office."

"Can you just ask the officer whether he has a moment to speak to me? I think his name is DSI Hayden."

"Did he say he wanted to speak to you?"

"No, he just asked me to leave this, but . . ."

She sighs. "Remind me of your interest in the case, sorry?"

I hesitate. "I'm a journalist," I admit finally.

Her face hardens, as instantly as if she'd pulled down the metal shutter.

"Can't help you, I'm afraid," she says. "All media inquiries are dealt with by the press office."

I suspect the police press office is as sick of talking to me as I am of bothering them. They probably thought that if they finally agreed to take Sophie's phone into evidence, I would go away for a while.

"But can you just clarify whether this means you are reopening the case?" I'd asked.

"No," the press officer had snapped firmly. "The line is as I gave you last week. If there's any change in our position, I will be in touch."

I press my fingertips down into the ledge in front of the glass door, until the flesh around my nails turns white.

"Please," I say, leaning into the acrylic hatch. "Just give DSI Hayden this." I slide the letter under the hole in the glass. The woman moves her fingers away from it, and wrinkles her nose.

"If you could move aside," she says.

Defeated, I turn away, push the glass doors open. A blast of freezing air hits me in the face. As I head for the bus stop, I hear a male voice from behind me, a thick east London accent.

"Excuse me, love. I think you dropped this."

I turn around. A tall man in a police uniform is holding out a folded piece of paper. I take it automatically, before pausing. I'm sure I didn't drop anything.

"Actually," I say, "I don't think that's mine."

"Oh yes," he says, meeting my eye. "It is yours, Miss James."

The tall man locks his eyes with mine, then turns on his heel. I notice his stab vest is slightly too short for his body.

By the time I unfold the paper, the uniformed man is already gone, disappeared back behind the glass doors of the police station. I stand in the street, staring at it, until my hands are cold.

Tash

———❦———

"SO A MAN CLAIMING to be a police officer wants you to go alone to a pub on Woodberry Down and not tell anyone about it."

I look at Tom in the mirror. His arms are folded.

"Yep." I brush my eyelashes with mascara. When Tom doesn't reply, I turn to look at him properly. "What? Finn's in bed. There's that curry in the fridge."

"It's not that! It's unsafe, Tash! Do you even know his name?"

"Adam."

Tom rolls his eyes. "Adam what? How do you even know he's a real police officer?"

"I know he is a police officer," I say. But privately, I wonder if I really do know that. He was there at the station, wearing what looked like a uniform. He could still be a mad stalker, for all I know.

"Look," I tell Tom, "that's how it is with sources. You don't want to push them for more details straightaway. They might back out."

"More details like a surname?"

"Yes, like a surname! If you were going to whistle-blow to a journalist, would you want to give your surname?"

Tom is silent. It is a pointless question. Tom would never whistle-blow to a journalist. He does everything by the book.

"I just worry about all this, Tash. After you got those horrible text messages." Tom is rubbing his nails over the back of his head.

"I know. But you know where I'm going. I'll message every twenty minutes or something."

I stand on tiptoe to give him a kiss on the cheek. As I pull my coat on, he wanders into the kitchen, puts the steaks he has bought into the freezer. I blow him a kiss and he smiles sadly, then turns away.

The Happy Man pub in Woodberry Down has the air of somewhere long abandoned. The paper on the walls is peeling away, revealing an underside stained yellow by tobacco. The floor seems to be on a slope. Deep cracks spread over the ceiling like tree branches.

The police officer I know only as Adam returns from the bar with a pint and a glass of wine. A purple-faced old man turns on his stool to heckle him.

"What's the weather like up there?" A ripple of laughter escapes from the crowd around the slot machine.

"I'm used to that." Adam shrugs cheerfully as he sits down.

"I bet. How tall are you?"

"Six six."

Adam perches awkwardly on the stool. He glances doubtfully at my glass of wine as he hands it over.

"I hope that's all right. I'm not sure there's usually much call for wine in here."

"I'm sure it's fine."

As I set it down, the table wobbles. Adam puts out an arm to steady it. He inspects the legs to work out which is short, then starts to fold a beer mat between his hands.

"Nice choice of pub," I mutter. "Looks like it's been condemned."

"It has, actually," Adam replies from under the table. "It's being demolished. There's some kind of appeal, but they won't win." He reemerges and sits back on his stool. "Making way for the next phase of the big development."

"Jesus." I should probably have known this, included it in the gentrification piece. I've gotten sloppy, I realize. Distracted by Sophie.

"I know. Bit of a dump, though, isn't it? To be fair." Adam places his glass on the table, then repositions it slightly with his thumb and forefinger, so that it is exactly centered.

"Are you going to tell me why we're here, Adam?"

Adam's expression clouds a little. "Um, yes. Sorry. It's just—I know you've been asking questions about Sophie Blake. We had a message from the press office. DSI Hayden told us all not to talk to you. He won't help you, by the way. No chance." He pauses. "But the truth is, I'm sure he got it wrong. I'm sure something happened to that girl."

Sophie

Four months before

IT WAS BOREDOM, IN the end, I think, that made me agree to go on the date. That, and the thought of another night in the annex alone with my phone.

The air in the house was becoming suffocating. Claire barely spoke to me. She seemed to barely speak to anyone. Our afternoons together were increasingly painful. I watched her spend nothing-filled hours with Beau, checking and rechecking her phone, while the rain flicked at the glass at the back of the house and the clock ticked out the minutes and hours of his babyhood, until it was time to collect Jude from playgroup.

I could see there was something wrong with her. Sometimes I caught her sitting in silence next to where Beau lay on the mat. His little legs were kicking, his eyes searching for her, left and right. But Claire's face would be fixed on her screen, checking and rechecking the time as if she was willing the hours to pass. I longed to scoop him up in my arms, read him a story, sing him a song. I couldn't understand how Claire didn't feel the way I did, caught between wonder and grief for every little stage of his that slipped by, watery and fast, impossible to stop or go back. Already he was getting too big for the things I'd dressed him in at the beginning, the sleepers covered in jungle animals, the tiny hat with bear ears.

The air always changed when Jez walked in, like a window being opened. He strode in, laden with shopping bags, rolling up his shirt-sleeves, tipping Jude upside down, the energy of his world outside the house still on him, like whizzing, invisible particles. He'd take Beau from my arms and kiss his fluffy hair, then jog upstairs to put the bath on, draw the curtains in the boys' rooms, find their pajamas. He would come and see me, too, ask quietly how I was. Occasionally, he put a hand on my shoulder, or my back, just briefly. It struck me as significant that he only did this if Claire wasn't looking.

Jez seemed determined to convince himself Claire was fine. "I think the breastfeeding is really taking it out of her," he said to me once, coming home to find Claire in bed again. It felt to me like an excuse, though I wasn't sure what for.

Sometimes if she was in bed, Jez would sit on a stool in the kitchen and talk to me while I cleaned up. It became my favorite part of the day. I made a point of having the kitchen spotlessly clean ahead of this moment, something fragrant in the oven. I liked to hear him exhale with the relief of it, the relief of having me there, the house perfect, the food done. He would pour himself a glass of wine, and I'd tell him about all the funny little things they'd done that day. Jez loved silliness. Claire didn't know how to be silly. I would flick through the photographs of the boys I'd taken on my phone. In the park, on the swings, at a music class. Jez would lean in to see better, the blue of my screen glowing on our cheeks, our lips. Close enough that I could feel the warmth of his chest through his work shirt. Close enough that I was sure he would catch the lingering scent of cocoa butter on my skin, coconut shampoo in my hair.

The night of the date, I made sure that Jez saw me in my dress. I came out of the annex and stood in the hallway, pretending I wanted to use the mirror to apply my mascara before leaving. I waited for his footsteps on the landing, then watched him do a double take, start to say something, then press his lips together and formulate something else. Later I played the moment over and over in my head.

"You off out tonight, Sophie?"

"Yep."

"Anywhere nice?"

"A date. Dinner. In town."

Jez's eyes locked with mine. Understanding. Accepting the challenge.

"Have fun," he said.

I smiled.

"I will."

Tash

—————◦◦◦◦◦—————

"LOOK, WHAT DID I know?" Adam says. "I'd only been on the force a few months. But I felt there were clear signs she'd been deliberately killed."

"Like what?"

Adam hesitates. I sense we are moving into confirm-or-deny territory.

"Did you look at the people she met on the dating app?"

Adam inhales. "You found that, then. Yes. We pulled the records. She was in contact with a few people . . ."

"Names?"

"I can't, you know I can't." Adam is shaking his head. "There was no evidence on her profile that she actually met anyone in real life. She could have deleted messages, of course. If it had been a murder inquiry, they'd have done a deep-dive on her communications, but . . ."

"But they didn't. Because the pathologist couldn't find evidence of unlawful killing."

He nods. "Bodies in water can be particularly difficult. All pathologists say that."

I pull the phone report from my backpack and hand it to Adam.

"I had this done on her phone," I say.

He looks at it, then back to me. "Who did this for you?"

"I'm not sure what his name was. A guy from Blackstock Road." Adam raises an eyebrow, but makes no comment. He reads the messages, then looks up at me. "Can I take this, have a look at these numbers?"

"Sure." I take a gulp of wine. I am not sure whether this is allowed, but I decide to leave Adam to worry about that. He folds the paper carefully once, then again, then puts it into his breast pocket.

"So you don't buy the coroner's assessment?" I ask him. "That Sophie went swimming, got in trouble, and drowned?"

Adam winces. "No," he says. "I just don't see it. There'd have been CCTV of her closer to the wetlands, I'm sure there would. There's nothing."

"Did you ask the estate for their CCTV?"

"We did. A lot of what should have been there was missing. Cameras in some of the key spots had been vandalized."

"Cameras?" I immediately think of Jez's company. "Didn't you think that was suspicious?"

"Of course. But Hayden didn't agree. Said it had always been a rough area, still was, even with the fancy face-lift."

"Wasn't Jez Henderson's firm responsible for the CCTV cameras? Graphite Security Solutions?"

Adam gives me a look. "He insisted not. Said Graphite had been contracted to install the security system, but that they had subcontracted the ongoing running of them to another firm. Graphite builds stuff all over London. They're a massive company—they turn over a hundred million a year. We couldn't find anything to contradict his account."

"Hmm."

"I know," he says miserably. "But Hayden said it all stacked up."

"It seems a bit of a coincidence, doesn't it? Jez being her employer, one of the last people to see her alive, and he's been involved in the site where her body was dumped?"

"It does." Adam gives me a slight smile. "And I don't believe in coincidences. All of that rang alarm bells for me. If you're in a hurry to dump a body, you tend to choose somewhere you know pretty well, right? But Jez insisted he was barely ever at the wetlands himself, that his firm had projects all over London. Which, as I said, they do."

I paused, considered this. "Did you look at him? At him and his wife?"

"I looked at their movements, the movements of their car, for any evidence it went near the wetlands that night," Adam says. "I looked into every minute between Sophie's last sighting and her being found dead. But their car hadn't moved. And I couldn't place either of them anywhere near the wetlands. I even got the cadaver dogs to have a sniff around the trunk of their Land Rover."

"Wow. Really?" I can't imagine Claire was too happy about that.

"Yeah. The sarge told me off for that. Said it was heavy-handed."

We exchange a look.

"And the dogs found nothing?"

Adam shakes his head. "Not in the car, not anywhere in the house. So that killed my theory, you see. If there'd been a body kept in that house, or that car, they'd have smelled it."

This makes sense to me. I have never really believed that Jez or Claire could have killed Sophie, dumped her body in the wetlands. But nor do I believe she went swimming. Something else happened that night.

"Look," Adam says, leaning in to me. "In the end, you've got a married couple who are each other's alibi—it wasn't ideal. But there was nothing else substantial to undermine them, either. Nice, wealthy couple. Nothing on their records. Totally cooperative, charming, consistent under questioning."

"Which could just be because they are telling the truth, of course."

"Of course," Adam says. "And that was Hayden's view."

We sit in silence for a while. I take a gulp of wine. The pub is quiet now, the traffic noise from the road outside more distinct in my ears.

"What about other cars? They had friends at the party that night—did you check their cars? Did you look at whether any of those went back and forth to the wetlands, after the party?"

"There were fifty-odd people at the party, Tash, all friends and family of the Hendersons. This was me on my own, remember, not a murder investigation with a big team. Sophie went missing on a Friday and wasn't found until three days later—it's a huge time window in search terms. A search on a specific place is one thing, but going through all the movements of everyone at the party, for a whole weekend . . . Do you know how many officers that would take?"

"But then how was your boss satisfied Sophie went to the wetlands of her own accord?"

Adam grimaces. "How can I put this? DSI Hayden has a particular view of young women. And their alleged tendency to make daft decisions."

"For God's sake."

"I know, I know. I'm afraid . . . that sort of sentiment—it's not uncommon among my, um, police colleagues." He puts his pint down, straightens it again. "Look, he had a point in a way, Tash. We had no obvious dodgy boyfriend, the employers looked clean, no criminal associates, no drug habits. All we knew was Sophie had had a few drinks, it was a warm night, and she liked open-water swimming. Once the pathologist report came back saying cause of death was unascertained, but likely she'd fallen in and drowned, that was it. The way Hayden saw it, there was no investigation. He wanted it passed back to the coroner."

A bell sounds for last orders. We both ignore it.

"I can't look into this anymore, Tash," Adam tells me. "Hayden won't hear another word about it. But I think someone killed this girl. And that person is still out there."

"I think they are, too."

Adam looks up. "Why?"

"Because ever since I've been looking into Sophie Blake's death, I've been getting these."

I hand him my phone and open the messages up. Adam looks at them in turn. He raises his eyebrows.

"You don't know these numbers, obviously?"

I shake my head. "If you call them, they say out of service."

Adam nods. He pulls his own phone out, saves the numbers in his notes. "I'll see what I can do," he says.

"Thanks."

The pub is emptying out. I feel tired, and no further forward. I need to get home. I start to gather my things.

"Have you spoken to Jane?" I ask Adam.

"I did at the time."

"She thinks Sophie had a boyfriend. One that she kept a bit quiet about, for some reason." Plus I found her contraceptive pills when I was sneaking around my friend's house, I don't add.

"Interesting. I think she was seeing someone, too," Adam replies. "This is what I came here to show you. I wondered if you might be able to shed any light on it."

Adam pulls a laptop out of his bag and sets it on the table. "This," he says, "is the last image we have of Sophie alive. She is at Jeremy Henderson's fortieth birthday party, at the Upper Space art gallery, the night she disappeared. It shows her leaving the venue, with the kids—the two boys. To me, it looks like there is a man with her when she leaves."

I blink at him.

"Why was this picture never released?"

"Because it wasn't a murder inquiry."

Adam still hasn't turned the laptop around. I can see in his face that he is crossing a line, showing me something he shouldn't. But I can also see that he wants to, that I'm not going to have to push very hard.

"This man," he says. "He looks like he's got an arm around her. But the odd thing is, this bloke isn't on the guest list for the party, and we were never able to eliminate him from our inquiries. Claire and Jeremy have always insisted they have no idea who this man was. They have no explanation for why he was there at their private party. None of the people at the party seemed to have any idea who he was either."

"Is it a good enough image to ID someone?"

Adam nods. "It's a bit grainy. But it's good enough."

"Can I see it?"

Adam looks down.

"I can show it to you here," he says quietly. "I can't send it to you. I can't risk there being a record."

He glances pointedly down at my phone, and I see what he is saying. I should take my own picture. He is going to look away.

"OK."

Adam makes a few clicks, a little pool of blue light on his face. Then he turns the screen around. And there is Sophie, in her black lace party dress. And behind her a man, with his arm around her shoulders.

I gasp, dropping my phone, clutching the table.

It doesn't make sense.

"Are you OK?" Adam leans into his bag, grabs me a bottle of water. I take it gratefully, put it to my lips. I look again at the screen, wondering if I made some mistake. But there is no mistake. The walls seem to buckle.

"You don't know him, do you?"

I open my mouth, then close it again. I can't tell him.

The man with Sophie in the picture is my husband.

It is my Tom.

Tash

WHEN TOM GETS HOME, I am sitting at the table in the kitchen, still in my jeans and hoodie. Tom doesn't seem to see me, or hear me when I say hello, ask how his day was. He doesn't seem to notice I have been crying. Or that I have got the photo of Sophie that I found in his sock drawer in my hands, and am turning it over and over.

"Tom, can you come and sit?" I say. "I really need to ask you something."

"Not now, Tash."

"Tom?"

He turns away from me, shoves his hand into the bread box, starts rooting around. I have been working up to this all day. I need to get it over with.

"Is something wrong?"

He shakes his head. "It's total bollocks. I have no idea what's going on, Tash."

"What is? What's bollocks?"

"Just work. Fucking hell."

He shoves two slices of bread into the toaster, yanking the handle down so hard I wince. He stalks around the kitchen for a while, like a caged animal. Then he collapses into a chair, as if the energy of not telling me what's going on has suddenly defeated him.

"I've been suspended from work."

I stare at him, unable at first to process what he is saying.

"What?"

The toast pops. We both ignore it, staring at each other.

"Someone's made a complaint. A woman. She says I . . . I can't believe it. I'm actually shaking." He holds his trembling hands out in front of him, stares at them as if they belong to someone else.

"Who? What kind of complaint?"

"I don't know, it's anonymous. A patient. They just said it's a woman and she's made a serious allegation. They won't tell me anything else." He breathes out, brings his hands to his face, and pulls them down his skin, like a child making a face.

"But what's their complaint? What are you supposed to have done?"

"I don't know. They won't say. But it's obviously bad."

"They can't suspend you and not tell you why!"

"Apparently they can. Christ, I need to eat something. I haven't eaten all evening."

He works so hard. The fact that he still hasn't eaten anything for dinner at one in the morning breaks my heart.

He stands up abruptly and turns to the toaster. I watch the back of him, listen to the scrape of his knife against the bread. This is a bigger threat, I realize. An actual crisis, rather than one I am speculating might exist. This is our real life. Our home, our son. My income is nothing, barely enough to pay the playgroup, let alone live on. If Tom loses his job, it is not like he'll get another one. It's not like that for doctors. One complaint can ruin them.

I know I need to stay calm for Tom, but I am struggling, a juddering panic coursing through me. I can't imagine Tom as anything other than a doctor. He loves his work so much. This will destroy him. I will have to get a full-time job, copywriting or PR or something, anything to pay the bills. But what if it isn't enough? What if we can't pay the mortgage on our flat?

I swallow, try to organize my thoughts. "What happens now?"

"I've got a meeting with HR in two weeks. They'll tell me more then."

"And until then?"

"I'm on paid leave."

"So you're being paid?"

"For now." I realize he is trying not to cry.

"Oh, Tom. Come here."

I stand up and try to hug him. Tom hangs an arm limply around me, but he doesn't relax his torso into mine. After a few moments, I let go and sit back down. I sense neither of us feels better.

Tom sits opposite me and takes a bite of his toast. I stare at the semi-circle he has left in the neat, square slice.

"You said you wanted to talk to me about something." He squints at my face through his glasses, as if he is looking at me properly for the first time. "Tash, have you been crying? What's up?"

I think about the picture, the speech I rehearsed about it in my mind. Then I look at Tom's face. I put the photo facedown on the table.

"It's nothing."

Sophie

Four months before

THE PLACE HE'D CHOSEN was actually pretty fancy. There were white tablecloths held down with little silver clips, lots of different knives and spoons laid out, a big arched ceiling like a church.

The food looked incredible, but I found I couldn't eat much of it. After the third glass of wine—or maybe the fourth—I realized I was bored. It occurred to me that I didn't actually feel anything at all for this person. In fact, he was really starting to grate on me—complaining about his job, telling me how awful the mother of his child was, how she had been more bothered about her career than about him. I didn't care about him, about any of it. He was not the person I had built up in my head. All I kept thinking about was Jez. I kept wondering what he was doing at home, whether Beau was coughing, or Jude was having a nightmare. I couldn't remember why I was there.

I stood up, said I was leaving, but my legs felt unsteady. He tried to tell me to stay, but I wasn't listening. As I got up, I wobbled a little, so that I was glad of his hand. He took me to the elevator and pressed the button.

By the time I wondered why we were in an elevator, remembered that there was no need to get in an elevator because the restaurant doors opened onto the road, it was too late. We were in a corridor, and he was pulling me down it, his hand tight on my wrist.

"Let go, you're hurting me." My voice was all slow and slurry, like a broken cassette.

He stopped at one of the doors, pulled a key card out of his jacket pocket. Started jamming it into the hole in the hotel room door, again and again. The card wasn't working, the little light flashing red instead of green. He jammed it again. The way he was breathing made me frightened.

"I want to go home," I said.

"You're not well," he was saying. "I think you should lie down for a bit." His voice was so calm, so clinical. I got that feeling then, the bad feeling, like when you miss a turn-off, and then you realize you're hurtling down the motorway in the wrong direction at a hundred miles an hour, and you can't find a way back.

His hand was still on my wrist. "Let go," I said again. But it was like he couldn't hear me. I said it louder. "Let go!"

"Is everything all right here?"

Both of us looked up. There was silence suddenly, and calm. A lady had walked over to us, leaving her husband by the elevator. She had a lined face, bright blue eyes, a sparkling tunic top and matching necklace.

"We're fine," he said. But she was not looking at him. She was looking straight down at my wrist, where he was holding on to it. I pulled myself free, and with the lady looking, he did not resist.

"I wasn't asking you." The woman's voice was teacher-sharp. He cowered, and the woman turned to me.

"Why don't you walk with us, dear?" She held her palm out in the direction of the elevator. Her husband was watching us.

"We can walk you to the Tube station if you like. We're going that way."

Before I knew it, the woman had placed a bony arm around my shoulders and ushered me down the corridor. When I risked a glance backward, I saw he was still standing there, staring after me, clutching his key card in one twitching hand.

ONCE I was on the Tube, on my own, I was glad of the way everyone averted their eyes, pretended not to notice anything. I sobbed and sobbed, unable to stop. No one sat down next to me. I saw my reflection in the darkness of the Tube windows opposite. I saw exactly what I looked like. A silly young girl in a too-short dress.

It was after midnight by the time I got home. I couldn't find my key to the annex—maybe I'd dropped it somewhere. I climbed the steps to the main front door, turned my other key quietly in the lock. The cold air had sobered me up a bit. When I started to slip my shoes off, I saw the kitchen light was still on.

Jez was in the hallway before I could do anything about the mascara streaks, the wine breath, the puffy eyes.

"Sophie?" He could see straightaway that something had happened. "Jesus. What have you done to your arm?"

I looked down at my wrist. My arm was unfamiliar, shocking, four thick welts and a bruise on the inside. It was hard to believe this was an arm that belonged to me. I looked away from him, ashamed of what had happened to me, of what he must be imagining.

"Come here."

I didn't resist. It was such a relief to be held, to feel the solid warmth of him. Jez's hand started to move up and down my back, in between my shoulder blades. We stood there together for a long time. I felt so safe, at last. I willed it not to stop.

Tash

WHEN TOM FALLS ASLEEP, I turn the light back on to watch him. He is wearing his old university athletics shirt, his stubbly chin pointed upward, the lines around his eyes and eyebrows puckered, as if he is trying to solve a problem in a dream. I watch his chest rise and fall, trace the edges of his fingers—long and slim, just like our son's, a band of silver matching mine on his left ring finger. Then I lean over him, unplug his phone from the charger on the bedside table, and take it with me into the kitchen.

It can't have been Tom in the photograph, I decide. It just can't. I'll check our calendars for July 2017. We will have been together doing something dull that day, the day Sophie went missing. Taking Finn to the park. Ordering takeout and watching Netflix, like we do every Friday night.

I tap in Tom's PIN, find his calendar, and flick back to that week. There is nothing on the Friday at all. The only entry that week is for Thursday the sixth. "Tash and F flight: 6:15 a.m."

It takes me a moment to process. It was the week we went to my mum's in France, without Tom, because he had not been able to get the time off.

I take my own phone out then and check my calendar. The dates fit.

We'd argued about it, hadn't we? I had been upset that he hadn't gotten the time off, but more upset he didn't seem that bothered, that he was treating it like just one of those things. We had exchanged messages tersely all week, and when I got home he'd been distant. Both of us felt we'd been somehow wronged.

What had Tom told me about that week? Had I even asked what he'd been doing? I'm sure he said he'd just worked. Gone for drinks with Ravi.

I flick through to the photo I eventually took of Adam's CCTV image. Each time I look at it I think I'll see it differently, find something that proves it can't be Tom. But the more I look at it, the more sure I feel. The line of his jaw, the set of his shoulders. The tatty orange T-shirt I always beg him not to wear.

I send Ravi a message.

Hey, can you meet me tomorrow? Really need to speak to you about something. T

THERE SEEM to be so many stops to get to Ravi's. I knew vaguely that he and Abi had "moved out," as Tom was always saying, in search of an affordable house. But I'm still surprised the postcode doesn't even seem to be London, though it is—just—on the Tube. "No-brainer" had been Tom's verdict. "They've got four bedrooms now, a massive garden." I hadn't said anything.

I follow Ravi's directions across a huge park with a café in a mock-Tudor building in the middle, a queue round the corner of parents in sunglasses and puffer jackets, clutching takeout coffees. I am forced to grudgingly admit to myself that it has its charms. The play area is five times the size of our local one, with a zip line and a huge tunnel slide. On the other side, the tennis courts are full, the staccato thump of bats and balls mingling with a smell of damp, raked leaves.

Ravi comes to the door straightaway, enclosing me in a big hug. Then he leads me through a hallway covered in baby photos and into the living space at the back of the house. I note the huge island, the skylight over the dining space. I greet his three sweet children with as much enthusiasm as I can muster, ruffling each head of shiny black hair in turn.

"Coffee?"

"Please."

The children amble happily on walkers, Fisher-Price cars, and tricycles, bifold doors opening out to a neat paved patio with a dining table and barbecue. Ravi starts making coffee.

"Your message sounded very serious," he says quietly. "Everything OK with Finn?"

"He's fine. Sorry, I didn't mean it to sound so dramatic."

"That's good." Ravi sets a coffee down in front of me. "Come on," he says. "What's all this about, Tash?"

I haven't thought properly about how to ask the question. "I wanted to know if you remembered something. The summer before last, in 2017, Finn and I went to France without Tom, because he had to work, and while we were away, you and he went out for some drinks. Do you remember that?"

Ravi thinks for a minute, then his face clears. "Oh yeah—I remember. We ended up at that pretentious party. Did he tell you about that?"

"That's right." I sidestep the issue of whether I have talked to Tom. "Can you remember . . . how you ended up there?"

"Didn't Tom tell you this?"

"He . . . he said he couldn't remember." I'm fully lying now. There is no getting around it. But Ravi seems somewhat mollified. I know this isn't the first time he's been asked to relay the details of a night out to his friends. Ravi doesn't drink, so he's probably often the only reliable witness.

"Right," he says. "Well, it was a bit random. We started out in the pub. But then one of our mates from the hospital said there was this party with free drinks up in Angel, and that we could come if we wanted."

"Do you remember who?"

"Girl called Laura—she's a doctor in Tom's department, been working at the hospital a few years. She's sort of posh. It was a posh party."

Even though I know it is the only thing that really makes sense, it still feels like a punch in the gut. He went to the party with Laura, the night Sophie died. Laura, whom he claims to dislike, whom he always acts weird around. And when Laura told me about that night, she completely failed to tell me that Tom had been there.

That can't have been accidental. She purposely omitted that information. Why? Was there something more to their relationship? My brain rejects the idea, but I force myself to confront it. Even if that's true, it certainly doesn't explain why Tom left with Sophie.

"Why did Laura want you and Tom to go to this party with her?"

Ravi laughs. "I don't think she did. She was all dressed up, saying she was going to just have one, then head off to this party. She had this great big gift with her and everything. But then someone pointed out that there was a Tube strike. She looked gutted. She started stressing out, trying to get an Uber, but everyone in London was trying to get one. In the end, I told her I'd just drive her. It was on the way, pretty much. And I'd already told Tom I'd give him a lift home, so he came, too."

"But if Tom wanted a lift home, how come he ended up going to the party?"

"We weren't going to," he says. "But when we got there, it looked amazing, a big flower arch thing over the door, like a wedding. It was a nice summer evening, really warm. Canapés, trays of champagne, people spilling out onto the pavement. Laura said come in for a drink, I'm sure it's fine. I said to Tom, what do you think? He said, fine, let's just go for one."

So it was a coincidence Tom was there. Could this really be true? Or could Ravi be lying to me, and covering for something Tom has done?

"Anyway," he says. "I left soon after that. Abi was at home, pregnant, with the kids—I didn't want to take advantage. I didn't know where Laura had gone by that point, she just seemed really distracted, and then Tom disappeared, so—"

"Hang on—Tom disappeared?"

Ravi hesitates. "Well, I mean, just for a bit."

"Who with? I thought you didn't know anyone else there."

"I don't know, Tash." Ravi looks down. "Are you going to tell me what this is all about?"

I have made him feel awkward. I can feel my blood hot under the surface of my skin, but I know I can't push it. I need to keep Ravi on my side.

"Tom knows you're here, yes? You have talked to him about all this?"

I avoid Ravi's gaze, look away from him into the glass doors. I catch sight of myself in the reflection. I look dreadful, the shadows under my eyes purplish, my eyelids raw, cheeks sallow, hair unwashed.

"Tash . . ."

"Oh, Ravi, OK. I promise I will talk to Tom."

"Good," he says, relieved. "He's a mate."

"I know."

We sit in silence for a moment. I see Ravi glance over at the kids. They are starting to squabble over toys, rub at their eyes. I've taken up enough of Ravi's time.

"I'll get out of your hair. Thanks for the coffee." I ease myself off my stool. "Can I just ask you one more thing before I go?"

Ravi makes a face.

"Did you find Tom in the end? Did he leave with you?"

"You need to talk to Tom, Tash."

"I'm going to, I promise. But did he leave with you, Ravi?"

Ravi rubs at the back of his head.

"No, Tash," he says. "I don't think he did."

Tash

I AM HALFWAY UP the path from playgroup drop-off when I hear Laura's voice.

"Tash, wait! You left this!"

I turn to see her holding my laptop case. I feel a sick twist of horror at how careless I've been.

"God," I mutter. "Thank you."

"Sal had it."

"Sal?"

"She said you left it by the buggies. I said I'd give it to you."

"Thanks." I take the bag, feeling the reassuring weight of my laptop inside. All my copywriting work is stored on there. It's due in tomorrow.

"Are you all right, Tash? You look exhausted."

I force myself to look at Laura. As soon as I do, I can see she knows about Tom being suspended.

"How is Tom?" she asks gently.

"Not great." I look at her accusingly. "Do you know what it's all about, Laura?"

She glances down, fiddles with the little tassels on her pashmina. "Only that it was a woman who complained."

I close my eyes for a second before I face her. "Is he supposed to have done something . . . inappropriate?"

Laura bites her lip, looks away. "Look, Tash, we all know it's nonsense," she says. "Patients make things up. They almost always get found out."

I feel like I am going to be sick. *Almost always.*

She reaches out and squeezes my arm, but I feel worse, not better. I feel irritated at being the recipient of her sympathy. Your husband's the creep, I feel like shouting. Not mine. My husband doesn't watch porn when there are kids playing downstairs, or look for young girls on dating apps.

"Do you want to go for a quick coffee?"

"No," I say too quickly. "No, thanks." I'm just not sure how much I can trust Laura. It feels like there is a growing list of things she hasn't told me the whole truth about. Finn being pushed down the stairs. That she'd fallen out with Tom at work. The fact that Tom was at Jez and Claire's party the night Sophie died.

"OK," she says. "Take care, Tash." I watch as she walks away down the church path, her brown boots clacking against the cobbles.

I had intended to finish the latest lot of copywriting work when I got home. Instead, I sit at the kitchen table, staring out of the window. I try to make sense of what Ravi told me. I need to get everything straight in my head before I speak to Tom.

I decide to go through Sophie's social media again. You can still see a cached version of Sophie's old page, with a few images still available to view.

Of course there isn't going to be a picture on here of my husband that I've somehow missed. But there might be something else.

I search a long time. I don't find any pictures of Tom. But I do find something else. A person I hadn't noticed before, who has liked a lot of Sophie's posts. Lydia Gracie. When I run the name through the voter registration lists, I get lucky. Only one in the whole of north London, Aubert Park. A few minutes' walk from Claire's house. That can't be a coincidence.

I click on Lydia's own Instagram profile. She looks about my age. Lots of pictures of a toddler daughter, a small dog. I pick up my keys and pull on my coat.

LYDIA'S HOME is the best part of a tall, handsome Victorian house. I buzz the doorbell marked "B," stand on the black-and-white tiles, and watch as a figure moves behind the stained glass and slowly opens the door.

Lydia has a plain, round face, owlish glasses. Her hallway is littered with the toddler detritus I recognize from my own life: a scooter, a doll's stroller, a pair of abandoned leggings. Behind Lydia, a girl Finn's age is wearing a Disney princess costume over her T-shirt and playing on the scuffed stair carpet.

Lydia squints at me impatiently. "Hi," she says. She glances down, as if she expects me to be holding an Amazon package, or a clipboard.

"I was wondering if you might have a moment to speak to me. It's about Sophie Blake?"

"What? How did you get this address?" Lydia's squint curdles into a frown. Her hand tightens on the latch. I am suddenly reminded of my own reaction when Jane Blake appeared at my door.

"I looked your address up on the electoral register. I'm a journalist."

"A journalist?" Lydia's mouth hangs open. She glances behind me, as if looking for the paparazzi.

"It's just me," I say gently. "I'm sorry—perhaps this is painful. Were you and Sophie friends?"

Lydia makes a sort of snort, her expression incredulous. "I already told the police. I know nothing about Sophie Blake. Absolutely nothing."

"Do you mind me asking how you met her?"

Lydia snorts again. "Good question," she mutters. The girl on the stairs behind, tiring of the lack of attention, begins to whine something. "One minute, Zelda," Lydia says behind her.

She speaks again, more sternly this time, her hand still on the door. "Look," she says, pushing her glasses up her nose. "I don't know who you are and what this is about, but I don't want to be in any article." Lydia looks close to tears. "This whole thing—it's been horrible." She waves her palms in front of her face, as if trying to waft me away. "I'm sorry," she splutters. "I just don't want to hear about it anymore. I don't want to hear her name. I'm going to go now." She starts to close the door.

"I need to know if she had a boyfriend. Please."

I blurt it out almost without thinking. Lydia's hand slows on the door.

"Why?" she asks. "Why do you need to know?"

Because it might have been my husband, I think.

"Because she might have been murdered."

Lydia's face creases. She shakes her head. "No. No—I read the thing in the newspaper. They said it was an accident."

"Lydia, please, just answer me this one question," I beg. "Did she have a boyfriend?"

Lydia folds her arms. "She said she was with someone," she says eventually.

"Did she give a name?"

"She might have."

I feel sick. *Please,* I think. *Not Tom. Please.*

"Can you remember the name, Lydia?"

Lydia glares at me. "Listen," she says. "I seriously doubt any name I gave you would be helpful to you."

"Why not?"

Lydia leans out of her door.

"Because every single word that Sophie ever told me was a complete fucking lie," she spits. "All right? I have no idea who that girl was. If you ask me, she was a fucking psychopath."

Sophie

Three months before

I DECIDED TO GO and stay with Mum for a bit. I told Claire I was sick. I couldn't face being in the house with her, risk her asking questions about the bruises on my arm. I kept getting messages from the runner, saying he wanted to talk. I deleted them all. I thought about Jez, how he had held me when I'd gotten home that night, what it might have meant. A few times I typed out a message to him, only to delete the characters one by one.

At dinner, I pushed my food around my plate. Mum had made toad in the hole because I used to like it as a kid, but it looked so beige and colorless compared to the food I had gotten used to. I thought of the things I'd seen in Claire and Jez's fridge that week. Persian filo pastries. A slice of banoffee pie. Salads scattered with red pomegranate seeds, like tiny jewels.

"You not hungry?" Mum asked.

"Sorry." The sausage batter was tough and cloying in my mouth. The mixed vegetables—in Lego-bright shapes of yellow, green, and orange— tasted of nothing.

Mum looked down, the sides of her mouth twitching, trying not to show she minded.

"How's that new baby, then?"

I look up, force a smile. "He's cute."

"What's his name again?"

"Beau."

Mum wrinkles her nose. "Honestly. Names these days. I blame celebrities. How's the mum getting on?"

I shrug. "She just mopes around. Doesn't do anything with him."

"What d'you mean?"

"She doesn't take him anywhere."

Mum laughed. "What do you want her to take him to, for crying out loud? He's a newborn, isn't he?"

I stab at my sausage, exasperated. "You can do loads of sensory stuff, Mum. There's research. He needs exercise—"

"Exercise?"

"Yes, Mum! Babies need time on their tummies from birth, to build their muscles. You don't know." In my voice, I heard the sulky teenager I always felt like in front of Mum. She snorted and passed me the jug of instant gravy.

"Anyway, it's not like you to stick up for her," I said pointedly, taking the jug. She was usually sniffy about Claire and Jez, their fancy house, their fancy food, their waste-of-money takeout coffees.

"Yeah, well, I feel for her," Mum said gruffly. "Having a baby's not easy, Sophie."

"But she could at least have a shower, crack a smile. Wash up once in a while."

Mum gave me a sharp look. "Ain't you being paid to do that?"

"I'm not a maid."

"Oh, Sophie . . ." Mum made a noise like she was exasperated. "Everyone's a perfect mum before they actually are one."

I blinked at her. "What do you mean?"

"I just mean, I know you think you're the world expert on children these days. But you ain't never had one of your own, have you? There's some things you only learn by going through it."

I made a huffy sound but didn't say anything. Mum sighed.

"Can't you just give her a break, Sophie? Just—I don't know. Take the baby round the block for fresh air. Claire needs rest, and that baby don't need anything else, whatever you heard at college."

CLAIRE DIDN'T say anything when I returned. She didn't ask about my fake illness, whether I was feeling better. I suppose she had her own problems. The morning after I got back, I found her with the baby on her lap in the front room. She was holding her cracked, red nipple pinched between the knuckles of her middle and index fingers. Her teeth were gritted.

"Come on," she was saying through her teeth. "Come on." Beau was turning his tiny face away.

"Claire, I don't need to get Jude until three. Shall I take Beau out in the buggy so you can both get some sleep?"

Claire stared at me. Her hair looked like it had been painted onto her head, her skin gray and slick and sweaty.

"He won't feed."

"But he's been up feeding through the night, hasn't he? I heard you getting up with him."

Claire paused, then nodded.

"Do you think he might just be overtired?"

Claire covered her face with her hands. Her fingers were so slim, her skin so pale you could see every bone inside.

"I'm terrible at this," she breathed through her fingers. "I can't do it."

"That's not true," I said. "You just need rest."

Claire dropped her hands into her lap and looked at me. "OK," she said weakly. "Thanks."

I went into the kitchen and made a formula bottle and a cup of chamomile tea. Claire didn't know about the bottles of formula I gave Beau sometimes, but what she didn't know wouldn't hurt her.

Claire zipped Beau into his thick, padded snowsuit, and started trying to clip him into the stroller. Beau was looking up at her, his little eyes searching for her face. But Claire wasn't looking at him. She was frowning at the clips, holding the parts like pieces of a puzzle she couldn't fathom.

"I'll do that," I said. "You go to bed."

Once Claire was upstairs, I took Beau out of the stroller and put him in the sling on my front. I had worn him like this before when Claire wasn't around. I found it soothed him. As soon as I started walking, his pale eyelashes drooped, his tiny head lolling onto my chest.

I walked up to Highbury Barn, dodging the skeletons of discarded Christmas trees on the pavement. By the time I got there, Beau was snoring quietly, his miniature nose in the air. I looked down at him, the top of his head snug in the center of my chest. His milk spots had cleared up now, and his scalp wasn't so scaly. His hair was kitten-soft.

The windows of the fancy deli were still filled with Christmas lights. There were benches set out inside, a smell of coffee and croissants. I felt for my expenses card in my pocket. I hadn't had any breakfast.

As I stepped inside, everyone smiled at me. I felt like I'd just walked into a surprise birthday party.

"Oh, congratulations! He's so sweet!" A woman sitting in the window blinked at me through an owlish pair of glasses. She was wearing a baby, too, a bit bigger than Beau. The tangle of white lights at the window shone around them both like a halo.

"How old is he?"

"Nine weeks."

"Blimey! So little! You're doing well to be all dressed and out and about!"

I could have just told her he wasn't mine. Of course I could. But somehow, the gaps between her talking didn't seem quite big enough.

"This is Zelda." She motioned to the baby strapped at her front. A flopping head of dark hair, two dangling legs in candy-striped tights, as soft and fat as sausages. "And I'm Lydia. Do you want to sit? We can squeeze up."

"Are you sure?"

"Of course! Come enjoy your coffee. I'm sure you need it. Nine weeks! Christ!"

As I bent to sit, Beau's sock fell off. A passing woman took a dive for it and handed it to me with a smile, mouthing the word "gorgeous."

A man in an apron appeared. "Can I get you a coffee? Decaf, I assume?" He was grinning at me. It took me a moment to realize he thought I was breastfeeding, that he was literally thinking about my breasts.

"Oh," I said. "OK. Yes. Cappuccino. Thanks."

Lydia scooted up on the wooden bench. "Nice to meet you . . ."

"Sophie."

"Sophie. Do you live around here?"

"Highbury New Park."

"Oh, amazing! We're Aubert Park. Not far at all!" Lydia looked delighted. "We're on our way to baby cinema. You should come! Zelda sleeps through the whole thing. They bring you tea and cake and you have a whole sofa. It's literally the most relaxing hour of my week!"

The man in the apron returned with my decaf cappuccino. Lydia looked at me.

"Do you fancy it?"

I looked up. "Sorry?"

"Baby cinema. There's plenty of space. It starts soon."

I hesitated, then smiled. "OK," I said. "Sounds great."

"Great." She turned toward apron man. "Sorry—can my friend get that to go? Thanks."

We were friends, then. Just like that.

As she stood up, Lydia glanced at my stomach.

"Whoa," she murmured, shaking her head. "You look incredible. So slim! I could barely get dressed when this one was nine weeks old. You've got makeup on and everything!"

I could have, should have, said something. But I had agreed to the cinema, the decaf coffee. It felt like the moment had already passed.

"What did you say his name was?"

I paused. I privately agreed with Mum about Beau. I thought it a strange choice of name. What if Lydia asked me how I'd picked it? I wouldn't know what to say.

"Teddy," I said eventually. "His name's Teddy."

That's what I would have called him, you see. If he was mine.

Tash

WHEN I GET HOME from seeing Lydia, Tom is pulling clothes out of the dryer.

"Tom! I thought you were going to call me after your meeting."

"I did."

"Oh." I pick my phone out of my pocket and see the three missed calls. "Sorry. How did it go?"

Tom stares grimly into the drum of the machine. "I don't know really."

"Did they tell you any more about what you are supposed to have done?"

Tom's shoulders slump like a puppet's, his hands tangled in a bedsheet.

"I don't even remember her," he says quietly. "It was just a routine exam. She declined a chaperone, and we were busy, so I just went ahead. So stupid . . . and now she says . . . She says I . . ."

"She says you what?"

He takes his glasses off and rubs his eyes.

"She says I sexually assaulted her."

"What?"

I instantly regret my horrified tone. Tom recoils, as if I have dealt him a physical blow. I sink down next to him on the floor and pull him into a hug.

"Oh, Tom, it'll be fine," I say, even though I am not sure it will. "You didn't do anything, so it will be fine. They will see through it. It'll be dismissed."

"Will it?" Tom pulls away from me, his eyes wide with terror. "How do you know? What if they believe her? Isn't the rule that you have to believe the woman now? What if I lose my job, Tash?"

"You won't—you can't. It won't come to that. Anyway, I'll get more work," I say as cheerfully as I can muster. "I just got paid for that wetlands piece I did at New Year's, the one that was your idea."

"Oh yeah?"

"Yeah." The truth was, I'd made them pay me for the work, even though it hadn't made the paper. "And this copywriting thing is good money."

"Is it?"

"Really good. If I do a good job on this batch, they've said there's sure to be more. I could approach other firms, too. I could just do that full time, if we needed—I think it would be a decent salary."

Tom sniffs. "OK. Thanks, Tash. Hopefully it won't come to that anyway."

"Of course it won't," I tell him confidently. "They'll see this is all nonsense. They'll have to."

That night, Tom goes to bed early, the lamb chops I cooked to try and cheer him up left barely touched on his plate. I clear up, pour myself a glass of red wine, and open my laptop. I'll send off the copywriting work tonight a day early, I decide. I can invoice for it tomorrow, tell Tom the money is on its way. It will be one less thing for him to worry about.

Oddly, though, I can't find it. I can't locate the folder where I saved all the work. I try the search bar instead, type in the name of the folder, but that draws a blank, too. I go through all the likely places, but it isn't there. Annoyed, I log into the cloud, where I keep all my backups.

There is nothing there either.

Amid the hot, heart-thumping terror, I force myself through the motions of checking and rechecking, and checking again. I keep doing it long after it becomes obvious, to my rational mind at least, that it is gone. There is simply nothing there anymore. Everything I have been working on for weeks. Thousands of pounds' worth of work that was going to save us, even if the worst happened. Work that is due in tomorrow.

It is all gone. The only thing left in my cloud is a single Word file, named "Tash."

I click on the file, feeling a familiar sickness, and read it. It contains only two lines of text:

You were warned. But you didn't stop.
What comes next is on you.

Sophie

⸻

Nine weeks before

"YOU CAN DEFINITELY AFFORD to eat this," Lydia said. "Unlike me." She looked sadly at the brownie that had been placed on the little sofa arm between us.

"Don't be silly. You look great." I cut the brownie in half, pushing the larger piece toward her.

My trips to baby cinema with Lydia were now the highlight of my week. I loved the deep, red sofas of the premium seats, the little menu of cakes they came over with, the hot chocolates bobbing with miniature marshmallows.

"I don't look great. I look like I've just had a baby," Lydia muttered. "You, however, look like some hot young nanny."

I froze, my hand hovering over the brownie. Beau's eyes flicked open on my chest, sensing the tension in my body.

"W-what do you mean?" I stuttered. But when I dared to glance at her, she was chuckling away to herself. It had been a joke. She was joking. She was entirely oblivious to the fact I was holding my breath, that my hand had started to tremble.

Beau let out a halfhearted cry. I shushed him, patting his bottom through the sling.

"Little Teds," Lydia cooed, leaning over to him. "He is so adorable. Just wait until the others see how big he's gotten!"

Gradually, my heart rate slowed, and Beau settled again, snoring softly on my chest. The colored lights from the screen flickered bright against his pale cheek.

It had been easier at first, all this. When it was just me and Lydia. I hadn't counted on her introducing me to her mates. There were loads of different activities that the babies could do, it turned out. Not just the sensory classes, where a woman blew bubbles and shone lights at the babies to a tinny backing track on the floor of a dusty church hall. There were all sorts: music classes, baby Spanish, baby French, baby Mozart, baby yoga, baby massage even. I followed Lydia to them all, copied the way the other mothers rolled out cotton blankets over the mats before they lay their babies down, readying wipes and bibs in case they vomited on their tambourines. I linked the app where you paid for the classes to Jez and Claire's joint account. I was sure they never checked it.

After the morning activity, the babies would sleep in their strollers, and Lydia and the other mothers would find a café to sit and drink coffee and eat cake. I tried to speak as little as possible about myself, but even so, the lies were piling up, and it was getting more difficult to keep track. But I found it was weirdly addictive, being part of their club. There was something comforting about the sugary dullness of it all, the easy camaraderie. I told myself I wasn't doing anything really bad by deceiving them all—Jenny, Margot, Lydia. I could just ghost them eventually, say that "Teddy" and I had moved away.

"Didn't you and Teddy get on with breastfeeding, Sophie?"

Jenny, one of Lydia's prenatal class friends, was staring at my formula bottle. Her head was tilted to one side, her ponytail swinging behind her, her infant clawing at her exposed breast.

"I've never really had much milk," I said, looking away. I mean, this was true.

"They're better off fed," Lydia said supportively, rolling her eyes at me in Jenny's direction when she wasn't looking. I smiled. "At least Sophie can get some help at night from . . . Was it James?"

"Jez." I coughed. I wish I'd made up a fake name for him, too.

"Jez sounds like such a great dad," Lydia simpers. "I wish Olly would do that. I've expressed a bloody freezer full, but he never offers."

"Does he get that unusual hair color from Jez, Sophie?"

Ponytail Jenny was smiling sweetly, but there was an edge in her voice.

"Yep," I said, stroking Beau's head. "He looks so much like his dad."

"Aren't genes funny?" Margot, another bobbing ponytail. "I wonder if his eyes will go brown, like yours."

Of course, I should have told Lydia the truth the first time I met her, but it wasn't as if I could undo it now. Also, she'd never have wanted to be friends if she knew I was just the nanny. Coffee invites were for mums only. Nannies were expected to seek out their own.

One day, when we stepped out of baby cinema, Lydia asked if I wanted to go to a playgroup with her. The sunlight was disorienting. It was a spring day, the warm air like an answered wish after months of cold. I glanced at my phone.

"Sure. I've got an hour or so," I said.

"Oh, great. It's called Cuckoo Club. It's down near Highbury Barn. Apparently it's on every week. I'd never heard of it—have you?"

I froze. I couldn't go to Cuckoo Club. Sal might be there.

"Oh, do you know what, I've just realized I can't. I need to get back."

"Oh, OK. No worries." Lydia looked at Zelda sadly, rocking her to and fro in the stroller. I got the sense she just didn't want to go home. She always seemed to be hoping for another coffee, another walk. She was forever scrolling her phone for more infant activities we could do, baby-friendly cafés we could visit. She never seemed to want to be home alone with Zelda. I guessed that Lydia was a bit lost and lonely, possibly a bit bored. She reminded me of a friend I had at college who never wanted to go home at the end of a night out because she always wanted one more drink.

"Any plans this weekend?" Lydia asked.

"Um, not really. Might be heading out for dinner."

"With your perfectly domesticated husband? Lucky you." I averted my eyes to the floor. "Oh, sorry, no, I've noticed before you don't wear a ring, do you?" Lydia gabbled. "Sorry, there's no reason why you should be married."

"Yeah, Jez and I just, um, never got round to it."

Lydia was hungry for more detail, I could tell. The trouble was, I couldn't remember exactly how much I'd told her about Jez, or what, and it felt like dangerous ground.

For once, Lydia took the hint that I didn't want to talk.

"Oh well, enjoy your night out." She sighed. "Olly and I still haven't managed to go out for dinner since Zelda was born."

This was the thing about Lydia—everything always became a conversation about her in the end. Which had its uses when your own life was something you had stolen from someone else.

Tash

I STAY UP MOST of the night, trying to cobble together as much as I can. But it isn't enough. In the end there's nothing I can do except send what I have, at four in the morning, along with a groveling email.

I can't bear to tell Tom about it. I rush off early, strapping Finn into his stroller while he is still chewing his last mouthful of breakfast.

"The bloke is coming this afternoon to fit the bars on the windows," Tom reminds me. "He's throwing in the creepy doorbell half price, too."

"Great."

I think about the pictures in the horrible security catalog we'd chosen from. The bay window was the nicest thing about our flat. From now on, it was going to look like a cage. But then I think about the message I got last night, and I look at Finn, a piece of toast in his little palm, looking up at me from the stroller.

"Have a good day." I give Tom a quick hug. He clings to me for a second in a way that is not like him at all, before letting me go.

As soon as I'm outside, I call Grace's bank and ask for the woman who commissioned me to do the copywriting work.

"I'm literally just taking it in now to one of those laptop places that specialize in recovery," I tell her. This isn't quite true, but it's very much what I intend to do, as soon I've dropped Finn. I am pushing the stroller with one hand, holding the phone with the other. "Even if it's not retrievable—you know, um, worst-case scenario—I remember most of it. I can get the rest of it to you within twenty-four hours. I'm sure I can."

I try not to sound like I'm panicking. I hear the woman's voice harden from courteous to glacial as she absorbs the horror of what I am telling her. She says she will call me back, and I know from her voice that if I don't sort this today, there will be no more work. Not ever.

When she hangs up, I start calling around to laptop repair places. I get a string of voice mails. Nothing opens until nine.

As I drop Finn off, I give him a tighter squeeze than normal, wishing I could just spend the day with him at home, feed the ducks in the park. But he squirms away and dashes inside, as he does now, without a second glance, and for once it's me with tears in my eyes, feeling abandoned.

As I turn away, I walk straight into Jez. He has just dropped off Beau.

"Hey, easy." He steps backward, his arms placed lightly on my shoulders. "Are you all right, Tash?"

I nod, unable to speak. I try to catch my breath.

"Are you sure? You look really upset."

I open my mouth to say I am fine, but find I have to look away, pinching my lips together.

Jez rubs the back of his head. "Is there anything I can do?"

"No," I tell him, forcing myself to swallow. "Unless—do you know anywhere I can take a laptop? I need to recover some work I've lost. There must be places. I don't think anywhere is open yet. I've tried searching online . . ." I trail off. My voice has reached a panicked, squeaking pitch; to my horror, a sob escapes my throat.

"Hang on, hang on," he says. "Slow down. Why don't you come over? I know a bit about laptops. I can see if I can help."

I hesitate.

"Come on," he says. "Got to be worth a try, right?"

I bite my lip. "I should probably take it to a shop or something," I mutter.

Jez stretches his arm out, revealing a glint of silver watch. "Doubt anywhere will open before nine," he says, cocking his head to one side. "Come on. It's got to be worth a go."

IT IS strange to be in Claire's house without her. Jez doesn't mention where she is, and I'm too choked up to ask. I sit at the kitchen island, the marble cold under my hands, and try to steady myself. I watch the wind moving in the trees at the end of their garden, where the wood-and-glass building is. Jude is playing outside, a woman I don't recognize crouched beside him.

While the laptop fires up, I distract myself by watching Jude for a bit. He is clutching a battered teddy, walking it up and down the garden steps, then throwing it. He seems a little old to be playing with a teddy like that.

"Jude not at school?"

"No." Jez clears his throat. "He sees someone on Tuesdays, at the house. A therapist." He gestures outside. "He hasn't been speaking much, since . . . well, for a while."

I can see this conversation is painful for Jez, that maintaining his usual, genial tone of voice is an effort. I wonder if he's talking about Sophie's death. Whether that was when Jude stopped speaking.

"That must be a worry," I say. "I hope it works out."

Jez gives me a pained smile, resets his voice to its normal, conversational pitch. "Thank you. Now, what do you need? Coffee? Something stronger?"

"Coffee would actually be great, Jez. Thanks. If you've figured out the machine."

"We'll soon find out."

While his back is turned, I move my Sophie folder onto a memory stick. I check twice that I've saved it there, then I delete it from the laptop and put the stick in my pocket. When he returns with two mugs, I turn the laptop to face him.

"OK, let's have a look." I watch Jez go into my settings. "You should probably set up two-factor authentication on here. Could anyone else have used your laptop?"

"No. No one uses it except me. Occasionally Tom, but he has his own, so . . ."

"Finn couldn't have been mucking around with it?"

"I honestly don't think so."

"OK. Let's see."

I give Jez the file names, and he starts tapping. "I'll just run a standard file recovery program first. If it's on there, we should be able to find it."

"Thank you." I hesitate. "Do you mind if I use your bathroom?"

"Not at all. Go ahead."

Upstairs, in their bathroom, I decide to check the drawer again, the one with the bottles. But when I open it, all I can see in there are Claire's expensive face creams and serums, her teeth-whitening kit, a pair of exfoliating gloves. The pill bottles have all gone.

I head back down the hallway. At the end, I pause. There is a room with its door ajar. It looks like a study. There is a desk by a window, a pile of papers on top. I look down the hallway, then back at the papers, feeling the weight of my phone in my pocket. I take a step inside, intending to flick through the pile of papers on the desk, maybe take a couple of pictures, but then I think I hear a noise on the stairs, and I slip quickly back into the hallway. I don't see anyone, but I've missed my chance. I can't risk it.

When I get back to the kitchen, the light of the laptop is glowing on Jez's face.

"I'm sorry, Tash," he says. "I can't understand what's happened here. The files you want were deleted yesterday morning. Could have been accidental, although they've been deleted from the recycling bin as well."

My stomach twists. And the cloud. It *can't* have been an accident. This was done to me, by someone who wants to cause me harm. Laura said Sal had my laptop. Could Sal have done this?

"The thing is," Jez says, "my program's thrown them up, but it's telling me I can't recover them. It looks like they've been corrupted somehow."

I walk around to his side of the island. I can see the files he's found are the ones I need. But they are in gray, the same error message popping up every time he tries to click on them. I feel sick.

"How did this happen?"

Jez shakes his head. "It's not clear. Could be a virus, some kind of bug in your system. I can get one of my guys to take a proper look, if you like. It might take a day or two, but . . ."

I shake my head, unable to speak. I can't wait a day or two. I'll lose the contract. All of a sudden, it is too much. The threats, the lost work, Tom's suspension, the worries about money, the horrible new bars on our windows. Is a false accusation against Tom part of this, too? But what about the photo of him with Sophie?

I find myself overwhelmed by it all. Before I know it, I am consumed by sobs. I clap my hand to my mouth, as if I can somehow stop it, but my shoulders are shaking.

Jez's eyes are wide with horror. "Oh my God, Tash, I'm sorry. Please don't cry."

"I'm sorry."

"I seem to have a talent for upsetting you."

"It's not you." I find I'm too choked to say anything else.

He scratches the back of his head. "Do you want me to drive you home?"

"I don't—I don't know where is safe," I say. "I'm sorry—"

Jez frowns. "Safe? What do you mean?"

"It's—someone has done this to me. This thing with the laptop. I know they have."

Whoever it is, they are winning. Adam said he would look into the messages for me, but every time he's phoned, I've canceled his call because I'm too scared he will ask me about the man in the picture. And I can't tell him the truth. I can't tell him it's Tom. Not until I can prove that Tom has nothing to do with this.

Jez stares at me. "I wish there was something I could do."

I shake my head, feeling the tears on my cheek. There is nothing anyone can do.

Jez doesn't touch me for a long time. When he does reach out his hand, he stops it, midair, before it reaches my back. He doesn't look at me as he does it.

As he pulls me into him, it feels important to me that my hands are at my sides. I don't move them up or down, I don't move anything. I know that if I move, something is going to happen, and the realization is both thrilling and horrifying. This has not been in my head. The danger was real. We have been picking through a forest, tinder-dry. It will take only the smallest spark.

I feel the scrape of my cheek against his shirt as I tilt my chin upward, toward his face. For a moment I am not sure whether it is already done, the line already crossed. I breathe in the air of him. He reaches out his hand, and pushes a strand of my hair behind my ear.

"Tash." As he says the word, his mouth touches the edge of mine.

The contact, the sound of his voice, makes everything too real. My senses refocus. This is ridiculous. I am not this person.

I pull away, as if burned, and mumble that I have to go. I feel my feet take a step back. I snatch up my laptop and back into the hallway toward the door.

Outside, a mizzling rain has started. My hands are shaking on my bag, my laptop. I haven't got a hood or an umbrella. But it is a relief when the door closes behind me to gulp in the cold air, feel the rain on the hot skin of my face.

Only after I start down the stone steps do I realize that Jude is there. He has walked around the house and is sitting on the top step, clutching that ragged old teddy by the neck again.

I freeze. Should I knock, make sure Jez, or the therapist woman, knows he is here? There are big locked gates, but surely Jude shouldn't be out here alone, in the rain.

"Hello, Jude. Does your dad know you're here?"

I hope I sound normal. I do not feel normal. I want to be away from here, as quickly as possible, but I don't feel I can just leave a six-year-old boy here like this.

I walk to the bottom of the steps. Jude watches me. Then he starts to walk the bear along the stone banister. It should be sweet, but it isn't. It is the game of a much younger child. And Jude does not look like he is playing.

Then Jude throws the bear down the steps. The movement is sudden, deliberate. Violent. The bear falls to the bottom of the steps, into a filthy puddle. Its head is left at an odd angle, its arm over its head, one leg propped up. Jude looks fixedly down at it. His curls are darkening in the rain. In my mind's eye, I suddenly see Finn at the bottom of the base-ment staircase, blood streaming from his face. I open my mouth to speak, but can find nothing to say.

Jez opens the door. He looks from me to Jude, then down at the teddy. He doesn't ask what Jude is doing. He doesn't seem surprised. He just sighs deeply, his shoulders sagging.

"Come on, Jude," he says. "Stop that now. Come out of the rain."

I turn away from them, open the gate, and pace down the street as quickly as I can. I move so fast I nearly trip over my feet, without fully knowing where I am going, except away, from him, from Jude, from that house. I find myself at the Clissold Park coffee kiosk. I mutter an order, then collapse into one of the metal chairs, my heart still racing. The place is empty except for me and a homeless man I see around here sometimes. He and I sit, clutching our coffee cups, watching the water drip from umbrellas overhead. Sheltering from the rain, with nowhere else to go.

Sophie

Six weeks before

I SAW THEM IN the queue for coffee at the café in Clissold Park. I'd taken Beau for a walk. He was wanting to be propped up in the stroller now, craning his neck when I pushed him around, a little neckerchief tied under his chin for early teething dribbles, a milk bottle tucked in next to him. Claire seemed to have gotten the hang of breastfeeding now, and was still mostly feeding him that way, but Jez had started making him bottles occasionally. I'd heard him marveling to Claire about how easily Beau had seemed to take to it. I had kept my mouth shut.

It was the first really nice spring day, and the café's outside tables were busy, the raised flower beds studded with snowdrops and nodding daffodils.

I heard Laura before I saw her. I gripped the push bar of the stroller, ready to make my escape from the queue, then I hesitated a moment. She seemed to be having a sort of argument with the girl in the kiosk.

"There must be some mistake," she was saying to the girl. "There must be enough on that card. Can you just check?"

Nicole was with her. She was looking from Laura, to the girl at the till, and back again. I could see this wasn't the first time she had watched an interaction like this.

"Put it through again. That card should be fine." Laura's voice had that squeaky, high-pitched quality I'd heard the night she came over with the nonalcoholic wine.

The girl in the kiosk tried again, then shook her head. Within a second, Nicole was reaching across Laura with her own card, settling the bill. Telling Laura it didn't matter. Laura was still muttering, shaking her head.

"It's—he's done this again, he always does this," Laura was saying now to Nicole. She looked like she was about to cry.

"Don't worry about it," Nicole was saying. "You'll figure it out."

I paused for a quick look into their strollers, curious to see the babies their bumps had turned into. Nicole's contained a sleeping dark-haired girl, Laura's a chunky, dungaree-clad boy, bibbed and chewing on a strap, like Beau. I readied myself to leave, but I had left it a beat too late. Nicole had turned around. She looked straight at me.

"Sophie! So good to see you!" Nicole moved toward me quickly, beckoning Laura to follow. "Do you have a minute to sit?"

A couple stood up, deserting the table next to us, the lids of their coffees blowing off into the flower beds as they collected their plates. Nicole motioned me to take their spot. I sat down slowly, the metal seat hard and cold through my jeans.

"How's Claire doing, Sophie?"

She and Laura were staring straight at me, smiles pinned tightly to their faces.

"Um. You know. I think she's OK."

I did not think this. Claire was much the same. She was looking thin, much thinner than when the baby was born. Her jogging bottoms, which she wore constantly, hung off her hips. When she bent over, you could see the lines of her rib cage, the bumps of the vertebrae in her back.

"Have you guys not seen her for a while?"

"We've barely seen her since the baby was born," Laura said.

"She's not returning our calls," Nicole added. Her eyes narrowed, as if I might be in some way responsible.

"Oh." I looked away, fiddled with Beau's blanket.

"Do you really think she's all right, Sophie?"

I was taken aback by how much Laura's question annoyed me. I was doing Claire's laundry, her cooking, her dishes, her shopping. I was caring for her baby and her stepson, while she lay in bed most of the day. I was trying to put on a cheerful face for her husband, trying to cover up how crap she was being just so he wasn't too horrified when he got home. How was I to know if she was OK? No one ever asked if I was OK. I didn't want to be part of this conversation anymore.

"You'd have to ask her," I said. "I'm sorry, I really need to go."

I stood up, wiped my hand on my jeans. Nicole's gaze followed my hand.

"Is that Claire's jacket you're wearing, Sophie?"

I froze.

"Claire gave it to me." I had said it too quickly. I sounded guilty, even though it was the truth.

"Sophie, wait," Laura said. "Can you just hang on a second?" I was already turning the stroller around, flicking up the brake. She came to my side, placed her hand on my arm.

"We're really worried about Claire. I'm wondering if she might have postnatal depression."

Hearing Laura say it out loud made me hesitate. She was right. The way Claire had been behaving since the baby wasn't normal.

"Maybe you should speak to Jez," I said. "Have you been in touch with him?"

Nicole and Laura glanced at each other. Laura withdrew her hand from my arm.

"We haven't spoken to Jeremy, no," Laura said. I noticed the use of his real name. Was she telling me off for referring to him so informally? I felt annoyed again. What did Laura know about what Jez and I had to deal with?

"I think maybe you should talk to him and Claire," I said to Laura.

I started to move the stroller away from the table. My heart was pounding, my palms slippery on the push bar.

"Hey! Sophie!"

I turned around. Nicole was right behind me. She had followed me. Laura was still at the table, out of earshot, but watching us both, stirring her coffee. Even from here, I could see the deep line between her brows.

"What's the big rush?" Nicole's voice was chilly.

"I'm meeting someone."

"How lovely. Your day for the monkey music class at Clissold House, is it?"

Nicole's voice was light, but her gaze was not. She stared at me, twisting the end of her long ponytail around her finger. I felt the prickle of adrenaline.

"It's so strange. A friend of mine, Jenny, told me the other day that she'd met a Sophie at that class. A pretty young mum, with a little red-haired boy."

I gripped the push bar of the stroller.

"I'm sure she was thinking of you. She was surprised when I told her you were just a nanny, though. She seemed to think you were his mum."

I forced a laugh. "That's funny," I managed to say.

Nicole didn't smile. "She said you had told everyone you were his mum. That Jez was your husband. And that the baby's name was Teddy."

I told myself to breathe.

"She obviously just got it wrong," I said. "I never said anything like that. I just said Jez was his dad. And Teddy's just a nickname. Like Teddy bear. Claire and I call him that all the time."

Nicole stared at me. The silence was heavy.

"Teddy," she repeated eventually. "How cute. I must remember that. For when we see her."

I swallowed, forcing a smile.

"Well, I'm glad I ran into you. Good to clear it up."

"Of course."

"Thank God." She grinned, zipping her jacket. "For a moment I thought Claire had some kind of psycho nanny on her hands, trying to steal her life! Can you imagine!"

I held my breath.

"I'm sure I'll see you around," Nicole called as she walked off. "Highbury is such a small world."

I took a breath and marched the stroller out of the park. I needed to tread carefully from here; I saw that now. Very carefully.

"Stupid bitch," I muttered, once we were at a safe distance. "She doesn't know the half of it, does she, Teddy?"

Tash

AS I WAIT FOR Abi in the restaurant, I find myself going over it again. Technically, of course, nothing happened. That's what I keep reminding myself. And yet, I have never done anything like that before. I have become fixated on it, replaying it over and over.

I find myself imagining it from different angles, trying to recall exact details. How much, I keep asking myself, had been Jez, and how much had been me? It feels important to establish, somehow, the exact allocation of blame. Had I, in fact, made the first transgression, when I tilted my chin up, into him? Perhaps he had been reprimanding me when he spoke my name. But no, because then he had touched my hair. Had it just been my hair? Or had he touched the skin of my face, or just my ear, or the back of my neck? The memory of it was hot under the surface of my skin.

Abi arrives, breaking my train of thought. She looks exactly the same as she did before kids, her skin just as smooth and clear. When I lean to kiss her cheek, she smells clean and soapy, medical rather than fragrant.

"Thanks for coming," I say, feeling strangely stiff. I haven't seen Abi since Nisha was a newborn.

"Not at all." She grins, sitting down. "It's my first lunch out since I've been back at work. It's a treat."

As she sits, Abi stills the ID card hanging from the blue NHS lanyard at her front. I notice it reads Pediatrics, where Tom's says Accident and Emergency, but doesn't refer to her being a child psychologist.

"I think I'll have the salmon." She sets the menu down, folds her hands in her lap.

"No starter?"

"I'd better not." Abi's eyes flick toward the time on her phone. "So, how can I help?"

Abi has been too polite to remark on the fact that I've never suggested we go for lunch, or even a drink, before, despite the fact that our husbands are so close.

"I was hoping you could help me with something," I say. "Something to do with your—professional knowledge."

"Oh. You're not worried about Finn, I hope?"

"No, no. Nothing like that."

I tell Abi about Jude. What I'd seen that day—him walking up and down the steps in the garden, throwing his bear down them. And what Finn had said, about being pushed.

"I hope this doesn't sound completely mad," I say. "But it just didn't look like normal playing to me. And after what Finn said about being pushed—on the stairs?"

Abi fiddles with her lanyard. At first, she doesn't say anything.

"Do you have any reason to believe he has experienced a trauma?"

I consider this. "I mean, it's possible." I pause. "He lost his mother at an early age, and then his nanny died, who I think he was very close to."

"Poor child." Abi is shaking her head. "Do you have any reason to believe the trauma involved the stairs? Someone falling, or being pushed?"

"I don't know." I hesitate. "Would his . . . behavior suggest he'd seen something like that?"

She looks thoughtful. "Well, that sort of unresolved trauma would present differently in different children. One child might react by obsessively avoiding stairs. Another sort of child might—as you seem to describe—become obsessed with them."

"What do you mean, obsessed?"

"The child might become fixated with walking on stairs, rolling down them. He might incorporate stairs into play—building a staircase from blocks, reenacting toys falling or rolling down the stairs. He would be doing this to process what he has seen, and make sense of it."

"And he might . . . involve other children in those . . . games?"

"Exactly. He might want to play at falling down stairs—either falling down himself, or throwing a doll or a teddy. Or—yes, it's not inconceivable he would want to throw, or push, another child."

I hold my breath.

"It's easy to imagine that he might get so caught up in the game that he would fail to notice another child becoming scared, or starting to withdraw," Abi says. "These games might be repeated, and might become even more dangerous, or violent, with repetition."

The food arrives. I ignore it, the thought of eating a bowl of pasta now unimaginable. I think of Finn's scream, his bloodied lip. I think of Sophie's head injury. Could Jude have seen Sophie pushed down the stairs? Could that have been what really killed her? And if so, who pushed her?

"Can I ask you something in return, Tash?"

I look up at Abi. She is hesitating, her knife and fork poised above her plate.

"Ravi says you came to see him the other day. Asking about some party?" She raises her eyebrows. "Is everything OK with you and Tom?"

"Fine," I say automatically.

Of course, everything is very much not fine with me and Tom. It's not just his suspension from work. Or the picture of him with Sophie, which I still haven't asked him about. The thought of what happened with Jez intrudes again, like a shadow blocking the sun.

"I'm glad," Abi says. Her words seem pointed somehow. "Tom is a good man, you know."

Before I can reply, my phone rings. It's Adam. I grimace. I can't just keep ignoring him.

"Go ahead," Abi says, taking a forkful of salmon.

I take the call outside.

"Hi," I say. "Look, Adam—"

"Just hear me out," he says. "I found out the name. The person your messages came from."

Sophie

Four weeks before

HE ASKED TO MEET me in the wetlands. I pointed out that I'd have the baby with me, that I was supposed to be working. But he'd insisted.

I got to the café early so I could put some makeup on while Beau slept in the stroller. My stomach was swimming too much for coffee. It had been going on for a few months now, but I still got like this, whenever I was seeing him. That's how I knew this was different, that what I was feeling was real.

I loved this side of the wetlands, with the café and the brand-new flats looking out over the water. The surface was sharp and glassy in the sunlight; it made me squint to look at it. A heron was poised on the railings of the wooden walkway, its neck tucked in an elegant S shape into its gray feathers. As soon as I spotted it, it took off across the reservoir, its wings wide and beautiful.

Jez had told me about the flats loads of times, about all the high-tech features he'd worked on. It wasn't just security. Other stuff, too. The lights knew when to come on; you could talk to the music player and the TV. The internet of things, he called it, or something. He loved to talk about his work.

I wasn't really listening a lot of the time. I preferred to think about what would happen when he left Claire, when we could finally be together. I had looked up how much their house was worth. I guessed he would have to give her half, and we'd have to share the boys, but even half was enough for a lovely place. We could even get one of the flats here, so I could start doing my swimming again, like I used to before I got so busy with the boys. Three beds would be best: the boys could share when they stayed, and we would have a baby of our own, in time. I was already fantasizing about coming off the pill, surprising him with a positive test. Yes, I could see us in one of the nice ground-floor properties, the ones with sliding doors facing the water. It wouldn't have to be huge. It just had to be ours, mine and his.

The bell on the door jangled and he stepped in, raised a hand and both eyebrows at me. "Sophie," he said, smiling blandly. "Ah, you've got a coffee already, great. I'll just grab one."

I was confused by the way he was speaking to me, like we were here for a work meeting. Then I realized that that's probably just what he wanted everyone in the café to think.

He returned with his drink and sat opposite me, planting his feet apart. I started to speak, and he went at the same time. We both laughed.

"Sorry," I said. "You first."

"All right." He had stopped smiling. "It's about us, Sophie. All this. I can't do it anymore. I really can't."

After the initial stab of panic, I told myself to keep calm. He'd had this before—attacks of guilt about Claire. It had never taken much to divert him, when it had happened at home, or in his office. I only had to slip my hand inside his trousers, or unbutton my dress a little, show him what I was wearing underneath. I loved watching him come, shuddering as he buried his head in my chest, crying out as if he were in pain. I imagined what he was used to with her—stretchy beige maternity bra, pajamas, and glasses. Sometimes I wondered whether it was this thought that thrilled me the most. The thought of getting one over on Claire, Laura, Nicole. Lydia. Margot. All those smug ponytail mothers.

"I'm serious, Sophie," Jez was saying. "It's over. We need to forget this. Move on."

My mouth started to twitch at the corners.

"You don't mean that," I said. "Look, Jez, I know it's complicated. I know people will get hurt, but—"

"No, no." He was speaking more firmly now. "Nobody needs to get hurt."

"But . . . but . . . I know you're not happy. With her."

He leaned in toward me. When he spoke, his words were thick with danger.

"Sophie, listen to me," he said. "Claire is my wife. I would lose everything. My home. My boys . . ."

"You wouldn't! We would—"

"Sophie . . . this was just a mistake!"

I felt my jaw fall open. My expression must have shocked him into a different tack. He softened his tone. He took my hand under the table, started to move his finger up and down my wrist.

"It's my fault, all this," he said. "Everything is too complicated. You're just a child, I—"

"A child?" I pulled my hand away.

"Young. I just mean young. Keep your voice down, Sophie, please."

"You know, I don't think I will." I didn't care about the people in the café. I didn't care about them at all. "Do you actually have any idea what I do all day?"

I stood up, took the push bar of the stroller, and shoved it toward Jez, so hard that he gasped.

"Here's your son," I tell him, pointing at Beau. "Fast asleep at the appropriate time, in the soft, clean clothes I chose for him. There's his toy, tucked by his hand. There's the warmed bottles I made him this morning, underneath, for when he wakes. There's the homemade baby food, the weaning spoons, the diapers I replenished this morning, the spare blankets I washed and dried over the weekend."

Jez clenched his jaw.

"I think you'll find I'm the adult in this scenario, Jez," I hiss. "And thank God for that! Somebody needs to be their fucking mother!"

I saw a muscle in Jez's cheek flicker, one I'd never noticed before. His mouth opened, then closed again. Then he stood up and strode out of the café.

Tash

IT IS BUSY AT Cuckoo Club, and at first I think perhaps Sal hasn't come. I pay my three pounds entry fee wordlessly. The gum-chewing girl at the trestle table at the front doesn't bother asking why I don't appear to have a child in tow.

I make my way past the grubby carpet with roads printed on it, the fake kitchens and plastic food, the craft tables covered in paint and glue and glitter that I tend to steer Finn away from.

Sal is sitting at the back in a makeshift window seat with a chipped mug of coffee. The glass behind her is smeared with children's handprints. The twins are tottering around in front of her, mashing at buttons on plastic walkers.

Sal smirks as I sit down next to her. "Fancied a go on the slide?"

"Very funny," I mutter. "I was looking for you, as it happens. I know it was you. I know about the messages."

She looks blank. "What?"

"And I know what you did to my laptop . . ."

"Your laptop? Yeah. I found it. A thanks would be nice."

I laugh. "Oh, sure. So you didn't do anything to it? Put a virus on it? Delete my work, thousands of pounds' worth of work?"

"I literally don't know what you're talking about," she says in a bored voice.

"Right. Just like you don't know about the text messages."

"Oh, that again! I told you, I never sent no messages."

"Except I know you did. The police traced the numbers for me. They were registered in your name."

At the mention of police, Sal's head snaps up.

"What? That's bullshit!"

I ignore her. My voice is shaking. "I've been trying to work it out. Why would a supposed friend of Sophie's do all this to someone who was just trying to find out the truth?"

Sal makes an outraged noise. "You think I don't want to know who killed Sophie?" Her voice is different now. Thick with anger. "Sophie was my friend, Tash. Not yours. You didn't even know her."

The children at the craft table look up in surprise at the hostility of our conversation. We throw them matching bland smiles, then turn back to each other.

"Why did you send me those messages?"

"I told you," she spits. "I didn't!"

Sal and I stare at each other. Behind her, the breeze picks up, scattering leaves across the church parking lot.

"What happened to Sophie?"

Sal gives me an incredulous look. "Why? Why do you need to know?" She shakes her head, brushes some imaginary dust from her leopard-print leggings. "I'm not interested in talking to you. None of us are. We all know you're a journalist, just after a story. And anyway, I don't know who—"

Sal glances at the toddlers, then lowers her voice to a whisper. "I don't know who killed her."

"But you know *someone* did. What did they do? Was she pushed down the stairs? Is that what killed her?"

Sal opens her mouth, then closes it again. The twins have veered off toward the craft table. Sal stands up and follows them, busies herself rolling their sleeves up, handing out different-shaped sponges, little plastic bowls of paint. I follow her to the table.

"Tell me who the boyfriend was," I demand. "Was he there that night? At the party?"

Sal lifts the paintbrush for Aiden, makes a show of doing the painting with him, even though he is losing interest. She won't meet my eye.

"I knew what was happening," Sal says eventually. She takes a dollop of red paint and mixes it into the blue.

"I knew she wasn't safe. I knew he was bad news. I should have done something. Stopped her."

"Stopped her doing what?"

Sal keeps painting furiously, daubing stroke after stroke of purple paint sloppily over the paper. In her fingers, the paintbrush is shaking.

"Sophie found something out," Sal says. "I told her something. She was going to confront him. I think that's why she was killed. For what she knew."

I lean toward Sal. "What? What was it? Who was she going to confront? Please, talk to me."

Sal shakes her head. "You should leave this, Tash. You should leave it alone."

"Why? Why should I? Who has told you not to talk about this?"

Sal carries on daubing marks on paper with the brush. She looks up, around the room, then toward the door, as if checking if she is being watched.

"What are you looking at?"

I try to follow her gaze, but I can't see anyone. I look back at her. She is still jabbing at the page with her brush, breathing heavily, her cheeks flushed, as if she is about to have a panic attack.

"What is it, Sal? Who are you so afraid of?"

Abruptly, Sal stands up and plucks one twin onto each hip. "We're going," she mutters. "Don't forget your picture." She thrusts the painting in front of me onto the table, the paint still wet. I look down, confused. Then a jolt shoots through me as I see what she has daubed on the page.

"Wait—what? Sal, wait!"

Sal is already retreating through the double doors, the twins in the stroller protesting that they want to stay. I try to push through to where she is, but am blocked by one stroller, then another, before nearly tripping over a woman changing her baby on the floor.

"Do you mind?" she mutters. She glances, disapprovingly at my heeled boots, my laptop case, my lack of child. "This is a baby and toddler group, you know."

When I finally get outside, Sal is already way down the street. I shout after her, but her eyes are glued to the pavement. She is refusing to look back.

Blood pounds in my eardrums. I turn away, toward the park. I take a moment, standing in the street, waiting for my senses to recalibrate.

It's then that I see the woman on the other side of the road. She is standing in the shadow of a doorway overhung with a thick bank of ivy. Dark leggings, dark glasses, despite the overcast sky. A shiny black puffer jacket. Her hair is tied up, her cap pulled low.

She is hiding. Why else would anyone stand in a doorway like that? Then I look more closely, and realize who it is. It's Nicole.

I avert my eyes, pretending I haven't seen her. I walk off, turning down the nearest side street. Then I double back around the next corner and head down a different side street, so I can watch her unobserved.

Was she the person Sal was looking at? The person she was afraid of?

Nicole pulls her cap down over her face and sets off sharply in the direction of Highbury Barn. I follow at a safe distance, tracking her as she crosses over the road, walks along the parade of shops. But when I expect her to head over the park, toward her house, she instead steps into a coffee shop.

I pull my own hood over my head, and duck into the launderette opposite. I stand close to the window, pretending to fumble in my bag for coins for the machine. After a few moments, I risk a glance across the street.

They are all there: Claire, Laura, and Nicole. Claire is talking an unusual amount, gesturing, Laura nodding back. Their faces are illuminated by a single pendant light hanging over their circular table. They are leaning into the center of it, their faces painted with the yellow light, and for a moment, they don't look like the women I know. They look like strangers.

Sophie

Three weeks before

SAL AND I HAD taken the boys to the soft play, a huge maze of cargo ropes, ball pits, and slides, with a clown's face looming large over the entrance. Claire never took Jude or Beau to places like this. She said they were full of germs.

Jude knew I was upset about something. He'd kept close to me all week, snuggling up to me on the sofa and taking my face between his hands as if he was trying to work out why I was so quiet these days, why my eyes were always red.

While the older boys played, Sal and I sat and sipped our instant coffee from Styrofoam cups and shared a chocolate muffin. Beau and Eliza napped silently in their strollers.

The more I thought about what had happened between Jez and me, the more the soft edges wore off. I found myself remembering the embarrassing physicality of that first time, in the annex, when I'd gotten home after that horrible night with the runner, my makeup all smudged. I thought how obvious my inexperience must have been. How I'd had to push my backpack and the Tupperware I used for sandwiches off the bed, how I couldn't undo my bra at the back. The squelching sound when he pulled out of me that neither of us acknowledged. How I felt him flinch slightly when I went down on him and my teeth accidentally made contact with his skin.

I obsessed about how I had looked the last few times. His office. The darkroom. I thought endlessly about how recently I'd showered, whether there was any possibility I could have smelled.

More than anything, I thought about what I'd allowed myself to imagine, my childish fantasy of what I'd told myself would happen next. A little place in the wetlands development, doors out to the front, a blue bedroom with bunk beds for the boys. He hadn't wanted any of that.

"You're very quiet today," Sal said.

When I didn't reply, Sal took a bite of muffin, looked around the room.

"This place reminds me of a contact center," she muttered.

"Hey? A what?"

"Oh, don't worry about it." Sal placed the muffin down, brushed the crumbs from her hands. "Come on, spit it out. Whatever it is, it can't be as dumb as some of the shit I've done in my time."

I tried to laugh, but I could feel my lip wobbling. "It's nothing. I've just been a bit stupid, that's all."

The tears started before I could do anything to stop them. I snatched the plasticky napkin from the sticky red table and held it against my face.

"Jez, is it?"

It wasn't in Sal's nature to comfort, but she didn't gloat either, even though she had tried to warn me. Just listened and nodded, her face grim.

"I'm such an idiot. Such a stupid, stupid idiot."

Sal shook her head. "We all make mistakes. You're young. Put it down to experience."

"I feel so stupid, though, Sal."

And of course, that was a big part of the hurt. I wished more than anything that nothing had ever happened, that I had just kept him and me safe in my mind. Unreal, undamaged. Perfect.

"He's the one in the wrong. You do know that, don't you?" Sal sighed. "It's just what he's like. Here, have one of these, your mascara's going."

I took the wipe from Sal's bag gratefully. I was crying unattractively now, my face wet, snot-filled, embarrassing. People were looking, but I couldn't seem to stop.

When I caught my breath, I asked her what she meant.

"Hmm?"

"You said this was just what he was like. What did you mean?"

"Oh. Nothing," she said quickly. "I just meant—you know, I'm sure you're not the only one."

I turned to face her. "Who else? Who else is there?"

"Oh, I wasn't—I just meant that's what men are like. Men in general. Forget I said anything."

The boys reappeared. Billy was sobbing, clutching his arm, wailing something about Jude hitting him. Jude was racing ahead to plead his innocence. Sal scooped Billy into her arms and shoved the remains of her half of the muffin into his hand.

"You should get out of that house, get away from them," she said to me over the boys' heads. "I can't see it ending well, Soph. I really can't."

I couldn't forget what Sal had said. I thought about it all that week. I thought about it when I watched Jez put his tie on in the morning, when I saw him checking his phone on the sofa. And when, one evening the following week, Jez announced he was going out, I thought about it again.

As soon as he was gone, I crept up the stairs. Jude was asleep, and soft, snoring sounds were coming from Claire's bedroom. The door was slightly ajar, and I could see her and Beau side by side in the bed, a makeshift circle of pillows around the outside.

The door to Jez's office was ajar. His desk was immaculately tidy. I opened one drawer, then another. Pens, paper clips, an old glasses case. Then I pulled the bottom one, and it jammed.

I studied the keyhole. Tiny and round. Nothing on his desk, or in the top drawer. So I pulled a bobby pin out of my hair and started on the lock.

Tash

THE THUNDER BURSTS OVER my head as I reach the long brick balconies of Sal's estate. I pull my hood up and squint into the rain, trying to remember which is her door.

Eventually I recognize it, the one at the end, with the washing line outside, loaded with little boys' pajamas and tracksuit bottoms. They are getting soaked, the colors deepening, droplets forming on the ends of the socks.

There is no answer when I bang on her door. The orange cat leaps onto the back of the sofa just inside the window and scratches at the frame as if to get out.

The lights in Sal's front room aren't on, despite the darkening sky. I knock again. Still no answer. I glance at my phone. It is three minutes past seven. It was definitely a seven she daubed on the paper.

I call Sal's phone, and I hear the faint sound of it ringing inside, just by the window. No one answers. I decide to clamber around the junk on her front patio to look into the window from the other side.

Sal is there. She is right next to her phone, curled into the back of the sofa. Is she asleep? I call the phone and its surface lights up, but Sal doesn't move. There is a taste of metal in my mouth. A shudder passes over my skin.

I don't notice my hood has fallen to my shoulders until I feel rain on my cheeks, my lips. I take a step back just as the roar and crack of thunder comes. Then I throw myself, shoulder first, against the door.

Incredibly, it works. The door is flimsy, the lock easily broken. I feel myself stumbling over her step, reeling from the impact, the pain in the top of my arm. The orange cat is around my legs immediately, purring and meowing. I push it away.

"Sal?"

As I call her name in the darkness, I am still hoping I have somehow gotten it wrong, that she is going to emerge from the front room, switching on the light and rubbing her eyes, asking me what the fuck I am doing breaking into her house.

But she doesn't.

A sound is coming from the door to the patio outside; is someone in the backyard? Her kitchen door is definitely open; I can hear the sound of it banging against the fence in the wind, the howl of the storm at the windows.

On the sofa next to Sal, her phone is still buzzing, rotating slowly with each ring, my name, Tash, on the lit-up screen, the room's only source of light. The phone drops to the floor, and I jump.

"Sal?"

Her chin is tucked into her chest, her face right up against the back of the sofa. It looks wrong, but even then, as I place my hands softly on her body, I think that she might perhaps come to.

Instead, I feel myself pulling her toward me, her limp body rolling heavily onto her back, her left arm swinging down beside her. I gasp, pull my hands away, and jump back. Her eyes and mouth are open, her T-shirt wet with vomit. The smell hits me, sharp in my nostrils.

I fumble for my phone. Somehow my fingers can't find the edges of it. I dial 999, but when the voice comes through, asking for my location, I can't answer. My mind is white and cold, like a blank page.

The back door slams again. A sound is coming from outside, like something is clattering, or loose. The kitchen floor is wet. Clutching my phone to my ear, I step outside into the small, paved yard at the back of Sal's flat. I can't see anything, or anyone. Just a darkening sky, the twitch of lightning behind the clouds.

"Hello?"

I stammer a reply to the 999 responder, giving the name of the estate. "I can't remember the flat number," I hear myself say. "It's Sal Cunningham—I think she needs an ambulance." I hear myself say it even though I know no ambulance is going to help her now.

A low roll of thunder sounds. I step back into the kitchen. I hear the crackling voice from the phone I am still holding to my ear, asking again if the person is conscious, if the person is breathing.

Only then do I notice the empty wineglass on the counter by the fridge, and next to it, a pile of brown, labeled bottles. White pills are scattered across the stone surface, like a handful of children's sweets.

Tash

THERE IS A RECEPTION at the community center on the estate after the funeral, but I can't face Sal's friends and family. People know I was the one who found her. I feel their eyes on me in the church, in the parking lot, as everyone files out at the end.

I know now that something is very wrong, that I am out of my depth. But Sal, my only real hope of finding out the truth, is gone. I have no idea which way to turn.

As I walk down the path, Christina catches up with me. "Can you come for a drink?"

"I'm not going to the thing," I tell her. "Sorry. I can't."

"Me neither. But I need a drink."

There's no way I'll get anything else done today. I have nothing to lose.

We walk in silence through the park. It feels inexplicable that it is a sunny day, that life is carrying on as usual, when we have just buried Sal. Street sweepers are still sweeping, drivers still honking their horns on Green Lanes.

I follow Christina into a pub on the other side of the park. It is nearly empty, just a few committed day drinkers, one leaning on the bar, another staring up at the horse racing on the TV from a small corner table, a wrinkled betting slip in his hand. She asks for a bottle of white wine, even though it is barely midday, then carries it and two glasses wordlessly to our table.

Christina unbuttons her coat and sets it over the back of the chair.

"So," she says. "You found Sal."

It doesn't seem worth replying.

"What were you doing at her house that night, Tash?"

"What?"

"I wasn't aware you were friends with Sal."

"I wasn't, exactly."

"I'm just trying to understand what happened."

We both know what the official explanation has been. Sal was depressed, and took an overdose of prescription drugs. The drugs had not been prescribed to Sal; the presumption is that she obtained them in street deals. There is still dealing on Sal's estate, despite the best efforts of police and residents to stamp it out with increased security. Inquiries continue.

I gaze into the glass of white wine Christina has poured for me. Clouds of condensation gather at the sides.

"I don't buy it," Christina says.

"Don't buy what?"

"What the police are saying. Sal would never have killed herself. She'd never have done this to Billy. Never."

At the mention of Billy's name, Christina's eyes redden. She cups a hand to her mouth. I close my eyes and try not to think about the little boy in school trousers that pooled at his ankles, holding the hand of his nan, looking at the black oblong of the casket and wondering where his mummy had gone.

Christina is looking past me, over to the bar.

"I have a spare set of keys to Sal's flat," she says slowly. "A few days before she died, they went missing."

"Keys to Sal's flat?"

"Yes. Two at the front, one at the back."

"Where'd they go missing from?"

"My bag. Someone took them."

Christina sets her glass down between us, like a chess piece.

"Are you sure—"

"Of course I'm sure. I don't lose things."

"Where had you been?"

"Normal places. Home. Work. Playgroup."

I try to think who I'd seen at playgroup pickups and drop-offs last week. They'd all been there, all the mums. I think about Nicole outside Cuckoo Club, the way I'd seen them talking in that café. But surely they couldn't have been involved in something like this.

"Did you tell the police? About the keys going missing?"

She shoots me a look. "Did you tell them what you were really doing at Sal's that night?" She tilts her head. "How did you get in, anyway?"

"What? You think I stole your keys?" I almost laugh. "Jesus, Christina. No. I saw her in there. I could see something was up. So I broke the lock."

"It was locked from the inside?"

"Not double-locked. Clearly."

We look testily at each other. I take a sip of my wine.

Christina presses. "You still haven't told me what you were doing there in the first place."

I take a large gulp of wine and swallow it. "I was asking her about Sophie Blake."

Christina's eyes narrow. "Why, Tash?"

"Because I'm a journalist," I snap, exasperated. "That's what I do. I ask questions. Even ones people don't want to be asked. In fact, especially those."

Christina's eyes flick to the floor.

"I know someone killed Sophie," I say. "I think whoever did it wants to scare me into dropping it. I've been getting messages, threats—"

Christina looks back up at me. "What kind of threats?"

I decide there is nothing to lose. I tell her about the text messages, the missing files on my laptop, the broken glass. I watch Christina's legal mind considering and weighing each item in turn.

"The numbers were registered in Sal's name, but when I confronted her, she insisted they had nothing to do with her."

"When did you confront her?"

"The day she died. At Cuckoo Club."

Christina stares at me blankly. "What the fuck is Cuckoo Club?"

"It's a stay-and-play, in Highbury—oh, never mind. The point is, I went to find Sal there. I wanted to confront her about the messages. She said she hadn't sent them, but that she wanted to tell me something— that Sophie had known something she wasn't supposed to know. That she thinks that's why she was killed."

Christina's head snaps up. "Did she say what?"

I shake my head. "No. But she was going to tell me. She painted a message on some paper, told me to come to her house that night, at seven. I went, like she asked. When I got there, she was dead."

Christina opens her mouth, then closes it again.

"You know, don't you?" I say. "You know what Sal was going to tell me."

Christina snatches her phone and keys from the table, her ringless fingers rapping against the wood. Then she takes her coat and storms out of the pub, the door swinging behind her.

THAT NIGHT, I run searches on Christina. This time I do a proper job. As I suspected, she is on the voter registration lists at the wetlands development. She has lived there since Eliza was born. I pull the birth certificate for Eliza, using my old login for the genealogy site we always used at the *Post*, hoping no one notices. Eliza Imogen Sandwell was born in 2016, like Finn. No father is named.

From her LinkedIn profile, I find the name of Christina's office. I pull up its website again, and look through it more carefully this time. Christina's headshot is striking among a grid of mostly older white men.

I click on a link to an award Christina was nominated for. I flick through the galleries of the awards ceremonies until I find 2011, the year Christina was nominated. I scroll through dozens of group shots. Finally, there she is, wearing a long green dress and standing with another female lawyer, being handed a prize by an old gray-haired man in a tuxedo.

I scan the caption. Then I stop and reread it:

Christina Sandwell at the Family Law awards 2011 with fellow barrister Emily Henderson, also of Eden Court Chambers, holding the Family Law Junior Barrister of the Year award.

I look closely at the picture. The curly hair, dark, intelligent eyes, porcelain skin. Emily Henderson.

The woman in the picture with Christina is Jude's mother. Jeremy's first wife.

Sophie

Nineteen days before

IT WAS ALL EMILY, all of it. The whole drawer was full of pictures of her. I picked one up that was near the top. She was small and pretty, curly haired, dimple cheeked, smiling. She looked clever and mischievous, like Jude. One of her hands was curled upward to meet Jez's as it hung off her shoulder. The other rested on a swollen stomach.

The Jez in the pictures was younger. His skin was smoother, with no bags under his eyes, as if he'd been airbrushed. He was so handsome. Everything would have been different if I'd been older, if I'd met him sooner. But this younger Jez had his arm around someone else. Someone who didn't look like me, or Claire.

My hands shook as I sifted through photo after photo of Jez's first wife. Then I started to find other things. A will. Letters from a solicitor. A quote from a funeral director. Beneath them, a booklet of some kind. I picked it up, then immediately dropped it. It had a photograph of Emily on the front, and the words underneath said:

In memoriam
EMILY LOUISE HENDERSON
8/8/1980–2/12/2014

It was the order of service from Jude's mother's funeral. I felt sick. I shouldn't be touching these things. What was I doing?

I started to push the drawer closed, then froze. There was something else inside. A phone, an old one. It was switched on, with full signal.

I knew what it meant when a man had a second phone. It meant he was having an affair. Except I already knew that. He was having an affair with me. But we'd never needed phones. We lived in the same house. Besides, I was the nanny. Calls between us were hardly suspicious.

I picked the phone up and tried the PIN I'd seen Jez enter on his phone many times. It worked. But there was nothing. No numbers saved. No message history.

Who was he talking to on this phone?

Tash

LAURA AND I ARE standing at playgroup pickup. Laura is holding a coffee, but she isn't drinking it. She stirs the surface of it with her wooden stirrer, upsetting the perfect barista swirl of white and brown, until it is long past cold.

I suspect I know what she is thinking about. The same thought has been in all of our minds all week.

"I can't get over how awful it is," she says eventually. "Poor Billy. What he must be going through."

The talk is that Billy is living with his nan, Sal's mum, for the foreseeable future. He hasn't yet been back at school, Claire says, but there has been a special assembly about it.

"It's the stuff of nightmares, huh?" I say grimly. "Leaving your child parentless."

"It really is, isn't it?" Laura sounds choked with emotion. "You'd do anything to spare your children that."

Laura adjusts her scarf, as if to indicate that it is the scarf to blame for the choking noise in her voice, the tightness around her mouth. I reach over and squeeze her hand. It feels cold and slight in mine.

The doors open, and Oscar and Finn barrel toward us. Simultaneously, Laura and I reset our faces to happy, crouch down to kiss our boys, ask them how their day was, express our delight over the drawings they are clutching in their hands, straighten the jackets and backpack straps that flop down over their shoulders.

Behind Finn, I spot Christina hurrying away with Eliza, almost dragging her by the arm. I haven't spoken to Christina since the day of Sal's funeral, even though she is at playgroup pickup every day now for Eliza.

When she arrives, all the other mothers fall silent. The squeak of her bike brakes is deafening.

I feel sure now that Christina is the key to this. She knows what Sophie knew, the secret Sal thought had led to her death. It must be significant that Christina had known Jude's mother, had worked with her in the same offices, that Sophie had a photograph of Christina. But I can't work out why, and she won't talk to me. I'm still not getting any answers. Just more questions.

As we stand up, Laura glances at me.

"You got time for another coffee, Tash? In the park, maybe, so the boys can run around?"

I hesitate. I'm still not sure I can trust Laura. I think again about the day Sal died, how I saw her and the others after Cuckoo Club.

"Mummy, can we go and play with Oscar?"

Finn is tugging at my hand. I know he'll throw a fit if we say no. And anyway, maybe it wouldn't be a bad thing to have a coffee with Laura. Maybe it'll help me work out what the other day was all about. What she and the others were up to the day that Sal died.

LAURA AND I sit at a metal table by the grass where Oscar and Finn are playing. In the days since Sal's death, spring has burst into life along the park, the paths scattered with pink and white blossoms, the beds dotted with the purple, yellow, and white of municipal spring bulbs: crocuses, snowdrops, daffodils. It is merciless, how the world moves on after the death of a person, how they can disappear without a trace, like footprints in the melting snow.

"I find it hard to believe she did it," I say after a while. "Don't you?"

"What?"

"I just find it hard to believe Sal would have . . . done something like that."

Laura makes a face, squints over at the boys. "I don't know. Depression is such a terrible thing. It really is an illness. Some people just can't beat it."

"I suppose."

Laura looks nervous. She is rolling a paper tube of sugar between her fingers. The paper splits, surprising her in a scatter of grains across the metal surface of the table.

Laura turns toward me, her hand shielding her eyes from the sun. "Are you guys still coming to Cornwall?"

I'd been so thrown by Sal's death and Tom's work crisis that I'd been deliberately putting off thinking about Cornwall. It felt kind of unimaginable to me now that we would spend a whole week under the same roof as Jez and Claire—not to mention Nicole, after I saw her following me, plus Laura's husband, Ed, who I had now mentally reclassified from supportive flexible-working father to possible weirdo. But when I'd told Tom I wasn't sure we should go, he had looked really disappointed.

"Oh. But I've booked surfing lessons for Finney and me."

"Isn't he a bit young?" I said. "He can't even swim."

"I'll hold him." Tom grinned. "He'll be bodyboarding by the end of the week."

I felt a sick roll of dread in the pit of my stomach. I could see the thought of time away was really lifting Tom's spirits, and I was relieved. I had been starting to worry that Tom was getting really down. I had told him only a brief outline of what was going on at the playgroup. He'd never met Sal, so while he was shocked by the news of her death, he hadn't asked many follow-up questions. He had been told at his last meeting with bosses at the hospital that they were still waiting for the complainant to come in for a formal statement, before deciding on "the next steps." I had told myself that maybe a vacation, any vacation, was worth enduring if it would take Tom's mind off it all.

"Oh please come," Laura says. "It would be really good to have you there, Tash. Plus, Ed can't come now, so I'll be solo parenting." She rolls her eyes.

"Ed's not coming? Why not?"

"Some work thing." Laura shakes her head. I pause. That's one less thing to worry about, I suppose.

"I . . . I think we are coming," I tell Laura hesitantly. "It would . . . certainly be nice. To get away."

Laura smiles weakly. "I'm glad, Tash. It's been such a strange few weeks. It'll be good to be somewhere else."

I couldn't disagree with that.

THAT NIGHT, when Finn is in bed, I join Tom in the kitchen. I can smell soy sauce and sesame. There is a sizzle of frying onions, a pot on the stove into which Tom is tipping a pack of noodles. A curl of smoke drifts in the air below the single working spotlight in the ceiling.

I open a window. The wood of the frame feels cold and damp, as if it might crumble away in my hand.

"Hey," I say.

Tom throws a tea towel over his shoulder and leans back against the counter, his fingers curled around the edge. When he looks at my face, he gives me a quizzical look.

"What is it?"

"Tom," I say. "I need to ask you about what happened when I went to France with Finn, the summer before last."

Sophie

Thirteen days before

I WATCHED THEM FROM the stairs. Claire was in the front room, watching TV, her back to Jez. He placed a hand on her shoulder.

"I've got to head back to the office."

"OK," I heard Claire say. "Will you be late?"

"Might be. Sorry. But Sophie's here."

I had to do this. I had to know who she was.

I used the annex door when I left so I wouldn't be heard. It was raining, a soft June rain, more like a cloudiness. I pulled my hoodie over my hair and followed him.

By the time I turned the corner, Jez was halfway down St. Augustine's path. I followed him, tacking close to the high walls of the church, fragrant with damp and moss, staying at the edges, in shadow.

Jez walked quickly. By the time we reached the alleyway between the New River and the wetlands, I felt out of breath. The gravel path was noisy underfoot, so I stuck to the beds on either side.

Jez crossed the boulders and the grasses, toward the newest, smartest part of the development. But when we reached the office, with the rushing silver fountain outside, he didn't go in there. Instead, he pulled a key card from the breast pocket inside his suit jacket, waved it in front of a sensor outside a glass door opposite, and headed toward an elevator.

I followed just close enough to shove my sneaker in the gap between the glass door and the frame as he stepped into the elevator. My heart was pounding as I watched the numbers rise steadily, then stop.

I went to the next elevator, tried to call it. But nothing happened. The elevators were controlled by a key card. I couldn't get up.

I made my way out, hitting the exit button to open the glass door. The wind pulled my hair across my face. I rubbed it from my eyes and headed to the path.

From there, it was easy to see inside. The windows were floor to ceiling, the penthouse lit up like a theater stage, a floating box of light. I could see everything: the curving arch of the floor lamp, the glint of copper on the lights over the kitchen island. And I could see two figures. One fair-haired, and one tall and dark, her hair flowing out behind her as she reached up to him and he kissed her lips.

I couldn't see her face, but I knew it was her. The same person I'd seen that day in the café, watching Jez with Claire. This was Jez's other woman. And what did that make me? The words rustled in my ears like the sound of the wind. Nothing. Nothing. Nothing.

Looking up at them, I finally felt the full, sick sucker punch of it. It was as if all the blood had flooded to my face in one final hot, sick sting of humiliation. Of rage.

Tash

———✦———

"IS THIS FOR REAL, Tash?"

I hold up my printout of the CCTV photograph.

"This is you," I say. "Leaving the party with Sophie Blake. Hours before she died. What were you doing with her, Tom?"

Tom takes the printout in his hands. He looks up at me, his voice is low. "Tash," he says slowly. "Have you completely lost your mind?"

I think in my head I expected some cataclysm. Instead, as the words come out, it does slightly feel as if the whole mad narrative that has grown up in the dark corners of my mind is collapsing in on itself in the light of our normal evening in the kitchen.

"Are we really having this conversation? Is this really you asking me if I had an affair with some girl we met once, and then . . . what, murdered her? Because of this?"

He waves the paper at me. It's not printed properly at the edges, and the lines that make up Tom's hand have thinned slightly where the ink cartridge was running out, like a faded bar code.

"I'm just asking what happened. Why you never mentioned that the week I was out of the country with Finn you went to a big, fancy party. A party hosted by Claire and Jez—who, at Christmas, you acted like you'd never met before."

"But I hardly even—"

"And then I find out you went missing that night, abandoned Ravi—"

"Ravi?" Tom looks stunned. "When did you talk to Ravi?"

"—and left the party with your arm around a very pretty girl—"

"My arm . . . what the hell are you—"

"—a girl that we had met a few weeks earlier when we visited the playgroup. A girl who was then found dead, and whose picture I then found in your sock drawer!"

"I never had my arm around anyone!" Tom is staring at me. "Where did this even come from? No—do you know what, Tash, don't even tell me. I don't care about your bloody investigation."

"Tom, I'm just—"

Tom tosses the paper onto the counter and holds his palms up between us. "We have been married five years—we have a child!" Even in his fury, he lowers his voice, careful not to wake up Finn, and the fact of that twists at my heart. "Do you actually believe there is a possibility I could have killed someone?"

"Of course not—I didn't say that!" This is true, I realize. I never really believed he could have killed anybody.

"Then what the hell is this?" Tom points at the crumpled photo, now lying facedown by the sink, dishwater soaking into the edges.

"I just want to know what happened that night," I say after a few moments. "That's all. I'm not accusing you of anything. I just need to know."

"Fine," Tom said. "I'll tell you exactly what happened."

Tom tells me the same story I've heard already from Ravi. He went for a drink with some people from work, Ravi included. Laura asked Ravi if he would drive to "some fancy party." He had promised Tom a lift, but Laura had "wheedled away, said that we could both come along to some fabulous party instead if we drove her there, and get free champagne, even though no one—least of all Ravi—wanted free champagne."

"The only reason Ravi said yes," Tom says, "is that he is too nice for his own good, and the only reason I was there was the lift—it was the Tube strike that week. You can look it up."

"But why did you never mention any party to me? When we came back from France?"

Tom groans. "Because you were already pissed off with me about the trip, and I knew what it would sound like. Like I was living it up while you were hauling Finn to France and back on your own." He rubbed his eyes with his hands. "But honestly, Tash—it was just a posh, boring party. You know I hate that sort of stuff."

"But Laura must have introduced you to Claire and Jez. It was their party!"

"If she did, I wasn't paying attention! I wasn't bothered about meeting Laura's posh friends . . . you know what I'm like at parties!"

"And then what? What happened at the end of the evening?"

"I got bored of Laura prattling on, looking over her shoulder for—well, I don't know who, someone else she was clearly much more interested in talking to. I went off for a piss, and then I went home. That was it. This"—he plucks up the piece of paper—"is a picture of me holding open a door for a girl who was leaving at the same time as me. I do remember it, actually. She had a baby in a buggy—he looked about Finn's age. I might have asked about him. It made me miss Finney." Tom's voice is cracking a bit. "All I did," he says, "was help her get through."

"You didn't recognize her? From our tour of the nursery?"

Tom shakes his head slowly. "No, I didn't. And the photo thing—you know Finn hides stuff. Takes your work papers and puts them away." Tom works his jaw, as if he's trying to contain his rage. "You know, I have never actually said this out loud, because I knew how you'd react, but I am pretty sure he does that because he hates you working every single second of the evenings and weekends, when we're supposed to all be together."

I gasp.

"That's not true."

"Maybe, maybe not." He locks his gaze with mine. "It's just a coincidence, Tash. Whatever happened to Sophie Blake, it had nothing to do with me. I'm not keeping anything secret from you."

He pauses, looks away from me, out of the window with the horrible new bars.

"Can you say the same, Tash?" he asks quietly. "Can you honestly say you're not keeping any secrets from me?"

I frown at Tom. "What do you mean?"

"Anything you want to tell me about your secret credit card? About selling your dad's pictures?" He looks back at me sadly. "Or should we start with you and Jeremy Henderson?"

Sophie

———— ❦ ————

Ten days before

WHEN IT BECAME CLEAR to me how stupid I'd been, how I had humiliated myself, even more anger started to seep into my sadness, like a clean wound going bad. I found myself smiling less, not bothering with please and thank you. I found it strange that I had ever bothered to please people, to make their lives comfortable. I was ashamed of myself for how obsessed I'd been with Jez's and Claire's approval, how hard I'd worked to help make their beautiful house more beautiful, their easy lives easier. And now look. Look what they had done to me.

One day Sal found me outside the playgroup, waiting in the bike shelter for the rain to stop. The sound of it on the metal roof was soothing somehow. I rubbed at my eyes. They felt raw and red. When Sal saw me, she shook her head.

"He shouldn't get away with it," she said.

The rain dripped from the dips in the metal, onto the asphalt path. I kept imagining Jez in the penthouse with that woman, gazing out of the big glass windows over the rainy city like a god. While down below, Sal and I looked after these children all day, filled their bellies, wiped their bottoms, returned them at the end of the day, fed and clean and happy. Their lives were kept clean and silent and perfect because of us.

I saw what he and Claire had been doing now, for what it was. Using me as whatever they wanted—a surrogate mother, a bit on the side— then dismissing me when it suited them. I hated myself for how grateful I'd been for the crumbs of their perfect life that they had tossed me—the odd glass of white wine, their leftover granola, a used cashmere sweater, an old clutch bag in a color that no one wore anymore. They'd thought they could buy me. I hated them both.

"What do you want?"

I looked at Sal, at the two of us in our cheap Primark clothes, our cracked phone screens, our chipped fingernails.

"I want them punished," I said. "I want them to lose everything."

Sal nodded. "All right," she said. "What do you want me to do?"

Tash

GRACE AND I SIT in the kitchen of her new house. Cardboard boxes are stacked in towers around us like building blocks. She has made us tea from a kettle plugged in on top of a chair. With her hair pulled back in a ponytail and her contacts abandoned in favor of glasses, she looks less like her adult self and more like the geeky girl I knew at school—except for the bulbous stomach.

"So," Grace says once Ben is out of earshot. "Has Tom forgiven you yet?"

I shake my head, cradling my mug. "I don't think so."

I don't know if I'd ever intended to tell him about any of it, if I could help it. Not the credit card debt I'd racked up. Not the picture of Dad's that I'd secretly sold to try and pay a bit of it off. And definitely not about Jez. But Tom had found the receipt from the hotel spa—a bill in my name for nearly a thousand pounds, paid for by a J. Henderson—and the whole thing had unraveled.

"How did you find the receipt?" I'd asked miserably. Tom looked like he was nearly in tears.

"It was in your pocket. I was doing your laundry."

I winced at that.

"Are you sleeping with him?"

"What? No! How can you even ask that, Tom?"

"Well, you just asked me if I killed someone, so I guess we're even."

I had gasped at that. It wasn't like Tom to talk like this. None of this was like us.

"What am I supposed to think? You told me it was a spa day with the other mums—and then I find this!"

"It was a spa day! You can ask them—ask Laura! Jez was just there using the gym, and—"

"And he paid a bill for you? Of more than a thousand pounds? Must have been some fucking spa day."

I was silent, my cheeks burning. How could I explain to Tom my decision to go and spend this sort of money, so pointlessly, on myself? It had been awful; the whole day had been horrible. Why hadn't I just canceled? What the hell was I thinking?

"Tom, I had no idea it was going to be that much," I said eventually. "Jez was just there, and I think he just . . . he could see how horrified I was when the bill came. He felt responsible because Claire had organized it. They're rich—he knows we're not. He was just trying to help out. I tried to say no but, but . . ."

Tom sighed. "It's not just that that you've lied about, though? Is it?"

He'd looked in my purse after he'd found the Corinthia receipt, found the credit card I'd kept secret from him. Then he'd looked through my emails, trying to find a statement for it, and instead found the emails between Dad's agent and me about the picture. I couldn't even blame him for snooping. I had looked at his phone. I'd done the same.

"I thought it was a complete no-go, selling the pictures," Tom said. "Otherwise, what the hell are we doing in this flat?"

I had been trying not to think too deeply about what I was really doing, about how I could be losing something that meant so much, for things that meant so little. I felt tears pricking my eyes.

"It was only one picture . . ."

"It was worth two thousand pounds, Tash!"

"I know, and I'm sorry . . ."

"I found your credit card statement—I looked it all up. Ruby's, Ottolenghi, Sweaty Betty, Petit Bateau. I'd never even heard of half these places! What does it all mean? Where the hell did two thousand pounds go? On what?"

And of course, I had nothing to say. Because the truth was that I had spent two thousand pounds on lattes and croissants, trinkets from the shops in Upper Street. Fancy new leggings. A cutaway designer swimsuit.

Hot-yoga classes and manicures. A stupidly expensive coat for Finn. I had spent two thousand pounds on absolutely nothing. I was filled with a self-loathing so intense I started to shake.

Tom had slumped down into a chair. "Tash, what is going on? I feel like I barely know you anymore. You hardly speak to me, unless it's because you need me to look after Finn because you're going out on yet another investigative mission. Which I wouldn't mind, except it's all you ever want to do." He hung his head. "I thought we would try for another baby this year. I don't even know if we should now."

I had no answer for him. I felt tears in my eyes.

"I'll do whatever you want," I said. "Tell me how to fix it."

Tom buried his head in his hands.

"I want you to stop it. All of it. All this crazy spending, this obsession with these rich women, and with digging around about Sophie Blake. You need to concentrate on us. For God's sake, Tash! I'm here, sick to death worrying about losing my job, about not being able to pay the mortgage. And meanwhile you're cashing in your family fortune without bothering to tell me, to fund spa trips and, what . . . yoga classes? I could understand overspending on Finn, or a vacation, or . . . I don't know. But this is just . . ."

I opened my mouth to try and explain. How keeping up with the playgroup mothers and looking into Sophie's death had become one and the same thing, without me noticing. I'd gotten in too deep, and didn't know how to get back. But as I started to say it, I realized I couldn't even make out how much of that was really true, and how much of it was a lie. Because there was a part of me that really did see them as my friends. And another part that had just become addicted to it. The coffees in their lovely houses, the trips to private members clubs in their flashy cars. The drama of trying to scratch beneath the surface of their perfect lives.

"I don't know who you are, Tash." Tom was shaking his head. "I don't understand you caring about this stuff. Can't you see how meaningless it all is?"

"Tom . . ."

"No, Tash. I can't even look at you, I'm so fucking angry."

"You and Finn are everything to me—you know that!" But even as I said it, the words felt false. When was the last time I'd ever really thought about him, about us?

"Apparently not," he muttered. "Apparently we're not enough."

It had, without a doubt, been the worst argument we'd ever had. I felt traumatized in a way that was almost physical, like whiplash. It was as if Tom had discovered something hideous about me, an ugly underside to myself that even I had never fully acknowledged, but that now lay exposed. In the days afterward, I found myself shrinking from people, as if they could see the ugliness in me, too.

"I mean, I guess the pictures do belong to you, Tash," Grace says hopefully. "It's up to you what you do with that money."

But as we sit in her pretty new home, the dappled light from the window playing on the bare tiled floor, we both know this is just not true. I am supposed to be a partner, a wife, a mother. Part of a family.

Grace leans forward, wincing at the baby underneath her hips. She wraps a warm hand around mine.

"Hey," she says. "Don't give yourself such a hard time. He'll calm down."

"He was so angry, Grace."

"Oh, sure. But he loves you. You love each other."

Is this true? I am starting to wonder. The way he looked at me, it was as if he was seeing someone else, someone he wasn't sure he even liked, let alone loved. The thought of not being loved by Tom is too frightening to contemplate.

I try to think about the last time I'd put any real energy into our relationship—the last time we'd done something nice together. I ended up thinking back to Christmas, sitting in that deserted square in France, with the holiday lights festooned around us. We'd had a good couple of weeks after that, but we'd barely even touched each other lately. As I looked at Grace's belly now, I thought for the first time how nice it would be to share this with her. How lovely it would feel to look forward to holding a tiny new baby again.

"I thought you must have had a lot on your mind," Grace said. "Seeing as you hadn't harassed me about Ed Crawley since our drink."

I realized this was true. I'd been so focused on what Tom had done, and what Christina was hiding, that I'd almost forgotten about Ed.

"Did you finally find out why he left?"

"I did, as it happens." I see a flicker of pride cross Grace's face, then hesitation. "None of this came from me though, OK, Tash? Everyone was told to keep quiet about it. I think the bank managed to hush it up. Even though, really, it should have gone to the police."

As Grace tells me the story, I realize I am listening to a tale so grimly familiar that any woman could fill in the blanks. A senior man in the office, people who turned a blind eye, even though everyone knew what he was like. Until the day it went too far. A younger trainee, a flirtation that had raised eyebrows, then work drinks that turned into a few too many for her. Ed had put her in a taxi, told her friend they were going the same way, he'd get her back safely.

"A few days later, it all came out," Grace continues. "She ended up in tears in the restroom, confessing to one of the senior women what had happened. She had passed out drunk, she said, and then she'd woken up to find him . . ."

I think about Laura at the dinner party, her facial muscles flickering with discomfort at her husband. Their relationship had always seemed odd. Now it was unfathomable.

"And then what?"

"The girl was adamant she didn't want the police involved," Grace says. "I think the firm was in a pretty difficult position. I know they took legal advice."

"I bet they bloody did."

Grace takes a deep breath. "The next thing anyone knew, he was gone. The girl, too—she wanted a fresh start. The rest of us have been sent on some kind of gender relations training, which you can imagine we're all thrilled about."

I exhale, pressing the tips of my fingers against my eyebrows. "My God, Grace," I say. "I know his wife, Laura. I know her really well."

"She must know this happened," Grace says, shaking her head. "Surely she must know."

"Surely. But honestly, Grace—she's smart, educated, beautiful. How could she stay with him?"

"Didn't you say they had a son?" Grace says quietly, raising an eyebrow.

"Yeah."

She shrugs. "There you go, then. That's how."

I tell myself Grace is wrong. But then I think about Tom, and wonder if I can really be so sure. Because my husband stands accused of molesting a female patient, and I have never even considered the possibility that this woman—whoever she is—is telling the truth.

Sophie

Six hours before

ON THE DAY OF the party, Claire spent the morning at the venue, making sure everything was ready. In the afternoon, she messaged saying it was cold. Could I come and drop off her long cardigan?

It was a typically unreasonable request—it left me with less than an hour to get there and back before I'd need to collect Jude from the playgroup, and Beau was whiny, unsettled. But obviously, I complied, strapping a confused Beau into the stroller, his big blue eyes watching me, wondering where we were going. When I was halfway there, she sent me a message asking why I hadn't arrived yet.

When I got to the gallery, it was weirdly cold inside, my footsteps echoing around the empty space. Claire was arranging flowers in a huge vase, great spiky orange ones, their jaws open. They looked as if they might take your hand off.

"It's very chilly in here," I said to Claire as I handed her the cardigan.

"It's for the flowers. It'll warm up once everyone is here." She gave a little shrug. "I'm leaving now anyway. I need to go home and get ready."

"I thought you said you needed this."

"I didn't think you'd take so long."

Claire and I looked at each other. I wondered how things between us had gotten like this.

We stepped outside the gallery. I was pulling the stroller out backward when I heard the voice.

"Sophie, hey!"

Lydia was trotting down Camden Passage, her stroller laden with shopping bags, wheels bumping on the cobbles. Ludicrously, I tried to duck down, pretending to get something out from the bottom of the stroller. But it was too late. She had seen me.

By the time Claire had followed me out of the door, Lydia was crossing the road toward us, one hand on the push bar of her stroller, the other waving.

"Oh my God, it's been ages since I've seen you, Sophie," Lydia said. "How are you guys doing?"

I can get away with this, I thought, breathing hard. I just need to control the situation.

"This is Claire," I said, primarily to cut Lydia off before she could say anything else. "Claire, this is Lydia."

"Hi," Claire said shortly, eyeing Zelda. "Cute baby. How old?"

"She's nearly a year."

"Ah, a bit older than Beau, then."

A confused expression flitted across Lydia's face.

"It's so good to see you, Lydia," I gabbled. "We've got to get back, but let's catch up again soon, OK?" I flicked the brake off the stroller.

"OK," she said. "Sounds good. Bye, Sophie."

Claire was looking at her phone. She'd lost interest already. For a moment, I thought it was all going to be all right.

Then Lydia leaned into the stroller, touching Beau on the cheek. Claire looked up at Lydia.

"Bye-bye, little baby Teddy," Lydia said in a singsong voice. "Me and your mummy will have to have another of our cinema dates soon, won't we, Sophie?" She grinned at me. "Bye, guys!"

Lydia walked away. Claire and I stood frozen to the spot. The noise of the cars passing behind us felt loud.

"You've been telling people he's yours."

It was a statement, not a question.

"It was . . . she just assumed," I said. "I just played along. I hardly know her."

"She said you went to mother and baby cinema!" Claire's eyes narrowed as she took a step toward me, snatching the push bar of the stroller out of my hands. I gasped with the violence of it. Then she brought her face close to mine.

"I knew there was something going on," she spat. "But even when Nicole told me, I didn't believe it. It was too much. No one would do that, I thought. No one would take my baby around and pretend he belonged to them."

"Claire, I—"

"Do you know the worst thing? Jez thought I was the crazy one!"

Claire started pushing Beau away furiously. I chased after her, panic quickening the breath in my chest. I'd lost Jez, and now I was about to lose my job, my home. The boys. I was about to lose everything.

"Please, Claire," I said. "Let's talk about this. Claire!"

But she didn't turn back.

Tash

"NO COFFEE TODAY?" CLAIRE is standing with Laura and Nicole at drop-off. She tilts her head to one side questioningly. "You're always racing off these days."

"Ah, I'm sorry, I really can't, Claire. I'm just slammed with work at the moment."

Since the argument with Tom, I am avoiding all expensive coffee dates and lunches. I have been going straight to the library every day after drop-off, my head down and my thermos in hand.

"Just a quick one maybe? We've hardly seen you."

Laura sticks her bottom lip out in exaggerated dismay. Nicole tightens the belt on her coat, fixing her eyes on my face.

"I've just got a lot to finish before we go away. But see you soon!" I wave behind me, heading down the path before they can voice any more objections.

Claire smiles weakly, Laura gives me a halfhearted thumbs-up. Nicole is unsmiling.

It's not true that I've got a lot of work to finish, of course. As of this week, Grace's firm is no longer returning my calls. I fear that the missing copywriting project has proven fatal to my chances of any more commissions. Without that stream of work, I know I need to redouble my efforts on getting freelance articles placed. But I feel bereft of inspiration, my focus clouded by Sophie.

Back home at the kitchen table, I try to fit the pieces together. Sophie had a secret—a secret Sal was planning to tell me about on the night she died—a secret she believes Sophie was killed to conceal. Whatever this was, it's obvious from the way Christina acted after the funeral that she knows something about it, too. I know Christina is linked to Claire and Jez's past somehow, through his first wife, Emily. And I'm convinced Sophie sensed Christina was significant in some way when she took that photograph of her.

Then there's Ed, who I now know has been accused of a violent act against a woman in the past, and who was on the same dating app as Sophie, and who was actually there at the party, the night Sophie died. Could he and Sophie have been seeing each other? Or maybe he followed Sophie back to Jez and Claire's, and attacked her after she refused his advances? Pushed her down the stairs, in front of poor little Jude—leaving Jude traumatized, like Abi said?

But why would Claire and Jez cover for him, after coming home to discover something so awful? Did Ed have some sort of hold over them? Was the secret Christina and Sal knew about linked to that in some way?

In the end, I call Adam. He answers within two rings.

"Tash," he says breathlessly. "I didn't think I'd hear from you."

I hear blood in my ears, throbbing, like a drumbeat.

"Did you confront Sally Cunningham about the messages? Why did you take off like that in the pub? Do you know who the man in the picture is?"

"Sal Cunningham's dead."

"What?"

I clear my throat. "Look, Adam—I just need to ask you one thing. Please."

Adam makes an exasperated noise.

"All right," he says eventually. "I'm listening."

"Ed Crawley. Did you ever look at him?"

There is a silence on the line. "The name doesn't ring a bell. Who is that? Is that the man in the—"

"No," I say. "But I think he was at the party that night. And might have done this sort of thing before." I take a breath. "You might . . . look into whether a complaint was ever made against him, a few months before. By a girl who worked with him, at Schooners investment bank."

Grace said the girl at Schooners hadn't wanted to report it, but that was months ago. She could have changed her mind.

I hear the scratch of a pen.

"I'll check it out," Adam says. "But, Tash, wait—"

"I've got to go." I hang up and immediately turn off my phone. I can't risk him knowing it's Tom in the picture, not yet. Not until I can prove to Adam that he has nothing to do with all this.

The thought of going on vacation with the others had already made me feel uneasy; now it makes me feel physically sick. But Ed isn't coming. I tell myself that that's the main thing. And I can't cancel the trip, the only thing Tom is feeling positive about. I'm hoping it might help us.

I'd never been seriously worried about me and Tom before. I've always thought we're just not the sort to get divorced—we didn't even used to argue. But now, communication between us is almost nonexistent. I've spent the week exhausting myself trying to be perfect, getting through all the laundry, setting it out in neatly ironed piles, ready to pack. I resist the urge to buy anything new, resurrecting all our nicest things and making sure they are clean and ready. I fill Tom's drawers with freshly balled socks and folded T-shirts. In the evenings, a rotating menu of his favorite dinners, cooked cheaply with ingredients from the Turkish shops along Green Lanes, are ready on the stove.

"Tom," I say, a couple of nights before we're due to go away. "I know you're still angry with me. But I can't go on like this."

I feel the tears prick at the sides of my eyes as I say it out loud. Tom looks at me and his face softens.

"Come here."

He holds me so tight it is bordering on unpleasant. I have the uncomfortable thought that he is trying to physically hold our marriage together, like a building at risk of collapse.

"I really am sorry," I tell him.

"I know."

"It feels like you can't forgive me."

Tom sighs. For a while he doesn't say anything.

"I do forgive you, Tash. But I also think things need to change."

I nod. "I'll do whatever you want."

Tom pulls back to look at me. "All right. I want us to try for another baby."

I hold my breath. This wasn't what I expected.

"I really don't want Finn to be an only child, like we both were. We always said that. And we always said we wanted them close together—Finn's going to be three next month."

"But, the flat . . ."

"That's the next thing," he says. "I want to sell the flat. I'm over it, Tash. I want to live somewhere we can afford a real home."

"But where—"

"I want us to move out of London, away from here. I don't care about London. I want a proper family house."

"But what about your job, Tom?"

"I've been offered a post at John Radcliffe."

"John Radcliffe? What's that?"

"John Radcliffe Hospital. In Oxford."

Tom pauses a moment, lets this sink in.

"When you said you might look at other jobs, other hospitals, I assumed you meant in London."

Tom looks away. "I honestly didn't think it was worth telling you about this one. I thought there was no way I'd get this job. But John Radcliffe is a really prestigious hospital. Obviously, they don't know about the complaint, but when—if—that's dropped, I want to take the post, Tash."

"But . . . hang on! Oxford is *your* place, Tom. I don't know anything about Oxford."

"I know. But we'd get to know it, together. It would be an adventure."

I gape at him. "But . . . what about our friends, our lives? What about Finn's playgroup?"

"I want to take Finn out of the playgroup."

"But . . ."

"Ever since he started there, things have been different. Since you've been hanging around with those women."

I hesitate. I know what he's talking about, but in some faraway place in my mind, an alarm bell sounds. Is Tom really telling me who I should and shouldn't see?

"They are my friends," I say sullenly. "And you're the one who was so keen to go on vacation with them."

"That was before all this!" Tom is pacing the room. "And another thing, Tash. I need you to promise you'll leave this Sophie Blake thing alone, now. I could understand if it was for an article. But there's no story. Is there?"

I have no answer. I had been sure, for so long, that there was a story here. But Tom's right. This has become something else. Something bigger than that.

"I mean it. I've never seen you like this, Tash. You've become obsessed with it, and it is hurting us."

"It might be a story," I insist stubbornly. "And I'm not obsessed. You're exaggerating."

Tom explodes. "You asked me if I'd had something to do with her death! Can you honestly not see how crazy that is? Of course you're obsessed with it!"

My phone rings.

"Who's that?"

"I don't know," I say. "Unknown number." I glance at him. I know the conversation with Tom is more important; I should offer to cancel the call. But something makes me hesitate, my thumb hovering over the screen.

Tom turns away from me. "You might as well get it. I'm getting a beer."

I answer the call.

"Is this Natasha Carpenter?" It is a male voice, businesslike, unfamiliar.

"It is."

"I'm Richard Jeffries, the solicitor for the estate of Sally Cunningham. I have a document in my possession which she seems to have intended for you. It was in her living room when she was . . . discovered. In an envelope with your name on it."

Tash

WHEN WE ARRIVE IN Cornwall, we park the car and walk up the gravel path to Claire and Jez's imposing stone farmhouse, Tom carrying a sleepy Finn on his shoulders. There is no answer at the front door, no sign of anyone in the bay windows, so we trudge around the back.

Suddenly the house looks completely different. It has been extended to create a huge open-plan space, with a farmhouse kitchen, island, and large wooden dining table on one side, a wood burner and sofas on the other, and full-length windows facing the sea. Through the glass, I see Claire at the kitchen island with bunches of dried herbs hanging. She is rubbing oil and salt into the yellowish skin of a chicken carcass. Beau is on the stone floor, playing with trucks. Tom clears his throat, balls a fist, and knocks gently on the glass. Both of them look up, delightedly, and Claire says something that can't be heard. I watch her walking over to the door, like an actress in a silent film.

Claire throws the door open.

"You're here! Wonderful!" Her smile looks a bit strained, the creases around her eyes deeper than I remember noticing before. "Come in, come in. Sorry, we don't use the front entrance, did it confuse you? You're the first here! You've done so well! Jez isn't coming until the weekend, but the others should be here tonight." She doesn't mention Jude.

Finn is desperate to go straight down to the beach. "Let's go, then!" Claire washes her hands, throws a jacket on Beau. "He'll want wellies. Here, don't unpack, have some of ours."

A wooden gate at the bottom of their garden leads directly to the sandy coast path. It runs up the cliffs in one direction, and down to the beach in the other. Higher up the cliffs, the path looks like it has been sealed off, a twist of black-and-yellow tape flickering in the wind.

Claire leads us down to the beach. Finn and Beau race ahead, whooping with delight. Green and purple heather shimmers on the path on either side of us. The waves in the bay are huge and foaming. It doesn't look like a beach where a child would be safe to swim.

I hang back a bit, tapping out a text to Grace. She is staying in our flat—she and Ben are having their kitchen remodeled—and I have made her promise to call when the letter from the lawyer arrives. Infuriatingly, the lawyer has refused to discuss the contents of the envelope, insisting it had to be sent, registered delivery, to my home address.

"Tash? Is everything OK?"

Tom is at my side. There is no disguising the edge in his question, the implication I shouldn't be on my phone.

"Fine. I was just trying to get some phone reception."

"I don't think you can here. I asked Claire already. Their Wi-Fi isn't working, apparently. You have to walk up onto the cliff path to get a signal."

"Really? The cliffs?"

"It doesn't matter, does it? We can put our phones away for a few days."

I force a smile, shove my phone into my pocket. "Sure," I say. "Of course." The thought of having no phone signal is more alarming than I feel I can let on to Tom, though. My stomach clenches.

Claire has grabbed waterproof-backed blankets, a large flask of tea. We sit on the sand watching while the kids chase each other giddily around the windy expanse of beach. Finn shouts for Tom, pointing with a stubby finger at something in the wet sand close to the sea. Tom jogs ahead to join him.

"Be careful of the waves," I call after him. The wind is up, the waves like huge walls of gray-green water smashing themselves against the sand. I have read too many news stories about things like this. It would only take a second.

Claire pulls herself up beside me. She is wearing expensive wellies and a big waterproof jacket that must belong to Jez.

"This is stunning, Claire. Thanks so much for asking us."

"Of course." She squints at me. "Everything all right with you guys?" Claire has to raise her voice over the wind, pushing a stray lock of hair behind her ear. I scuff the sand beyond the blanket with the tip of my sneaker.

Tom is heading back over, and Claire turns to me, lowering her voice. "Talk later? With wine?"

I force a smile. "OK," I say. "Sounds good."

I HEAR Laura and Nicole arriving as I am putting Finn to bed, their luggage clattering on the stone floors. I fear the noise will unsettle Finn, tucked in his little folding bed. But he is exhausted, his eyes drooping shut before I have even turned off the light.

When I pad back downstairs, Tom is sitting on one of the sofas drinking a beer, and Ed is opposite him, kneeling on the floor and throwing a log into the wood burner.

I stop in my tracks. The shock must show on my face. Tom throws me a confused look. Ed smiles, stands up, dusts off his hands, and sits down next to Tom.

"Hello, Tash," he says.

"Hi," I mutter. I don't want to sit. "I thought you weren't going to be able to make it."

"Managed to swing it after all."

I feel the hairs on my arms stand up, a prickle at the base of my head.

"Was just saying to your husband." Ed smirks. "Natty little car you've got there."

Ed jerks his head in the direction of the window looking down toward the drive. Our rental car is parked beside the others' sleek vehicles, its branding plastered across the sides.

"What's wrong with it?" Tom says, smiling as if Ed's joke isn't at our expense. "It's fine."

"Bit of a pain for you both, isn't it? Not having your own car?"

"We did have one, a while back," Tom says. "But we got rid of it in the end. We decided we didn't use it enough to justify it."

Claire walks in from the kitchen. "Ah, Tash, Finn's down! Great! Laura's just getting Oscar settled, and Beau is asleep, too. They must all be exhausted. Time for wine. What would you like?"

"Whatever you're having." I glance at her glass. It looks like she is just drinking water. "Or some red." As I say it, it occurs to me we should have brought some.

"Is there anything I can get for tonight?" I ask Claire hurriedly. "Some drinks, maybe? Is there a shop nearby?"

"A what? At this hour?" Claire laughs. "There's nothing for miles. This is the countryside, silly!"

I smile faintly, the feeling of queasiness returning to my stomach.

"No kidding," moans Ed, swiping at his phone. "No 4G signal, either."

"Oh, come on, Londoners!" Claire winks at me. "I'm sure we'll all survive the week!"

DINNER IS served, and more wine poured. Through the windows, steamy with warmth and breath, I can still make out the lurid yellow branding of our rental car. It's been bugging me all evening.

"You OK?" Tom is leaning to fill up my water glass, giving me a squeeze on the knee.

"That wasn't what happened with our car," I say to Tom under my breath. "What you said to Ed."

He looks confused. "What?"

"Our old Corsa," I say. "You said we'd decided it wasn't worth having it anymore."

"We did, didn't we?"

"No. You told me it had broken down when you were driving it. That you took it to the garage, and they said it needed scrapping. That it was going to cost more to replace it than it was worth."

"Yes," he says slowly, as if unsure what I'm asking. "That's what I said.

And then we decided it wasn't worth getting a new one. Isn't that the same thing?"

The truth is I can't remember now how we ended up getting rid of the Corsa, because I wasn't there when the car broke down. It's been bothering me ever since he said it. Why would Tom have been driving it without me?

"When did it happen?" I ask him.

"When did what happen?"

"The car breaking down and having to be scrapped." I pause. "Was it . . . was it when I was in France with Finn?"

Even as I say the words, I know that I am right. It was that week. The week Sophie died. I came back from France, and Tom had gotten rid of the car. He said it had been worn out and had had to go, and that was it. I never saw our car again.

"Not this again," Tom is muttering.

"But why were you using the car?" It didn't make sense to me. We only really used the car when we needed to take Finn on long journeys. "Where were you driving?"

"I can't remember."

I exhale, irritated. "Can you try and remember?"

Tom shakes his head and stands up. "I'm getting another beer."

After dinner, everyone moves into the living room. Tom is among the first to go, leaving me behind without a second glance. When I look into the living room, I see that he is sitting with Ed again. I decide to stay in the kitchen with Claire, help her load the dishwasher.

As I collect the wineglasses, my stomach is churning. I can't stop thinking about the car.

"Is this yours?" I ask Claire, seeing her wineglass looks unused. "Are you not drinking?"

Claire hesitates. When I look up, her cheeks are flushed pink, a half smile on her face.

"I might as well tell you—I can't exactly keep it a secret the whole vacation," she says. "I'm pregnant."

It takes me a moment to process what she is saying. I force myself to recover, to search for the appropriate reaction. Even as, to my horror, I realize there is a tightening in my chest that feels very much like jealousy.

"Oh, Claire!" I reach out to hug her. "Sorry— I didn't think— But that's amazing! I'm so pleased for you. How are you feeling?"

"Oh, you know." She grimaces. "Terrified."

Claire sits down at the table, her fingertips brushing her belly. I see it now, a tiny rise under her clothes, barely noticeable.

"I'm sure it'll be easier this time," I say gently.

"Well, I certainly hope it's nothing like the first time."

I sit next to her. "You'll know what to look out for, won't you?"

"I guess." We sit in silence for a while, listening to the low thrum of the dishwasher, the rise and fall of the conversation in the next room.

"When did you . . . When did you get help, in the end?"

Claire smiles sadly. "Laura helped me. When I finally told her. But it had been months and months by then. I was such a mess, Tash. I'd have been a goner if it wasn't for her getting me . . . what I needed."

I nod, slowly, as what she is saying sinks in. So this was what the pills were for, the ones Tom caught Laura stealing. The shock must show on my face, because Claire looks down, as if I have admonished her.

"I mean it," Claire says. "I should have gone to the GP, but I was so worried that they'd take Beau away—I didn't want anything on my medical record. Of course, that was crazy of me. But I wasn't thinking straight. I was having so many dark thoughts. About Beau, about Jude, about Jeremy . . . even about our nanny."

"Your . . . nanny?"

"Yes. Her name was Sophie . . ."

I try to stop myself gaping. Claire is talking about Sophie, just like that. I have to say something. I can't miss my chance.

"I heard . . . that Sophie died."

Claire looks straight at me. "Yes," she says. "She died."

"That—must have been awful."

"Yes," says Claire. The words seem automatic somehow, as if she is reading from a script. "It was a terrible tragedy. She was found in a reservoir. No one really knows what happened to her."

Before I can say anything, Laura is in the room. When she speaks, I see her glass of red wine has stained her teeth.

"What are you two gossiping about?"

"I was just telling Tash our news." Claire smiles, touching her belly.

"So exciting." Laura grins at Claire and winks at me. She sits down in one of the dining chairs.

"Anyway, Tash," Claire says. "What's going on with you and Tom?"

Laura glances at me, surprised. I shift in my chair. I really don't want to talk about this with the two of them. Claire was one thing, but talking to Laura—whom I know Tom doesn't trust—feels like more of a betrayal.

"Tom . . . thinks we should move to Oxford," I say eventually. "We've sort of been arguing about it."

"What?" They both look at me, horrified.

"Oxford?" Claire gives her head a little shake. "But why?"

"He's got a job offer there," I say carefully. "He thinks we need a fresh start."

"Hang on, I thought you loved London, Tash," Claire says. "It's where you're from."

"And I don't think you'll get much more for your money in Oxford, I'm sorry to say," Laura chimes in. "If that's what he's thinking. Not if you want Summertown, or North Oxford. That's where all the schools are."

I blink at her. I don't know anything about Oxford.

"What have you told Tom?" Laura asks.

"That I'll think about it."

Actually, I had been starting to think Tom was right. Maybe we do need to move, have a fresh start. But the idea of leaving London, selling my dad's pictures—it feels like rubbing out a bit of myself. What would I do all day in Oxford? Whom would I talk to? We wouldn't know anyone there. I wouldn't have anyone except Tom.

"Why does he think you need a fresh start?" Claire asks.

I hesitate. "I think—well. He thinks I spend too much time on my work, for one thing. That I spend all my time on my job or Finn, and there's nothing left over for him, I suppose—"

"What?" Laura makes an indignant noise at this. Even Claire, who always tries to be evenhanded, looks shocked.

"That came out worse than it was when he said it," I say. "Tom just thinks that— I guess between seeing my friends a lot—"

"Does he mean us?" Laura asks, her eyes widening.

I shift in my chair. "I think he just feels we should reset our priorities?"

"That sounds like he means your priorities."

I search for a response. As I say it out loud, it does sound bad. I watch as Laura and Claire exchange a look.

"Sorry, Tash," Laura says gently. "You know how highly I think of Tom, but . . . it doesn't sound very fair to me."

"Didn't you say that Tom went to Oxford for uni, Tash?" Claire's brow is furrowed.

"So it's his place," Laura says, folding her arms. "Not yours. How can he ask you to move so far away from your friends, your career, your network?"

The answer to that makes me feel uncomfortable, even in the confines of my own mind. Tom wants me to stop investigating the death of Sophie Blake. I think of the messages. *Stop digging.*

I stand up, take a clean glass from the cupboard, and help myself to a drink. The window over the sink is dark, the scenery outside black and unknowable, the wind straining at the window locks.

WHEN I get to the bedroom that night, there is a single bar of signal, and a message from Adam.

Can't find any police log re: the allegation against E. Crawley, he says.

Shit. So Grace was right. The girl never went to the police.

Something else I could look at?

Quickly, I tap out a reply. Can we run license plates?

Adam replies straightaway. I can try.

OK. Couple for you to check.

I take a breath. I note down the plate of the BMW X5 parked outside the window, illuminated by the outside lamps. The one that belongs to Ed. Then, my fingers shaking, I add a second plate number. One that I know by heart. The plate of our old red Vauxhall Corsa. I press send, pinching my eyes closed.

Sophie

Four hours before

AS I GOT THE boys dressed in their party outfits, I could feel Claire's eyes on me. Makeup didn't really suit Claire. It made her face masklike, hard and unfamiliar.

Once they were dressed, I sat the two of them on the floor and read them stories while we waited for Jez and Claire to be ready. I scratched the raw skin on my hands and thought about the piece of paper in my rucksack, the one Sal gave me. It was there, in black and white. I'd held off until now. But I was starting to think that now I had nothing to lose.

A message pinged through from Lydia. Was I OK, she wanted to know. I hadn't seemed myself. She wanted to meet up soon. I flicked it closed. I knew I would never see her again.

Beau was whining, refusing to settle on my lap. He'd barely touched his dinner either. He was too ill to be going to a party. He had caught a summer cold and had that pinkish, viral look around his eyes, a cough that made people wince at him at bus stops. Claire seemed almost cross with Jude for giving the cold to him.

"Maybe Sophie should stay here with the boys, if Beau's not well," I heard Jez tell Claire in the hallway.

"No, I want him with me," she replied firmly.

Jez said nothing, but he was still looking at Beau, who was rubbing his eyes, slumped into my chest.

"We won't keep him there long," Claire said, relenting. "We'll get him into bed early."

By we, she meant me, as usual. But maybe this was the last time she'd let me put him to bed. She would get this party out of the way and then I'd never be allowed near the boys again. I could feel it. The thought of it made me feel physically sick.

Jez didn't seem to notice Claire was being off with me. He didn't seem to notice me at all, in fact. I could hear him whistling upstairs while he had a shave. The longer the whistling went on, the more furious it made me. When he finally emerged, he came down the stairs in the dancelike way he had, in his suit, the shirt unbuttoned, no tie. His shiny shoes tapped on the hallway tiles as he went back and forth fetching his wallet and his keys from the hook. I heard the music of the ice cubes in Claire's glass, the hushed whisper of her spraying the perfume she kept on the hallway table. The exclusive sounds of an exclusive life that I was no real part of.

"Wow. You look beautiful, Claire."

"Thanks, darling. Can you do me up at the back?"

I was right by the door to the hallway, now. I heard the sound of the zip, and then of lips making contact with skin. I imagined the feeling of his fingers on the skin of her back.

"Are the boys ready, Soph?"

I couldn't bear to hear him say my name. I worked Beau's spare sweater in my hands, the skin on my fingers chapped to bleeding between my forefinger and thumb.

Claire scooped Beau up and carried him out into the Land Rover. She left me to see to Jude, then climb into the back between their two car seats, like an older, unwanted child. The roads were jammed, a Tube strike clogging the arteries of the city. The weather looked ominous, too, cloudy but warm, the sort of humidity that got under the material of your top. Claire hadn't said a word to me since we'd argued on the pavement.

I didn't understand what I was doing at the party, or why the boys had needed to come. Jez had said something about how the family wanted to see them. But apart from Michael and Wendy—who saw Jude and Beau all the time—none of the other guests showed much of an interest in them. Most took a cursory glance at Beau—"Oh, doesn't he look sweet in his outfit!"—then wandered off, eyes trained on the canapés.

I'd packed a mat and a bag of toys for them, but couldn't find anywhere to set them out. Jude ended up sitting under a table, eyes fixed on his iPad. The floor was too hard for Beau to play on—he was crawling, but had still not taken his first steps—so I had to keep him strapped into the stroller. He kept straining against the straps.

Claire and Jez seemed to be going to some lengths to avoid interaction with me. Jez ignored me when he came over to see Jude, who was by now sitting on the floor next to me, looking miserable in his smart checked shirt and trousers, eating chips from a cupped hand.

When no one was looking, I plucked a champagne flute from a passing silver tray, then snuck off to the bar, away from Jez and Claire, and downed it in one, the bubbles cold in my throat. I assumed I wasn't supposed to be drinking, but I felt I needed to steady my nerves. It didn't work, though. I just felt dizzy and sick.

I turned around, intending to get back to the boys, then froze.

He was there. Standing between me and the entrance, his legs apart. He was talking to some other man, taking a canapé from a passing tray, shoving it into his mouth with a grin. Then his eyes met mine, and his face darkened.

Tash

THE NEXT DAY, AFTER breakfast, Claire leads us on a walk over the fields—safer, she explains, than the cliffs. "There have been some rock-falls up there lately. I think it's better not to risk it."

We walk in single file along stony footpaths and tracks of down-trodden grass, our conversations shouted along the line, our shoulders wearing the legs of toddlers. Claire's skinny arms reach ahead for haw-thorn branches and stray nettles.

Jez is arriving today, Claire says. He'll either catch up with us on the walk or meet us back at the house. When I asked what was happening with Jude, Claire said he was with his grandparents. I noticed she didn't meet my eye.

We cross into a field studded with cabbages, the sky stretching in all directions, the distant shimmer of wind turbines on the hills inland. At last a bar of signal appears. I hang back, pull out my phone, and text Grace.

All OK at home? Any news? X

After a few moments, the little blue dots appear to show she is typ-ing, then a reply flashes up.

All fine here! No baby, no letters of note. Will message if that changes! G x

"Tash? What's going on?"

It's Tom. Finn is on his shoulders, waving a piece of grass in his hand.

"Nothing. I'm just sending a text."

"We're supposed to be on a family vacation. You're on your phone the entire time."

"I am not—this is the first time I've had a signal!"

"Is it about Sophie Blake?"

I look at him.

"Well, is it?"

"I just texted Grace to ask her how things are." I feel the eyes of the others glancing back at us and I hope desperately that they're too far ahead to hear that we're arguing. Tom doesn't reply.

"Tom, can we not do this now? Jesus!"

I turn around, aware of someone running up to us from behind.

"Hey, everything OK? Are you all right, Tash?"

I hadn't seen Jez arrive. He has jogged to catch up with us. His face is flushed, his lips parted.

"We're fine," I say. "Hello, by the way."

He smiles faintly. "Hello." He glances at Tom, then back to me with a searching look. Tom looks furious.

"Hey, guys!" Claire shouts from a stile ahead. She is gesturing at a farm building at the end of a stone wall. "That's the farm produce shop, OK? Next field. Oh, hi, darling!"

She waves at Jez. I give a thumbs-up to acknowledge the location of the farm stand and she and the others continue.

Tom looks from Jez, to me, then back to Jez. He pulls Finn more firmly onto his shoulders by the ankles and turns away, leaving Jez and me alone.

Jez frowns at me. "You OK?"

I nod miserably. "Fine."

"You look a bit cold," he says.

I rub my arms, feeling the goose bumps on them. I didn't think about the wind. Should have brought a sweater.

"Here." Jez encloses his hands around my fingers, then blows gently on them. I glance up ahead. The others are too far ahead to see.

"A hand house." He smiles. Despite myself, I smile back.

WHEN WE get back to the house, Claire shuffles all the kids into a cold utility room that smells of Barbour jackets and damp laundry. We strip off their mud-caked trousers and wellies before settling them in front of the TV. I feel shaken, jittery. The more I think about the way Tom spoke to me on the walk, the closer to tears I feel.

"Do you mind if I sneak off for a shower?" I ask Claire.

"Sure, although I think Tom just said the same," she says. "He'll be in the one in your room. Use our en suite if you like, at the top of the stairs. There's shampoo and stuff in there."

The piping hot water on my cold skin is instantly soothing. I linger long after I've washed my hair, enjoying the feel of Claire's expensive coconut-smelling conditioner and the luxury of a few moments alone. When I shut the water off, I hear that the rain has stopped. From below come the muffled sounds of Nicole, Laura, and Claire ordering the children outside. I hear Finn laughing as he chases Beau and Oscar. He is having a great time. I just need to get through the week. That's all. In the small bathroom window, I can just make out the bay through a maze of rooftops, puffs of white spray rising from the rocks each time a wave crashes, like little breaths.

I wrap Claire's towel around myself and gather up my clothes. I open the door and find Jez standing in the bedroom, his shirt undone and an open suitcase on the bed.

"Oh fuck," I say. We both say "Sorry." We both laugh. "Claire said I could use the shower," I blurt. I am extremely aware of my wet hair, my damp skin, my bare, scrubbed face.

"I assumed it was Claire in the shower."

"I think she's outside."

"Right."

I shift, pulling the towel up as much as I can over my front. I need to leave, and I can't quite work out why I haven't done it yet.

"I'll just, um . . ."

Neither of us moves. From far away, I can hear the crash of the sea against the rocks, as the tide inches closer and closer to the beach.

Tash

WHEN I WAKE UP the next day, Finn has already abandoned his folding bed and gone to play outside. I get out of bed and walk over to the window. I can see him in the garden with Oscar. Claire is there with them. She has put a fleece jacket I don't recognize over Finn's pajamas to keep him warm. I feel a lurch of guilt as I creep back into bed.

Tom rolls toward me under the covers. "God, this bed is comfortable," he says.

"I know," I say. "Why don't we have a mattress like this?"

"I think we're probably due for an upgrade. I'll treat you to one when we move to the burbs."

I swat at him, somehow managing a laugh. I know that he will apologize, now that I have signaled I'm ready to forgive.

"I'm sorry about being an arse on the walk, about your phone," he says. "I just wanted to not think about all that stuff this trip, that's all."

"I know. Apology accepted."

We both hear a shriek from the garden that is unmistakably our son's. We exchange a smile.

"Little scamp," Tom says. "He loves it here. Is Claire with them?"

"Yeah." I hesitate. "Tom, I have been thinking about Oxford."

"Oh yeah?"

"Well, I suppose being here has shown what a difference it makes to Finn—a bigger house, a real garden. Space to play."

Tom smiles. "I think he'd love it."

"I just . . . I know what this sounds like, but—London is my whole world. I don't know anywhere else."

Tom makes a face at me. "You know Oxford. You visited me enough times."

"I know, but our life was so different then. I only really remember the bars and that awful club, the fish-and-chips van, and your horrible college digs."

Tom laughs.

"London is my home, and Finn's now," I say. "It's where I grew up, and apart from my miserable Cardiff years"—Tom smiles knowingly—"it's the only place I've ever lived, and I . . ."

"Come here." Tom pulls me onto his chest, laughing. "It's not a complete cultural wasteland outside the M25, you know. Oxford has all the things you like. Coffee shops, and bookshops, cafés with pretentious breakfast food."

"OK, OK," I mumble. "But, Tom, if we do move, if we do try for another baby, it would be a fresh start, wouldn't it? We could forget about the past. All the other stuff." My throat feels thick, a lump rising that I can't swallow.

Tom pulls me closer into him. "I really want that, Tash." I can hear the emotion in his voice.

"OK," I say. "I'll think about it. Really. I promise."

And then Tom is kissing me, and then his hands are moving down my body, our movements assuming a familiar rhythm. Afterward, listening to his breathing and the sound of the sea, I think that maybe I can do this, I can give this thing to Tom. I can make it what I want, too. And at the thought of that, I feel still somehow, and peaceful, in a way I haven't in a long time.

WHILE TOM is in the shower, my phone rings. The signal must be back. I snatch it up from my bedside table before the signal goes. It is Grace. I answer, but as soon as I do, the signal cuts out.

"Fuck," I say.

A few minutes later, one tiny bar of signal reappears, and a message pings through. It's from Grace.

Got your lawyer letter. Call when you can.

Tash

—⟡—

THE SIGNAL DOESN'T RETURN. That night, or the next day. We are mostly confined to the house, rain hammering on the skylight windows, bubbling into the gutters. The wet beach shines like sealskin.

In the evening, Tom volunteers to put Finn to bed. While Nicole and Laura make dinner, I go and find Claire in the utility room, hanging the wet clothes on hooks.

"Claire, have you had any signal at all? I know the Wi-Fi's bust, I just wondered if there were any good spots in the house I should try."

Claire frowns. "The Wi-Fi's not bust. Didn't Tom tell you? It's the Vodafone one. The code is on the router behind the TV."

I stare at her.

"He asked me about it the first day," Claire says. "Sorry—I assumed he'd tell you."

I feel sick. I don't have time to think about why Tom has lied to me. I need the Wi-Fi signal; I need to speak to Grace. I find the router, type in the password, and call Grace. I get her voice mail. "Fuck," I mutter. "Grace, call me as soon as you get this."

I head back to the kitchen. The children have all gone to bed. Claire pours drinks for Laura and Nicole as they emerge smiling from bedtime stories.

When Tom returns, Ed stands up. "Shall we go to the pub for an hour or so, let the women have a gossip? Jez, Tom, you up for it?"

I flinch at "the women," but Claire doesn't seem to react. "Fine with me," she says. "We'll eat around eight thirty."

"What's the local like?" Tom asks Ed.

"It's an acquired taste." Jez grins.

"You can say that again," Ed laughs. He slaps Tom on the back, squeezes his shoulder.

My phone buzzes. I pick it up. It is a text from Adam—sent hours ago, but only just coming through. Two missed calls from earlier, too. Fuck.

CALL ME. URGENT.

I step into the hallway and try and use the Wi-Fi to call Adam. But his phone doesn't accept Wi-Fi calls. I need a proper phone signal. I need to get out.

When I return to the kitchen, Tom is standing with Ed, his jacket already half on. It looks as if they have just shared a joke. He catches my eye, grins, and makes a "What can you do?" gesture. He looks pleased at the prospect of male adult company, a trip to the pub.

I wait until Ed has moved away and speak into his ear. "Please don't be long," I say.

"Why not?"

I don't know why not. But I have a strange, jittery feeling tonight, an unfocused sense of panic.

"Why are you so pally with Ed all of a sudden?"

Tom looks at Ed, then back at me, confused.

"I'm not," he says.

"Why did you tell me the Wi-Fi wasn't working?"

"Because Claire told me it wasn't working," he says slowly. He pauses. "What? What now? What's going on, Tash?"

I glance at Jez and Ed, waiting for Tom at the door. When I look at him, Jez averts his eyes, pretends to fiddle with his watch. Ed returns my gaze. I'm forced to look away.

"OK," I whisper. Something makes me grab Tom's hand. "Just please, don't be long, Tom."

He frowns at me, confused, then glances over my shoulder at Jez and Ed. "All right." He gives me a quick kiss, and is gone.

I sit down next to Nicole on the sofa. She pours me a glass of wine. Laura emerges from the hallway.

"Let me guess, Ed's gone to the pub," she says.

"They all have," Claire says.

"Best place for them," Nicole mutters.

Rain starts up again at the windows. There is something flimsy about the glass all around the kitchen addition. It doesn't feel like enough of a match for the wind that is coming in off the sea, rattling at the windows, trying to get in.

"Oh dear. They'll be soaked," Claire says. She is curled in a corner of one sofa, legs tucked up underneath her, drinking a chamomile tea. She looks over at me and smiles blandly.

"Serves them right for abandoning us!" Laura laughs. "Can I do anything more for dinner?"

Claire shakes her head. "It's all done."

Behind us, in the kitchen, a pot of potatoes on the stove is bubbling, steam clouding the windows. The wind rattles them again. Claire brings a protective hand to her belly. There is a knot in my stomach. One of them is lying. Her, or Tom.

There is a hiss from the stove. The potatoes have boiled over.

"I'll get them," Laura is saying. She presses a hand on Claire's knee as she gets up.

I can't stand it any longer.

"I need to get some air," I croak, standing up. Three sets of eyes look up at me. Then I see a glance pass between Nicole and Claire, just a flicker. I need to get out.

"Are you sure that's a good idea?" Nicole says as I pull on my coat. "It's pouring rain."

I avoid her gaze. "I won't be long."

As I leave, I look Laura in the eyes. "Laura. You'll be here for Finn, won't you?"

"Yeah, sure," she says, looking puzzled. "But what—"

"Please, Laura. Promise. You'll look after him. Won't you?"

"Of course, but—"

Before she can say anything else, I've closed the door behind me.

AT THE bottom of the garden, I reach the path that goes both ways, down to the beach and up to the cliffs. Below in the bay, I can see the boarded-up café, wave after wave of rain sweeping over its shuttered windows. The festoon lights shake. The chairs for the outside tables are stacked. Puddles gather at the feet of the open-air pizza oven.

I head up, on the path to the cliffs. There will be a signal up there. I need to call Adam. I need to know what he has found out.

The cliff path is muddy, glassy rivulets of water running down each side, the way strewn with trailing brambles. One slices into my hand as I hold out the flashlight on my phone. I realize I am relying on it for light, but the battery is low, and it is getting wet.

As soon as a bar of signal appears, I place the call.

"Hey, Adam? I got your message. What is it?" As I say it out loud, I feel the sobs start, heavy in my chest. "Just tell me. I need to know."

Adam doesn't say anything.

"Adam? Can you hear me?"

"Yeah, I hear you, but I'm confused. We spoke a few hours ago—remember?"

I think I've misheard him. "No—we—you sent me a message saying I needed to call urgently."

"And you did. This afternoon. Remember? I looked into the plates. I found something. I told you all this. We spoke."

"No, no. We haven't spoken today, I . . ."

"But I . . . you answered . . . Tash? It . . . it sounded just like you."

"When was this?"

"This afternoon—three, four hours ago, max?"

I had left my phone in the kitchen to charge. How long had I left it there? Half an hour? An hour? More? But now there's barely any battery. Someone obviously unplugged it. Who had been in the kitchen then? It could have been any of them.

"Someone else must have answered my phone."

"What?"

I feel choked by panic. "Adam, what did you tell them?"

Adam is breathing heavily. "I said I'd found something," he says. "Something about Ed Crawley."

Sophie

Three hours before

FOR A MOMENT, THE party seemed to slow. No one else was in the room. It was just me and Ed.

I thought about all those times I had seen him, running in the wetlands. The nice things he'd written to me at first. Then I thought about that hotel corridor, the crack of his hotel key as he tried to force it into that lock. How frightened I'd felt. Something had happened to me since then, though. I didn't feel fear anymore. Just rage.

Before I could speak, Ed's head jerked to the entrance. I followed his gaze, tried to work out who he was looking at. And then I saw Laura. And as Laura walked up to him to brush something off his jacket, all the pieces fell into place.

"Ed, darling, come and talk to Jez," I heard her say to him.

Ed pulled his gaze away from me to his wife. "Sure," he said. "Just a moment."

Laura looked annoyed. She glanced at me, smiled tightly, then walked back over to Jez and Claire, wobbling a little in her heels.

I moved toward Ed. I felt the champagne warming me, making me brave.

"Wow. You fucking liar."

"Keep your voice down." He looked over my shoulder, smiled at someone, as if to reassure them everything was fine. His face was flushed, his temples sweaty. In that moment, I couldn't work out how I'd ever found him attractive.

"On the brink of separating, are you? Funny. I've got a feeling that might come as news to Laura." I did the math quickly, in my head. We were messaging even before Beau was born. Laura must have been pregnant.

Ed's eyes widened at my use of his wife's name.

"How do you . . . ?" He glanced over at her, then back to me, straightened his tie. "Look, we can talk about all this—"

"I don't want to talk to you about anything," I spat. "I'd much rather talk to your wife. Maybe she'd like to see the messages you sent me. Or the pictures? They didn't do a lot for me."

The color of Ed's face deepened.

"Hello, excuse me? Sophie?"

I hadn't heard Laura approach. She was standing beside Ed, looking from me to him, then back to me. Ed's eyes were wide, amphibian. Laura frowned at me.

"What's going on, Sophie?"

Tash

I REACH INSTINCTIVELY FOR the crumbling stone wall. It feels cool against my palm. I hear myself breathing.

"Nothing for the Corsa?"

"Nope," Adam replies. "It wasn't anywhere near the wetlands that weekend. In any case, it was scrapped some time ago, that car."

I breathe out, then in again, my heart pounding. Tom never lied to me. Tom was telling the truth.

"So what did you find, Adam?"

Adam makes an exasperated noise, like something catching in his throat.

"Adam?"

"I—it was the first plate you gave me," he stutters. "For the BMW X5, registered to Ed Crawley. It was caught on camera, late that night, near the Hendersons' address. Then later that weekend, it was driven to the wetlands and back. Parked right by where the CCTV cameras were so conveniently vandalized." He pauses. "I told you . . . I thought it was you . . . they sounded just like you, Tash."

I take a breath. "Are you sure? About the car?"

"I'm sure. Look, there's still work to do. But to me, this looks significant. Really significant."

There is a crackle on the line. The signal is dropping. Adam pauses.

"Tash? Did you hear me? Tash?"

I felt a thump of terror. One of the women in the house had answered my phone. Had heard all this. One of them knew that I was looking into Ed. That I knew what he'd done.

"Adam, what did the person who answered the phone say when you told them all this? Was it definitely a woman?"

"Of course it was a woman. Fucking hell, Tash." I've never heard Adam swear, and it doesn't suit him. "They said they'd call me back. Thinking about it, you did sound . . . I just thought it was a bad line." He exhales loudly. "Who had access to your phone?"

"I don't know. All of them."

"All of who?"

I am silent. They were all there. Claire, Laura, Nicole. It could have been any of them.

"So . . . Was it Ed?" I am speaking to myself as much as Adam, trying to unravel it all.

"Maybe, maybe not," Adam is saying. "But I think he was involved. I think it was his car that moved the body."

Sophie

One hour before

I WASN'T SURE HOW much she'd heard. I could have told her. Of course I could. But I realized that actually, I just didn't care enough. About either of them.

"I'm taking the boys home." I walked away from Ed and Laura, ignoring the heat of their gaze on my back.

I found Jude on his own still, under the table with his iPad. He looked up at me, his eyes tired.

"Are we going home now, Fee?"

I nodded, held out my hand, and pulled him up. He was so tall now. He would be going to school in September. He wouldn't need me anymore. Nobody would.

Beau was in Jez's arms, whining, his face puffy and red. I told Claire and Jez I thought I should take them home.

"Fine." Claire pretended to busy herself packing their things. I held my hands out for Beau. Jez passed him over awkwardly, avoiding my gaze. I realized he was trying not to touch me. The pain of it stabbed anew in my heart.

"Thanks," he muttered. I forced Jez to catch my eye, just for a moment. He looked ashamed, embarrassed, and actually, a tiny bit frightened. In that moment, I could see it was going to happen. They were going to let me go. Claire had wanted to for ages, and Jez wouldn't resist it now. I had become a wrinkle in their perfect lives, to be ironed out and erased.

Beau was so sleepy he didn't protest about the stroller. As soon as I gave him his pacifier his eyelids drooped.

"Come on, buddy," I said to Jude. "Let's get home." I took him by the hand. Suddenly I was holding a sob in my chest, my eyes blurry with tears. I couldn't see how I was going to get through the next few hours, or what was going to happen after that.

"Are you OK?"

When I looked up, I saw it was one of the scruffy doctors who had arrived with Laura. He was wearing an orange T-shirt. He had a beard and glasses, and a kind face.

"Fine, thanks." I rubbed at my eyes, embarrassed.

"Bad party?"

I looked at him and half laughed, half sobbed. "The worst."

The doctor laughed. "Not exactly my scene either," he said. He was looking down at Beau with an expression I couldn't fathom. Then he looked back up at me, and squinted a bit.

"Sorry." He shook his head. "I thought I recognized you from somewhere—maybe not." He sighed, reached behind me. "Come on," he said. "Let me get the door for you."

BY THE time our black cab arrived home, Beau was deeply asleep in the stroller. I left him there in the hallway while I put Jude to bed. I read Jude his favorite story:

> Stick Man is lonely, Stick Man is lost.
> Stick Man is frozen and covered in frost . . .
> He can't hear the bells, or the sweet-singing choir . . .
> Or the voice saying "Here's a good stick for the fire!"
> Stick Man is lying asleep in the grate.
> Can anyone save him before it's too late?

I wanted Jude to have stayed awake long enough to hear the happy ending, but his eyes had closed. I imagined his dreams flitting over his eyes like shadows. I had a sudden sense that I didn't want to leave him in this cold, lonely house. A house full of secrets. Full of lies.

I went downstairs, lifted Beau from his stroller, a warm rag doll. I carried him up to his beautiful bedroom, and onto the soft mattress of his crib. I brushed his pale hair away from his eyes, even though they were closed, and blew him a kiss in the darkness.

I went back to check on Jude, by now snoring softly. "I love you," I told him. The words snagged in my throat.

I'm glad he didn't know, when I pulled his dinosaur cover over his chest, that it would be the last time I did it. I'm glad he didn't know it when I kissed his hair, turned out the light.

I heard the key in the door, the shift in the air as it creaked open. The sound of footsteps on the tiles in the hallway, the brief music of keys hitting the bowl on the hallway table.

All night, Sal had been messaging me. Telling me not to do it, not to use it. *You don't know what they'll do.* But it was time for the truth. If not now, then when?

I took a deep breath, headed down the stairs, and finally opened my mouth.

"I need to talk to you."

Tash

THE STORM IS LOUD in my ears, the sea below the cliffs dark and un-still. I hold my phone tightly to my ear, try to cover it with my hoodie cuff.

"Was it Ed?" I find I am almost shouting at Adam over the wind. "Could he—have killed her? He was seeing Sophie? And then he got violent when she ended it?"

Adam pauses. "Or there could be another explanation. I ran a financial search. Ed had some pretty severe money problems. Until Jeremy Henderson gave him a job at Graphite, soon after Sophie died."

"You think . . . that was some sort of payback?"

"It could have been."

"So . . . Jez could have been involved?"

"He could have. He could have gotten Ed to help him cover it up, in return for money."

I swallow.

"I'm hoping I have enough now," Adam is saying. "To persuade the higher-ups to look into the case again. But, Tash . . . you need to steer clear of these people in the meantime, OK? All of them. Just in case we're right."

"Oh God, Adam. I can't! I'm here with them in Cornwall. With Ed and Jeremy. I'm in their house. Finn's here with me and Tom."

I look back at the house, alone on the cliffs, the little yellow squares of light in the windows illuminating the curtains of water washing wildly off the sea. My son is in there with them.

Adam is incredulous. "What? Why? Can't you leave?"

I will call Tom now. I'll tell him to leave the pub, get home. He can make up some emergency. We can say Finn is sick, that we have to leave. Anything to get him out of there.

Adam is still on the line, but his voice is faint and tinny, the line distorted.

"Tash?" he is saying. "How soon can you leave?"

"I don't know, I . . ."

Before I can finish, I hear the line go dead.

My fingers are cold and shaking as I close the call and ring Tom. It goes through to his voice mail. I feel like I want to scream.

"Tom, we need to leave. Call me back. I need you to get Finn, to meet me somewhere, with the car . . ."

The signal cuts out before I can continue. I stare at the screen, willing a bar to appear, but there is nothing. The wind whips past again, nearly knocking me off my feet. I fumble for the flashlight again on my phone. As I do, I see that a message has come through from Grace, accompanied by some images.

Can't get through to you. Sending images of the letter. Hope it makes more sense to you than it does to me!

I have to zoom in on the images with my thumb and forefinger. At first, I can't make sense of the different columns, the lists of numbers, references to allele sizes, genetic markers. But other parts are clear:

Child: Eliza Imogen Sandwell.
Alleged father: Jeremy Mark Henderson.
Probability of paternity: 99.9999 percent.

I think of Eliza, strapped onto the back of Christina's bike, eating chips on the sofa with Billy, in her Elsa dress at the Christmas play. Her little pigtails, so fair, so pale and translucent. Hair that is nothing like her mother's. But that is just like Beau's.

Christina in the audience that time, craning her neck to look over to where we were sitting. She hadn't been feeling left out of our group. She hadn't cared about that at all. She had been looking at the father of her child, watching their daughter, in her first nativity play.

This must have been it—the secret Sal and Christina knew. The secret Sal told Sophie, then decided she didn't want Sophie to use it, for fear of what might happen. I don't think u shud use it Soph. U don't no what they'll do.

Sophie must have gone ahead anyway. She must have confronted Jez over it, over his secret child.

What if Sophie had threatened to expose Jez's secret, and Jez had gotten angry? What if he killed her? Got Ed to help him cover it up—take the body—and in return, he made Ed's money troubles disappear.

This is the only thing that makes sense. And then I feel my hands, still clutching my phone, with the image on the screen, start to shake. Sophie was killed because of what she knew. And I know the secret now, too. Which means that I'm in the same danger she was.

I need to get through to Tom. I need a signal. Maybe if I climb higher up the cliffs. I pull my hood up, squinting into the rain. I flick on my phone flashlight and hold it out in front of me to light the way.

And that's when I see, through the silvery rods of rain illuminated in front of me, a lone figure on the cliffs ahead. Waiting for me.

Sophie

Forty-nine minutes before

CLAIRE STARED AT ME. She looked as if she had just been woken from a dream she'd been in for the last year.

"What?"

"We've been sleeping together," I tell her. "At his office. And here, in this house."

"You and Jez?"

Claire's face was a mask of horror and disbelief, as if she had been bitten by a family dog she thought would never turn.

"No," she said eventually. "No. He would never."

"He would. He did. Many times. But actually, it's not me you need to worry about."

Claire was frightened. I could see it now. I was powerful, suddenly. All the stuff that she had, that I didn't. I was holding all of it in my hands. One move, and it all smashed to pieces.

"He's been having an affair with someone else. A woman called Christina Sandwell. It's been going on years. Way longer than me."

Claire's eyes narrowed. "You're way off the mark," she spat. "Christina is just an old friend of Jeremy's. She was best friends with Jeremy's first wife, Emily." But I could see the doubt behind her eyes, hear the wobble of it in the pitch of her protest. Claire was not stupid. I could tell from the way she paused, waited for more. She had had her doubts about this woman before.

"Her baby—"

"She had that baby with a sperm donor." Claire's voice was harder now, snapping like an animal.

"No," I told her. "Christina's daughter is Jez's. Eliza is Beau's half sister."

Claire froze for a moment, then actually laughed. "What rubbish! You're making this up!"

"I'm not."

I unfolded the piece of paper in my pocket, the copy of the one that Sal gave me. I placed it in front of Claire. She backed away.

"You don't want to know the truth, do you?"

Claire looked up at me. She still hadn't looked at the paper.

"You," she said. "Ever since you came, nothing has been right. I haven't felt right—"

"But, Claire, I've tried to help, all the time, and you—"

"Liar! You don't want to help me." She shook her head. "You want to take the boys from me! And Jez, and this house . . . I see it now. I see what you want!"

I held up the paper, but Claire turned her head, refusing to look at it, to read the names.

"You're wrong," I told her. "I don't want your life. Your life is a lie."

"Get away from me. I don't want to hear anything you've got to say."

"Because you don't want to hear the truth!"

"Get out. Get out of my house."

"This is my house, too!"

My dad always said you should never say you hate someone. If you hate someone, that means you want them dead. But with the look she gave me then, Claire didn't have to say the word. I could see it, feel it all over my skin. But she didn't say it. Instead, she turned away and started up the stairs.

Tash

———

"TASH, IT'S NOT WHAT you think."

Although I can see it is Laura, the voice doesn't sound like hers. It sounds like something from far away.

"I t-thought you were looking after Finn," I stutter.

"Tom's back," she says soothingly. "I waited until they were back to come."

I don't know whether I can believe her or not. I have no idea whom to trust.

"You've got it all wrong, Tash," she says. "You think you know, but you don't."

I take a breath. "Did you answer my phone? Before?"

Laura looks at me steadily.

"Why did you do that?"

Laura bites her lip. She says nothing.

"Answer me! I know you've been lying to me, Laura—you all have! About Sophie. And about how Finn got hurt that day at Claire's. What's going on, Laura? What else have you lied about?"

"Tash, listen. Come this way—away from the house, away from the others. Trust me, Tash." Laura's voice is breaking, her face tortured, contorted.

I hesitate, but when I look at her face, I believe the pain etched on it; I can see that it is real. Haltingly, I follow Laura up the cliff. The rain floods the path, water gushing down either side. I think of Finn. He's fine, I tell myself. Tom is there. He is tucked up in his bed. Tom wouldn't let anyone harm Finn.

Laura stops abruptly, then turns to me. "You have to believe me, Tash. I didn't want any part of this."

She moves closer and tries to take my arm. I pull away, as if scalded by her touch.

"Don't touch me."

"I'm not a bad person, Tash." Her lip is wobbling, like a child.

I feel myself shaking.

"Tell me the truth, Laura."

"It was an accident," Laura croaks. "It was all an accident."

Sophie

Thirty-three minutes before

FOR SOME REASON, THE way she turned her back on me made me angrier than anything else. I felt the cold grip of fury in my wrists, my jaw. I followed her, the paper grasped in my hand.

"Look! Look!"

I was screaming it now, pressing the paper into her face.

"Look at the paper!"

Claire was at the top of the stairs. Even as I followed her, I had the feeling that this was unreal, that this could not really be where we were, what we were doing. But the mist in front of me was thickening, and I could not stop. Even when I heard a key in the door, the voice of a man calling to us, asking us what the hell was going on. Even when I heard another door open on the landing, just a crack. A pair of dark eyes in a small, pale face.

Jude rubbed his eyes sleepily.

"Fee?"

"Go back to bed, Jude sweetheart," I said. "Go back." But my voice seemed to wake him up even more. "Jude, please," I told him, but he took another step toward me.

I looked back to Claire. When she turned her face was pink and wet with tears.

"Claire, listen!" I cried. I tried to reach out to touch her arm.

"Get off me! I want you gone!"

It happened quickly then. It was as if Claire hadn't seen Jude. Her eyes were fixed on me. She pushed me, hard, so hard that I was thrown against the wall. My head slammed against a corner of plaster. The pain was white in front of my eyes. My hand, still clutching the paper, was too slow to reach out and stop my fall. And so fall is what I did, over and backward, until I was at the bottom, my head slamming again, against the cold, hard tiles.

Tash

I LOOK AT MY phone. A single bar of signal has reappeared.

"I'm calling the police," I tell her. But as soon as I say it, Laura lunges at me, her eyes wild and glassy. She grabs my forearm and I gasp and shake her away. In doing so, I throw her off balance, and she drops to her knees in the mud and sobs.

My instinct is to help her up, apologize. But all the rules have changed; everything has shifted. I can't reconcile the Laura who cooks spaghetti for Finn, sits him down with a spoon and fork, lends him spare clothes if he gets mucky, has him over to play in her garden, with the person in the mud in front of me.

"Please listen, Tash," she begs. "I had no choice."

"What do you mean, *you* had no choice?"

Laura staggers to her feet, holds her hands up in front of her, fingers splayed, as if I have a gun and she is asking me not to shoot.

"What did you do, Laura?"

The tips of her fingers are shaking, the rain starting to darken the reddish color of her hair. I tighten my hand on my phone.

"We were ruined, Tash." Her voice is wavering. "We were fucking ruined. There was this girl, at Ed's work. She said he had . . . that he had . . ." She shakes her head. "It was nonsense—a lie, of course. Ed would never— But that didn't matter. They didn't believe him. He got sacked. You know what it's like now—men can't do anything . . ."

She is shaking her head, her chin wobbling, eyeballs shot with red in the light of the flashlight on my phone. I wonder if she really thinks this. Perhaps she has told herself this lie so many times she believes it to be true.

"He tried to get another job," she says. "But no other bank would touch him. We had nothing. We needed Ed's income. We were mortgaged to the hilt. We couldn't live on just . . . you know what doctors earn . . ."

Her shoulders sag. Living on what a doctor earns. Like us, in other words. Was this the horror she was trying to prevent? The horror of not being rich?

"You don't understand," she gabbles, seeing my expression harden. "We were going to lose the house, Tash. Our whole life. Oscar was only a few months old. I was still breastfeeding. I couldn't go back to work, not yet. We were in real trouble. My cards had stopped working, I couldn't even buy a coffee— I had these letters piling up. Neither of our families could help. All I could think of was Claire and Jez."

She hangs her head.

"I'd been trying to talk to them, to find the right moment," she says. "That's why I went over that night, after the party."

"Hang on," I say. "It was you who drove the car over to their house? Not Ed?"

She nods wordlessly, staring down at the ground.

"You drove the car," I repeat, my voice shaking. "You took her . . . you took her body." My vision swims. I feel sick.

Laura buries her face in her hands.

"Why, Laura? Why?"

"Please, let me explain," she cries. "It was all by accident. I had only gone over to try and talk to Jeremy, to ask him to help Ed. I'd wanted to find a moment to talk to him at the party, but it had been too difficult. I'd gone over that night to ask him—beg him, if I needed to—to help Ed."

"And?"

"I got there. I knocked and knocked. They ignored me. But I could hear voices inside. I knew they were there. And then I remembered where Claire kept her spare key, under that bay tree pot. So I let myself in. And when I opened the door, they were both there, and . . . and . . ."

"And what?"

My voice is uneven. I realize I am cold now, to my bones.

Laura looks down. "Sophie . . . she . . . she was on the floor. I checked for a pulse but it was no use. She was gone, Tash. It was over. There was nothing anyone could have done to change it."

"You said it was an accident," I spit, my teeth gritted. "If it was an accident, you would have just called an ambulance."

Laura drops her gaze.

"You knew it wasn't an accident. You knew she hadn't just fallen."

Laura meets my eye. "No, Tash. She didn't just fall. I could see she hadn't just fallen."

I feel myself wobbling under the weight of it. I reach out automatically for a handrail, or a wall, but there is nothing to hold on to up here.

"How could you, Laura? How could you have helped them?"

Laura looks away, ashamed. "Tash, you have to understand. If I'd called the police, what good would it have done?"

I want to tell her to stop. I can't bear to hear her rationalize it.

"All I could think was, we were all ruined," Laura says quietly. "Unless we helped each other. If I helped them, and they helped me. I'd have lost the life we'd built for our son. And those boys' lives would have been ruined, too. Beau was still so little, not even a year old—he needed his mummy. And Jude, he'd already lost one parent, about to lose another."

"So you told them you'd help them. What did they do for you in return? What was the price, Laura?"

"Tash, listen, I know it was wrong, but . . ."

"Well, now you can fix it," I tell her. I still can't look her in the eye. "You can come with me, to the police. We can tell them everything." I lift my phone to my ear, my hand trembling. "You need to do this. You owe it to Sophie's mum."

Laura is close to me again, trying to take my phone.

"Tash—listen. Just wait. We can't do any of this now. They know you're onto them."

"What?"

Laura glances down the cliff behind me. "Claire. Your phone rang, when you were in the bathroom, and Claire answered it. And now I think they . . . I think they . . ."

I hear her gasp, see her fingers fly to her mouth, before I feel my phone being snatched from behind and an arm clamped around my body, a hot palm putting pressure over my face. The light from my flashlight is gone, and from behind, I hear a voice in my ear, a voice I know all too well.

"I wouldn't do that, Tash, if I were you," Jez says. And his arm tightens on my neck.

Tash

———◦———

"I JUST NEED TO talk to you, Tash," Jez says. "I just need to explain."

Somehow I break loose of him and spin around.

"All right," he says, holding his palms up. "But please, let me explain." But I am not looking at him. I am looking behind him.

Their faces are so smooth, impassive. They offer no explanation. They edge closer in unison, their eyes glinting like deer. Claire first. Then Nicole.

I take a step back.

"I'm sorry," Claire says. "None of us wanted it to come to this. Truly, Tash."

My eyes cross from her to Nicole, then back to Claire, then to Jez.

"Tash," Jez says, "please, listen to me. I don't know what Laura has told you, but Sophie . . . it was a mistake . . ."

"You killed her." I pause, stare at him. "Was it because she found out about your little secret with Christina? Or had you been fucking Sophie, too?"

The anger is boiling over now, hot and throbbing on the surface of my skin, the insides of my ears. How could I have been so stupid? How could I not have seen what he really was?

"I would take it back if I could, Tash," Jez murmurs. "All of it." Jez looks at Claire. He reaches out an arm to her, and she takes his hand. They both hang their heads. I feel like I might be about to vomit.

I turn to Laura. "How? How could you help them?"

Laura sobs. "I know, I know. I was so desperate . . ."

"You took her body!"

Laura sinks down into the grass, her body racked with sobs.

"She did the right thing." Nicole is speaking now in a bored voice, as if we'd already spent long enough on the topic. My head is spinning. So she knew about this, too?

"The nanny was dead." Nicole shrugs. "There was nothing anyone could have done. No rational person would have thought it worth ruining everyone's lives over a mistake. No rational person would see any point in raking over it. Unless of course there was something in it for them." Nicole steps toward me. "When were you going to tell Claire, Tash? When were you going to mention the big article you were writing about us all? We've been waiting for it. The big reveal!"

Even in the freezing wind, my cheeks burn. A smirk forms on Nicole's face.

"No. Thought not. That's the thing, isn't it, Tash? You've been lying to all of us. From day one."

"That's not true," I say in protest, but my voice sounds weak.

She gives a snort of laughter. "Some investigative journalist. You really thought we just wanted the pleasure of your company? We knew your game. We needed to keep an eye on you, that was all."

Nicole takes a step toward me and brings her face close to mine, so I can smell the wine on her breath.

"You can tell yourself you were doing this for Sophie, out of solidarity for some lying little slut you never even knew," she says. "But I saw her for what she was. And I see you, too, Tash. I've seen you from the start. This was always about you! It was supposed to be your big story, wasn't it? Your big break finally, after years as a failed reporter?"

Claire pulls Nicole back. "That's enough, Nicole," she says. She turns to me. "We *are* friends, Tash. We've all made terrible mistakes—"

Nicole shakes her off. "Friends! What kind of friend is she to you, Claire? Snooping around in your house. Digging into your life behind your back. Cozying up to your husband." She points a finger at Jez, then flicks it toward me. "Don't think I haven't seen that, too."

I back away from Nicole, from all of them. I can feel underfoot that I am leaving the path—the grass is thicker, mattresslike. I have no real sense of where the cliffs end, where they give way to the rocks beneath.

"I tried to warn you," Nicole says, gesturing at me. "I told you to leave it alone."

I feel my jaw slacken with horror.

"You sent me those messages? You came to my flat?"

Nicole throws me one of her counterfeit smiles. "You should have listened, shouldn't you? Think how much better it would have been. For everyone. Especially your stupid husband."

The anger is hot now under the surface of my skin. It was her. She made the complaint. She is the one ruining Tom's career.

"That's enough, Nicole." Claire is speaking now. "What's done is done."

Laura sighs, mutters under her breath. "We told you that you were taking it too far, Nicole."

Nicole spins around to face Laura, her eyes illuminated with fury. "Not far enough, clearly! Jesus—you're fucking deluded, all of you!" She jabs a finger at me. "Can't you see how out of hand she's gotten?"

Claire shakes her head. "Nicole, please . . ."

"Oh, cut it out, Claire. You've been too out of it on your dumb pills to see what's in front of your face for months."

Claire shrinks from her, as if she's been scalded. Laura's eyes widen with concern. And in my mind, something starts to fall into place. The scattering of pills, like sweets, on Sal's counter. Pills that looked just like Claire's.

"Nicole," Laura says, "Claire's been through a lot . . ."

"Oh yeah, so what's your excuse?" Nicole snaps at Laura. A polished nail jabs in my direction again. "*You* were supposed to be handling *her*!"

I look up at Jez. Even despite everything, I find myself looking at him, for a safe harbor.

"Where is Tom?"

"He's back home. With Finn."

Jez sees my face soften. He takes a step forward.

"I swear to God, Tash," Jez murmurs. "It was all just a terrible mistake."

It is unmistakable, the guilt in his eyes. It is hideous. I start to shake.

"What about Sal?"

Jez fixes his eyes on mine.

"I asked you a question. What about Sal, Jez? Was she just a mistake, too?"

"Sal?" Claire's face is confused. "Sal killed herself." Claire looks at me, then at Jez, then back at me again. "Sal killed herself, Tash. That's nothing to do with any of this. Tell her, Jez."

"Of course I didn't kill Sal," Jez murmurs.

"Liar!" The rage is in front of my eyes, hot and white. It had to be Jez, I saw that now. He would have known that Christina had confided in Sal about Eliza. He had the pills—Claire's pills. He had access to Christina's flat—her penthouse flat, that he put her up in.

"Did you go to Christina's house just for the keys, Jez?" I demand. "Or are you still fucking her, too?"

I stare at Jez, watch his expression flicker as he makes his calculations, plots his verbal escape. And finally, it is gone, the heady suck of attraction. I see this man at last for what he is. A liar.

"Oh my God." There is a quiver in Laura's voice. "Jez, tell me this isn't . . . tell me Tash is wrong."

Jez comes to life, shaking his head.

"Right. This is bullshit. Laura, enough. Tash, I had nothing to do with Sal . . . I didn't even know her!" He is still holding my phone in his hand. As I glance at it, I feel pressure on my wrist. Laura has grabbed it and is holding me tightly.

"Tash. Please, believe me. I know I shouldn't have helped him, I—"

I push her away and lunge at Jez, managing to snatch my phone. I clutch it tightly to my chest.

"I'm calling the police right now, Laura," I tell her, my voice wobbly with adrenaline. "You can tell it to them."

"Don't do that, Tash!" Jez is roaring now, panting, edging closer to my face. He grabs at my phone and I swing away from him.

"Get off!" I scream.

"Please, let's just talk this through. You need to listen to me, not them. They are trying to manipulate you—it wasn't me—"

"You as good as admitted it was you!"

"It wasn't me, it was—"

"Stop lying!"

It comes quickly, like a struck match. The anger, the humiliation. Mine, and Sophie's together, a sudden flame that burns white hot. Jez lunges toward me, snatching at my phone again. Instinctively, I raise my hands to bat him away, and his hand misses the phone and slams against my face. I feel the nauseous thud of injury, the wetness of blood on my nose, my chin. He looks shocked, and for a mad moment, I think he is going to apologize, clean me up. But instead, his face hardens, and he lunges again for my phone.

I grab at the lapels of his jacket in an effort to keep him at arm's length, twist my body in a bid to stay on my feet, to avoid the force of his movement knocking me over. As I twist, I feel the crumble of earth and rock underfoot, giving way. Instinctively, I release my grip on Jez, pushing him away, and leap, as if scalded, away from the cliff edge. Moments later, the cliff edge disappears.

My strength was no match for his. But however I replay it in my mind, there is no escaping the fact that it was me who pushed him. It was me who pushed him over the disappearing cliff. Down the rockface, and into the darkness.

Sophie

AFTER THE FALL, THERE was darkness, just for a few moments. Then something between darkness and light. A hot, wet place at the back of my head. My fingers and feet felt cold. I looked up to the top of the stairs and all I could see was Jude's little face.

I tried to call out to him, to tell him I was all right. But I couldn't.

"Fee!" Jude started to scream, and then there was the sound of a door closing. Behind the door, I heard him scream my name again and again. Fee. Fee.

And then another door opened and closed.

A man's voice. It was him. Jez. I waited for him to save me, to pick me up, bring me back to life. But he didn't. He didn't touch me. He stood over me, terrified, looking at me as if I was something monstrous.

I heard them talking quietly, her sobbing, him pacing. His footsteps were loud in my ears. The two of them came close to me, and everything swam again. My eyes must have been open, but I could not focus on their faces now. Could not move, or speak. They moved away. More voices. More sobbing.

What are we going to do? Claire kept asking. *What are we going to do now?*

After a while, I thought I heard a third voice. An open door, the feel of the night air. A clanking on the tiles. But I could not be sure. Things were slipping away—the house, the windows, the beautiful ceiling roses. The marble, the glass, the rainbow-colored bookshelves.

Sometimes there was a beat of panic, and I tried to struggle, but more and more I let it lap at me, the warm water of it, and I let myself drift. Awake still, but no longer fearing sleep. Starting to want it, rather than fight.

Tash

CLAIRE SCREAMS INTO THE darkness beyond me. The sound is swallowed by the wind.

"Where did he go, Laura? Where is he? Jez!"

Claire is hysterical. Nicole holds her still, but even she looks at a loss.

"Where is he? Where is Jez?" I turn to Laura. My entire body is shaking. Laura doesn't answer me. Her eyes flit from me, to the cliff edge, then back again.

"What happened to him, Laura?"

She doesn't reply. But we all heard the scream. We all heard the crack of a body on the rocks. We all heard the splash.

"We need to get help," Claire cries. "Why are you all just standing here?"

"Just wait a minute," Nicole spits. "Let's just think about this a minute."

Laura puts her hand on my back. I shake it off. I don't want to be near any of them. Laura looks at my face, wounded.

"Tash, please. I'm sorry. I just wanted to protect Oscar. I didn't . . . I didn't . . ." She trails off, bringing a muddy sleeve to her eyes. "Did Jez really kill Sal, Tash?"

There is a flash on the horizon. Two white cylinders of flashlights, edging closer. A crunch of gravel underfoot, raised voices.

"Hello? Police!"

The sound of the voice is like waking from a dream. I look down at my clothes, the mud-soaked path. The rain is still falling, the wind still howling. My leg is shaking. How long have I been here? How long has it been since the splash?

"Police. Is anyone there?"

Laura grips my wrist again. She pulls her face close to mine, forces me to meet her gaze.

"Listen, I think there was an accident, Tash," she pants. "Do you hear me?"

I stare at her.

"Jez fell." Laura turns to Claire and Nicole. "Right? Are you listening, Tash? He fell."

Tash

THE TEA DETECTIVE WILLIAMS brought me has gone cold. The storm outside is starting to quiet; the rain settling into a slow drumbeat. Pascoe leans forward on the table, rests on his elbows.

"So," Pascoe says. "You didn't actually see him fall."

The room feels so cold. I long for sleep. I gaze down at the flecks in the blue linoleum floor. I could curl up on this floor, just here, in the corner of this room. I could pull my hood over my head. If they would just let me shut my eyes.

I shake my head.

"Speak for the tape?"

"Sorry. No. I didn't."

"It's extraordinary," he says, tilting his head to one side. "No one actually saw him fall. And yet, you all seem so sure that that's what happened."

"POLICE!" THE call had come closer. There had been a crack of thunder. Laura lowered her voice to a whisper.

"Tash came out to make a call and got lost on the cliffs," she said. "We all came looking for her. Jez lost his way. He fell."

"He fell," Nicole said. She glared at me, at Claire. Claire looked like she hardly knew where she was.

I looked at their faces, staring at me, waiting. I thought about the body at the bottom of the cliffs. And then I thought about Finn, about Tom. About the new life Tom wanted, far away from here. I saw the price that I would have to pay.

"Police!"

Laura had come closer to my face. I could feel the coolness of the rain, mingling with the blood coming from my nose.

"Are you hearing me, Tash? He fell."

I had looked at Claire, and she had looked away and howled into the wind.

I STARE at the glass on either side of the room. I want to know where Tom is. I long for him. I look at Pascoe, waiting. He has sat back in his chair now, his arms folded. He passes me a tissue for my face. I told him it was just a nosebleed. He keeps looking at it, making it feel hot on my face.

"It's like I told you before," I say. "It was dark. I heard a rock fall, where he was standing. I heard a noise like someone falling, a cry. I recognized his voice. Then I heard someone falling into the water."

The words are out, now. I have said my story, and the effort of it feels like a sucker punch.

"Please," I say. "Can I go home now?"

Tash

～

Four months later

"MUMMY, THERE'S OSCAR!"

Finn does a little jig in excitement at the sight of his friend. He races off toward him and taps him on the shoulder. Soon they are giggling together, running off under a trestle table covered in homemade cakes in Tupperware. With an effort, I raise my gaze from the red-painted toes and sandals at the foot of the table where they have disappeared, up to Laura's face.

Laura is looking at me, her smile tight in the scorching glare of the sun. She is wearing sunglasses, a new dress. She gives me a nodded hello. I do the same. I tell myself that this is the last time, the last thing.

The moving van arrived this morning. It's parked outside the flat, filling up with our furniture, including the last of Dad's pictures—we sold most of them, but some, the most special ones, are to be framed for our new place. I've left Tom to sort the endless baby junk I'd been tempted to give away or sell, but that we'll now soon need again.

Tom and I are leaving tomorrow, at first light. It all moved so fast once we got started—our flat sold over a single weekend. We will sleep in it for the last time, on roll-out mattresses, tonight. We'll order our favorite takeout, from the Indian place on Church Street, one last time. We are leaving London, and Clissold Park, and Ruby's, and Highbury Fields, and the wetlands. The keys to our new home in Oxford—a real house, with a garden and, most unbelievably of all, four bedrooms—are hanging on the hook by the door. I get a little thrill every time I feel the keys, the cold metal of them, their edges rough in the palms of my hands.

I was nervous about coming here, but the weather is due to break after today—a long, hot spell due to end in heavy thunderstorms—and Finn had been so excited about the summer fair. I thought he should see his friends one last time.

"Are you sure you don't mind finishing the packing?" I'd looked guiltily at all the toys, the books still on the shelves, the plates still stacked in the cupboards. But Tom had shaken his head. "It'll be loads easier with him out of the house. Anyway, I'm hardly going to let you lift any heavy boxes, am I?"

Luckily there is no sign of Claire. I don't think I could bear seeing her again. I spotted her a few days ago, at the ice cream van on Highbury Fields. She was queuing up, holding tightly to Beau's hand. In profile, her bump was like a perfect semicircle under her pale pink T-shirt. She was staring straight ahead, her lips pursed, as if she was still trying to work it all out.

Jeremy's parents were standing behind her with Jude. He was on his scooter, as usual, the blue one with the light-up wheels. I watched his grandfather hand him the ice cream, ruffle his curly hair. Jude is living with his grandparents in the countryside now, one of the other mothers told me, coming down to see his half brother every other weekend. Both boys are doing better than anyone dared to hope.

It had been enough to see them, to see the boys one last time. I had turned away and headed back up Highbury Fields. I hadn't wanted her to see my face.

Then, at the top of the Fields, I had passed Nicole's house. The wooden shutters are closed over the windows now, like eyelids. There is no agent's sign outside, but I know it has been sold. Their move, too, all seems to have happened with breakneck efficiency: a private buyer, a property scout. The last photograph Nicole posted on Instagram was her with John and the girls on the steps of the house, the smart painted door behind them. Lissy was on her knee and John was holding the baby, bigger now, her fist in her mouth. *Bye-bye, London Town*, the caption read. Nicole and Lissy were waving with both their palms, a broad smile on Nicole's face. She was washing her hands of us.

As I go to lure Finn back from under one of the fair tables, I brace myself for Laura.

"What do you recommend?" I ask, gesturing at the cakes.

"Definitely Bakewell tart." She smiles. "Although in this weather, most people just want the ice lollies."

"I can imagine."

"How are you all, Tash?"

"We're all right, I guess."

"Heard you were moving out."

"We are," I tell her carefully. "Tom took the Oxford job. And it seems we are in need of a bit more space."

Laura smiles again, glancing at my belly. "It seems so. Congratulations. I'm really happy for you both."

With everything that happened after that night on the cliffs—the police investigation, the inquest, the endless, endless phone calls from reporters and news desks who'd ignored my invoices for months and now wanted to be my best friend—I'd barely noticed the nausea, the exhaustion, creeping up on me like a looming shadow. When I'd had to stop on the way back from playgroup drop-off to be sick behind a horse chestnut tree at the edge of the park, I had finally realized. I'd bought a test, one of the expensive ones. I wanted to know how many weeks. It said five to six.

Cornwall, then, I'd said to myself out loud. It was too soon. I didn't feel ready. But when I touched my belly, I was sure I felt her, even as early as that. A fluttering, no stronger than the beat of a butterfly wing. She was there, and there was no going back.

Laura takes a knife and cuts me a slice, revealing the deep red line inside. She has been true to her word; Claire and Nicole, too. We all agreed to the story, and we stuck to it. When Jez's body washed up a few days later, a mile or two down the coast, there was nothing really conclusive. Bodies in water can be particularly difficult.

The inquest heard there had been a gale force storm that night. No moon, meaning it had been difficult to see the path. The coroner had recommended the erection of a safety fence, given the popularity of the route with vacationers, including children, and the growing evidence of rockfalls, coastal erosion. The police investigation had eventually been dropped.

I've kept my part of the bargain, too. There will be no new investigation into the death of Sophie Blake. No vindication for Jane, no award-winning podcast, no four-thousand-word magazine piece in the *Sunday Times* in which I lay out how I cracked a murder case on my own, in between my childcare commitments.

I feel my phone vibrate in my pocket. I ignore it. Somehow, I know who it will be. It's not the first time they have called today, and it won't be the last.

Laura holds the slice of tart inside a paper napkin, her fingers pinching either side. "Best excuse for sugar ever, being pregnant. Make the most of it."

I hand her a fiver and she waves it away.

"Don't worry."

"It's for the playgroup." I put the money in the Tupperware, weigh it down with some two-pound coins.

I find it difficult to meet Laura's eye. I am a journalist. I don't believe in secrets. But now, I've become part of one. Her secret, her lie. The lie that protects her and Claire, and keeps them safe inside their huge, beautiful houses. And I have no choice. Because now the lie protects me, too.

In my quietest moments, alone with it, at night, I have told myself that Jez's death meant that justice was done for Sophie—some sort of justice, anyway. I tell myself again and again that Jez as good as admitted he killed Sophie. Maybe he got the ending he deserved.

But plenty of other questions remain, questions that my reporter's brain finds impossible to silence. Like exactly how much Claire did. She was home before Jeremy, after all—or so she said. Was she really just a bystander, crouched with horror over the body of the nanny Jez had hurled to her death? Or did she do more than that? Did I really know the Claire of then? Or had Sophie known a different Claire? A person gripped by dark thoughts and paranoia. A person who had been on the edge, and ready to snap.

And then there were other questions. How exactly had Ed—or Laura, or both of them—dumped her body in the wetlands? Had Jez fixed the CCTV, to ensure they wouldn't be seen, or told Ed where the cameras were, and let him get on with it? And what was the nature of the deal Laura brokered? How much did Jeremy have to pay Ed to make all their problems go away?

Most perplexing of all was the question of Sal. Had I been right, on the cliffs that night? Had Jeremy really killed Sal, too?

I'd dared to ask Tom about it, weeks after, when things had settled a bit. We had been in the car on the way back from Oxford, one of our house-hunting trips, a pile of brochures on my lap, my bump snug under the seat belt.

"No," he'd said. "It wouldn't be possible to trick someone into taking an overdose like that."

"Are you sure?"

"Absolutely. Not that many pills. They'd taste it in a drink."

He was adamant. But the picture still doesn't fit. And I'm not the only one who thinks so. My phone vibrates again. It's Christina. A text message this time.

You can't keep ignoring me. Come to my place, tonight. We really need to speak.

I delete the message, put the phone back. We'll be gone tomorrow. This will all be over.

Laura dusts the tart crumbs from her hands. I'm not sure whether there are any crumbs, really, or whether this is just a gesture of finality, of tidying the last threads. "Good luck. In Oxford. In your new home. I hope you guys are happy."

At last, I manage to look her in the eye.

"Thanks," I say. "You, too, Laura."

We force the boys to say goodbye. Laura mumbles something about letting her know if we're ever back in the area. I confect a noncommittal reply. A sudden breeze lifts the tablecloth and Laura slams down a hand to steady it. I glance up at the sky to find that a swirl of dark clouds are gathering. The wind picks up, the bunting in the churchyard starting to flicker.

"Time to go," I tell Finn, and I steer us toward the gate. I hear the familiar creak, one in a long list of last times. I take one last look over my shoulder toward the park, the pretty view of the church spire, the tall columns of Clissold House, the bright green lawn where Finn took his first steps. It twists in my heart, leaving the place where he has grown up. But like I keep reminding myself, we have no choice.

"Bye," Laura calls. Oscar is in her arms now, and she makes him wave a floppy hand. The she puts him down and sets off back to her stall, her sandals slapping on the paving stones.

WHEN I get home, Finn is tired. I put him down for a nap on a little mattress among the boxes. As I bend down, I feel a wave of nausea. It's been so much worse this time. I feel as if I'm at sea, on a boat, and I can't get off. The heat hasn't helped.

In the kitchen, Tom is wrapping mugs and kitchen knives in paper and packing them into boxes. I fill an unpacked mug with water and ease myself into a chair.

"How was it?"

"Fine."

"Did you see Laura?"

"Yup."

Tom leans back on the empty sideboard, raises his eyebrows. "Rather you than me," he mutters.

I wonder if Laura really thinks we believe her, if she really thinks we haven't worked out by now just how far she went to destroy our lives. Because although she might have sent a few weird text messages, Nicole couldn't have been the one who got Tom suspended from work.

I'd done some digging after Tom was cleared. As I'd suspected, the hospital would never have taken the complaint so seriously if the name given hadn't been a genuine patient of Tom's. But it was—complete with NHS number, details of their treatment. Only someone with access to patient details could have made such a plausible false complaint. I knew it had to have been Laura.

That's when I knew it hadn't just been about frightening me, trying to keep me away from the Sophie Blake case. That wasn't enough. Laura hated us anyway. She hated Tom for what he had done to her. And after a bit more digging, I found out why. She was still under investigation for the overprescribing Tom had reported her for, by the Medical Practitioners Tribunal Service. She could still lose her license, though Claire is paying for a good lawyer. Tom might have ruined her career. Trying to ruin his was not just about scaring me. It was about payback.

I'd asked Tom which pills he had seen Laura overprescribing all those months ago.

"All sorts," he'd said. "Sleeping pills and benzodiazepines, mostly. Very dangerous."

I'd pressed. What would the drug names be? What would they look like?

"Zopiclone, I think. Maybe diazepam? They'd be in bottles, little brown ones. Why?"

It had finally made sense then—the rows and rows of pill bottles with no prescription labels. Laura had been giving them to Claire without prescriptions for her postnatal depression. What had Claire told me? *Laura helped me . . . I'd have been a goner if it wasn't for her.*

Claire had been terrified about having postnatal depression on her medical record. Instead of encouraging her to see her doctor, Laura obviously offered her a way around it, promising to secretly get her some pills that would help her sleep, would help calm her anxiety. Most likely, without proper oversight, they'd have done the opposite, Tom thinks. They can be highly addictive. Claire would have become increasingly reliant on Laura for her supply. For everything. And I think that must have been what Laura wanted—otherwise, why risk her career to steal the pills? Perhaps that had been her plan A, to use Claire's addiction to extort money out of her and Jez. Of course, that was before she had the good fortune to find them with a dead body on their hands.

All of which had convinced me, in the end, that we had no choice. We needed to get away from Laura. I should have listened to Tom. I had no idea who she really was. I could not trust her. Tom and I needed her out of our lives.

Tom gestures to a pile of stuff on the table. It's all my research into Sophie's death.

"I wasn't sure if you wanted to pack all this," he says. He picks up a document from the top of the pile. Sophie's postmortem report.

I hesitate a moment. "No. Let me sort it out, though. I'll have it all sent back to Jane."

"OK." Tom is still looking at the paper in his hand.

"What?" I ask him.

"Nothing. I just thought you always told me she'd died of a head injury."

"Well, the pathologist couldn't say definitively what Sophie died of," I say carefully. I don't tell him what Laura and the others admitted on the cliffs. How I really know she died of a head injury.

"Look." I point to the section of commentary on the pathology report, where it mentions the head injury. "See? It talks about it here. It was the only wound on her body."

Tom shakes his head. "Sophie wouldn't have died of that head injury, Tash."

I stare at him. "What do you mean?"

He gestures at the report's conclusions. "With a young person," he says, "you need a hard blow, sufficient to fracture the skull, to cause the death."

"So?"

"So it says here there was no skull fracture. That wound she had—it might have caused a period of unconsciousness, or concussion. But that wound didn't kill her. No chance."

I suddenly feel cold all over.

"What—what could she have died of, then?"

Tom flicks through the pages of the report. "It's not at all clear from this." He pauses on the final page, mutters almost to himself. "Strange no fracture to her collarbone, was there?"

I shake my head. "Why do you ask about that?"

Tom rubs his beard with his palm. "Look, it's not my area. Don't listen to me. I did a pathology module years ago. I've forgotten most of it."

"No, go on. What?"

"Well . . . it's just this part, where it talks about hemorrhages under her eyelids." He tips his head to one side, looks away, as if remembering something. "I'm pretty sure the only time I've ever seen those was on a case of strangulation."

"But she wasn't strangled."

"No," Tom says thoughtfully, putting the report back. He stands up, wiping his moist brow with the back of his arm, then takes a stack of cardboard boxes to the bedroom. "She could have been smothered, though."

I SIT for a while and sip some water, listening to Tom pack next door. I find my hand is trembling on the glass.

Maybe Jez still did it, I tell myself. He could have smothered her before he threw her down the stairs. Or after. Perhaps it doesn't matter exactly how it happened in the end. Sophie is gone, and if it weren't for him, she would still be alive. It's all his fault. Isn't it?

But that is not the only thing that's bothering me. There is something else. The slapping sound I heard when Laura walked away from me earlier today. It's a thing she does, I realize. A sound she makes when she walks. Sort of heavy-footed. And I suddenly remember when I heard that sound before.

I walk into the bedroom. Tom looks up at me from the floor.

"Tash? What's wrong?"

Tom stands up, rubs his hands on his jeans. I can see this is painful for him, revisiting this. He had hoped it was over.

"Tash," he says gently, placing his hands on my arms. "I thought we said—"

"I know," I murmur. "I know."

I rest my head against his chest for a moment. Then I pull away.

"But there's something I have to do."

Tash

THE SLOW BOIL OF thunder follows me across the wetlands. The reeds are bowed in the wind, the geese huddled together, their heads tucked backward into their feathers, their eyes closed. There is no rain yet, but I feel it is coming, the air close and stifling. I pass the playground, the fake Victorian lanterns. I head to the Heron tower, the tallest, the showcase, right on the water. I press the buzzer for the penthouse.

Christina's apartment is huge, the views from the floor-to-ceiling windows spectacular. The lights of the city blink and shimmer to the south, the wetlands now just a dark pool at the tower's feet. Three copper lights cast a glow over the kitchen island in the center, where Christina is standing, pouring red wine into three large tumblers.

"You came," she says. "I'm glad. You remember Adam, I presume."

I hadn't even noticed Adam. He is standing on the other side of the apartment, his face half in shadow, his hands shoved into his pockets. I feel hot blood rising to my cheeks, an alarm bell sounding inside my brain.

"How do you two . . . ?"

"I found him," Christina says. "His name was on the inquest documents. He spoke to me. Told me you had been ignoring his calls since what happened in Cornwall."

I avert my eyes, unable to meet Adam's gaze.

"I can't stay long," I say. "I just wanted to—"

"This isn't going to go away, Tash." She gestures to a stool at the island. "Why don't you sit down?"

Clumsily, I take a seat. Christina passes me a glass of wine.

"I'm not drinking," I say defensively.

"Oh yes, I see." She glances down, her eyes lingering on my belly. "How far along are you?"

I shift on the stool. "About four months."

Christina looks up. Her fingers twitch, as if she is counting down. "April, then," she says, smiling.

I return her gaze steadily. "The baby's due in January."

"That's what I meant," she says, no longer smiling.

I feel a prickle on my arms. I don't want to be here. But I need to know how much she knows. And what she plans to do about it.

"Christina, what do you want?"

"To share some information with you. And I'm hoping you'll want to share some with me. Would you like to sit on the sofa?"

She gestures behind Adam to her living room. A large, apricot-colored sofa, an armchair in a designer pattern, a curving floor lamp arched over a coffee table with a neat stack of art books. It must be four times the size of our flat. Eliza's toys are only just visible, tidied away in baskets.

"I'm fine here."

"Great. Let's start with Nicole DeSouza."

Christina starts pacing, holding her wineglass in her fingers. I have a sense that I am in her courtroom, though I'm still not sure what part I am supposed to be playing. Jury. Witness. Or accused.

"I'm sure you know by now that Nicole was behind the threats against your family," Christina says. "She took out the contracts for the burner phones fraudulently, in Sal's name—the evidence that Adam found, that he told you about. Easy enough to do."

I look over at Adam, hunched over the marble top of Christina's kitchen island. He avoids my gaze.

"I'm sure you've also worked out that only Laura could have been behind the complaint against your husband."

"How did you . . . How did you know about that?"

Christina ignores my question. I glance at Adam, and he looks away.

"Did your husband mention why he'd raised the alarm about Laura?" Christina asks.

"It was to do with prescriptions."

Adam clears his throat, speaks for the first time. "Are you aware, Tash, that the medications Laura was illegally overprescribing are the same medications that killed Sal?"

I take a breath, clamp my mouth shut. I manage a nod, but I can't speak. I feel as if I will vomit if I open my mouth.

How could I have been so stupid? No, it wouldn't have been possible for an ordinary person to trick Sal into taking an overdose. But Laura was cleverer than that.

"Did Laura ever try to turn you against Sal?" Christina asks. "Or undermine her, perhaps? Did she make any comments that would tend to suggest Sal was the sort of person that would kill herself?"

"Yes." It comes out as a croak. I think back to that day in Laura's kitchen. *I think Sal has got some . . . mental health issues. It's very sad.*

Christina raises her chin, triumphant. "Laura and the others knew Sal had been close to Sophie, and they knew Sal was also close to me. They knew it was likely Sal knew things that Jez and Claire didn't want to be generally known. About Jez and me—and my daughter. And about Jez's . . . relationship with Sophie." Christina gives me a hard look. "They tried to stop you from listening to Sal, Tash. But when you were determined to listen, they had to make her disappear."

Christina opens a rose-gold laptop on her marble countertop and puts on a pair of thick-rimmed glasses. "Adam," she says. "Perhaps you could show Tash the images."

Adam leans over Christina and makes a few clicks with the mouse. Christina moves out of his way, her hair falling over one shoulder. She looks beautiful, powerful. Terrifying. Behind Adam, the thunderous sky comes to life over the wetlands. Little seams of lightning twitch over the tall buildings of the city. The rain is suddenly loud against the glass.

Christina picks up the laptop and rotates it so I can see. It is a CCTV image, incredibly sharp. There is no mistaking whom it shows.

"This is an image from the concealed camera situated at the alleyway behind Sal Cunningham's flat," Christina says. "The alleyway that ad-joins the small patio at the back of her flat. The residents of her estate set up this camera to catch drug dealers, and I suppose, in a way, they have succeeded."

A muscle in Christina's cheek twitches. Her voice is brimming with anger. She looks at me.

"This image was taken on the day that Sal was found dead."

I look at the picture. A flash of green pashmina, hair the color of an autumn leaf. It was her, the *clack clack* I heard from the patio outside Sal's house, when I found Sal that day. Laura's brown boots, the heels she always wore. She was there that day. She was there when I came in. I missed her by a moment.

Laura knew I was going to Sal's that night. Because Nicole knew. Nicole was there that day, watching us at Cuckoo Club. She had seen the message Sal had written, and reported back to the others. Was that what they were deciding that day when I saw them in that coffee shop, under the round pendant light? Deciding that Sal had to be gotten rid of?

"It could only have been Laura, Tash," Christina was saying now. "No ordinary person would have been able to talk Sal into taking an overdose. But an experienced doctor? They could find a way."

I close my eyes and force myself to swallow.

"Laura intubated her."

Christina nods. "It seems Laura slipped enough diazepam into Sal's wineglass to knock her out. She was able to intubate her once she was unconscious and get the pills into her that way. It was expertly done. Looked exactly like she had taken the pills herself."

I shift on my stool, my heart beating fast. A sharp kick of heartburn forces me to move again. The baby feels huge. I already feel her pressing against my lungs, depriving me of space, of oxygen.

"So it wasn't . . . Jez had nothing to do with Sal." I know it to be true, but somehow the thought of it is so difficult to bear. After what I've done. What I convinced myself I had to do.

"Jez?" Christina almost laughs. "It certainly didn't have anything to do with him." She spoke more quietly. "Anyway, he was with me that night."

I look at Christina. There is no trace of shame on her face. In her mind, Jeremy belonged to her. Her lover. The father of her child.

"You're shocked," she says, refilling her glass. "But it was me and Jez before everything. Before Sophie. Before Claire. Before Emily." She gives me a hard look. "Before anyone else."

"Emily? You mean . . ."

"I introduced them," she says, smiling sadly. "I guess I came to regret that decision."

My head is swimming. I find myself looking at Christina's wine and wishing I could take a long, deep drink.

"Look, Emily and I were friends," Christina says throatily. "I gave him up. Then she died. We grieved her together, and then . . . well. I wanted my independence back then. I kept ending it. And he kept coming back. But I mean, Claire? She was never . . . She and Jez . . . They weren't right. Anyone could see that. Jeremy and I would have ended up together."

I feel unsteady as I step off the stool. I walk over to the edge of the room, the thunderous sky huge, the city spread out underneath. I stand close to the glass, close enough to feel the cold air on the other side of it.

I turn around, look back across the island to Adam, then to Christina, the wine bottle in the puddle of light under the eye-level copper lamps.

"The thing I can't understand," I say quietly, "is why she would agree to kill Sal. Just to cover up the fact that she and Ed helped hide Sophie's body."

Christina looks at me. And I realize it does make sense after all.

"She just . . . wouldn't have done that . . ." I say. "Unless . . ."

Adam and Christina exchange glances.

"Unless," says Christina, "Laura had done something considerably worse than just hide a body."

Sophie

One minute before

THEY WERE ASKING LAURA if I was dead.

She was the woman who'd come in, her shoes making that noise on the hallway tiles.

Oh no, she said. *Oh no. What's happened? What have you done?*

The ceiling was swimming, closer then farther away. My head hurt, where it was wet. It hadn't hurt before, but the hurt was coming back. The light was fading and growing, as if someone had their hand on the dimmer switch. Then the light went black.

They were asking her if I was dead. They were saying it over and over.

Sounds now, but no pictures. Someone beside me, kneeling. Two fingertips at my throat, pressing. A silence.

I'm sorry, I heard her say. *She's gone.*

I was gone. I was dead. So why did the sounds keep going, the light coming on and off? The pain, still, louder and quieter at the back of my head. A thump of blood. My heart was beating, wasn't it? But it couldn't be. She said I was dead.

We should call the police. The ambulance. Should we, Jez? What do we do?

Think, for a moment, Jez was saying. *We think. Take a beat.*

Then Laura.

Look. I can help you. Ed and I will help. Here's what we do. You take the body, and you put it in our car.

I was the body. I was going in the car. I waited for someone to tell her no. But no one did.

Take all your clothes off, put them on a hot wash. In a few weeks, wear

the same outfit, spill red wine on it, in front of witnesses, then get rid of it.
Clean up here. Only use products you already have. If you don't report her
missing until Monday, no one will be looking for her.

No one would be looking for me.

A man's voice. Jez. And I hear the smallness in it now. I didn't before.
Why are you doing all this?

A scratch, like a piece of paper. She was writing something.

This is the price.

Silence. Then Jez says something. I can't hear what. Then it's her
again. Saying something about no one would lose their house, or go to
prison. *Our lives can stay the same,* she was saying. *Everything can stay the*
same.

Pictures now again. Blurred, as if underwater. Some muttered instruc-
tion, something about Claire. A shape that was Jez, walking away. Talking
to Claire. Claire's crying louder, then quieter, a door closed behind.

She was kneeling beside me now. Laura. I could see her green scarf
thing. She was taking it off, winding it around one hand. She was going
to see I was still here. She was going to help. She was going to stop the
bleeding.

I felt sensations, then the cold floor. I felt it against my back, my fingertips. The pain at the back of my head.

Her fingers at my throat again. She was checking again. This time she
would realize I wasn't gone.

She put the scarf over my face, her hands over my mouth.

Softness, and a perfume smell. Then the pressure, and darkness. And
terror.

No more words then. No more pictures.

Tash

⸺

I WASN'T AWARE THAT I'd been crying, but I find my cheeks are wet, my voice unsteady as I look at Adam.

"Sophie would have lived?"

"Yes," Adam says. "If it had just been the head injury, Sophie would have lived."

"Laura could have helped her." Christina's voice is harder than Adam's. "Instead, she told Claire and Jez that Sophie was dead. She let them believe they were responsible for killing her. And then she smothered her."

This can't be true. Surely, it can't. Setting Tom up was one thing, but this—first Sophie, then Sal—surely she couldn't have been capable of this.

"The forensic pathologist thinks Sophie would have been unconscious, or minimally conscious," Adam explains. "A scarf or a pillow would have been sufficient."

I turn away, press my hand against the window.

"Laura needed Claire and Jez to be so indebted to her that they would do anything she wanted," Christina says. "It was the only way they'd give her the kind of money she needed to keep her perfect life intact."

"They couldn't exactly write her a check," Adam says. "Too obvious. Even Hayden would have picked up on that when we looked at the case."

"But by giving Ed a job at Graphite, they could structure the payment as a bonus," I say. "So it was able to go under the radar. Almost." I look away from Christina, suddenly ashamed. How had I not seen these people for what they were from the start? Not a friendship group, but a vile protection racket.

Christina studies my face. "I want to be sure you understand this, Tash," she says. "Laura killed Sophie. She killed Sal. And if things had gone according to her plan that night on the cliffs, she'd have killed you, too."

I stare at Christina.

"She had tried to warn you off, but it hadn't worked. You kept going. So she planned to get rid of you. I read all the documents at the inquest, Tash. I think Laura knew where the rockfalls were that night. I think she had led you to them."

I breathe in and out. I feel as if I have stepped off a roundabout, the ground buckling under my feet. Adam's phone rings and he leaves the room, mumbling an excuse, closing the door behind him. Christina and I look at each other.

"What do you want from me?"

Christina plucks her wineglass from the kitchen island and closes her laptop.

"I need you to tell the truth," she says. "About what happened on those cliffs."

So here it is, then. I feel strangely numb. The realization of my worst fear, of living my darkest nightmare. I thought I could make that night go away. But Christina knew what I did. She was going to make me pay.

"Why?" I whisper. "Why do you need me to?"

"I know you are frightened," she says. "I understand why you are afraid of her. But, Tash—we've got her now. All I need is for you to tell the police the truth." Christina comes closer to me. "Tell them, Tash. Tell them how Laura pushed Jez."

I look up. "What?"

"It's OK," Christina says. "Nicole told me everything. She told me it was Laura who pushed him off the cliffs that night."

My mouth hangs open.

Christina shrugs. "I went to pay Nicole a little visit. We suspected she'd probably cooperate when we told her we knew she'd taken out the burner phone contracts, and when we told her everything that Laura had done. We were right—she saw pretty quickly that she needed to play ball."

"But why did she do it?" This was something that still didn't make sense to me. How had Nicole gotten involved in the first place? Why would she have gone along with it?

"Nicole told me she'd found out by accident," Christina said. "She'd overheard Laura and Claire talking one day, and they'd realized, and then they'd been forced to tell her everything. She says they begged her to stay silent. Nicole told me she had agreed simply because they were her friends." Christina pauses. "She also said she sympathized with Claire because she'd—her words—'known that nanny was trouble from day one.'"

Christina gives me a meaningful look. I shake my head, ball my fists in anger.

"I believed her, though," Christina says, "when she said she had felt she had merely been protecting Claire from the consequences of one terrible mistake. I do believe that she didn't know the full extent of what Laura had done."

I imagined the scene. Christina at the smart steps of Nicole's house on Highbury Fields. Nicole's pinched brow, her clever, racing mind working out her best possible move. She could see what Christina wanted. She wanted a culprit. And Nicole had given her one. And in return, Nicole had been allowed to get her family on a plane to New York.

I think about our own escape. The moving van parked outside our house. Tom, sitting at home. He would be wondering where I'd gotten to with our last-night takeout. The keys to our new home in Oxford, our new life, on a hook by the front door.

"I don't want to be involved in this."

Christina laughs drily. "That's exactly what Nicole said." She folds her arms. "Unfortunately, that is not negotiable at this point for you, Tash."

"Please. You don't need me involved—"

"Oh no, I do," she says. "I made a deal with Nicole. This is the only way. It has to be you. And I think you will be involved, Tash. Unless you want me to recommend to Tom that he avail himself of the paternity testing services I used for Eliza. I'm sure the clinic will still have Jeremy's DNA sample on file."

Instinctively, I cup my palm to my belly. Christina tips her head to one side.

"You can thank Nicole for that tip-off, I'm afraid," she says. "The walls in Crugmeer House are thinner than you think, apparently."

Slowly, I walk back to the island and ease myself down onto a stool, my heart pounding. I had almost convinced myself it hadn't even happened, not really. Jez's cool fingertips on my skin, picking the towel from my hands and running down my body. The feel of his wet mouth on my neck, between my legs. My soaking hair on the pillowcase. The sound of the waves, crashing on the rocks in the bay.

When I finally speak, my voice emerges as a croak. "Why do I need to do this, Christina?"

"Because I had to make a deal with Nicole. The deal was that I'd leave her out of it, as long as she told me everything."

"But I—"

"I want Laura punished, Tash!"

Christina slams her hand down on the kitchen counter. The movement carries such force that I jump up. My head knocks the copper lamp, and sends it flying, its beam flashing alarmingly around the dark room. In the wild, flashing light, Christina's face goes from full beam, to dark, to full beam again.

"She killed Sophie. She killed Sal. And . . . and she killed Jeremy."

With these last words, her steely voice crumbles, her chin starts to shake, like a rock edifice about to fall.

"Jeremy was not perfect, Tash," she says, her voice thick with emotion. "But I loved him, and he was the father of my child." Then she glances down at my belly. "I wouldn't be so impolite as to speculate as to whether he is also the father of yours."

The copper light starts to still. I hear the sound of the rain outside. Tears prick at my eyes as I think about my kind husband, about our new house far away from here, with the pear tree in the back garden, the little window seat in the back bedroom I picked out for the new baby the first time we looked around the house. The baby who will be Finn's baby sister. Who I have told myself, in every sleepless night since that day, sobbing silently in the dark beside my husband, will belong to Tom and me. The baby will be ours. She will, she will. Whatever a test might say.

I think about what will happen if I tell the truth. And then, I think about what will happen if I do what Christina wants, and tell a lie she thinks is the truth.

I think about what I am, and who I want to be. Not a bad person, I do believe that, though I suppose everybody does. Not a victim, of course. Not really a journalist, probably, not anymore. Just a person. A mother. A wife. An adulteress. And a killer.

I was, in that moment, at least. I think I knew, deep down, that the cliff was breaking behind me. I think I knew that if I moved out of Jez's way, if I let him go, then he wasn't coming back. I knew it, and I let it happen anyway. I never wanted to see him again. I didn't want the complication of him. It was better this way.

But of course, it's not the truth that matters in the end. It's stories that matter. And whose is the most compelling. Hers, or mine.

Acknowledgments

I AM SO GRATEFUL to the many people who assisted me in researching and writing this novel, and who were so generous with their time.

In particular, the doctors, who—even amid the pressures of a pandemic—took the time to help me understand something of the life of a medic in the NHS. Thank you so much, Ben Crooks, Deepak Chandrasekharan, Aravind Ramesh, Simeon Innocent, James Ray, and Juliet Raine, for answering my (many!) questions so fully and thoughtfully. I am also grateful to Dr. Melanie Smart for her invaluable advice on childhood trauma and attachment disorders, and also to the brilliant nurse Lara Willis, who patiently entertained my many morbid medical inquiries.

The original idea for *The Other Mothers* came from an inquest I attended many years ago in South London as a trainee news reporter. Thank you very much to the coroner and coroner's assistants who helped me research that case, and to Tom Stoate and Nicholas Rheinberg for helping me better understand the work of the coroner and the coronial system in England. I am also most grateful to Russell Delaney for a fascinating insight into the work of a forensic pathologist.

The beautiful wetlands at Woodberry Down in Hackney, East London, which provide the setting of this novel, were created thanks to the London Wildlife Trust. I am very grateful to David Mooney, its director of development, for talking to me about the area's extraordinary transformation. I'm also grateful to Dr. Meri Juntti of Middlesex University and Simon Donovan of the Manor House Development Trust for their very helpful insights, and to Chris Smith at Thames Water for a hugely enlightening discussion on the dangers of managed waterways!

I am so lucky to have my brilliant agent, Madeleine Milburn, in my corner. No writer could ask for a better champion, especially over the past couple of years, and I always feel a thousand times better about everything after we've spoken. Thanks so much to the whole MM team, and especially Liv Maidment, whose helpful and encouraging feedback on the draft manuscript came just at the point when it was most needed.

I had three incredible editors on *The Other Mothers*, and it was such a privilege to work with all of them. Thank you so much to the brilliant Alison Hennessey at Raven, Alison Callahan at Gallery, and also Becky Hunter, whose input was so valuable. Thanks, too, to all those on the Raven and Gallery teams who have put so much work into its publication. In particular, I would like to thank Katherine Fry, Emilie Chambeyron, Amy Donegan, Ben McCluskey, and Francisco Vilhena in the UK and Nita Pronovost, Jackie Cantor, Bianca Ducasse, Taylor Rondestvedt, and Lauren Truskowski in the US and Canada. Last but certainly not least, thank you so much to Jen Bergstrom for your huge support and passion. It is a privilege to be among your writers.

Writing this novel in lockdown—with a newborn and a toddler in tow—would have been impossible without practical and moral support from so many people: my wonderful agent, my editors, and their publishing teams, but also my amazing family and our wider support network. Thank you to all those who helped, when it was permitted, to look after our girls so I could find time to write—especially Mum, Jo, Kirsty, Sue, Brendan, Lara, Megellene, Andi, and everyone at Coconut Nursery. A special mention must go to Aimee Perry, too, for not freaking out when I told her I was writing a book about the murder of a nanny. Or not too much, anyway.

Thankfully, the real other mothers in my life are nothing like those in my novel. Thank you to all the remarkable women with whom I am lucky enough to share the experience in all its undignified, unfiltered glory. Without our gallows humor, the coffees, the shared school pickups, and, most crucially of all, the wine, I'm not sure how I would get through any of it. I appreciate you all.

Thank you to Pete, for being the best, most equal partner and the most patient, present, and loving father. I am so lucky to have you by my side through all the tears, tantrums, and broken sleep.

And finally, to Emma and Maddie, who are worth every single moment.

This one is for you.

About the Author

KATHERINE FAULKNER, an award-winning journalist, studied history at Cambridge. She has worked as an investigative reporter and as an editor and was formerly the joint head of news at *The Times* (London). She lives in London, where she grew up, with her husband and two daughters.